# HALIA

KINGDOM OF FAIRYTALES
SEASON EIGHT

You all know the story of your favorite fairytale, but did you ever wonder what happened after the fairytale ending? Well we know. Not all afters end up happily, sometimes the real adventure starts much later...

Following famous fairytale characters, eighteen years after their happily ever after, the Kingdom of Fairytales offers an edge of the seat thrill ride in an all new and sensational way to read.

Lighting-fast reads you won't be able to put down

Fantasy has never been so epic!

KINGDOM
OF
FAIRYTALES
URBIS PRISON
SHIPLEY
THE VALE
AZREN
BADALAH
KISBU
DESERT
DRACONIS
ZHORE
MOSA
ABORIA
ELDER
AIRE
SKYLA
URBIS
AZURE
ENCHANTIA
EMERALD CITY
OZ
FLORIS
TULIS
THE FORGE
ARCADIA
RENAIS
MELFALL
ATLANTICE
ANTLA
W
E
S

ISBN: 978-1-989997-23-9
Enchanted Quill Press



Contaact the author at www.enchantedquillpress.com
Cover by Enchanted Quilll Press
Interior Formatting by Enchanted Quill Press
Editing by Rose Lipscomb

# QUEEN OF SONG

# 15TH JULY

I swallowed hard as I surveyed the tray for room thirteen. A bottle of Malbec, two glasses, three bowls—the first one filled with crackers, the second one with olives, and the third with different cheeses cut into even cubes. The food and drink was perfectly arranged, thanks to me wasting several minutes pushing the items around on the tray. No longer having a reason to procrastinate, it was time to bite the bullet and deliver the dinner to my guest, no matter how much it terrified me to serve him.

Taking a deep breath, I shoved the kitchen door open with my foot and walked up the rickety staircase to the first floor. My heartbeat quickened with each step I took to room thirteen and its occupant. Demons were terrifying enough in general, but our guest wasn't just any demon. He was an incubus.

*Don't look him in the eyes for too long, and you'll be fine,* I tried and failed to reassure myself as I knocked.

"Come in," a gruff voice said, and I exhaled. Normally, I hoped that my demon guests were in a good mood. However, with an incubus, it was preferable he was in a foul mood since it meant he might ignore me being female and forget to view me as an energy supply for his lodestone.

Balancing the tray against the wall, I pushed the door open and entered. I kept my eyes glued to the ground and put the tray on the table. "Here you are, sir. Is there anything else I can get for you?"

Footsteps neared me, and an icy hand reached for my face. Inching backward would only incur the incubus's wrath, so I stayed perfectly still, telling myself he would soon lose interest.

"Look at me, girl."

Not wanting to be thrown onto the streets, I did, silently counting to ten. The eye contact couldn't last longer, or there would be no chance for me to escape the incubus's mind control.

"You're a pretty thing, aren't you?" His red irises sparked with passion. His pitch-black hair moved, even though the window was closed, giving it the appearance of soft silk.

I glanced downward again. "If there's nothing else, sir, I'm afraid I must go."

He let go of my cheek. "Send up the girl."

I practically flew out of the room, forgetting to inquire what girl. As it turned out, I didn't need to search for her. On the ground floor, I saw a tiny thing, with porcelain skin and wide eyes standing in the entry to Madam's Boarding House, looking uncertain.

"Room thirteen," I said.

The girl gave me a shy smile. "Thank you."

I didn't return her smile. "A word of advice, get out of this while you can."

The girl flinched back, and then she scuttled past me and up the stairs.

I sighed. They never listened. I didn't know what the incubus was promising the girl in return for her life energy, but whether it was money or a dream reality that allowed her to escape her life for an hour, it wasn't worth it. It was best and safer for us normal folk to stay away from those who had magic. If I could stop seeking out the fae, I would. Unfortunately, I couldn't. I didn't go to Acacia out of convenience or to satisfy my desires, but out of necessity. If I stopped seeing her, I would die.

After serving the incubus, I delivered a few more dinners to mostly human guests. The only magical guests were a sprite and a goblin, and, thankfully, both left me alone. Sprites could be nasty, but only if they were attacked first. As for goblins, they were interested in those that had money, so definitely, not me.

Done with serving dinner, I headed to the laundry room to see if Tia needed help. My best friend was in the middle of folding sheets when I entered the furnace.

"How do you stand it?" I fanned myself.

She grinned. "I could ask you the same thing, Halia. I see the expression on your face when you study what occupants have requested room service. Yet, you always manage to go deliver dinner to the unholy creatures without turning into one."

"Haha." I waved her remark away. Best not to think about what fae and demons could do to us, especially now that more and more of them were coming to Arcadia. Was our kingdom attracting them? Or was it that I had lived a sheltered life before?

I snorted. Having a leaky roof over my head and sludgy porridge for breakfast, lunch, and dinner could hardly be considered sheltered. The orphanage had provided me with bare necessities and nothing else. Then, when I turned eighteen, I was kicked out without any notice or advice on how to find work. Tia decided to go with me even though she could have stayed one week longer. It was by sheer luck that Madam Fontaine was passing by the orphanage when we left and told us she was looking for two maids.

"And once again, Halia is one thousand miles away. What are you daydreaming about?" Tia asked.

I shook my head. No need to bring up bad memories of living at the orphanage. "Nothing."

She let it go and handed me a big stack of freshly washed linens, while she carried clean towels. Together, we walked to the ground floor where we loaded the laundry into our cart, which was already filled with cleaning supplies. Then, we began our evening routine of cleaning the rooms.

Tia and I alternated in who took care of the bathroom and who made the bed and tidied up the room.

"Yikes," I said as I opened the door to the first room on our list and choked on a mix of stale, rancid air. The first thing I did was thrust the window open and inhale a lungful of fresh air. Then, I began tearing off the sheets, wondering how in only one night, the guest managed to stain them with white, yellow, and red bodily fluids. I tried not to think too much about what had happened in the sheets, but my abundant imagination made it impossible. To distract myself, I began to hum. As usual, my humming turned into a song that I made up on the spot:

*There is a girl who cooks and cleans, cooks and cleans, to make a dime. One day, she hopes her road will take her to a better place. Her head tells her it's impossible, impossible, but her heart tells her anything is possible, even the word impossible is saying: I'm possible.*

"What are you singing?" Tia asked.

"Nothing special." I put on the fresh bed linens. "Just trying to distract myself from this gross mess." I held up the dirty sheets for her to see, and she wrinkled her nose in disgust.

"You should really do something with your voice," she said.

"Like what?"

"Go to a bar that has live music; see if they will hire you."

I chortled. "Why on earth would they hire me?"

"Because, Halia, you can sing, and you write your own songs."

I shrugged. "That's not enough. Look at me." I gazed down at my torn jeans and my bell-sleeved shirt that was put together from a bunch of fabric scraps. "I don't look anything like those gorgeous performers."

"Anyone can look the part when put in the right clothes, their hair and make-up done. But most people can't sing, and even fewer can write their own songs."

"Whatever. Even if someone would take me, I don't want to perform."

"You keep saying that, but I know you'd be great onstage." Excitement entered her face.

I turned away, focusing on the dusting. "Leave it," I whispered.

Tia didn't protest. Relief filled me, but it was tainted with a touch of sadness. I was being silly if I allowed myself to feel wistful about the stage. I'd never been on one. What would a girl like me even do up on a stage? Who did I think I was? I was an orphan and a maid. I was a girl trying to survive. I was not a singer. Singers were beautiful, rich, and lucky girls. There was nothing lucky about me. I was cursed, and twice a week, I had to pay a faerie to stop my curse from killing me. I glanced into the mirror hanging on the wall. My eyes were still a cornfield blue, but specs of gold were beginning to dot my irises. I needed to wipe out those golden specks before they turned into golden circles.

Tia and I finished cleaning the room and moved to the next. Since we had cleaned room eleven to fifteen in the morning, we had to do one through ten, which took us several hours.

"I need a drink," Tia said when we were finally done. She wiped the sweat off her forehead with the back of her hand. "I know what we could do." A smile lit up her tired face. "I heard a rumor that the bar on Port and Sanderson Street switched hands a month ago. Apparently, opening night is tonight, and the first fifty people will get a free drink."

"I can't," I said, annoyance trickling through me. I loved my friend dearly, but even though she knew about my secret, she seemed to forget that I couldn't go out on the nights before I visited Acacia. For the transaction between the fae and me to take place, I needed to get a good night's sleep. The few times I had shown up tired or hungover, she had sent me away, saying my emotions were too muddy for her to sieve through.

Noticing the dejected expression on Tia's face, I said, "I'll go next time."

She nodded. "All right. Do you want to take a walk tonight? I've heard there's a concert at the castle. If we get close enough to the wall, we might be able to hear it."

I felt my forehead wrinkle. "Really? With everything going on, they're still putting on concerts?"

She shrugged. "I doubt the king will attend it, but the court still needs entertainment."

How anyone at the castle could think about entertainment when our queen had gone missing almost a week ago was beyond me, but it wasn't my place to judge.

"I'm afraid I already have plans for tonight."

Tia crossed her arms. "Victor?"

I nodded. "He has a surprise for me."

Tia shook her head. "He's not good for you."

I twirled a strand of my wavy, auburn hair around my finger. "He's not perfect, but neither am I."

"You lack confidence and proactivity. He's a jerk. There's a huge difference between the two."

"He's not. He simply has strong opinions."

"You'd be better off without him."

"I have to go." I walked away without hugging Tia goodbye. She was wrong. Victor was good for me. He had rescued me that night in the alley when a customer had tried to rip off my dress. He chased down the elf who had tried to leave the boarding house without paying up and had made him pay us an extra 10 percent for trying to flee.

Victor was my only hope of escaping the life of an orphan and a maid. With his help, I could become a better version of myself. With his love, I could finally have my own family.

As I left the boarding house, a refreshing summer breeze greeted me, ruffling my long hair. I closed my eyes and stood still for a moment, savoring my freedom. The sun had long gone down, but my favorite time of the day was just beginning. The city was coming alive with lights, singing, and dancing. At the night market, vendors were selling their wares, and delicious scents of cinnamon, vanilla, and chocolate tickled my nose.

I strolled past the night market, taking my time since Victor was always late. In the center square, the acrobats balanced on their hand, contorting their bodies in positions that looked impossible while fire breathers swallowed whole swords.

Ten minutes past our date, I left the market and headed toward the lover's bridge where Victor had told me to meet him.

The center of the bridge was my favorite part. It was crowded with love-locks, some engraved with names, and others only revealing the initials of the lovers. How many of them were still together? Had the ones that broke up taken down their lock? Or did they hold on to their key, cherishing that, at least, they had known love even though they had lost it?

Would my and Victor's lock hang here one day? I doubted it. Unlike me, he wasn't into sentimental "crap." And while I liked the idea, a part of me was relieved that we weren't official on this bridge or anywhere else for now. Eventually, he would ask me to marry him. While on a logical level, I knew this was good, my soul found the idea terrifying, and my heart said no, even though getting married would mean security and not wanting for anything ever again.

*It's not worth it. Don't marry him.*

But if I declined, I'd have to stay at the boarding house. That was no life either.

I traced the top of one of the locks as if petting its head, ashamed that instead of thinking about sharing my life with Victor, I was wondering if he would come through and one day give me the music shop he had promised me. I knew he would never gift it to me as a wedding present. He believed gifts needed to be earned. By being his bride, I wouldn't have earned anything. I would have to first prove myself as his wife and a mother.

My stomach contracted. I couldn't be a mother yet. I could barely take care of myself. I needed time for myself, to explore who I was and what my purpose was in this lifetime before I could consider bringing a new life into this world.

Footsteps came from my left. I turned to find Victor marching toward me, still wearing his patrol uniform, his hair as black as the night, his already sharp features sharpened by the shadows the streetlamps created.

He stopped two feet away from me. "Halia, do you always have to stand in the middle of the bridge, making me come all the way to you?"

"N-no, I'm sorry." Had I been selfish? I guessed I should have been more attuned to his mood.

"I've had a busy day. I really don't need you to be difficult as well."

"I wasn't trying to—"

"Let's go." He grabbed my hand, none too gently and pulled me after him.

"Where are we going?"

"Dover's Tavern."

My steps faltered. Dover's Tavern was worse than the boarding house I worked at. Our guests might be nonhumans, and the house was old and creaky, but everything was clean, and we used fresh ingredients for our meals. The tavern, on the other hand, was populated by rowdy drunks and had been temporarily shut down a few months ago over claims of serving rat meat.

"Can't we go somewhere else?"

Victor's eyes narrowed. "What, are you too good for Dover's now?"

"No, but it's such a nice night out, I thought we could stay outside. And you said you had a surprise for me."

"Yes, well, the surprise will have to wait with everything I have going on. I'm hungry. Come on now, I need to eat."

Thankfully, I had already eaten. The benefit of the boarding house serving food was that I was allowed to eat it as well. However, to appease Victor, I ordered a French onion soup while he got the pig roast. I crinkled my nose as the dish was brought out, trying not to think about how the animal had been mistreated in his short life. The tavern wasn't known for its ethically sourced meat.

Victor wolfed down half of his dish before abruptly putting down his fork and looking up at me. "Aren't you going to ask me what is bothering me? Don't you care?"

"Of course, I do." But if I'd asked, you'd accuse me of being intrusive.

"We have lost another establishment."

"Really?" I tilted my head. "I didn't realize there was a fire."

He waved his hand dismissively. "No, nothing like that. A demon bought the bar on Port and Sanderson Street. As if it weren't bad enough that he's invading our city, he's renaming our bar. Who does he think he is?"

The bar had been renamed so many times, I didn't understand why it mattered if the name changed again.

"Guess what he called it? Daydream! Pure travesty!"

I tried to hide the smile that threatened to burst onto

my face. Daydream, I liked it. People could dream about going to the bar and having fun while going about their daily business and chores. It was clever and humorous.

“It’s simply atrocious.” Victor spit out a bone.

“Has this demon done anything illegal?” I asked.

“No.” Victor wiped away the gravy dripping down his chin with his fingers, ignoring the napkin in front of him. “But we don’t need another magical creature coming to Arcadia.”

I nodded. Arcadia had recently seen an influx of powerful, nonhuman immigrants. Where had they been all my life? And why were they all coming out now?

“Top me up.” Victor waved his beer jug at the bartender.

I stirred my now-cold soup, humming a song.

“What did you say? Speak up.” Victor lifted his head and looked down at me.

“Nothing.”

Victor gulped down his second beer. “If I weren’t a good man, I would try to convince you to come to my place after this.”

A shiver darted through me.

“But I’m an honorable man, and you’re an honorable girl. We’ll have to wait until we’re married.”

The relief I felt at us having to wait vanished as he said we had to get married. It was too soon. I wasn’t ready.

“Once I save up enough money to move out of my parents’ house and buy a place, we’ll have a wedding. Nothing fancy. No point throwing money out of the window, but it’s important to get the papers. We’ll be respectable people with our own home. And we’ll raise a respectable family.” Victor pushed his almost empty plate toward me. “Are you hungry? I told you to get the roast, not the soup."

I pushed my nailbed back. "I'm good, thanks."

"Then why are you staring at the food and not me?"

I rubbed my temple, feeling a headache coming on. "I'm just tired, that's all."

"Fine, let me walk you home." Victor threw down a few Marks and rose. I followed him out of the bar, busying my hands with the Rhombus cube Tia had given me last Christmas. I was still trying to solve it and kept it in my pocket.

Halfway through the walk, Victor grabbed my hand, sending the cube flying. "Why are you always fidgeting with that thing?"

I darted forward to pick up the cube. I shook off the street dirt and pocketed it. "I want to solve it."

"It's stupid. It doesn't have any real-life application."

"I suppose it doesn't. It's just fun."

Victor shook his head. "This nonsense has to stop. You're not still writing songs, are you?"

I opened and closed my mouth several times. "They just come to me. I never sit down to write them. I don't have the time."

"That's good."

Bubbles of anger floated up through my chest and popped from my mouth. "What would be so wrong with writing them down? It wouldn't hurt anyone."

"It's one thing to sing them while you work, but don't get a big head over it."

"Why would I?"

"I don't know. You're a woman. Who knows how your mind works," he said as we reached the boarding house. He opened the door, but I made no move to step through it.

"Why would you say that? Not all women are alike.

How would you feel if I said all men are the same?"

Victor threw up his hands. "Calm down. I didn't mean anything by it. Don't be so sensitive."

His dismissing me only enraged me further. "What if I do think I'm a good singer or songwriter, what's wrong with that?"

Victor let the door fall shut and stepped closer, pushing a hair strand behind my ear. He smiled, but his eyes were hard. "I really care about you, Halia. I don't want to see you get hurt. Girls like you, innocent girls, are easily taken advantage of by their environment. I'm afraid someone will promise you riches or fame, or who-knows-what, and you'll go with them, straight into a trap. You still remember the incident in the alley, don't you?"

The memory froze me into place. The stranger's hands shoving me, ripping the top of my dress. If Victor hadn't interfered, my virginity would've been taken by force in the best-case scenario. In the worst-case scenario, the stranger would've slit my throat afterward.

"Remember, the world is a dangerous place." Victor stroked my upper arm. "You're safe with me. I won't let others hurt you, but you need to be smart. You need to be a good and reasonable girl, understood?"

I nodded, too exhausted to contradict him.

"Good. I'll be busy for the next two nights, but I'll meet you at the night market on Sunday. We can go somewhere you like, perhaps that Mediterranean place that has the vegetable dishes."

I couldn't help the smile forming on my lips. Victor hated vegetarian dishes, but he was willing to go to Ali Ali, even though the few meat dishes they served were never spicy or salty enough for him. "I'd love that."

Victor leaned forward and pressed a quick kiss to

my mouth. Then he turned around and left. "I'll see you on Sunday."

"Yes." What would it be like to lay with Victor? Would he consider intimacy a duty? Would he try to get it over with quickly, and see it as something we had to do from time to time in order to produce children? Or would he want to do it daily?

My throat closed up. The idea of doing it terrified me. I didn't want to be naked and exposed. What if I hated it? What if it hurt? What if it was boring and awful?

I chewed on my lip. I'd have to ask Tia about it. Even though she had grown up with me in the boarding house and technically wasn't allowed to go out after nightfall, she had managed to sneak out and meet a guy last spring. For several months, she had spent her nights with him while I had to cover for her, until eventually, he moved away to live with his uncle who lived in a different city, leaving her behind. Afterward, Tia had insisted she didn't need a man in her life, but occasionally she would spend the night with someone. I never asked her how many, and I never cared why or what it felt like, but now, I needed to know. Was it always the same? Was it better sometimes? Was it different with different men? And if so, was there any way to know if I would like it with a person before committing myself to him in holy matrimony?

I had never asked myself those questions, but then, I had never spent time alone with a man until Victor. The orphanage was all-female, and I was too busy directing the female chorus. The chorus brought me a lot of joy and the orphanage a lot of money, which it desperately needed for new mattresses and kitchen repairs. Selfishly, I had hoped that if I oversaw the chorus, I would get to stay after I turned eighteen and be paid a small salary. Alas, the orphanage had other plans.

Victor was right. It was better not to get my hopes up. I could continue singing to myself, but there was no need to share it with others who might feed my unrealistic dreams and desires that would only bring me pain in the end.

## 16TH JULY

Working as a maid had its advantages. The daily physical exertion ensured I was asleep as soon as I collapsed in my bed and slept through the night until my clock rang.

With my shift starting at eight, my alarm was normally set for seven, but on days that I saw Acacia, like today, I got up at six.

I slammed down the alarm button on clock and trudged toward the basin. My eyes were half-closed, and I splashed cold water onto my face to properly wake up. Only then, did I shoot a glance toward Tia's cot. She snored and smiled in her sleep. Since she only snored after drinking, I guessed she'd had one drink too many and would appreciate it if I brought her a fresh coffee before our shift started. If it had been anyone else, I wouldn't have been too thrilled to share a room with them, but Tia was the only family I had, and I was glad we worked and lived together. It made me feel less lonely. I didn't mind her returning when the sun rose or eating garlic bread in her bed, even if it made our room smell like garlic for days to come.

I dressed in my gray dress, not bothering to put on my apron for now. Then, I made my bed and drank the glass of water on my bedside table that I always put out the night before. Then I tiptoed downstairs.

Acacia preferred it when I didn't have breakfast before seeing her, which was fine by me since I would rather not go into the kitchen anyways and risk someone seeing me and asking what I was doing up so early.

The only other person who knew about me visiting a faerie twice a week was Tia. I hadn't even considered confiding in Victor and wasn't sure I ever would even if we did get married. I supposed I should tell my husband the truth, but I really didn't want to. I had the feeling that Victor wouldn't appreciate knowing that his wife had strange golden circles around her irises, which she had to hide every three to four days with the help of a faerie. The way he had talked about magical creatures yesterday made me suspect he would blame me for having this abnormality, perhaps even accuse me of getting a sense of importance from it.

Obviously I had no control over what my eyes looked like, but still, I didn't want to risk hearing such accusations from him. The girls in the orphanage had teased me about my abnormality, and I never wanted to go through that again.

No, even if I married Victor, I wouldn't tell him. I would simply sneak out twice a week early in the morning to see Acacia. Or maybe I wouldn't marry him at all. But what would I do then? Did I really want to spend my life cleaning the boarding house? If only I had a skill that made me employable. Alas, all I was good at was singing, and there was no way someone like me could find the right contacts and make it as a singer.

Enveloped in my gloomy thoughts, I reached Acacia's rose-colored house in low spirits. I knocked thrice as the faerie had instructed me to do the first time I had met her. Several seconds passed before there was a rustling, and the door opened.

Acacia's sky-blue gaze scanned me. "You need to worry less, child. It's not an attractive quality." She waved me inside and walked down the corridor, her gauzy train brushing the ground, her knee-length hair glinting like liquid gold.

The corridor was narrow, allowing only one person to pass through at a time, but it was beautiful, decorated with stained glass and paintings that depicted merry fae families.

At the end of the corridor, was one single door that led into Acacia's workspace. The room looked like a pharmacy. It was lined with countless cabinets and tables that displayed multi-colored bottles and tinctures of all kinds of sizes and shapes.

The scents in the room kept changing as if different perfumes were being sprayed at one-minute intervals. At first, it smelled citrusy and refreshing, then the scent unfurled into a flowery bouquet, heavy on lilies. Next, it morphed into something heavier with luscious plum notes before turning into a spicy scent, then back to the citrusy aroma.

Even though the lamps looked standard, the light in the room also too kept switching. Mint light gave way to a light pink light, followed by a magenta blue, azure blue, and back to the green light.

Acacia motioned for me to sit down in the wooden chair opposite her plush throne, an opaque table separating us. She took my hand. I tried to relax and not think too much about what she was about to do. To distract myself, I studied the bottles arranged on the tables.

Acacia hummed as she read me, sifting through my emotions, deciding which one she wanted to take in exchange for making the gold flecks in my eyes disappear.

"How interesting." Her voice was tinkling, yet it also had a low quality to it. She was like the room we were in, constantly changing. As a mortal, I couldn't even begin to understand what it was like to be her and how her mind worked.

"Interesting," the faerie repeated. "You're practically bubbling over with emotions. Normally, when that happens, a person is driven by one emotion. In your case, however, there's excitement, fear, anxiety." She smiled wickedly. "And underneath all that is anger, something I haven't seen much in you, Halia. What triggered it, dear?"

None of your business. "Which emotion would you like to take?"

A crystalline laugh filled the air, but Acacia's face was void of amusement. "I'm tempted to take your anger since I have never tasted it before, and I would love to know what it tastes like. But I have a feeling you'll need it yourself, and I have many sources whose anger it is much easier to siphon off. Perhaps next time, when you're more enraged."

I flinched, pulling, or trying and failing to pull, my hand free from hers. "I'm not angry."

"Keep telling yourself that. Anyhow, I'll take some of your anxiety. I have several buyers for that."

I tilted my head. "Who would want anxiety?"

Another crystalline laugh. "Not for themselves, silly."

My jaw clenched. Somebody would buy anxiety to give it to somebody else, probably to control a person, and I was part of this disgusting manipulation.

Acacia pressed the spot between my wrist and my right thumb, a trigger point, drawing my attention toward her.

"Don't beat yourself up. If you don't give me your anxiety, somebody else will. But if I don't hide your eye color …." She didn't finish the sentence, letting the implication hang in the air.

I didn't want anyone to feel anxiety or suffer because of me, but I also wasn't ready to die, which I would if my true eye color came out.

"Do it," I said, giving the faerie the permission she needed before tapping into my emotion. Then, because I couldn't handle thinking about how my anxiety would be used, I allowed the past to wash over me, searching for justification in my memories.

I was seven years old, and the girl in front of me, a twelve-year-old, was pointing at me. "What's wrong with you? Do you have jaundice?"

"Why are your eyes so funny?" A second girl joined us. They were both so tall and big and mean.

"You're a monster!" a third girl yelled.

"A monster, a monster, a monster," they chimed in unison.

Hot tears stung my eyes. I darted out of the room, down the stairs, and out of the orphanage, managing to hold the tears at bay until I was safely hidden in an alcove. I cried for what felt like forever until a shadow leaned over me, and I jerked upright.

"Tia, you almost scared me to death."

She scanned my face. "It's happening again."

I lowered my gaze. "I don't know what you're talking about."

"Mrs. Woods told me to call her when it was time."

I peeked up from underneath my eyelashes, wondering if the girl I had played with on a few occasions knew how to fix me. "What can she do?" I barely remembered Mrs. Woods. She had shown up around Christmas, held my hand, and called me a brave girl. Then she told me to find her when I needed her. I had forgotten all about that until Tia brought it up.

"Where do we find her?"

Tia wrinkled her forehead. "I don't know. She made me promise to remind you. She said you would know how to find her. Did she give you anything?"

I shook my head slowly. "No." Suddenly, it all came back to me. When you need me, you only need to think about me and speak my name silently three times in your mind; then, I'll be there.

Not wanting the only girl who was willing to play with me to think I was a lunatic, I said, "I'm going to do something strange, please don't freak out."

Tia gave me a smile. "Stranger than Sister Catherine kissing the priest?"

I chuckled. That had been extremely strange. Our teacher had been so mad at us for walking into the church when we weren't supposed to that she made us take our meals in the corner for a week afterward.

"All right, here it goes." I closed my eyes and focused. *Mrs. Woods, Mrs. Woods, Mrs. Woods, please come. I need your help.*

There was a popping sound, and then Tia and I

were no longer alone in the alley. A woman covered in a powder-blue cloak stood before me. "So soon. It's only been half a year. I suppose I'll have to make my visits more frequent to you."

"I don't understand," I said.

She held out her hand, and I gave her mine. Something floated through me. It felt like a strong combination of a water drop, a fresh breeze, and the caress of rose petals. The sensation only lasted for a few seconds. Mrs. Woods dropped my hand. "You should be good for another six months, but let me know as soon as the golden specks in your eyes begin to show again."

"What are they? Why do I have them? None of the other girls do."

Mrs. Woods shook her head. "It's not for me to tell. All you need to know is that you must hide them. As soon as they appear, call me. Don't let your eyes ever get to the state where you have golden circles around them." She glanced at Tia. "You'll help your friend, won't you?"

Tia nodded solemnly. "Of course."

For a moment, I forgot all about my questions. All I could think about was that I had a friend. Tia was my friend.

"Good. Until soon." One moment, Mrs. Woods was standing next to us; then, she was gone in a cloud of dust.

Throughout my childhood, I wondered if Mrs. Woods worked for the circus and was able to perform magical tricks. It was only when I turned twelve that I realized she must be a magic wielder.

"What are you? Who sends you?" I asked again and again, but she refused to tell. At fourteen, I became so angry about not having any answers that after summoning her, I yelled, "Maybe I don't want to change my eye color anymore! Maybe I want people to see that I have golden rings around my irises!"

A deep look of sorrow entered Mrs. Woods' face. "If you do that, you'll die."

My burning anger transformed into icy fear. "Dead? How? Why?"

"I don't have permission to tell you."

"Why?"

Mrs. Woods didn't reply.

"Why are you helping me?"

Once again, she didn't reply. All she said was, "I must go now." Then she disappeared once again.

I tried a few more times to get the truth out of her, but, eventually, I gave up and accepted my fate. That was until the day before I turned eighteen, and Mrs. Woods came to visit me of her own accord, without me having to call on her. "I'm sorry, Halia. I won't be able to help you any longer."

"What do you mean?"

"I was only looking over you until you turned into an adult. My work is done. You must find a faerie that can hide the gold in your eyes."

"Why?"

"You know why."

I balled my fists. "If the gold in my eyes is killing me, then why are they always turning that way?"

"It won't be that way forever. You'll know when it's safe to show yourself."

"How will I know?"

She pressed her hand to her chest. "You'll know in here. When there's no fear inside of you any longer."

No fear. Was that even possible? Everyone in the orphanage lived in constant fear of the heat being turned off, or there not being enough food for everyone, or the teachers getting upset and smacking us.

"You'll figure it out. I believe in you." Then Mrs. Woods disappeared on me for the last time. She never turned up again, no matter how desperately I called her, no matter how many hours I spent in prayer, begging her to return. Since I had turned eighteen, I was on my own. Mrs. Woods and the orphanage no longer supported me, so I did what I had to survive—scrubbed Madam's Boarding House and met with Acacia twice a week.

And I was fine. I had survived. Many other girls who had once lived in the orphanage were now working the streets or with men that gave them new bruises daily. Others were drinking as soon as they got up or spending their earnings and going into debt for half an hour dream escape they bought from a fae, imagining, for a while, they were somebody else, somewhere else.

I had avoided all these pitfalls for several months. My life wasn't too bad.

"All done," Acacia said, and I realized that my sudden shift of mood wasn't due to myself but due to her siphoning off some of my anxiety.

That was the problem with feelings, wasn't it? Countless times I had wished to wipe away the sadness, and uneasiness. They were nasty parasites that led me to avoid others, gave me stomachaches, and sometimes paralyzed me to the point that all I could do was stare blankly into empty space. Yet, as hard as those emotions hit me when they came to me, they also had a purpose. Fear and anxiety protected me from danger, and anger helped me to stand up for myself. Perhaps the emotions I wanted to get rid of so desperately were blessings in disguise.

"Look at me."

I did, meeting Acacia's arctic-blue gaze. Her lips moved quickly, but silently for a few seconds, and then it was done. She handed me a mirror. The golden specks in my eyes were gone. "Thank you."

Acacia rose. "I'll see you in a few days."

"Yes." I had never dared to ask Acacia how long she thought I would need to come to her. She had been fair with me as far as I could tell, but she was still a fae. What if she wanted to continue tapping into my emotions and would tell me that I would need to always hide the natural pattern of my eyes? Or what if she didn't care about my well-being and told me I could stop coming to her at any time, and then I would die.

Somehow, I didn't think that my eye color would directly kill me. Mrs. Woods certainly hadn't made it sound that way. It appeared more as if I had to hide the golden rings in my eyes until it was safe to reveal them. But why? What did the gold in my eyes tell others?

Was my abnormality a sign that I perhaps had magic within me? A laugh escaped me at that preposterous idea, earning me a raised eyebrow from Acacia.

"Am I amusing you, child?"

I quickly shook my head. "Forgive me, it's just that my eyes are so strange, I wonder if I perhaps have some magic within me."

"Everybody has a drop of magic in them," Acacia replied solemnly.

I was so surprised by this response, I didn't respond. I exited her house, wondering if she really meant what she had said or if it was some fae philosophy. Perhaps it was even deception. The legend had it that because fae were unable to lie, they had become masters at manipulation.

How I wished Mrs. Woods would come to me one final time and answer my questions. Everything would be so much easier if only I could make sense of it. Confused and desperate, I stopped in an empty alley, closed my eyes, and focused hard. *Mrs. Woods, Mrs. Woods, Mrs. Woods, please come to me. I need your wisdom.*

I kept my eyes closed for at least a minute, but nothing happened. I waited for at least five minutes, turning at every bit of sound. Mrs. Woods didn't appear. She had forsaken me. She wasn't coming back. Just like my parents and the orphanage, she had abandoned me. Was I really that unlovable? What if the pattern of my eyes was my smallest problem? What if I was somehow rotten, wrong on the inside, and others could sense it, and that's why they went running for the hills?

Hot tears threatened to run down my cheeks, but I had no time to wallow in self-pity, unless I wanted to lose the roof over my head. I hurried back to the boarding house where I forced myself to swallow a couple of pieces of cheese, washing them down with a cup of coffee.

Five minutes prior to my morning shift, the door flung open, and Tia walked in, or more correctly, she careened into the kitchen, her eyes at half-mast. I grabbed her a mug and filled it to the brim with black coffee, the way she liked it.

"You're a lifesaver." She downed half of the cup in one go.

"You enjoyed the club then?" I asked.

She smiled widely, and her head lolled. Clearly, she was still drunk. "It was great. You really missed out."

I stared at my short nails. "I had some business to take care of this morning."

She nodded but didn't ask any questions. The only

time we ever discussed Acacia was when we were 100 percent sure no one could overhear us. I had no doubt that if Madam Fontaine found out about my strangeness, she would fire me on the spot. Tia would probably lose her job through association.

I rose. “We better get going. Don’t want to be late.”

Tia stuffed a piece of bread into her mouth and chewed rapidly as we walked up the stairs to the cleaning supply cupboard.

With Tia’s hangover, I offered to clean the bathrooms while she dusted. An hour later, my back was on fire from all the bending. Was that all my life would ever amount to? Scrubbing and cleaning? Would I always be an outsider and never belong anywhere?

Unable to keep the desperation locked within me any longer, I opened my mouth and sang quietly so that Tia couldn’t hear the words.

*They come and go as the wind. Come and go as the breeze. Only I remain; only I, alone, alone.*

“A new song?” Tia asked.

“It’s nothing special.” Tia was still happy from the previous night. The last thing I wanted was to bring my friend down with me.

By the third room, Tia had worked off the alcohol. Her movements were sharper and more energetic, and her pupils were back to normal. “Halia, why don’t you sing something for us? It always makes the time goes by faster.”

“Sure.” Even though I wasn’t in a cheerful mood, I began to sing an upbeat song I had come up with last week, knowing she would love it.

*You put your chains on me, but I broke free of them. You can’t hold me down. Never, ever will you hold me down.*

I teased out the last word, making my voice vibrate. All right, so maybe the song wasn't exactly upbeat, but rather defiant, but the tempo was fast, and Tia bobbed her head in rhythm, clearly approving of my choice.

We worked our way through all the rooms on our list before we mopped the corridor. Several guests opened their doors at the hubbub we made. My worries that anyone would complain about my singing were unfounded. Instead of glares and reprimands, I received smiles.

Tia jabbed me in the ribs. "Everybody loves it when you sing. You should do it professionally."

I sighed. "Not again."

Tia slapped herself on the forehead. "I almost forgot to tell you! The bar I went to yesterday, Daydream, is so cool. The owner is so nice and open-minded—"

"What kind of demon is he?" I interrupted.

Tia grinned. "How did you know he was a demon? Did you run into him?"

I tore off the dirty sheets from the bed. "Victor told me."

Tia tsked. "Did he? Did he make up a story about how Lorenzo eats little children for breakfast to keep you away from Daydream?"

"No, he simply doesn't appreciate demons owning businesses in Arcadia."

"Victor wouldn't be thrilled about anyone's success but his own."

I grabbed fresh sheets from our cart, nearly knocking it over. "Why do you have to say that?" On a rational level, I knew there was some truth to Tia's statement, but on an emotional level, I had to wonder why she had to badmouth the only man who had ever shown interest in me.

"You could do so much better."

Normally, I wouldn't have responded, but seeing Acacia always made me vulnerable, and Mrs. Woods refusing to show up when I called her didn't help my mood either. "Is that so? Then why did my parents give me up? Why did the orphanage throw me out? Why did Mrs. Woods stop helping me? Victor is the only one I have! He's the only one who hasn't given up on me. Maybe you don't need anyone, but I want to be loved."

"Is that what you think Victor gives you, love?"

I busied myself making the bed. "I don't know. How can I know what love is when I have never experienced it?"

Matching my quiet tone, Tia said, "You have me, but I guess that doesn't count because I'm not a man."

I dropped the pillowcase and stepped toward her. "You are the best friend anyone could ask for, but it can't be just you and I. I need other people in my life."

Tia gave me a sad smile. "I know. And I want you to have others in your life. Just because I don't want a man, doesn't mean you shouldn't have one. I just wish it would be anyone but Victor."

"He's not that bad." At her I'm-not-buying-it look, I added, "Really."

"How do you know? He's the first guy you ever dated."

I bit my lip. "He always tells me how much he cares about me. And he always makes an effort to see me."

Tia rolled her eyes. "He monopolizes your time, stopping you from meeting anyone else. We're going to change that. You're coming to Daydream with me tomorrow night, no excuses. If you have plans with Victor, cancel them."

"How expensive is it?"

"We'll go on a budget. Dancing is free. You deserve

to have some fun, and we need some girl time."

"I don't know."

She grabbed my hands. "Come on! It's going to be fun!"

Her smile was so infectious, I couldn't stay neutral. "All right." Little did I know I would come to regret my response the following day.

## 17TH JULY

Tia and I had cleaned all but the last two rooms on our list the following night when she dropped a bombshell on me wrapped in an innocent question. "Are you excited to go to Daydream tonight?"

"Yes, it will be fun." I wasn't as much of a dancer as Tia was, but it would be good to check out a new place.

"Great. I forgot to mention yesterday, it's open mic night, and I signed you up."

My chin dropped. "You what?"

Tia pushed the cart to the next room, acting as if she hadn't heard me.

I ran after her. "Why would you do that?"

"Because you're a great singer, and it's time you shared your wonderful voice with the world."

"No." I crossed my arms. "I'm not going to Daydream

to make a fool out of myself."

"You wouldn't be making a fool out of yourself." Tia motioned around herself. "Wake up, Halia! Every time any of our guests hear your voice, they come out of their rooms to listen."

"They're just curious."

"Is that why they stand outside their rooms, their eyes full of awe?"

I collected the dirty dishes strewn across the table and loaded them onto the cart. "It doesn't happen all the time. Only sometimes."

Tia gave me a look that said cut-the-crap.

I grabbed a cloth and wiped down the table, which was a mess of crumbs, sauce, and stains of wine. Had the last occupant never heard of how to use dinnerware?

"How about a bet?"

I turned around, intrigued by what Tia might propose. "You sing in the hallway a chorus of one of your songs, and if less than three guests come out of their rooms to listen, I'll delete your name on the open mic sheet."

I bit my lip. "And if more than three come out?"

"Then you'll go to Daydream with me. You don't need to sing, but I want you to at least go with me and listen to the other performers so that you can see how much better you are."

I wrung my hands. "There's no way I'm better than them."

Ignoring my statement, Tia held out her hand. "Deal?"

Knowing she wouldn't leave it alone until I proved her wrong, I shook her hand. "Deal."

Beads of sweat formed on my forehead as I considered what song to sing. Part of me wanted to sing something awful, something that would discourage anyone from coming out of their room. But the other part of me wanted to sing one of my better songs. This part wanted to believe Tia and longed for a confirmation that I had talent.

The trepidation within me made it impossible to think of anything joyful and easy-going. Instead, I settled on a song I had named "Torn."

I started with a low note, excited about belting out the higher ones.

*I don't know if you ever felt this way. I don't know if you'll understand. But for me, it's a constant battle raging on the inside. See, I'm torn. Torn. Unsure what to do. My head is saying no. My heart is saying yes. Should I take the risk, or should I stay? Should I leap, or should I stay down?*

*Just when I think I have the answer, everything flips. My heart is saying no while my head is saying yes. What part should I listen to? How do I decide? I am torn, so torn. I don't know if you ever felt this way, but I do, I do a lot. I am torn, oh, so, so torn.*

At some point during the song, I had closed my eyes and lost myself completely to the melody and the words. Done with the chorus, I stopped, not wanting to open my eyes, afraid of what I would see. I wasn't quite ready to go to Daydream, but I also wasn't ready for an empty hallway.

Applause sounded, and I could no longer remain blind to the outcome. I peeked through my eyelashes and counted not one, not two, but eight guests. All of them were clapping, big smiles on their faces.

Tia jabbed me in the ribs. "I won this bet fair and square."

I nodded. "I'll go with you to Daydream, but no

singing. I'll just watch."

"At least, consider singing."

I wrung my hands.

"Please?"

"All right, but I'm not promising anything."

Tia jumped up and down, sending her blue hair swinging.

"What's going on here?" The shrill voice belonged to Madam Fontaine. She glared at the guests, who disappeared behind their doors, then headed toward us.

I quickly grabbed a stack of fresh towels. "Nothing. We were just cleaning."

Madam's thin lips curled into a sneer. "I don't pay you to cluck. You better be done with all the rooms in an hour. I'll deduct a Mark if I see a spot of dust because of your inattentiveness."

"You won't," I said and dropped my head in deference.

Sensing that Tia was about to speak up, I pinched her hand. Nothing good could come out of arguing with Madam. On the contrary, it could cost us our jobs.

"Go back to work," Madam said even though we were already opening the door to the next room that needed to be cleaned.

"She's such a bitch," Tia said once we were inside the room. I shushed her, afraid Madam was still nearby to overhear, but Tia didn't stop. "Do this, do that," she imitated in a stern voice. "Perhaps she should stop stuffing her face with cakes and do some work herself."

"Don't say that! She's just big-boned."

Tia rolled her eyes. "Those four cupcakes she gobbled down yesterday made her big-boned?"

I dusted the counters and emptied the trash, ignoring my friend's rant. We weren't in a position to challenge

Madam or ask her to treat us differently, so there wasn't any point in getting upset in the first place.

"Does she even do anything around the boarding house besides bossing us around?"

I sighed. "It's none of our business."

"So because she pays us, she can say whatever she wants, and we need to remain silent?" Tia put her fists on her hips in a defiant pose.

"I'm not saying it's right. Being her employees doesn't give her the right to treat us with disrespect. But even though her treatment is unfounded and unfair, we have no choice but to bite our tongues. Please promise me you won't say anything. We need these jobs."

Tia exhaled loudly. "You wouldn't if you were a singer. Perhaps I could work at the bar." A big grin spread across her face. "We're going to have so much fun at Daydream." She took my hands and twirled us in a circle until I couldn't help but smile as well.

"I feel overdressed." I pulled on the straps of my silk dress as I walked next to Tia toward Daydream.

"It's perfect. The color looks amazing on you. Plus, I picked it out, and I have great taste." She chuckled.

I nodded. The turquoise, floor-length silk dress did compliment my blue eyes and pale skin. I liked how it flowed along my skinny frame, making me look almost like a fae. However, was it appropriate bar attire? I was certain the other girls would wear provocative dresses in black and red colors or something like Tia, who was clad out in a pair of jeans with studs and a black top that read, "Rock on." Neither the femme fatale nor the rock chick was my style, but I was afraid that I would stand out like a sore thumb in my choice. The dress was brand new. Tia had somehow saved up to give it to me as a birthday present. I loved it, but I hadn't had an opportunity to wear it until today. As nervous as I was to fit in, I was worried about sticking out like a sore thumb. Still, I was excited to wear it and see how people reacted to me when I wasn't in my daily clothes.

Perhaps Victor was right, and I was provocative. As if thinking of him had conjured him up, six patrolmen marched past us, one of them, Victor.

I pulled Tia into an alcove.

"What?"

I shushed her, my eyes glued on Victor.

"Oh." She fell silent.

With bated breath, I watched as Victor and the other soldiers dragged away two teenage boys with dirty hands. What had the youngsters done? Were they thieves? Stealing wasn't all right, but what if those children didn't have anyone to provide for them? With their countless rules, orphanages didn't work out for everyone. What if those two boys simply couldn't sit still, follow all the commandments, and pretend the nuns didn't hide forbidden romance books or hit children for eating cookies with dirty hands?

"That was close," Tia said once Victor was out of sight.

I shook my head. "I'm not hiding."

"Sure. You just didn't want him to see you because you knew he would disapprove of you going to Daydream. Tell me again how he's not controlling."

I shook my head. "You don't understand. He's protective of me."

"He's treating you like you are his possession."

I tore a hangnail off my middle finger, making it

bleed. As much as I wanted to disagree with Tia, Victor could be restrictive. But then again, wasn't that proof that he loved me? Wasn't every relationship like that? One gave up some of their freedom to get love in return. The orphanage had been strict with lots of rules, but they took care of us. Then when we were allowed to do whatever we wanted because we turned eighteen, we were kicked out.

If the choice was between being loved and receiving safety in exchange for which I had to follow rules versus being all on my own without any support, how could I choose the latter? I wasn't strong like Tia, not needing anyone. I wanted to care about someone and to have someone care about me. Perhaps I was too soft for this world. Perhaps I should harden myself.

Tia touched my shoulder gently. "Hey, I'm sorry. I didn't mean to upset you. Can we put this aside and focus on having fun tonight?"

"Yes." I hugged my friend. As hard as it was to hear her opinion, I was glad I had somebody I could talk to who didn't mince her words. Perhaps Tia was too hard on Victor, but it was nice to have a second perspective. Sometimes Victor's forcefulness and loudness snuffed out my personality. He was so righteous, so steadfast in his beliefs that my flexibility was a trait that disappeared in the background while his ideology took the foreground.

Even though it was half an hour past eleven, Daydream didn't have a line to enter and no bouncer to admit the guests.

"It's not very popular, is it?" I asked.

Tia shrugged. "It was packed when I came here the other night. I've heard the other bars aren't happy about a demon buying it and are trying to sabotage it by offering ridiculously cheap drink specials." She shook her head. "They're losing so much money just to spite Lorenzo."

Lorenzo. Was that the demon's name? It was too melodic, too nice. I had expected something sharp and lethal. Shaking off the random thought, I asked, "Isn't it better to go to one of the other bars first?" Money was always tight.

Tia gave me a knowing smile. "You're not getting out of this. Believe me, it's going to be fun. And with us the first to arrive, we'll get the best seats and have time to talk to each other without having to shout."

I supposed Tia had a point. Plus, she had won fair and square. So if she wanted to go to Daydream now, we'd do it.

She pushed open the lacquered, black door, and I followed her inside, my mouth dropping open in wonder. I had expected black and red decor, something that looked like a fun version of hell. A pink and purple decor wouldn□t have surprised me either since the name Daydream lent itself to a Sugarland theme. Even a simple, minimalistic black and steel décor with a large stage was within my range of expectations.

What I didn't imagine was that Daydream would sport a thousand different shades of blue. The smooth floor was reminiscent of an ice rink. The stage glowed in an electric light that made it look like a magical lake, while the main floor was decked out in detailed ice sculptures of demons. One spitfire, another wielded a sword, while yet another rode on a dragon. And amidst all those magical creatures were two human sculptures—our king and queen.

Victor would say this was blasphemy. Liberal Arcadians would say it was cool that magic creatures stood alongside our rulers. The bar was progressive and lived up to its name. The demon who had bought it had made the conscious decision to appeal to both humans and magical creatures to create a place where both felt at ease.

Mesmerized by the sculptures, I stepped closer. There was a woman who looked like a nymph. She stood on a seashell and was surrounded by waves, dolphins, and smaller fish. Next to her, was a demon with a triton in his hand and a crown upon his head.

Two-winged fae were flying toward each other, the ice sculptures supported by clouds that reached the ground. Its neighbor was an incubus who struck a suggestive pose and stuck out his tongue. To his right was a demon that looked like a goat and one that looked like a half-lion, half-bird.

At the end of the display were our king and queen. Ella's blonde hair was arranged in an elegant chignon. Her smile was sweet and gracious. Behind her stood her husband, his hand on her shoulder. Even though they were made of ice, there was nothing cold about them, quite the opposite, they radiated warmth and love. How I wished I could see the king and queen once in my lifetime. Rumors had it that nobody was as generous and understanding as Queen Ella. Even though I had only heard tales about her, her sudden disappearance last week felt like a dear friend had been ripped from me. Whatever had happened to her, wherever she was, I prayed she returned home safely.

"Isn't she beautiful?"

I whipped around at the melodious voice, coming face-to-face with a man half a head taller than me, one with violet-green eyes and silver hair. Not a man, but a demon.

"I'm Lorenzo, and you must be Halia." He extended his hand, and I shook it, releasing a breath when nothing happened at his touch besides my heartbeat quickening. Still, given his sharp chin, high cheekbones, and muscled body, I was certain he was an incubus, which meant it was best to stay away from him. I inched backward, bumping into the statue behind me.

"I'm so sorry." I stepped aside, far away from him and the statue.

Lorenzo smiled. "They're sturdier than you might think. The artist is a dear friend of mine. He'll create a replica if I need it."

"I'd never be able to pay you back the cost."

He tilted his head, amusement swirling in his eyes. "Is that so? Your friend Tia swore you'd double my nightly earnings with your singing."

I cursed silently and scanned the room for Tia, who was nowhere to be found. Why did she always have to go around, bragging about me?

Lorenzo must've noticed my agitation, because he said, "Don't worry. Your friend went to the ladies' room."

"Are you an incubus?" I blurted out, immediately regretting my question. It was probably very uncouth to ask such a question after meeting a demon only minutes earlier, but I needed to know. I needed to know if I was daft enough to be attracted to a demon or if my need to trace his lips was something he was responsible for.

Lorenzo threw his head back and let out a carefree, unrestrained laugh. "Would you like me to be?"

I shook my head vigorously, sending my untamed hair flying. "No. I hate how they're able to…." I trailed off. What was wrong with me? Was I set on making this conversation as awkward as possible?

"I'm not an incubus."

"What kind of demon are you?"

Lorenzo's smile disappeared, and I wanted to kick myself. I might not want to sing at Daydream, but there was no point in pissing off an influential demon who had just moved to Arcadia.

"I think it's easier if I demonstrate my powers to you. Hopefully, then you'll stop acting as if I could pounce on you at any moment. You know, I don't appreciate being accused of taking advantage of or hurting women, especially when I have not given you a single reason to believe that's who I am."

I opened my mouth to apologize, but he was already gone. Was he like Mrs. Woods? Could he disappear and reappear at will?

"Behind you."

I followed his voice to find him next to the flying fae statues. Then he was gone again. I pivoted around my axis, unable to find him until there was the rattling coming from the bar. Lorenzo was standing behind it. Lazily, he swirled ice cubes in a tumbler. "What can I get you?"

Ignoring his question, I asked, "How were you able to do that?"

"I teleport."

I blinked, shocked that this was even possible and at how casually he spoke about it.

As if he hadn't just revealed his power, he proceeded to casually pour purple, yellow, and amber liquid into a mixer and shook it vigorously. He poured the concoction into a martini glass. "I'm glad my powers don't terrify you, but just so you know, not all incubi are evil. Only some of them."

"Just like humans."

That earned me a long look I couldn't decipher. He

pushed the martini toward me. “Try this.”

“What is it?”

“Why don’t you tell me?”

I took a seat at the bar but didn’t touch the drink. Sure, I had seen him mix it in front of me, and all the ingredients looked legit and not like any suspicious powder that could be poison, but if he could disappear in one place and reappear in the other, he could easily add something potent to my drink.

Sensing my reluctance, he grabbed a shot glass and poured himself some of my drink, then gulped it down. “Satisfied?”

I nodded and finally took a sip of the concoction. Black currant and citrus exploded on my tongue and were washed down with something that tasted like liquid sunshine. “Delicious. Lemon, black currant, and the best bourbon I’ve ever tasted.”

He smiled and showed me a bottle called Star Rush.

“Never heard of it.”

“It’s small batch. Very limited.”

Immediately, my joy turned to worry. “How much do I owe you?”

“Nothing. The first drink is on the house.”

I shook my head. “I don’t need a handout.”

He leaned forward. There was a challenge in his gesture, but nothing about it was threatening or made me want to pull back. In fact, the warm buzzing in my stomach made me want to lean forward into him.

“I’m not in the habit of pitying a pretty and smart girl, especially when I’m told she has the best voice in Arcadia.”

I licked my lips, my throat suddenly parched. What was it with this guy? He might not be an incubus, but it appeared as if he had done an apprenticeship with one.

I took another sip of my drink. “My voice is nothing special.”

“You’re not going to address the other compliments I gave you?” His tone was so playful, so easy-going that I wanted to joke in return, yet I couldn’t come up with anything funny.

Normally, I would have said that I wasn’t all that pretty and that I most certainly wasn’t smart. Sure, I had some common sense, and I knew how to highlight the gifts Mother Nature had given me, but I was nothing special. But with Lorenzo, it was hard for me to say those things. It was hard because if he truly saw me as smart and pretty, I didn’t want him to stop seeing me that way.

I traced the drops of condensation running down my glass. “What brings you to Arcadia?” It was safer to redirect the conversation toward him and way more interesting.

Several emotions crossed his face—sadness, wistfulness, and determination. “I felt the call.” At my confused expression, he elaborated. “My otherworldly nature tells me where to go. We all have a role to play in the game of the universe, and I felt the call, so I followed it.”

“You’re here to help someone?” Perhaps he would bring back our lost queen.

He gave me a sad smile. “When I feel the tug, I’m never told why; that’s for me to figure out.”

I motioned around the bar. “Why did you buy Daydream?”

He shrugged. “That was a personal decision. I always wanted to own one, and this one was perfect for me.”

I pondered his response, trying to make sense of it. “You’re very intuitive.”

He tilted his head, his violet-green eyes sparking. "That seems to surprise you. Are you not?"

I shook my head. How could I trust my intuition, how could I trust the voice inside when whatever I did never seemed to impact my environment? I had tried to be a good girl, and yet I had been thrown out of the orphanage. I was a good employee, and yet Madam yelled at me almost daily.

"You might want to work on that."

Defiance raised its head within me. I didn't need advice from a stranger who didn't know me and had no idea what it was like to be mortal, vulnerable, and without a family. "No, thanks. Intuition is dangerous. It makes you do stupid things."

"Like what?"

His voice caressed me, pulled me in. I needed to redirect the conversation. "Do all demons and fae have influence over humans?"

He propped his hands against the shelf behind him and leaned back. "You must have had a very bad experience with an otherworldly if you keep coming back to this question."

"Better safe than sorry."

"No, not all of us possess mind manipulating abilities, just as not all people are skilled at manipulation. And before you ask, I have no ability to manipulate others, but I am keenly aware of their desires. Not because of any evil power within me, but because I am attuned to my own emotions." His voice was tinged with hurt, and I realized I had gone too far.

"I didn't mean to offend you."

He ran his hand through his silver hair that almost reached his shoulders. "I can move past this if you can."

Could I? He was asking me to put my suspicions

aside. He was asking me to let my guard down and trust him, a demon. I bit my lip. "You're very direct."

He chuckled. "That I am."

"And you're very comfortable with your..." I waved my hand in the air, unsure how to word my thought.

"My masculinity? I don't need to act like a macho to feel like a man."

I liked that. I liked that a lot, and I liked him. He challenged me, and yet, he made me feel at ease at the same time. Sort of like Tia did, but in a more exciting kind of way. Talking to Lorenzo was almost like singing, a heady rush that pulled me out of my shell.

# 18TH JULY

Before I could ponder whether I was all right with Lorenzo pulling me out of my shell, Tia finally emerged from the ladies' room and strolled toward us, her gait relaxed, as if she had no care in the world. A clock on the wall told me it was already past midnight, and yet, the night was young. Nightclubs in Arcadia opened late at night but stayed open until the first light.

"Did you two have a good talk?" she asked.

I pushed my cocktail over to her. "You must try this. It's delicious."

She took a sip and leaned forward onto the bar, pressing her elbows into the ebony wood. "I can recreate this."

Lorenzo chuckled, apparently not the least bit

offended. "Please, be my guest." He motioned for her to go behind the bar. "If you manage to recreate it in half an hour, I promise I'll let you work tonight."

"What's going on?" I asked.

Tia smiled. "Lorenzo and I had a deal. If I brought you in, he would let me experiment behind the bar. If I impress him, he'll give me the chance to bartend for him tonight."

I felt as if she had just punched me. "I thought you said tonight was girls' night."

She grabbed my hand. "I'm sorry I didn't tell you everything, Halia, but we need to get out of the boarding house. And while your talent is obvious, I'm still trying to figure out how I can earn a living. I was always interested in cocktails. I need this chance." She looked at me with pleading eyes.

"I understand." I forced a smile. I had no doubt Tia would make a great bartender. But what would I do? Even if I had a talent for singing, it didn't mean I would be able to support myself as a singer. The entertainment industry was fickle and unpredictable. If Tia left me, I would be all alone at the boarding house. She made the depressing and boring work doable. She cheered me up and was there if I needed to talk after serving a creepy client or being reprimanded by Madam. If I had to continue working at the boarding house without her, my days would become pure bleakness.

"Why don't you give it a try?" Lorenzo's voice tore me out of my thoughts. I bit my lip as I realized he was pointing his head toward the stage.

"I couldn't."

"Why not?" He made a show of glancing around us. "There's no one here. What's the worst thing that could happen? Or do you care that much whether I'll like it or not?"

Gosh, this guy, demon, really knew how to push my buttons. "I don't care what you think." I pushed off the barstool and headed toward the stage. Even though my fear grew with each step I took, my determination to show Lorenzo he had no effect on me was bigger. With his good looks and charming smile, he already had a big head. I didn't need to add to his exaggerated confidence.

It was only once I was up on stage, the microphone in my hand that I realized I had no idea what to do.

Lorenzo materialized next to, making me almost drop the microphone. He reached for it, and our fingers brushed, electricity darting through me. I licked my lip. So much for not showing him how much he affected me.

Thankfully, he didn't say anything. Instead, he grabbed the guitar that was lying at the back of the stage. "Go ahead. I'll come in as soon as I figure out the melody."

I stared at him blankly. I had never sung on a stage, into a microphone, let alone with anyone to accompany me.

"But you don't know the song. I don't have sheet music or anything like that."

"Don't worry about it. There's no one here. This is the time to make mistakes."

I turned to the empty bar and focused my eyes on Queen Ella's statue. "This is for you," I whispered and sang the first note.

*Through the darkness, I must go; through the darkness, I must go. Find a way to reach the lights, find a way to reach the lights.*

Behind me, Lorenzo strummed the guitar and hit a

G chord.

*I thought I was on my way, I thought I'd found my path, but now, I'm more confused than ever.*

My voice grew fuller as I realized that singing on stage wasn't all that different from singing in the boarding house.

*This life, it ain't easy, ain't easy. How do I know which path is right? How do I know the light is real? Through the darkness, I must go; through the darkness, I must go.*

I sang the full song without stopping, and Lorenzo kept up. When I was done, I turned to him, bracing myself for his critique only to be met with a smile.

"Your friend was right. You, Halia, are a singer."

Before I could reply, a group of giggling girls stumbled into the bar. "Are you open yet?" one squeaked.

Lorenzo nodded. "We are." He jumped off the stage to serve them while I put the microphone back into the stand and hurried toward Tia.

"You were great," she said, pausing her cocktail mixing.

"Really?"

She squeezed my hand. "Really."

"I still don't want to sing in front of an audience." I sat down on the barstool, busying myself with smoothing my silk dress.

Tia took a sip of one of her concoctions and wrinkled her nose. "What do you think is missing?" She pushed the drink over to me, and I took a sip.

"Too syrupy. But aren't you supposed to figure that out on your own?"

She rolled her eyes. "Not all of us have been practicing their talent for years. No one has ever given me access to a bar until today."

"I didn't mean to discourage you."

She used a shaker, making conversation impossible. At the other end of the bar, Lorenzo was serving the still giggling girls who had ordered fancy umbrella drinks that equaled probably half of my weekly salary.

With a loud sigh, Tia put down her latest creation. "Maybe we're both not ready." She stepped from behind the bar to my side. "Maybe we should just stick to girl's night out, instead of trying to get jobs."

I bit my lip. As much as I didn't want to sing in front of a large group of people, I couldn't just watch Tia's dreams wither. "I can entertain myself. You don't have to worry about me. If being a bartender is what you want to do, I think you should keep on trying until you get it right. Maybe ask Lorenzo for some guidance."

She turned to watch him. "He's a bit busy at the moment, but I appreciate your support."

"I'll always be there for you." I swallowed the rock in my throat. "Even if I'm not ready for you to move on."

She hugged me sideways. "I'm not leaving you. Even if I worked here, and you stayed at the boarding house, we'd see each other daily."

"It wouldn't be the same. We wouldn't be working together or sharing a room."

"Guess, you'll need to quit too and really give this singing thing a go."

I chuckled, imagining Madam's flared nostrils if Tia and I quit on the same day.

"Just imagine, you could become Arcadia's newest star, and I'd win the cocktail of the year award," Tia said her eyes shiny with hope.

I liked the sound of that, but I was afraid to let myself imagine what life would be like if I could leave Madam and the boarding house and make it as a singer. Hope was a treacherous thing. It lifted one up, but it also meant that one was open to being crushed. Optimism made one temporarily stronger but also weaker. If I stayed realistic and accepted the life I had been given, my potential pain would be much smaller.

As if we had made a pact not to talk about the future, Tia and I both began people watching as more patrons streamed into the bar.

"Who do you think they are?" she pointed at three girls decked out in leather and velvet.

I shrugged. "Probably some merchants' daughters who snuck out of their piano lessons." We broke down in hysterical giggles.

The bar grew crowded. A switch had been flipped, and within minutes, Daydream had gone from empty to full capacity. Even though Lorenzo had several employees, he never stood still or simply yelled orders, but was always tending his bar. He seemed to enjoy the work and didn't appear to have bought the establishment to boss people around or squeeze customers dry, but because he truly appreciated bars.

Tia studied him and the other employees. Lorenzo hadn't asked to taste her cocktail, and she hadn't offered. As much as I believed in my friend, I didn't think she was ready for cocktail mixing, especially on a night as busy as this. However, the longing in her eyes as she watched the servers made me certain she should still try to get her foot in the door.

"Go ahead. I'll be fine," I said.

"But, I sucked."

I shook my head. "Nobody becomes a master on their first try. Perhaps your claim to emulate Lorenzo's cocktail was cocky, but you can make up for it. Ask him what he needs help with."

She threw me a grateful smile and headed behind the bar where she exchanged a few words with Lorenzo that I couldn't hear. Minutes later, she was cutting lemons into slices. A while later, she restocked bottled beverages. For the next hour, she refilled the ice, replaced the glassware, and even poured wine. I was so proud. Tia had just finished our regular shift at the boarding house, and yet here she was, giving 100 percent for the chance to get hired.

"Saturday night is open mic night." Lorenzo's voice carried from the stage across the vast bar. "Please put your hands together to welcome our first act of the evening: The Jives."

A group of four guys with spiky hair walked up onto the stage.

Lorenzo placed another cocktail in front of me. This one had notes of strawberry and what I believed to be rum. Not letting me reach for my wallet, he nodded toward Tia. "It's on your friend."

I wasn't looking for a handout, but not accepting Tia's offer would be insulting, almost like saying her working tonight wasn't worth anything.

Thus, I sipped on my delicious drink and watched the band. Their style was unique and memorable, but their notes could be cleaner, and their vocals weren't quite there.

After the band, a male singer came on stage. He wasn't quite able to hit the high notes of "Striking Midnight," a popular song that was much harder to pull off than most singers anticipated. He was followed by a female who was more of a dancer and mostly moaned into the microphone. Perhaps I was too harsh, but as a fellow singer, I couldn't help but spot weak spots and consider how they could be improved. What would other singers think if they heard me? That my voice was too bright and young? That I was too simple? Would they think I hit the notes just right or tried too hard? Perhaps they would focus on my shyness and lack of stage persona.

Lost in the music and halfway through my second drink, my body relaxed, and my mind became soft like cotton candy. A female band finished their upbeat song, and Lorenzo walked onto the stage once again and said, "This was such a fun night. I hope you enjoyed it as much as I did!"

There were screams of protest, and my stomach sank. I hadn't wanted to sing; yet now, I was sad the opportunity had passed me by.

"It's final call, so get your drinks together, and please welcome with me our last performer of the night."

I studied the stage area with curiosity, unable to see anyone getting ready to sing.

"Please give a warm welcome to Halia."

I froze. I must've misheard him. But no, Lorenzo was staring right at me. He motioned for me to come up on the stage, and everyone turned into my direction.

Unable to remain sitting and take the scrutiny, I headed toward him, fully intending to tell him off and tell the audience this was a mistake, that I was not a performer. But as soon as I was up on the stage, he handed me the microphone and strummed the first few chords of *Through the Darkness,* the song we had practiced earlier. Something shifted within me. I was shaking, but I no longer wanted to leave the stage. I wanted to stay. I wanted, no, I needed to sing.

Not daring to look at the sea of faces in the club, I remained with my back turned to them as I sang the first line. Sweat dripped down my back, and my heartbeat as fast as a gazelle's, but my throat didn't constrict, and my voice flowed freely.

Lorenzo walked past me, gently taking my free hand and turning me so that I was facing the audience.

I only glanced at the audience below me briefly, then closed my eyes and focused on the words and melody as if they were an anchor.

*Through the darkness, I must go; through the darkness, I must go. Find a way to reach the lights, find a way to reach the lights.*

Halfway through the song, I dared to open my eyes. Still not quite ready for the audience's reaction, I switched between eye contact with Lorenzo and keeping my gaze on the ice sculptures. It was only when I sang the final note that I allowed myself to survey the audience. They erupted with cheers and applause. Warmth spread through me. I was on cloud nine. I was whole.

"More! More!" the crowd demanded.

"Are you up for doing another one?" Lorenzo asked softly.

I nodded. "This one is called "Hope."" Since Lorenzo hadn't heard it before, I started on my own, my voice echoing through the space as the crowd grew quiet.

*Sometimes, it's hard. Sometimes, it's painful. Sometimes, I wish hope would leave me alone. Its false promises tear me up from the inside out, the inside out.*

*But then another day comes, and I'm glad for it. The sun rises, and my heart fills with joy. The trees explode in bloom and chase away the winter. You smile at me, and I feel hope. Hope that carries me through the dark times.*

The song ended much too soon, but the feeling of floating and finally having reached paradise didn't. Humans, goblins, and sprites cheered and clapped as I walked down the stage steps, and several came over to congratulate me.

"That was fantastic!" a troll exclaimed.

"Your voice is so beautiful!" a young woman said.

A pixie beamed. "I hope to hear you sing again!"

Tia made her way through the crowd toward me and fell around my neck. "You were amazing! I always knew you could do it!"

We hugged for a long time. When we finally pulled apart, Lorenzo said, "I do hope you'll sing for us again."

"I will." Overflowing with joy, everything felt possible.

Tia lifted her foot and circled her ankle, her face contorting. "I would love to celebrate your singing and my giving bartending a go, but my feet are killing me, and it's already two in the morning."

I gasped. Where had the time gone? "We need to get back; otherwise, we'll fall asleep on the job tomorrow."

Tia grimaced. "Tomorrow is going to kick my butt."

I smiled at Lorenzo. "Thank you."

"You're welcome. We should do it again. Soon."

"Yes!" Tia sidled up to him. "Can I pour some beers and mix long drinks next time?"

He chuckled. "It's a deal." He took my hand and brought it to his lips. "I'll send you the details."

Shocked, I watched him leave. Had he just kissed my hand? Why? Was it a demon thing?

Tia jabbed me in the ribs. "I know he's a hottie, but if we don't leave now, you'll have to give me a piggyback ride."

I shook off her remark. "He's all right. Come, I'll make a salt bath for your feet."

Leaning on me, Tia hobbled out of the bar while I felt as light as a feather, still high on performing.

We didn't speak on our way back. I didn't know

what was on Tia's mind, but all I could think was that I had done it. I had performed in front of an audience. I wasn't sure I could do it again, but for once, I wasn't fretting over the future. The present moment was too precious. If only I could bottle it up and relive it whenever I wanted.

Inside the boarding house, we climbed up the stairs to our attic bedroom. I was about to grab the Epsom salt when Tia stopped me.

"Don't. I'm too tired. I'll fall asleep, and then I'll catch a cold from the water getting cold."

"At least put on the salve."

I handed her a sample of an expensive herbal ointment Acacia had given me during one of my visits. Tia slathered her feet in it, and I turned off the light. Not a minute after collapsing in my bed, I was fast asleep.

My alarm clock went off way too early.

I groaned and turned to the other side to escape it to no avail. Lying on my belly, I reached out with my hand. My clumsy attempt to hit the off button only led to me knocking over the clock.

Reluctantly, I pushed myself out of bed and put an end to the buzzing.

Tia was still sleeping peacefully.

I sat down on her bed. "Get up." No response. I shook her. "Get up! We're going to be late."

"I'll skip breakfast. Just pick me up when you're done."

"It's quarter to eight," I said, and that finally made her throw back the covers. "What?"

"We came back so late, I decided sleep was more important than having a proper breakfast, so I set the alarm for half-past seven. It must've been going off for fifteen minutes before I heard it."

We dressed with lightning speed and ran downstairs toward the kitchen, more concerned about getting our fix of caffeine than filling our bellies with food.

Tia and I gulped down two mugs of lukewarm coffee, and I grabbed an apple that I ate as we got the cart ready while she wolfed down a piece of toast with blueberry jam. We started our shift at eight exactly.

We were cleaning the first room when the door flew open.

"Housekeeping. We're almost finished," I called, warning the guest only to find Madam storming toward me.

"What is this?" she demanded, waving a piece of paper in front of me.

I put down the broom. "I can't read it."

She shoved the paper into my face, and I had to take a step back to make out the white words printed on the black background.

**July 21**

**The Daydream presents Dark Quartet**

**10 p.m.**

***Entry: 5 marks***

***Opening act: Halia***

"Where did you get that?" I asked, feeling faint. Was this a joke?

"A flyer girl left a staple of those at the front desk." Madam put her fists on her hips. "What is the meaning of this?"

"I don't have evening shift that night," I said calmly.

She snorted. "So, just because you're not working, you think you can be an opening act at a bar?" She spit out the words as if they were bile.

I clasped my hands together to stop them from shaking. "My contract doesn't say anything against working a second job."

She raised her chin, and her nostrils flared. "You're not forbidden from going there, but your common sense should prevent you from doing so. Why would you make a fool out of yourself? Why would you bring shame to the boarding house?"

"She won't," Tia chimed in. "Halia sang yesterday and did an excellent job."

I pressed my teeth together and shook my head no. Arguing with Madam wouldn't lead to anything good.

"Is that so?" Madam gave me a fake smile. "And how does your young man feel about you gyrating on stage, begging a demon to give you a chance, and doing who knows what in exchange for the favor?"

"She didn't," Tia began, but I shushed her.

I forced my lips into a tight smile. "He'll be fine with it, once I explain."

Madam's dark eyes filled with cruelty. "Good luck with that." Her tone dripped with derision. Having trampled all over my happiness, she left the room.

Tia ripped the dirty covers off the bed. "She's a crazy old hag! I can't wait to get out of here!"

I didn't reply but focused on dusting the floor.

"You're not going to take to heart what she said, are you?"

"It's fine. She has a right to her opinion."

Tia took the broom from me. "She's a bully!" She reached out, but I stepped back. "Listen to me, Halia. You were amazing out there. You should be proud of yourself. Don't let anyone take your spark, not Madam and not Victor."

I shook my head. "Yesterday went well, but that doesn't mean I can be an opening act. What if yesterday was a fluke? What if I'll do terribly? Being an opening act is completely different from singing one song on stage for open mic."

"You did two."

I took the broom from her and attacked the area underneath the bed, discovering a discarded receipt, breadcrumbs, and a hairball. "Yes, two songs. Opening act would be at least five."

"So what? You have more than that in your repertoire."

"What if I suck? What if I make an idiot out of myself and prove Madam and Victor right?"

Even though Tia was crouching, holding the dustpan in her hand, she exuded authority. "Stop being a coward. Yes, you can fail. But if you don't try, you have already failed. You only have a chance of winning if you try. And if you fail, what's so bad about that? I failed at making the cocktail, but I still got to work behind the bar. If you fail, you try again, tweak something, and see if you succeed."

I shook my head. "It's different for you."

"Why, because bartending is less important?"

I sat down on the ground. "No, I would never say or think that. But as a bartender, there's a smaller risk of embarrassing yourself. If you mess up, only one person notices. If I mess up, everyone in the bar will know and the day after, everyone in Arcadia. Gossip travels fast in this town."

She chuckled. "Ditto on the gossip, but even though the risk in your case is higher, the potential reward is bigger too."

I pressed the heels of my palms into my forehead. I loved Tia, but sometimes she was beyond frustrating. "I'm not like you. I don't want thrills and danger."

"I'm not telling you to sing in front of the king. Being

an opening act is the next natural step after crushing open mic."

"I wasn't—"

"Yes, you were the best, and you know it." She thumped her chest. "You know it right here. Stop allowing your head to limit you. But anyway, the point isn't whether you were the best or not. The point is you have been given a chance, and it would be a crime not to take it."

"I guess." She was right. I could fail, but I could also win. And if I failed, so what? Yes, people would make fun of me, especially Madam, but it wouldn't last forever. Sooner or later, they would move on to ridiculing someone else. As for Victor, he wouldn't be happy, but he would get over it eventually.

"You need to start believing in yourself, Halia. You don't need the permission of others to go after your dream. If you wait for others to approve of your choices, you'll never get anywhere. You need to first believe in yourself, and then when you do, others will believe in you too."

I was speechless. No one had ever put it that way. The orphanage had always communicated that if others didn't believe in me, I wasn't worth it. If others didn't love me, I wasn't lovable. But what if Tia had a point? What if I had to have self-confidence, self-respect, and self-love first before I could expect others to believe in me, love me, and respect me?

# 19TH JULY

Deciding that maybe Tia was right, and a lot of my unhappiness was coming from my uncertainty and lack of confidence, I was determined to try a new approach to life.

Starting small, I went ahead and braided my hair even though Victor preferred it loose. It took me an hour and four tries to master the intricate French style, but it was totally worth it. The braid lay on my right shoulder, and the top of it snaked like a crown around my head. Certain that even Victor would like this new hairstyle, I left the boarding house with a spring in my step and a wide smile.

In less than ten minutes, I reached the night market where I was supposed to meet Victor. As usual, he was late, but I didn't mind, excited to browse the various merchandise stalls. Most of the goods, Badalan silks, pearls, and fragrant teas on balanced scales, I couldn't afford, but it was still fun to look at and know what the latest trends were.

I was browsing through turquoise rings when someone cleared their throat behind me.

"Excuse me, are you Halia?"

I turned around, not recognizing the twenty-something girl. "Yes. Are you staying at Madam's Boarding House?"

She shook her head. "No, I saw you perform at Daydream. You were amazing." She motioned her friend over who was tasting a fig jam. "It's really her—Halia."

"Oh my gosh! You're amazing." The girl threw away the disposable spoon and pulled out a notepad from her backpack. "Will you sign this?"

I blinked at her stupidly, unable to do or say anything.

She handed me a pen. "It's to Marisol."

The notebook was completely empty. "Are you sure? This is brand new."

She smiled. "Yes. I plan to fill it up with my poems. It was so inspiring to watch you on stage. It would really mean a lot to me if you could autograph it."

"Sure." I took a moment to consider what to write.

*To Marisol, all the best with your poems! Halia*

"Thank you."

Marisol's friend handed me a romance book. "Would you mind signing this?"

I took the romance novel. "But I'm not the author."

She shrugged. "I know, but I don't have anything else with me, and I'm not sure when I'll get to see you again."

This was still confusing, but I decided to go along

with it. "What would you like me to write?"

"Whatever you want. My name is Carrie."

*To Carrie, I hope this book brings you lots of hours of joy! Halia*

Judging by Carrie's big smile as she read my inscription, she seemed to be satisfied with what I had written.

"Are you going to perform again?" she asked.

"You're the opening act on Friday, aren't you?" Marisol chimed in.

"Ahem, yes." Word sure was spreading fast. A tingle in my forehead made me look past the girls to find Victor striding toward me. I needed to get rid of the girls. This was so not the way I wanted him to learn about my singing.

"At Daydream?" one of the girls asked.

"Yes. I'm sorry, I must go now."

"Oh." They sounded disappointed.

Not wanting to appear rude, I said, "I have a date."

The girls giggled. "Of course, you do."

Unsure what they meant by that, I gave them an apologetic smile and walked toward Victor, feeling their gazes on me.

"Who were those broads?" Victor asked, his face a storm cloud.

"No one. Just some girls I ran into." My voice was too high-pitched. I needed to take it down a notch.

"Then why were they acting as if they were your best friends?"

I glanced backward. "I just met them." The girls chose that moment to wave the book and notebook I had signed.

"What is that?"

I groaned and faced Victor, who was squinting. Even

though I doubted he could make out my signature, I had the feeling the cat was out of the bag.

"They asked me to sign something for them."

"Why?" His tone was annoyed, but his face showed puzzlement.

"Let's go somewhere quieter, and I can explain."

He took my hand and led me to an empty bench. As soon as we sat down, he faced me. "Tell me what's going on."

I crossed my legs and then recrossed them. "It's nothing bad. In fact, it's something good. I went with Tia last night to Daydream."

He scowled, and his eyes narrowed to slits. "You went to a bar owned by a demon?"

"He was really nice."

Victor jumped up. "Do you hear yourself? He was nice? Have you lost your mind?"

My arms trembled, and an apology was on the tip of my tongue, but I didn't give in. Instead, I stood up and raised my head high. "I did not lose my mind." I enunciated each word. "Lorenzo is very nice. He gave me the opportunity to perform on his stage."

Victor face-palmed himself. "You embarrassed yourself in front of everyone?"

Tears sprang to my eyes. They weren't tears of fear or pain, but tears of fury. "Why do you assume that I embarrassed myself? Is it so hard to imagine that I did well?"

Victor took a step back, scrutinizing me from head to toe. The urge to flinch, grab his hand, and take back my words was overwhelming, but I held firm. I had to stand my ground. Tia was right. I had to be strong if I wanted others to respect my wishes and values.

After the uncomfortable silence dragged on for a

while, Victor stepped toward me and took my head in his hands. "What has happened to you, Halia? I've never seen you like this. Are you unwell?"

Was I overreacting? Was I embarrassing him and myself by having this outburst?

Quietly but firmly, I replied, "I like to sing. And I'm good at it."

"I didn't say you weren't. It's just that it's a very tough industry, and people can be very mean." He brushed my cheek. "You're sweet, kind, and sensitive. I don't want anyone to take advantage of you, chew you up and spit you out."

I glanced away. What if my success at the open mic night had been a fluke? Had the girls really wanted an autograph from me, or were they making fun of me? It wasn't normal to ask someone who had performed at one open mic for an autograph. I wasn't a star. I wasn't even officially a singer.

"I really care about you, Halia. The world we live in is dangerous and cruel. I'm a patrolman. I see every day what people are capable of. I don't want anything bad to happen to you."

I glanced back up at Victor. There was so much sincerity in his eyes, and yet, as much as I craved and wanted his care, I also wished he would take it down a notch and let me breathe. "I'm performing again this Friday."

He let out a loud sigh, then brushed his lips against my forehead. "Did the demon name his price?"

I stepped back, confused. "What do you mean?"

"What does he want in return for letting you perform?"

"Nothing." My anger from before sparked alive anew. "He thought I was really good. He asked me to sing because he wants good performers at his bar."

Victor stuck his lower lip slightly out in a poor-you expression. “You have no formal training. No manager. Yet you believe this demon is hiring you because you’re the best? Not because he hopes to get…” He didn’t finish his sentence, but his gaze roaming over my body made it very clear what he was implying.

“Lorenzo isn’t like that!”

“And you know that after meeting him once?”

My cheeks heated as I remember Lorenzo’s hand brushing mine as he handed me the mic. Then there had been the banter between him and me. Despite this, I didn’t feel like he expected me to do anything I didn’t want to just because he was giving me an opportunity. I didn’t feel any pressure from him. We had engaged in a mutual, playful give and take, enjoying each other’s company.

Apparently, my emotions showed on my face because Victor’s hands dug into my shoulders, and he shook me. “Wake up! You’re under his spell!”

“No.” I tried to free myself from Victor’s grip but couldn’t.

“He has given you something, mixed something into your drink. Did you accept any food or drink from him?”

“Yes, but—”

“I knew it.” Victor’s grip on my shoulders tightened enough to bruise. “He’s messing with your mind. I’ll kill him for this!”

I shoved my hands against Victor’s chest. It wasn’t as much my physical strength, but the shock of me fighting back that made him let go of me. He wasn’t used to me resisting. I wasn’t used to standing up for myself, but I liked how it felt.

I crossed my arms, stepping far enough away that Victor couldn’t touch me and used my firmest voice. "Lorenzo didn't put a spell on me. He was very professional and friendly."

"That's what he wants you to think. Then, once he gets you into his bed, he's going to throw you away like a dirty sock."

"He isn't like that!"

Victor smirked. "Did he tell you that? Or could you sense it?" His words dripped with mockery. "You know what will happen once he's done with you?"

I shook my head, not wanting to hear what he had to say.

"Once he uses you and throws you away, you'll be damaged goods. Nobody will want you." Victor advanced, and I stepped back. "I care about you, Halia. I want to marry you. But I don't want a demon whore for my wife or the mother of my children."

Even though he hadn't touched me, it felt as if he had slapped me across my face. The emotions bubbling up in me were too much. Unwilling to break down in front of him and let him win, I turned around and sprinted, my feet barely grazing the ground as hot streaks of tears slid down my cheeks.

At first, I didn't know where I was running to. At first, I was simply running away from Victor and the painful feelings swirling within me. Yet somehow, in the end, I found myself right in front of Daydream.

A part of me wanted to back away, return to the boarding house, and throw myself onto my bed. But I wasn't ready to explain to Tia, who was having a night in after a busy week, what was going on. I wasn't ready to face her and tell her about Victor's reaction. I also didn't want her to solve my problems. I had to confront this head-on. If even a tiny part of me believed that Victor was right, I needed to talk to Lorenzo. This issue had to be brought out into the open.

I wiped away the tears on my cheeks, took a deep breath, and entered the bar.

Without any live music going on and it still being fairly early in the evening, there were only a few people sitting at the bar, having drinks by themselves or speaking quietly with a friend.

A female bartender I hadn't met last time was pouring a glass of wine. Lorenzo was nowhere in sight.

I stepped to the bar. "Can I speak with Lorenzo, please?"

"He's in his office," the white-haired girl replied. Even though she looked like she was no older than fourteen, I had the feeling she was much older, at least, in her mind. Her black eyes were a stark contrast to her flowing, almost waist-length hair. "I can let him know you're here."

"Please do. I'm Halia."

She turned and slipped behind the black door. Returning a minute later, she motioned for me to follow her. "Lorenzo will see you now."

My stomach tightened. Was it wise to go into Lorenzo's office by myself? Was this a trap? Nonsense. I was just allowing Victor to get into my head, letting what he had said to me affect me.

The door closed behind me, and I found myself in a small office illuminated with gas lamps. Cabinets lined one wall, and a large, oak desk occupied most of the space. Lorenzo was sitting behind it, poring over some papers. When I entered, his gaze shot up toward me. "Halia, please take a seat."

I did, sinking into the soft leather. Unsure where to begin, I folded my hands in my lap and surveyed the cabinets, wondering what they held.

"What's going on?" Lorenzo tilted his head.

"I need to talk to you about opening for the Dark Quartet."

He nodded. "Are you upset I put you down without talking to you first?" His voice was filled with genuine concern.

"No, I'm grateful for the chance, but I don't understand why you chose me."

He leaned back in his chair, a slow smile spreading across his face. "I believe in you. I think you can do it."

"Did you expect me to do anything in return?"

Lorenzo's silver brows furrowed. "Well, I hope you will put on a good performance."

I shook my head. "That's not what I mean. I want to know if you expect me to give you something in return for providing this opportunity."

He chuckled. "If I did, I would be a very bad salesman for not having mentioned it until now." His mirth disappeared. "Why? What do you think I want in return?"

Heat streamed into my face, and I turned away, unable to take his intense violet-green gaze any longer.

"I see." Lorenzo rose from the table and headed over to the cabinets. He opened one and, ignoring the decanters filled with alcohol, poured himself water from a jug. After emptying his glass in one go, he faced me. "I thought we had settled that question last time. Not all demons are bad or into deception."

"We have, but..."

He crossed his arms. "Is that what you plan to do, question me every time you see me? How would you feel if I questioned your goodness every time?"

I rose and stepped toward him. "It's not like I don't trust you."

He gave a tiny shake of his head. “Hard to believe, given your words and actions.”

I looked down at my hands, pushing my nail bed back. “I’m seeing someone. I think he’s jealous of me working with you.”

Lorenzo sat back down at the table. “I see. Do you expect me to talk to him and explain that my intentions are pure? That I’m only trying to run a business here and give a rising talent a chance, not steal his woman?”

His words made me want to disappear into thin air. He must think me a spineless coward. How I wished I hadn’t started the conversation. If only I believed in myself more, I wouldn’t have let Victor undermine my confidence and convince me Lorenzo could only be interested in me for ulterior motives.

I sat down once more and forced myself to look Lorenzo straight in the eye. “I grew up in an orphanage. I’ve never had anyone besides Tia to show any interest in me. When I came here a few months ago, Victor rescued me and made my life easier in many ways. But lately, he’s been moody. I think he’s under a lot of stress from his work. I don’t want to ruin what I have with him for a possibility that is only real in my head. I want to sing, but I don’t want to mess up my life. The opportunity you’re giving me is amazing. I know I should be overjoyed, and I am, but I’m also terrified.”

Lorenzo leaned forward. “If what you have with this guy is real, how could you ruin it by pursuing your passion?”

Tears welled in my eyes, but I swallowed them. I had cried enough for one day. “I don’t know. He doesn’t want me to sing or perform.”

Lorenzo was silent for a long moment. “Do you want to sing?”

"More than anything." The fervor of my words surprised me, but once they came out, it was as if a dam had broken. "Singing is my thing. It gives me joy. When I was on the stage, I felt alive like I had never before. I was on top of the world."

"Do you think any man is worth giving up your dreams for?"

I swallowed hard. "Doesn't love require sacrifices?"

Lorenzo gave a bitter chuckle. "I used to think so. A long time ago, I contorted myself for a female. It nearly destroyed me. I can't stop you from making the same mistake I did. But ask yourself this: If tomorrow, either your voice disappeared forever or the man you're seeing, which would devastate you more?"

I reached for my throat, guilt overwhelming me as I whispered, "My voice. It would be like a part of me was ripped from me." I shook my head quickly. "I'm an awful person for thinking this. I'm too attached to my talents and needs."

"No, that's your healthy sense of survival and self-esteem. You should develop that." Lorenzo smiled, and his violet-green eyes sparkled with warmth. "Your voice is an integral part of who you are. It's much bigger than you know."

"I don't understand."

"You'll see. The world is changing, and so are you."

I didn't know how to reply to this cryptic statement, so I simply asked, "You really think I'm ready to perform in front of a huge audience?"

"Yes, I do. But at the end of the day, it's not what I believe or what your boyfriend believes; it's what you believe. Do you believe in yourself? Is your dream stronger than your doubt and fear?"

If I walked onto the stage on Friday, I could fail

miserably. I could embarrass myself in front of everyone. But if I didn't try, I would lose immediately. I rose from my chair. "I'll be here." I smiled at Lorenzo. "Thank you."

The urge to hug him was overwhelming, but I didn't. It would be inappropriate. If I wanted to sing and stay with Victor, I had to prove to him that there was nothing between the handsome demon and me. And there really wasn't. Because no matter how charming, kind, and thoughtful Lorenzo was, he was an immortal, and I was a mortal. Relationships between one person who was aging and another who wasn't could never end well.

"I'm looking forward to hearing you sing again," Lorenzo said as I reached the door.

"I'm looking forward to performing." With you, I thought.

I exited Daydream feeling light and calm. Strange how I had gone from completely depleted to being filled with positive energy in one evening.

# 20TH JULY

The fog hung heavy over me like a stifling blanket as I trudged through the streets of Arcadia. All around me were people who walked straight ahead, their faces emotionless. What was going on? Where were they all going? Every time I was close enough to touch one of the zombies, the person disappeared. We kept walking in circles around the night market, and with each circle, the tension within my chest increased. What was the meaning of this? Why couldn't I talk to anyone?

Buzzing sounded, and one by one, the people vanished, and the fog grew heavier until I couldn't see anything. The buzzing grew louder. Trying to escape it, I turned to the left only to fall onto the ground.

Ouch. I blinked a few times, realizing the noise was coming from my alarm clock and that in my desperation to escape it, I had tumbled out of bed.

I rubbed my lower back, slowly remembering that I had set my alarm this early because today I had to go back to Acacia's. I pushed off the floor and stepped toward the mirror. The pronounced golden specks in my eyes told me I was pushing it. The spots were so close and big they almost formed a circle.

Not wasting any time, I washed my face and threw on my clothes, then hurried downstairs. I had to walk down the entire length of the guest floor before I reached the stairs that led to the ground floor and outside. To not draw any attention, I kept my gaze downward even though I didn't expect anyone to be up at six in the morning. To my surprise, there was a rustling, and two women strutted toward me, their heavy dresses way too fancy for our boarding house.

"This is a shithole," one of them was saying. "How does Mother expect us to stay here?"

"She's handling it. She said our room is the biggest and has the best view," the other replied.

I dared to peek up from underneath my eyelashes to find two faces marred by disgust. The two girls both had tiny, beady eyes, large and wide noses, and hair that was combed so high a wig would've looked more natural. Given how similar they looked and them saying that their mother couldn't expect them to stay here, I assumed they were sisters. Strange, our boarding house wasn't exactly known to be the place to stay for women traveling by themselves, especially women who had money.

"I wish we hadn't come," the first sister, who was the shorter and plumper one moaned.

"Shut up. It will get better soon. Give it a few months, less if we're lucky, and everything will be restored to order," the taller one snapped.

"It better be faster."

As they passed me, I had to press myself into the wall since they walked in a way that took up the whole corridor. With a sinking feeling, I left the boarding house, hoping the sisters would change their minds and stay somewhere else. They seemed like very difficult customers, and I could easily imagine them complaining that the sheets weren't ironed enough, that the bread wasn't fresh enough, and demanding snowdrops in the middle of July.

At least, they weren't here with their mother. In my experience, children who allowed their parents to make decisions for them after they were grownups, had parents that were ten times worse than the children themselves were.

Since I tended to arrive at Acacia's around half past six in the morning, I never had to wait. As a fae, she chose to run her business during the night hours, opening around eight in the evening and closing in the early morning. Many people frowned upon those that did business with the fae, so most of her clients preferred to arrive protected under the cover of darkness. However, when I knocked that morning on her door, she said, "Please wait in the hall. I need to finish up with a client."

"No problem." I didn't mind waiting as long as I wasn't standing outside where I ran the risk of someone who knew me spotting me and asking me why I came to see the fae. With no chair to sit down, I remained standing and studied the beautiful stained-glass art, wondering if it was made by a fae. After a prolonged silence, voices carried toward me. I didn't mean to eavesdrop, but I also wasn't willing to wait outside.

"I feel so energylcss as if I have aged by ten years in

one night," a female said in a sad voice. She sounded like a middle-aged lady, which surprised me since older people were even more suspicious of fae than the younger generation. "And I look much older. It's as if I have gone gray overnight."

"Are you sure you didn't take anything that might've caused this?" Acacia asked.

"No, I already told you. I don't drink alcohol or take any tinctures. The only treatment I use to fall asleep is chamomile tea."

"Did you fall asleep quicker yesterday than usual?"

There was a pause. "Well, yes, but that was probably because the full moon had ended."

"Did anyone have access to your tea?"

Another pause. "Ever since my husband died, I had to sell my house and move into a women's house. We share the kitchen. But why would they put anything into my tea? What little money I have is in the bank, and none of my belongings were taken."

"Why, indeed?" Acacia wondered aloud. "Here's what I'm going to do for you. I'll prepare a brew for you. It should help, for now; however, it won't do much good long-term. You need to move out of this women's house."

"Why? Where would I go?"

Acacia sighed. "New times are ahead of us, and unfortunately, those that are coming into power are willing to exploit the helpless."

"I don't understand. What would anyone want with me? I don't have anything."

Acacia didn't reply immediately. Instead, there was rattling, as if she was mixing the brew. After a few minutes, she asked, "How old are you?"

"I turned fifty last year. Why?"

"You have at least twenty years to live, perhaps more. Someone who knows how to harness life energy could use twenty years for dark magic."

I gasped as the middle-aged woman exclaimed, "Who would do such a horrible thing? And why isn't anyone stopping them? What you're talking about is murder. Murder!"

"I've told you everything I know," Acacia replied calmly. "Take this brew. It should help you temporarily. But once again, I urge you to move out. Find another house, move in with other people to save money, but leave the place you're at now. It's not safe."

There were footsteps, and I quickly retreated to the end of the hallway and lowered my gaze. The client stalked past me without a word.

Acacia closed the outside door behind her. "Come in, Halia." She shot me an appraising glance. "I see you left this until the last minute."

Normally, the statement would've made me feel guilty, but today my curiosity took precedence. "What did you mean by times are changing?"

Acacia sighed. "Haven't you noticed? There are a lot of newcomers in Arcadia."

I took a seat at the table. "A lot of magic wielders. I would think you would view this as something positive."

She screwed a bottle cap shut. "Not all magic wielders are good. It feels as if a protection spell has been lifted, and everyone is able to come into Arcadia, including a lot of bad people." She shook her head. "I've been here for eighteen years, and something has changed in the last few months. I don't know exactly what is happening, but it's not good."

I shifted in my seat. "Do you really think somebody is taking life energy from unsuspecting people while they sleep?"

"Yes. Those who practice dark magic could do it easily and won't have too hard of a time finding victims." She shut one of the drawers forcefully. "Arcadia's citizens are spoiled. They don't know to look for the danger."

"This dark magic, is it performed by fae? Is it similar to what you do?"

Acacia had been putting away potions, but now halted mid-motion. "I don't know if fae are behind this. Energy stealing relies on a similar magic as emotion siphoning, but there's a huge difference. People who come to me know what they're getting in return. They enter willingly into a mutually beneficial relationship. I'm not a parasite. I don't exploit others. I offer them the option to escape their lives for a little while or to make their life easier, as in your case." She lifted her chin. "If you no longer require my services, you're free to go."

"I didn't mean to offend you. I was only trying to understand." Why was I always so damn clumsy? Either too shy or too forceful. Would I ever find the right balance?

Acacia's face softened, and I added. "It's not safe for me to show my true eye color yet, is it?"

She gave a tiny shake of her head.

"Do you know when it will be safe?"

"That's not for me to decide. Only you will know."

I bit my lip, people kept saying that, but I had no answers. Even when I tried to listen to my inner voice, my intuition, there was nothing.

I hadn't planned on talking about my dream but figured I had nothing to lose. Perhaps it was a puzzle piece to whatever was going on. "Last night, I dreamt about walking in circles around Arcadia. Thick fog surrounded me, and every time I tried to touch one of the people who acted like zombies, they would disappear. Any idea what that might mean?"

Acacia took my hand. "I'm not a clairvoyant. A witch might have the information you seek." She focused on my palm, and a tiny crease appeared between her eyebrows as she sifted through my emotions, deciding which one she would like to take.

"Less anxiety in you today, a little bit more anger than last time." She smiled. "There's confidence and positivity."

I jerked my hand backward.

"Don't worry; I won't take that from you. I know you need it."

I relaxed and rested my hand in hers.

The crease between her eyebrows grew. "Sadness. Such beautiful sadness, a melancholy for something that never was. I think I'll take that."

"I accept." She could have all the sadness she wanted.

Her lips moved rapidly and silently, and I closed my eyes, leaning into this exchange.

With each passing second, I grew lighter and lighter, and my happiness floated to the surface, toward the space my sadness had vacated.

"All done," Acacia said after a few minutes.

I opened my eyes and met her arctic-blue gaze. Her lips moved quickly and silently as she said the incantation. I looked into the mirror. The golden specks in my eyes were gone.

"Thank you." I rose from my chair, ready to leave.

"Before you go, take this." She handed me an amethyst quartz rock, half the size of my palm. "Keep it in your bedroom, preferably close to your bed. Don't let anyone see it. It will protect you."

"Thank you so much." I searched my pocket for coins, but she shook her head. "I can't accept this, it's too big."

A feline smile spread across her lips. "Consider it a favor."

I swallowed hard. If I accepted, I'd be indebted to a fae. But if I didn't... "Do you think somebody will try to steal my life energy?"

"I don't know, but they would be idiots if they didn't try. You have a lot of magic within you, and it's only growing with each passing day."

I shook my head. "I had a strange dream. It can hardly be described as a vision, and I most certainly cannot move objects with my mind or hear other people's thoughts."

A tinkling laugh. "Why are you humans always so obsessed with witches when there are so many other types of magical creatures out there that are much more fascinating?"

I wrinkled my forehead. "Because that's the only thing I could be. I suppose somebody could turn me into a vampire or werewolf, but neither bit me. The fae folk are born the way they are." Just like sprites, goblins, and elves. As were demons. For the first time, I wondered what world Lorenzo had come from. Was he born here? Had he traveled to hell or perhaps even heaven? Who were his parents? What was his life story? I've been so obsessed with my problems that I had neglected to ask him anything about himself besides what his powers were, afraid he would use them on me.

"You're none of those things." Acacia brought me back to the present. "I'm not sure what you are, but I know you have magic within you. And it's growing."

I twisted a strand of my auburn hair. I was odd,

nothing more. I didn't have any magical abilities. I wasn't a magic wielder.

"Don't worry about it. The time hasn't come yet to uncover your heritage."

My heart fluttered, and hope rose within me. Was there a chance I might discover who my parents were? The orphanage didn't keep any records, so I had given up trying to find my parents a long time ago. But if there was a chance, even the slightest chance of finding any answers, I would give anything to know where I had come from.

"For now, follow your path." Acacia placed her hand on her upper stomach. "Follow your intuition. It will guide you where you must go, and it will keep you safe."

I almost asked whether she was talking about my performance tomorrow but didn't. Fae liked to communicate in riddles, and I was already overwhelmed by all the pieces of information I had gathered today. I was also feeling slightly light-headed from the emotions she had taken from me, and I didn't want to be late for my shift. I thanked her again and made my way back to the boarding house.

I was about to enter through the front door when Tia rushed out of it. "You're just in time!" She shoved a piece of paper and a basket into my hands.

"What's this?" I scanned what appeared to be a list.

Pink roses,

Honey from wildflowers

Turkish delight

Hazelnut chocolate

Lavender hand cream

"We need to get this in the next half hour before our shift starts. We have new guests with very high demands."

I sighed, immediately knowing to whom Tia was referring. "The sisters decided to stay."

"How do you know about them?"

"I saw them complaining when I went to see Acacia." I whispered the last word.

Tia's forehead wrinkled. "Hurry. Madam won't be happy if we're late for our shift. I'll start cleaning now so that we finish on time."

"Maybe I should do the shopping later?"

She shook her head. "No, Madam will be furious if she finds out we didn't run the errands immediately."

Tia was right. As much as Madam acted like a fire-spitting dragon toward the staff, she treated her guests like royalty. Still, the items on the list weren't exactly cheap or reasonable. "She's all right with us buying all of this? Maybe we should run it by her first?"

"I almost forgot." Tia handed me a coin bag that was much heavier than I expected it to be.

"The sisters must be paying a lot of money to stay with us."

"They're not paying anything at all."

"What?"

"They're Madam's daughters. Now hurry." She gave me a gentle push, and I started toward the market, confused by this new turn of events. If Madam Fontaine had children, why hadn't they visited her until now? And why had they suddenly decided to stay with her?

Acacia's words came to my mind. *It feels as if a protection spell has been lifted, and everyone is able to come into Arcadia, including a lot of bad people.*

As far as I could tell, Madam and her daughters were annoying, but harmless humans. Or were they? Just because they didn't possess magical abilities didn't mean they couldn't exploit people. Icy fingers tap-danced down my spine. I shook the sensation off, unwilling to give in to the panic. The sisters and Madam were a pain in my behind, but that didn't make them dangerous.

Even though Arcadia's market had everything one could wish for, it took me a while to check everything off the list, given how precise the sisters' instructions had been. I hurried from stall to stall, but there was no way I could make it back by eight.

My basket filled with luxuries I would never be able to afford, I returned to the boarding house's reception desk to be greeted by Madam's scowling face.

"Who do you think you are, Halia?"

"I bought what your daughters have requested." I held out the basket to her, and she snatched it from me.

"You were supposed to do that before your shift." She glanced meaningfully at the clock hanging on the wall. "When does your shift start?"

"At eight. But—"

"And what time is it now?"

"Half-past eight."

"So, you're half an hour late."

"No, I left at half-past seven. I started my shift half a half-hour earlier to get the shopping done."

"Not another word. You should be ashamed of yourself. You can't expect others to do all the heavy lifting while you coast by."

I balled my fists. I'd had enough of standing down and letting others intimidate me.

"Would you have preferred I didn't get those items for your daughters?"

Madam's nostrils flared. "How dare you suggest such a thing? You are supposed to get them and return here on time."

"This is a very extensive and precise list. I did my best to fulfill this task in my free time to start my shift punctually."

Before Madam could retort, the front door opened, and a young man peeked his head in.

"We have no free rooms," Madam snapped.

"Oh, I'm not here for boarding." He smiled at me. "I was wondering if I could get an autograph, Halia."

I shot him a pained smile and whispered, "Later." This was the worst timing ever.

"An autograph! Is this a joke?" Madam advanced, and the young man quickly rushed out of the door. She whirled on me. "That's it. I've had enough. You are suspended from room service. From now on, you'll be working in the kitchens."

"But—"

"Because of your disrespectful attitude, your friend is demoted to kitchens as well."

"But she hasn't done—"

"Not another word unless you want to get fired immediately."

No, she couldn't do that. Our meager salary had made it impossible to save up any money while working here. If she kicked us out, Tia and I would have to live on the streets until we found work somewhere else.

Madam smirked. "I didn't think so."

"Go and tell your friend to finish up the rooms by herself. When she's done, she'll join you in the kitchen."

I didn't trust my voice, so I left without a reply. I climbed up the stairs to the second floor and found Tia in the third room.

"You're back!" she exclaimed. "I tried to clean as fast as I could, and so far, Madam hasn't checked up on me." She stopped as she noticed the look on my face. "What happened? Were you not able to get the items on the list?"

"No, I got them, but Madam threw a fit; she said I was late. Then a guy walked in, asking for an autograph." I shook my head. "I got demoted to the kitchen. And you as well."

Tia's jaw clenched. "What? I'll go talk to her." She tried storming past me, but I grabbed her hand.

"If you do, she'll fire us both."

"She can't do that!"

"She can, and she will. It's her boarding house. Tia, we can't argue with her. We need this job unless we want to live on the streets."

"Yes, but working in the kitchens will cut our pay significantly. We'll be barely able to scrape by."

"I know." My voice broke. "I'm so sorry."

"You've got nothing to be sorry for." She pulled me into a hug, and unable to hold in my tears any longer, I released a sob.

"If I hadn't argued with Madam, if I had apologized, it wouldn't have come to that. I should have never given an autograph to the girls at the market. What if somebody else comes around asking for an autograph?"

"Then we'll figure it out. This isn't your fault. It's Madam's. Can't you see, she's filled with anger and she's looking to unload her misery on whoever is close by? It's unfortunate that it was you who crossed her path, but it isn't your fault."

I pulled out of the hug, appreciating her trying to make me feel better, but knowing that if we were caught not working, we would lose our jobs immediately and be thrown out onto the streets.

"Madam wants you to finish up the rooms before

you help me in the kitchen," I said in parting.

With heavy steps, I trotted downstairs. Was I making everything worse for Tia and myself? It had felt good in the moment to stand up for myself, but if I hadn't, Madam wouldn't have become so furious with me. If I had backed down, I might have run into the young man by myself and given him an autograph without her knowing. If only I had returned earlier from Acacia's instead of dawdling, I could've run the sisters' errand on time. I sighed. There were so many "coulds" and "shoulds" in my head, but they wouldn't help me now. I couldn't turn back time. I had gotten myself into a serious mess, and now I needed to find a way to dig myself out of it.

I had thought that I would be all by myself for kitchen duty, but when I entered, I found a middle-aged woman I hadn't met before standing by the sink, scrubbing a deep dish.

"Hi, I'm Halia. I'll be working with you today." And hopefully, not forever.

She nodded but didn't respond. Her shoulders were hunched, and she worked quietly as a mouse. I gently prodded, "What's your name?"

She just shook her head.

"You don't have a name?"

The corners of her mouth turned downward and trembled. Was she painfully shy or a mute?

"I don't mean to upset you, but I need to know what I can call you." She still didn't respond, and I decided there was a reason why she didn't want to share her real name. Taking a moment, I tried coming up with a pretty, temporary name she might like. "How about Doris?"

She smiled, and I felt a bit better. "Doris, it is. Now,

let me help you." I stood next to her and began cleaning the dirty pans, scrubbing away the grease and the food morsels stuck to them.

Since Doris didn't seem in the mood to talk, I began to hum a tune, which soon turned into a song.

*You say I should dare, you say I should put myself out there, but when I do, I'm met with closed doors, when I do, I'm met with nos.*

*You say to believe in myself, you say to try, try, try again, but what if I can't go on? What if I can't?*

*It's not that I don't want to; it's that I'm not sure I'm strong enough.*

*I want to be stronger; I want to be better, but I'm not sure how.*

*Can you teach me the way? Please, teach me the way.*

When I stopped singing, Doris squeezed my hand, her eyes filled with joy. Even though she hadn't spoken a word to me, I didn't think she was mute. The haunted look on her face told me something bad had happened to her and led to her not speaking. What horrible fate could've befallen her that she lost her voice? I wished I could find a way through to her, to tell her that if she shared her pain, it would grow lighter.

Was that how Tia felt about me when I had difficulty speaking up? How many steps had I been away from becoming someone like Doris?

Right then and there, I decided I didn't need anyone to show me the way. I didn't need anyone to teach me how to be brave. I had to find the strength within me. If people like Doris and I remained silent, people like Madam would only become louder, and the world would hear only their words. I didn't want to live in a world run by Madam, so I needed my voice to be heard.

I cleaned the dishes on autopilot, thinking about the set I would play at Daydream. I came up with a list of five songs. As soon as I was finished here, I would head to the bar and practice each of the songs with Lorenzo. Hopefully, he would agree to accompany me on the guitar again.

Doris and I were on the last dish when Tia came through the door. Her hair was a mess, and her hands were red from the cleaning supplies. Still, she asked, "What can I help you with?"

"We got it," I said. "Tia, this is Doris. Doris, meet Tia." The two exchanged nods. "How did you get on with the rooms?"

Tia collapsed onto a chair and rubbed her lower back. "It was awful. Madam expected me to be done at the original time, so I had to work twice as fast."

I cringed. "I should have never confronted her."

"I'm glad you did. Being demoted to the kitchens is the push we needed to finally leave this place."

I put the clean dishes away and dried my hands. "We need to find a new workplace first before we hand in our resignation."

"We have one. Daydream."

I shook my head. "Even if Lorenzo agrees to let me perform regularly, I doubt the money will be enough to make a full-income salary."

"So work with me behind the bar. I'm sure there are lots of things you could do."

I chuckled. "You don't even have a job at Daydream, yet you are already offering me one?"

She smiled, some of her weariness melting away. "I believe in us. I know there's something better for us in this world than scrubbing dirty dishes in the kitchen."

I glanced at Doris, hoping Tia wasn't offending

her, but Doris showed no signs of listening to our conversation. She had retreated to the corner and was staring into empty space.

"All right," I said. "I wanted to head over earlier anyway to practice my setlist with Lorenzo. I suppose we can leave now, and see if he has work for us at the bar or if he knows of anyone who would employ us."

"Great, we need to stop by the clothes donation shop on our way."

At my confused look, she said, "A couple left their suitcases behind."

"Which room?"

"The one that the sisters are staying in now."

Doris trembled, and I put on a pot of water for her. Hopefully, she wouldn't get sick. "Wasn't the couple in that room supposed to stay until the twenty-fourth?"

Tia shrugged. "Something must have happened for them to leave so abruptly and not even bother to take their suitcases."

I didn't like this one bit. It sounded like our guests were on the run from someone, and they had been discovered in Arcadia. Acacia was right. Whatever spell had been protecting Arcadia and made it a joyful, safe place was falling away. Dark times were ahead for us.

## 21ST JULY

After dropping off the clothes at the donation shop yesterday, Tia and I had headed to Daydream only to find it closed. We waited outside for half an hour, hoping someone would let us in or respond to our knocks, but no one did, so eventually, we left without talking to Lorenzo.

Even though a lot of establishments were closed on Mondays, I was stressed all of last evening and tossed and turned through the night. What if Lorenzo had left town? What if I wasn't performing today after all? The worries stayed with me as I scrubbed plates in the kitchen.

Tia was uncharacteristically quiet, probably practicing her speech for why she should be hired as a bartender or barback. Doris still wasn't talking to either of us and scurried around like a mouse.

There was something familiar about her, but try as I might, I couldn't place her. Was it her eyes? Or face? Had I seen her at the night market before? Perhaps she had worked at one of the stalls. Or maybe she had been a guest once at the boarding house? Either way, even though she was working efficiently, her soft hands didn't make me think she had led a life of manual labor. What had happened to her for her to become a kitchen maid?

I shook my head. It was none of my business. She would tell me when she was ready, and right now, I had more pressing matters to attend to anyway.

The setlist I had created yesterday didn't sound good any longer. I hummed through all the songs I had ever written, tweaking and rearranging, trying to come up with the best flow while wondering if the concert was still happening. Of course, it was. It had to be. It didn't mean anything that Lorenzo hadn't been at Daydream the night before, right?

Distracted and worried, I spilled soapy water all over my clothes and the floor, creating more work for myself. By the time my shift was finally over, my hands were red and cracked from all the dishes I had washed and my mind was a wreck.

"Tia, if you don't mind, I'd like to take a walk before going to Daydream." I needed to get rid of the nervous energy coursing through me.

Tia nodded. "No worries. I'll see you at Daydream."

"Are you still going to ask him for a job?"

She gave another nod, but her face stayed weary. Being demoted to the kitchens had taken a toll on us both. It didn't help that the boarding house had practically radiated tension ever since the sisters' arrival. This place was toxic. We needed to get out.

I took off my apron and pulled my hair out of its braid. "I'll freshen up, and then the room is all yours."

I was at the door when Tia said, "Good luck. You'll do really well."

"Thanks," I said, even though what I really wanted to ask was, "Aren't you going to be there earlier? I need you there." I swallowed my words. Tia had enough on her own plate. I had to find the strength within me to weather nerve-wracking situations, not use my friend as a crutch.

I rushed up the first flight of stairs only to halt on the guest floor as the two sisters came my way. I pressed myself into a shadowed alcove, my gut telling me I needed to hear this, needed to understand why they were here.

"I can't wait to get out of this pigsty," the shorter and rounder one said.

"Patience, Bernadette."

"Get off your high horse, Georgette. I know you want it too."

"Shush." Georgette smacked her sister on the hand. "At least, I'm not pathetic enough to dance around with a diadem on my head, practicing court etiquette."

Bernadette pouted. "There's nothing wrong with having some fun."

"There's no room for fun or balls. This time, everything will be different. Being an airhead won't get you anywhere. That was cute eighteen years ago when the prince was searching for a bride, but there's no prince anymore. To live at the palace, we won't need to look pretty, fake niceties, or force our feet into stupid glass shoes. It's all about power now. Survival of the fittest."

Bernadette perked up. "Yes, we'll be powerful. Mother will see to it."

The two sisters strutted past me, and I looked after them, unsure whether they were delusional for thinking they would ever live at the palace or if they were a threat to the crown. Should I report their conversation? If they truly planned to act on what they had said, they were committing treason. I bit my lip. If I told one of the patrolmen, they would laugh at me and tell Victor, who'd admonish me to mind my own business. I needed to keep an eye on the sisters and Madam and wait until I had proof before I said anything.

I sighed. How could a woman that was running a boarding house be a threat to the king? Madam was mean, but I had never seen her use any magic. The only threat she presented was if she rallied together a group of demons and fae that were willing to rise against the king. I shook my head. Why would demons and fae help Madam Fontaine? I was over-thinking this and putting my nose where it didn't belong. If I didn't want to remain a kitchen maid forever, I needed to focus on my concert tonight, not on the real or imagined machinations of my employer and her daughters.

Banishing the drama of the boarding house from my mind, I freshened up and put on a pair of jeans that were fashionably torn in the knee area and a green top with a tropical pattern that I tied around my nape and mid-back.

I left my hair loose and slipped into a pair of second-hand wedges I had snatched up a month earlier.

Not giving myself the chance to rethink my ensemble, I left the boarding house and made my way to Daydream. I hummed, going through the songs I was planning to perform when a hand grabbed my shoulder. Startled, I let out a yelp.

"Relax, Halia. It's just me."

I turned around and met Victor's gaze, which hardened as he took in my outfit. "You're going to Daydream."

I straightened. "I am. This is really important for me. I understand your concerns, but I need to do this."

His jaw tightened, and he didn't respond for several seconds. "Fine. I'll come with you to ensure nothing bad happens."

I shook my head. "I don't think that's a good idea."

"What? Are you telling me you don't want me to be there?"

"I think it's best if we take a break, Victor." Only when the words left my mouth did I realize how much I meant them. I needed to breathe, find out who I was, and I couldn't do that with Victor around.

He puffed his chest out. "Break? Do you know how many women would be honored to be with me?"

"I'm sure there are a lot of ladies who would welcome being courted by you. I understand if you want to pursue them."

"Is this because of the fight we had last time? This is stupid." He tried to take my hand, but I disentangled myself from his grip and stepped backward.

"We have a lot of disagreements. You're used to me giving in, but I'm done doing that. I want to pursue my passions. I want to be able to do what I love without having to apologize or worry about how you feel about it."

"You want to be selfish. Everything I did was for your own good! You're being very ungrateful."

"I need to be on my own. Goodbye, Victor."

I started turning around, but he grabbed my shoulder

again. "If you leave now, Halia, there's no going back."

I removed his hand from my shoulder. "I know, Victor. And I'm ready to accept the consequences of losing you."

"You're throwing away everything we built in the last few months. You're throwing away your future for one stupid night of singing."

"I'm no longer willing to give myself up for security, love, or acceptance. You want somebody who is subservient to you, and I'm not that person. I would rather have no support than be with someone who doesn't allow me to express myself."

"You're an ungrateful bitch!"

As I walked away, an unexpected smile curled my lips. It was good to finally hear the words out loud that Victor had silently communicated to me so many times. It wasn't just in my head. I wasn't too sensitive. Victor was controlling. His facade had finally cracked to reveal who he truly was.

I reached Daydream but didn't step inside. If I asked Lorenzo for a job at the bar, I would be binding myself completely to him, almost in the way I had done with Victor.

I didn't want that. Also, I wasn't interested in bar work, and I didn't want to abandon Doris. I needed to find a job that allowed me to stay in touch with her while also giving me insight into the developments of Arcadia. Something bad was happening to our kingdom.

Perhaps I couldn't do much, but it was my obligation to help my country in whatever way I could. Also, I had the feeling that the mystery of my eye color would be revealed soon. I wanted to know what the golden rings meant. I wanted to know why I was different.

There was one job I could think of that was easy

to obtain, would allow me to keep an eye on the boarding house, and gain a better understanding of the happenings in Arcadia.

Hoping my performing outfit wouldn't be off-putting, I entered the post office.

"Do you have an opening for a mail carrier?" I asked the woman behind the counter who was weighing a package.

She pointed me toward a form. "Fill this out. Be ready to start the day after tomorrow. Oh, and I hope you're an early riser. Shift starts at 5 a.m."

I grabbed a pen. "Sounds perfect."

I left the post office in a much better mood, relieved that I could hand in my resignation to Madam next time I saw her. She would throw a hissy, but there was nothing she could do to stop me from leaving. My contract stated explicitly that both parties had the right to terminate the employment without giving notice. It had probably been an oversight on Madam's part to allow her employees to do that, or perhaps she was legally required to provide this option if she wanted to exercise the right to fire them whenever she wanted. Either way, it was my ticket to freedom. Excited to never be bossed around by Madam again, my pre-performance jitters only hit me when I walked through the heavy door into Daydream where I was bathed in azure and turquoise hues of blue light that weren't in the least bit cold, but rather calming, like a lake on a beautiful, sunny summer day.

"Good luck," the statues murmured.

"Thank you." I took the time to make eye contact with each of them.

Lorenzo was talking behind the bar with Tia, who was nodding eagerly before disappearing behinds the door to the restocking room. I guessed her interview had gone successfully as well.

I stepped toward Lorenzo. "How are you?"

His gaze slowly traveled from my face down my body and back up to my face, making a pleasant warmth fill my belly.

"I'm good. You look different."

I stuck my thumbs into the front pockets of my jeans and rocked back and forth on my wedges. "Is my outfit all right?"

A slow smile spread on his mouth. "I didn't mean the clothes. There's something different about you. After last time... I wasn't sure if you would return."

"I'm fully committed to this." I stepped forward. "Thank you for giving me this opportunity."

He raised an eyebrow. "You're no longer worried about what that boyfriend of yours will think?"

"We just broke up."

He whistled. "Lots of changes, huh? Tia told me you're also quitting the boarding house."

I nodded. "We were unfairly demoted to the kitchen, which finally gave us the push we needed to leave."

He hesitated. "I'm starting Tia on a mix between a barback and a bartender, but I'm not sure that's the right thing for you."

"You don't need to worry about me. I've already found a job as a mail carrier."

He tilted his head. "You're full of surprises today."

I shrugged. "It will be good for me. Something new." A week ago, I would've never considered it, certain I wouldn't be able to find all the addresses and deliver the mail correctly. A lot has changed during the last week. Besides my newfound confidence, Arcadia was molding itself into a new town. There were those that oppressed the innocent, like Madam and her daughters. Those that were victimized like the middle-aged woman who had aged overnight, the silent woman in the kitchen, and the couple that had disappeared from the boarding house. And then there were those that could either help rebuild or destroy Arcadia, like Lorenzo and Acacia. I was done standing back and looking on. This was my home, and I would help defend it from whatever darkness was trying to encroach on it.

"Arcadia isn't changing for the better," I said slowly. "Whatever has been protecting our kingdom for eighteen years is falling away."

Lorenzo's eyes narrowed. "How do you know this?"

I bit my lip, unsure about mentioning Acacia. Fae and demons were famous for disliking each other. "I have my sources. Do you agree then? What happened eighteen years ago? What spell was put into place to protect us?"

"I don't know, but it wasn't just Arcadia. Everywhere I've traveled for the last eighteen years, I've found prosperity and blooming kingdoms. Then, a few months ago, things started shifting."

"Why did you come here?"

He sighed. "Changes are coming everywhere. When that happens, it's best to be surrounded by your own kind, even if you don't like all of them."

"Arcadia has the biggest demon population?"

"Correct."

I ran my hand through my auburn waves. "Do you know what's going on?"

He shook his head. "Evil forces are awakening. Why or what they plan, I don't know. But I do know that you'll play a part in this new world."

Only a day ago, I would have met a statement like that

with denial. Now, however, anything seemed possible, so I simply said, "Perhaps. But that's not something to worry about tonight."

He smiled. "I'm glad you're finally ready to embrace your calling."

I stepped toward him, so close that only an elbow-length remained between us. "Thank you for taking a chance on me."

Something sparked in his green-violet eyes, and the temptation to lean closer was overwhelming. My interest in him unbalanced me, especially because I was certain it was all coming from me and not from some magic he used on me. Whatever was transpiring between us was real and natural, no matter how much it terrified me. Something to examine later.

I took a deep breath and headed for the stage, calling across my shoulder, "Are you coming? I want to show you the songs so that you can accompany me."

For once, I wasn't waiting, or asking, finally, I was leading.

Lorenzo and I went through my setlist, his musical talent allowing him to pick up the right chords halfway through the songs. Even though we had never played the songs together until today, I was confident we would be a great team.

Just as we finished, the first people streamed into Daydream. It wasn't long until the bar was filled with humans, demons, fae, elves, goblins, and sprites. My heart swelled with joy. I had expected a small crowd to show up to hear me perform, but it seemed that everyone who had bought a ticket to see the Dark Quartet had decided that I, too, was worth their time. This was an honor I wouldn't squander by wondering if I was good enough or worrying if I deserved it. I would show my gratitude to those that have paid to hear me play by giving the best performance I could.

I might not have an agent, or a manager, or even much experience, but I had fervor. I was the queen of song.

I sang the six songs Lorenzo and I had practiced, "Chains," "Through the Darkness," "Torn" "My Path," "Hope" and "Teach *Me* the Way."

When I was finished, the crowd hollered and clapped. "More! Encore! One more!"

I turned to Lorenzo, who grinned at me. He looked so carefree and young like he was my age and not an immortal demon. "Do you have another one?"

I nodded. "I do. I came up with it today."

"Are you ready to share it?"

I smiled, grateful for him asking for my preference instead of putting pressure on me. "Yes. It might not be perfect, but I really want to share it."

I took the microphone from the stand and said, "This is a new one. I composed it today. Let me hear you make some noise if you want to hear 'Queen of Song.'"

The crowd went wild, and behind me, Lorenzo chuckled. "You're a natural. Are you sure you've never performed?"

I threw my hair across my left shoulder and winked. "It's not what I did in the past or what I'll do in the future; it's about seizing the present moment."

The tenderness that shone on his face made it painful not to lean forward and kiss him. Maybe if we had been alone, I would have done it, even if it was too soon, even if he was a demon. As it was, the thundering crowd stopped me from giving in to my crazy impulse.

I faced Arcadia's citizens, my family, and sang:

*Once upon a time, there was a girl who liked to sing.*

*She didn't have a home, she didn't have kin, but she had a voice. Her blessing terrified her, for it gave her hopes and dreams she was told were impossible.*

*Years passed, and the girl only shared her voice with her closest friends, only shared her voice when it was lost in a choir. Then you came along, and you challenged the girl, you told her it wasn't right not to share her blessing, you gave her strength, you gave her confidence. You allowed her to lean on you, and she became the queen of song, she became the queen of song.*

The applause went on forever. Tia ran up onto the stage and hugged me tightly, making it hard to breathe. "Was that dedicated to me or Lorenzo?"

I chuckled. "Why can't it be dedicated to you both?"

As the Dark Quartet set up, I made my way through the crowd, signing shirts, booklets, and even forearms.

I had never felt so joyous, and yet something kept nagging at the back of my mind. I was signing a t-shirt a girl was wearing when my gaze landed on the king and queen statue behind her, and that was when I knew what was bothering me. The queen statue. The high cheekbones, the small nose, and the shape of the chin. I had seen those features recently. Not in a newspaper or a poster. No, I had seen those features on the silent woman in the kitchen. Doris looked exactly like our missing queen.

# HEIRESS OF MELODY

## 22ND JULY

It was my last shift at the boarding house, which meant that I had to accomplish several things. First, tell Madam Fontaine that I was quitting. Second, figure out why the silent woman in the kitchen, whom I had named Doris, looked like our missing Queen Ella.

With these goals in mind, I stopped at the reception desk first before going into the kitchen and scrubbing the never-ending amount of dirty pans and dishes. "Any idea when Madam will be here?" I asked the young man who had started working behind the front desk a week ago. I would have been ashamed to not know his name hadn't Madam's staff-turnover been legendary and if this wasn't my first time meeting him. If he lasted more than a few weeks or a month, he would get to join the ranks of what was considered long-term employees. My friend Tia and I had lasted nearly three months before deciding to quit.

The young man shrugged. "Madam won't be in until later. She told me she had several things to take care of."

"Could you let her know that I need to speak to her? My name is Halia."

"Sure."

I thanked him and headed toward the kitchen. I didn't like the conversation with Madam hanging over me like a black cloud, yet I was also relieved that I wouldn't get to talk to her until later. She wouldn't be pleased that I was quitting and would make my last shift miserable.

I entered the kitchen to find Doris was already there, scrubbing away at greasy pans.

"How are you today, Doris?"

She nodded in acknowledgment and gave me a smile. So far, I hadn't pushed her to speak to me. She had piqued my curiosity because she looked so much like our Queen Ella, who had suddenly disappeared over a week ago. But because this was my last shift, I no longer had the luxury of waiting for Doris to come around.

Sensing that demanding that Doris talk would get me nowhere, I decided that I had to trick her. It felt a bit cheap, but I didn't have a choice. She might know something that could help our kingdom, which had seen a lot of strange activity lately.

I started singing a song that was extremely popular and catchy:

*The sun is out; it's summertime. Let's come together, in this beautiful weather; let's have some fun. Throw away all your worries; let's have some fun.*

*Fun, fun, fun in the sun. The days are long; the nights*

*are even longer.*

*Forget your worries and come out with me to have fun, fun, fun in the sun.*

I repeated the chorus and the first verse and then pretended to leave the room. I was by the door mid-chorus and stopped singing. Doris kept on humming.

I whirled around. "I knew it!" I hurried toward her.

With her mouth wide open and eyes even wider, she looked like a terrified doe.

"It's all right. It's fine to speak."

She shook her head.

I took her hands. "I don't know what happened to you, but I can only guess it was something horrible." Her face contorted with pain, and my heart swelled with compassion. "I can't erase the past, but I guarantee you that you will feel much better once you share your sorrows."

She shook her head rapidly.

This wasn't working. I needed to slow down. "Are you from Arcadia?"

In response, she extricated herself from me and took a step backward. I sighed. I wasn't getting anywhere. It was time to lay my cards on the table.

"Listen, I found a new job. I'm going to work at the post office. Today is my last day at the boarding house. I'm sure I'll come by here occasionally to drop off the mail, perhaps even daily, but I won't have much time."

She gave me a smile and an approving nod as if she thought it was good for me to leave this place.

"My friend, Tia, also quit. She's going to work at Daydream, the bar. I'm sure they could use more people if you want to switch jobs."

Her eyes widened again, and she shook her head vigorously.

All right, clearly, she wanted to stay here, even though I didn't understand why. The only explanation was that she was trapped, same as I had been, in believing that working at the boarding house was the only other option besides living on the streets.

"I promise other employers would be happy to have you. You're dedicated, hard-working, and sweet."

She turned away and grabbed a fondue pot.

I bit my lip. None of my approaches were working. Perhaps I should simply ask her the question that was haunting me. It couldn't get worse than her not talking to me.

"When I performed last night at Daydream," I began, "I had a chance to study the ice sculptures that decorated the space."

She glanced up at me.

"They're beautiful. You should come and see them sometime. You don't even have to stay at the bar or get a drink, just come inside and have a look at them."

She tilted her head sideways as if considering my offer.

"The owner is very friendly. Anyhow, two of the ice sculptures were made to look like our king and queen."

She stiffened at that, and I took a step closer, needing to see the expression on her face when I made my next statement. "The queen looked a lot like you."

Doris inched away from me until her back hit the wall.

As much as I didn't want to intimidate her, I needed to know. "Queen Ella has the same cheekbones, the same face, the same eyes as you. It's like you two could be twins or at least sisters." I searched Doris's face, which had gone blank. Her arms trembled. "Please, tell me what you know. The queen has been missing for over a week now, and bad things have been happening in Arcadia. People are disappearing, while others are aging overnight. The queen's disappearance is connected to this. I think the queen had some magic that protected us, and now that she's gone, Arcadia is falling apart."

Tears welled in Doris's eyes, and she wiped at them quickly, but still, she didn't speak.

I stepped closer. "Please, I need your help. Arcadia needs your help."

Doris rushed past me and out of the kitchen.

I sank to the floor. "That went well. Not."

Doris returned half an hour later. For the next few hours, we worked side-by-side, but now, she wasn't even looking at me as if I didn't exist.

I didn't dare to broach the topic of Queen Ella's disappearance or Doris's resemblance again. The last thing I needed was for Madam to blame me for distracting her employees or for Doris running away. She knew something, and, sooner or later, I would find a way to uncover her secrets and help Arcadia.

I had just finished cleaning my last plate when Madam entered to inspect our work. She nodded her approval at the clean dishes. "Very well. However, you'll have to do the after-dinner clean up as well since your friend quit."

This was all directed toward me. Madam acted as if Doris was invisible. "I'm quitting too," I said. I wasn't prepared to work a double shift for the meager salary she was paying us. "Today was my last shift."

Madam's generous chest heaved, and a vein popped out on her meaty neck. "You can't do this to me!"

"My contract states that I can quit at any time."

"Unbelievable!" She pointed her finger in my face. "Don't come back begging for your job when your singing doesn't work out."

I tried hard to hide the smile that threatened to erupt on my lips. "I'm not just relying on my singing. The post office hired me as a newsgirl."

Madam huffed. "You'll be walking the streets, rain or shine, snow or heat. I'll give you a week, max."

"I don't think so. It can't be worse than here, and I've survived months here."

Madam's upper lip curled back into a snarl, revealing big, uneven teeth. "I'm not going to pay you your salary for mouthing back at me!"

"Fine." I wasn't about to beg for today's pay. "I'll be back soon to check on you," I whispered to Doris. Grateful for Tia's foresight to collect our meager belongings from the attic room, I stalked out of the kitchen. It looked like for the next few nights, I'd be sleeping on a barstool. It might be uncomfortable, but it was preferable to being in a snake's den.

Outside the boarding house, a carriage pulled up, and a round man climbed out, heaving a trunk that was almost as big as he was. He waved at me. "Excuse me, do you know which room the sisters Bernadette and Georgette occupy?"

"Room one." I held the door open for him, disgust welling up in me. The trunk of clothes was probably why Madam was so greedy. She squeezed her employees dry so that her daughters could afford countless dresses they wore only once.

After being cooped up for the whole day in the dark kitchen without any sunlight, I decided to wander the streets of Arcadia before going to Daydream. Plus, if Tia and I were to sleep at the bar, we would have to wait until the last customer left, which was hours away.

I headed toward the night market. It always cheered

me up, not because of the countless goods one could purchase, which were interesting to look at, but unaffordable for someone like me, but because of the artists congregating there.

Tonight, there were several painters, caricaturists, and pottery makers at one end of the market. I walked between their displays, enjoying the beautiful views they had captured. Some of them had painted the king's castle with its high turrets, heavy gate, and dark-blue roofs. Others had painted beaches and seas, or mountainous and forest landscapes.

Those that could afford the paintings probably didn't find any of the depicted places exotic, but I found them fascinating. I had never ventured outside of Arcadia. All I knew was this city and the outside of our castle, never having been allowed to step foot past the gate.

I had never felt the sand between my toes, swam in the salty sea, or hiked through a luscious forest.

Would I ever get to see other kingdoms? Arcadia was gorgeous and my home, but suddenly, the need to see the world overwhelmed me. And then loneliness hit me. If I wanted to see those places, I would have to go on my own.

With a bit of luck and convincing on my part, I could join a traveling group of musicians, but Tia wouldn't come with me. As a bartender, it was best for her to stay in one place and establish herself.

Could I leave my best friend behind? She was like a sister, and we had spent every day together in the eighteen years of our lives.

"What about Lorenzo?" a quiet voice inside my head asked.

I wanted to snap back at the voice and say he didn't matter, that I barely knew him. Yet, even though I had met the teleporting demon less than a week ago, he did matter, and I didn't want to leave him. Lorenzo brought out the best in me, my playful, carefree side. He helped me believe in myself. He supported my singing ambitions.

I had never come across anyone like him. I wasn't ready to leave him. I wasn't ready to throw away whatever was growing between us. He made me feel alive. With him, I was the best version of myself.

"Let me go! Let me go!" A boy's screams pulled me back to the present. I scanned the market to find a scrawny boy who couldn't be older than ten years of age cuffed and being dragged away by none other than Victor, my ex-boyfriend and one of the patrolmen of Arcadia.

I didn't want to talk to Victor. We hadn't exactly parted on amicable terms, but I couldn't just stand by and do nothing while he dragged a young boy to prison. Whatever the kid had done, it couldn't justify getting a mark on his record.

I pushed past the market-goers until I reached Victor and his partner Thomas. Thomas, with his wispy brown hair and average height, looked like a friendly schoolteacher compared to Victor, who was very tall and all sharp angles. As luck had it, Thomas noticed me first. I nodded at him in acknowledgment.

"Why are you arresting this boy?" My question was directed at Victor since he was the one holding the boy.

"He's a thief." Victor showed me a loaf of bread.

"He was probably hungry or trying to help his parents." I leaned down to the level of the boy. "Who do you live with?"

"My mom, but she's been sick lately and unable to work."

I straightened to my full height. "See," I said. "He didn't do it out of ill will; he was simply trying to provide for himself and his mother."

Victor's jaw locked. "Maybe the circle you run in nowadays permits stealing, but it is still illegal in Arcadia, and it is my job to uphold the law."

"He's just a boy."

"If I allow him to get away with stealing, others will soon follow suit."

Anger simmered within me, but before I could reply, Thomas stepped in between us. "He's right, Halia. Where are we supposed to draw the line? Is it all right for a twelve-year-old to steal? Is it all right for a fifteen-year-old girl to steal because she hasn't found a position of employment yet? And what about the old people. Do they get to steal as well because they're too old to work, and their pensions are meager?"

I bit the inside of my cheek. "I'm not asking you to abolish rules, but there has to be a way to uphold the law without letting our citizens starve or throwing them into prison."

Victor glared. "Yes, and it's called work."

"He's too young!"

"Then he should go to an orphanage. They'll take care of him until he's eighteen."

I shook my head. No child would willingly go to an orphanage if there was another option. "He has a mother. He can't just leave her."

Victor shrugged. "If she can't provide for him, she should give him up. It would be in everyone's best interest."

The boy started to shake, and a sob escaped him.

I knelt in front of him and wiped away the tear from his cheek. "It will be all right."

I wasn't crazy enough to think I could overpower two men or outrun them with the boy. I couldn't take them with brute force, but I could bring them to their knees with my wits.

Using the trick from earlier, I began singing:

*The sun is out; it's summertime. Let's come together, in this beautiful weather; let's have some fun. Throw away all your worries; let's have some fun.*

*Fun, fun, fun in the sun. The days are long; the nights are even longer.*

*Forget your worries and come out with me to have fun, fun, fun in the sun.*

I glanced around myself, smiling at the people nearby and motioning for them to join in. Some were already humming or tapping their feet and heads rhythmically. With my encouragement, the crowd joined in, one by one. By the time I repeated the chorus, half of the market was singing and dancing, inching closer toward our foursome.

"Stay back," Victor yelled while Thomas looked torn between admonishing the citizens and joining in.

With the patrolmen distracted, I whispered to the boy, "Grab his key. It's on his belt buckle." Victor was busy swinging his baton, yelling, "Stop it; stop it right now!" and the boy was able to grab the key undetected and hand it to me.

Still continuing to sing, I unlocked his shackles. I motioned for the crowd to come closer, then grabbed the boy's hand and ran.

"Hey, where did they go?" Victor's voice thundered behind us, but he wasn't able to see us through the thick crowd, and technically, he couldn't prove that it was I, who had taken the boy.

We ran to the edge of the market and down a side

street.

"Where does your mother live?" I asked the boy, gulping down air into my burning lungs.

"I'm not allowed to bring strangers home. Thank you." With that, he took off, his soles flashing as he disappeared into another side street.

I gazed after him until I realized the singing in the market had stopped. I needed to leave before Victor spotted me.

No longer in the mood to stay outside, I headed toward Daydream. With it only being eight at night, the place was still fairly empty. Tia stood behind the bar next to Mikka, a white-haired bartender with black eyes whose childlike features—tiny nose, wide eyes, round cheeks—made her look much too young to tend a bar. Despite this, she seemed to know her stuff and appeared to be teaching Tia how to mix a martini.

I approached the bar, and Tia's face lit up. "How did your last shift at the boarding house go?"

I shook my head. "Not good. I didn't get Doris to talk. Madam threw a fit at me for quitting and refused to pay me the money for my last shift."

Tia's eyes narrowed. "I'll go over there right now and demand she give you the money."

"It's not worth it."

"But—"

"We have bigger problems to think about, like where are we going to sleep tonight."

She hesitated, and I knew she hadn't thought this one through. My friend was great at taking the initiative, but she wasn't exactly the practical type.

I turned to Mikka. "Is Lorenzo in his office?"

"Yes." Mikka made no move to let Lorenzo know that I wanted to see him, so I simply stepped behind the bar and knocked at his office door. “It’s Halia.”

“Come in,” he called.

Lorenzo was sitting at his desk, his silver hair flowing like silk onto his shoulders, his violet-green eyes brighter than gemstones. “Stressful day?”

Did I look so bad that he could tell that after a quick glance without me opening my mouth? I sat down across from him. “You could say so.”

He waited for me to continue.

“Since Tia and I are no longer working at the boarding house, we can’t stay at our room there. I was wondering if we could perhaps spend the next few nights at the bar until our earnings allow us to rent a room somewhere.”

“I’m not letting you stay at the bar.”

I blinked, surprised by the firmness in his voice. Lorenzo had been nothing but kind in the past. Was my request that unreasonable?

“I have a spare room upstairs in my apartment. You can stay for as long as you want.”

“That’s very generous of you, but I doubt we could afford the price.”

“You and Tia are working for me. It’s only fair that I take care of your accommodations, and it’s convenient for me to have my employees nearby.”

I shook my head. “We wouldn’t want to impose.”

“Nonsense.”

I opened my mouth again, but he stopped me.

“Stay for a week. If you don’t feel comfortable, we’ll figure out something else once the week is up.”

All right. I supposed we could do that. “Thank you.”

He tilted his head, studying me. “Now that this is out of the way, would you like to tell me about the stunt you pulled at the market?”

I cringed. “How did you know?” It never failed to

surprise me how quick news traveled in Arcadia.

"A little birdie told me that two patrolmen lost a boy because somebody started singing and used the crowd to get the boy out."

"He was so young. They wanted to throw him into prison for thievery. It wasn't fair."

"I agree, but what I'm more interested in is how you managed to control the crowd."

I shrugged. "It was nothing special. I started singing a popular song, *Fun in the Sun*, hoping the market-goers joined in. And they did."

"You don't find it strange that they flocked to you, heeding your call?"

I shifted uncomfortably in my chair. "I had good timing and luck on my side."

Lorenzo pressed a slender finger to his lips. "It was magic."

I shook my head. "I don't have any magic. I'm human."

"Is that why you go to see the fae, Acacia, twice a week?"

I jumped up from a chair. "How do you know that? Have you been spying on me?" Unable to contain the adrenaline rushing through me, I paced the room.

"I saw the amethyst protection stone in your bag, and I knew immediately it was from her. I was concerned about your well-being and what you were doing with her, so I went to ask her what kind of relationship you two had. She told me you come to her twice a week, and that I would have to find out the rest from you."

I crossed my arms. "My business with Acacia is personal."

Lorenzo brushed a hand through his silver mane. "I didn't mean to upset you."

"Then you should've asked me directly and not gone behind my back."

"You're right, but I needed to be sure you weren't addicted to fae dreams before I offered you this." He pushed a few pieces of paper stapled together across the table.

I glanced at the papers, realizing they were a contract. "You want to manage me? Why?"

Lorenzo didn't reply immediately. Finally, he said, "Because even in good times, it's best to have an agent, somebody who is willing to negotiate on your behalf, do the business side so that you can focus on the creative stuff. Given the recent happenings in Arcadia, you need someone to keep you safe. As your manager, I would be able to come with you to auditions and performances and protect you."

Warmth spread through me at his words, but I wouldn't agree before I knew all the facts. I had made that mistake with Victor once, not realizing that his support came with strict control. "Do you know who's behind the issues in Arcadia?" Images of a couple disappearing from the inn, and a woman aging overnight flashed through my mind.

"No, but whoever they are, I think they're responsible for Queen Ella's disappearance."

I fought hard to keep my face neutral. I couldn't reveal my suspicions until I knew what his interest was in this. "Why do you care about our human queen and king?"

"Because every kingdom needs a ruler. Someone who is smart, strategic, and good. I believe our king and queen have all of those qualities."

"Wouldn't you prefer a magic wielder on the throne?"

A feral grin spread across Lorenzo's mouth. "Just

because I'm a demon doesn't mean I believe in the supremacy of our race. I don't think magic wielders are special. At the end of the day, we all have magic; some of us simply have way more than others."

His words were an echo of what Acacia had said to me a few days earlier, the fae claiming that every person had a drop of magic and that I had more, which made me an asset and a target.

"What makes you think I have magic?"

Lorenzo smiled. "Isn't it obvious? Your voice, it's not just beautiful, it's mesmerizing. When you sing, you compel those around you."

"No, I don't." I was not some evil mind manipulator.

"You might not be doing it consciously, but you are doing it. Don't tell me that today at the market was the first time. You knew, with certainty, the crowd would help you if you sang, didn't you?"

My cheeks heated as I thought about how I had tricked Doris into humming the tune. Had I really just chosen a popular song, or had I willed her to sing with me? And what about all the times when I had been singing while working with Tia, my intent to cheer up my friend, only to see her smile a while later as she mopped and got rid of bodily fluids on the sheets.

"So, if I'm able to..."—I searched for the right word, not wanting to use compel or manipulate—"influence others with my singing, what does that make me?"

Lorenzo leaned forward, his gaze boring into me. "That's for you to find out. I've met fae and demons with similar skills, but if you were either of those things, I would have smelled it on you."

I let out a sigh of relief, glad that I was still human.

"I strongly doubt that you come from a line of witches or anything that can be considered human. Witches need to use incantations and spell books, while your voice is an internal gift, which makes you other than human."

"But I am human! My skin isn't odd, my ears are normal, I don't have horns on my head..." I trailed off, focusing on Lorenzo's violet-green eyes. As much as I didn't want to admit it, I could see how my blue eyes with golden rings were a lot more similar to his than the eyes of other humans. If my eyes were nothing special, Mrs. Woods wouldn't have hidden the golden rings and told me to find a faerie to continue the masquerade after she abandoned me.

I bit my lip, coming within an inch of telling Lorenzo about my secret. My cautionary nature held me back. There was no advantage in rushing into that, but once I told him, there was no way of taking it back.

In fact, it would be easier to show him. By tomorrow morning, the golden specks in my eyes should be pronounced enough to show him if I chose to or for me to sneak out and find Acacia to magic away my otherness.

I faked a yawn. "Would you mind showing me my room? I'm really tired."

Ever the gentleman, Lorenzo nodded and led the way.

# 23RD JULY

I woke up feeling refreshed. It had been a long time since I woke up full of energy. I'd never felt this good. Neither the orphanage nor Madam's Boarding House had comfortable beds. Lorenzo's furniture, on the other hand, was heavenly. The blanket covering me was as soft as a feather. The pillow had just the right amount of stuffing, and the bed was so big, I could turn over both ways without falling out.

It was perfect. When Lorenzo had shown me Tia's and my room, I had protested, saying it was too much, but he had reminded me that I had already agreed to stay here one week and then reevaluate the situation.

I had begrudgingly accepted, planning to argue the next day, but now that I had slept in this bed that was like a cloud, I doubted I could ever leave. Whatever

Lorenzo wanted for the room, Tia and I would pay it. Thinking of my friend, I turned around toward her bed, expecting her to be snoring softly, her body twisted in a strange position. To my surprise, Tia wasn't next to me.

I jumped up. Had something happened to her? Had she fallen asleep in the bar? Given the night owl she was, I was used to her returning when the sun rose. However, I found it highly unlikely that even she would choose to party after her first shift.

I glanced at the clock. It was 4:20 am. I had slept for over seven hours, and my alarm would go off in ten minutes, which meant I only had enough time to look for Tia downstairs before I had to report to the post office for my 5 a.m. shift.

Glad that I was an early riser, I stepped to the sink, washed my face, and glanced into the round mirror attached above it.

The golden specks in my eyes were pronounced but hadn't formed circles yet. I would wait until the evening to decide whether to go to Acacia or show Lorenzo my secret. Not wanting to dwell on the choice I had to make, I focused on what to wear. My wardrobe was half a suitcase, so there wasn't much to choose from. I put on my most comfortable pants, a shirt, and my sturdiest shoes. Outside my room, I paused and stared at the door that led into Lorenzo's bedroom.

Should I knock and ask him about Tia? No, he had probably gone to bed late. I didn't want to pay him back for his generosity by waking him up. Plus, it was unlikely he knew where Tia was.

There was another door on this level, but I didn't try to open it. Lorenzo hadn't told me who or what was behind it, and I wasn't about to put my nose where it didn't belong. Lorenzo, being a demon, the likelihood that this was a guest room where another demon stayed was high, and I was not stupid enough to disturb a resting demon.

I descended the spiraling, wooden staircase and unlocked the door at the bottom with the smaller key Lorenzo had given me. I stepped through into a corridor that had a door that led to his office, which was accessible from here and the bar, and a door that led to the bar. With the bigger key, I opened the second door and stepped into the bar.

Even though it was unlikely, I checked every booth and underneath every table to see if Tia had passed out. She hadn't.

I tried to calm the rising worry within me by telling myself that Tia had returned much later in the past. She was an adult. She would be fine.

I arrived at the post office fifteen minutes early, and the woman who had hired me, Mrs. Flanagan, seemed to appreciate my punctuality because she greeted me with a warm smile. "Glad to see you're wearing your sensible clothes. The last girl showed up in a skirt. How she expected to ride a bike wearing that is beyond me."

I blinked rapidly. This was the first time I was hearing about a bicycle. "Do I need to ride a bike?"

"Of course. How else do you expect to deliver all the mail on time?"

"I don't know how to ride one. I've never been on one." I had seen a few in the city, but that was the extent of my familiarity with the devices. Bicycles tended to be something that rich merchants' sons rode, and sometimes merchants' daughters if they had progressive parents. It was, most definitely, not something that a girl like me from the orphanage had access to.

Mrs. Flanagan tsked. "I hope you're a fast learner.

You'll never get all the work done on foot."

She must have noticed the look of terror on my face because she added in a softer voice. "You can go on foot today and even tomorrow if you must, but you need to find somebody who can teach you."

"Could you?"

She busied herself with putting away a pair of scissors. "I don't ride a bicycle."

So it was normal for her not to know how to ride a bike, but I was somehow expected to learn how to ride one?

Mrs. Flanagan walked around the counter and pushed a red trolley toward me, filled to the brim with letters.

Wow, I had never quite understood how much mail the citizens of Arcadia got. "Is this for the whole city?"

She let out a belly laugh. "Good one. That's just for our market quarter."

What did all those letters contain? Were those letters from family and friends? Letters between lovers? Business-related information? What a life it must be when you received correspondence weekly, or maybe even daily. Even though you hadn't seen your loved ones for months or years and were separated by hundreds or thousands of miles, you knew they cared about you. It sounded like a wonderful life, one that was unattainable to an orphan like me.

"There will be more coming in later today. Come back once you're done for your second run."

I tried to hide the panic her declaration elicited, but clearly, it showed on my face because Mrs. Flanagan patted me on the shoulder. "The first few weeks will be hard, especially if you don't learn how to ride a bike, but you'll get used to it. You do still want the job, don't you?"

I nodded quickly. "Of course. I'm just surprised at how much mail Arcadia gets."

"Well, the mail won't deliver itself. Better get on your way." Mrs. Flanagan was back to being all business. Was it her natural tendency to go between sweet and kind to business-like, or was she that way with me because I was her employee?

As I pushed the red trolley outside, I noticed our kingdom's insignia. A golden crown and underneath it, a glass slipper.

I swallowed hard. Without Queen Ella, there was no Arcadia. I had to find the missing queen. I needed to get Doris to talk.

An hour into my new job, I was ready to cry. I had thought I knew the city well, but it turned out that I only was aware of about 10 percent of the streets. Even though Mrs. Flanagan had kindly highlighted the path I needed to take on a very detailed map, it took me forever to find the right houses. Then I had to check my list, ensuring that I delivered all the regular letters, telegrams, and any newspapers they had subscribed to.

At most homes, I simply pushed the letters and magazines through the post box hole. At restaurants and inns, which didn't include the boarding house today, I went to the reception desk and handed the mail to the concierge.

The few houses that didn't have post boxes left me no choice but to shove the letters underneath the front door, hoping it was all right.

At one home, a humongous brown dog kept barking and snarling at me, making it impossible for me to get closer. The neighbors started coming out to complain about all the noise, and I finally saw no other option but to throw the letters toward the house. They landed with a thump two feet from the doorstep, but the dog snatched them up and ran into his yard. I hoped he would bring them to his owners, not shred them apart.

I was finally done by noon and absolutely starving. Unable to take another step, I stopped in the middle of the market and purchased a flaky croissant with ham and cheese. I sat on the sidewalk and chewed the fluffy goodness slowly as the sun warmed my face. Too soon, the pastry was gone, while I remained hungry. Unable to afford another one, I headed back toward the post office.

"There you are," Mrs. Flanagan said as I entered, or more correctly hobbled in. "I thought you decided to run off with the mail."

"Why would I do that?"

"Normally, the newsboys and girls are done way before noon."

I sighed. "I ran into a few difficulties," I confessed, telling her about my lack of direction and the black dog who wouldn't let me get close to the house.

"You did well. If the owners wanted their post in their post box, they should have chained up the dog."

My shoulders slumped a few inches at not being reprimanded.

"Seems like you did well for your first day, but you can't keep up all that walking." She thought for a second, then walked to the other side of the room, pushed back the kickstand of the bicycle, and wheeled it over to me. "Take this home and practice."

"What about the second batch of deliveries for today?"

She shook her head once more. "Girl, you're in

no condition to do any more work today. I'll give it to someone else."

I bit my lip. "Won't they be angry at having to take on my load?"

She shrugged. "The post office is an organization where everyone supports one another. There's no I or ego in team."

I smiled. How different she was from Madam, who was quick to accuse me of being a selfish, freeloading brat. "Thank you. I really appreciate it."

"I'll see to it that someone takes your second load for tomorrow as well, but I won't be able to do that the day after. You have today and tomorrow to learn how to ride the bike." She shoved it toward me, and I took it by the smooth handlebars.

I left the post office with mixed emotions. On the one hand, I was extremely grateful to Mrs. Flanagan for her support. On the other hand, I doubted I could learn how to ride a bike, let alone in such a short period of time. I was not athletic. Running myself ragged across the city might not be the best idea, but it seemed much safer than falling off the bike and breaking my neck.

Deciding that I was too exhausted to do anything right now, I wheeled the bike into Daydream's corridor. Then I dragged my body up the spiral staircase, nearly tripping several times, yet somehow managing to make it into my new bedroom and collapsing onto my heavenly mattress.

My last thought before I fell asleep was that I needed to check Tia's bed to see if it looked slept in. However, my head was too heavy to turn, and my lids glued together. I was out like a light.

I woke up with my mouth cotton-dry and my body covered in sweat. The brightness greeting me as I opened my eyes made me realize why I had gotten so hot. In my exhaustion, I had fallen asleep without closing the curtains, and now, the skin on my arms and legs that had been exposed to the afternoon sun had a pinkish hue. Grateful that I didn't get a proper burn, I rose and stretched, bringing my arms overhead. I rolled my neck and glanced around, noticing that Tia's bed still was untouched. Worry spiked within me, and I rushed downstairs.

It was five in the afternoon, and the bar would open soon. Right now, however, it was completely empty, no Tia or Mikka in sight.

With my throat parched, I poured myself a glass of water and gulped it down in one go, then poured myself another, emptied half of it, and hurried toward Lorenzo's office. I knocked but didn't have the patience to wait for him to call me inside.

I pushed the door open, to see his violet-green eyes widen, surprise on his face.

Realizing I probably looked like a mess, I tried to straighten my clothes as much as I could with one hand while still holding my glass. "Sorry to interrupt. Have you seen Tia? I don't think she slept in her bed last night."

He put a stack of papers aside. "I really don't think it's for me to tell you. You should ask her."

My eyebrows drew together. "Why?"

When he didn't reply, I stepped closer, put the glass down, and leaned forward on his desk. "Lorenzo, if you know something, please tell me. I'm worried out of my mind. I haven't seen her since yesterday evening."

Lorenzo shook his head. "I didn't mean to worry you. She's fine. I believe she's off somewhere with Mikka."

I released a breath and plopped down into the chair

opposite his, then finished my glass of water. "Why didn't you tell me so from the start?"

"You don't mind?"

"No." Did he think I was the jealous type?

His silver eyebrows rose so high, they almost disappeared behind his hairline.

Given his surprise at my answer, I must've really come across as the possessive type. "Of course, I don't mind. Tia can have as many friends as she wants," I clarified.

Lorenzo glanced away, a tiny smile spreading on his face.

Feeling like the joke was on me, I leaned forward and placed my hand on his. A pleasant wave of electricity darted through me, and I immediately regretted what I had done. Why had I touched him? Not a good idea to do anything to jeopardize our friendship and business relationship, especially if he became my manager, and I was to continue living at his place. I pulled my hand away and said, "I feel like something's going on, and I'm the only one who doesn't know what it is."

He was quiet for a second, his eyes hungry with... No, I didn't want to think what was swirling in his eyes. Then he blinked, and the emotion was gone. "Ask Tia."

I sighed. "Fine. I doubt she can get into more trouble with Mikka than she normally gets into on her own."

Lorenzo chuckled. He was really beginning to annoy me. I crossed my arms. "Spit it out."

"You do realize that Mikka isn't human?"

I was glad I was already sitting. "She's not? But she looks so..." I searched for the right word. "Normal."

"That's because she's a half-demon. She has half of the power from her demonic line and none of the looks."

Well, besides the white hair and black eyes, but I

had always assumed she had simply bleached her hair as a fashion statement.

"Are all demons able to make themselves look human?"

He shook his head. "It requires a lot of concentration and decades or centuries to master."

How old was he exactly? Despite his silver hair, he looked to be in his mid-twenties. Even though I had always guessed him to be much older, hearing him confirm it felt strange. As tempted as I was to find out more about him, this wasn't about getting to know him better; it was about making sure Tia was safe. "What kind of demon is Mikka?"

Lorenzo must've heard the worry in my voice because he said, "Don't worry, she won't harm Tia."

"What kind of demon?" I repeated.

He clucked his tongue. "So impatient today." At my hard glare, he continued. "Ever wonder how the ice sculptures are able not to melt, even though the bar is at regular room temperature?"

I threw my hands up. "I always assumed it was some demon magic you use."

"Really, you thought temperature regulation was related to teleportation?"

I shrugged. "You're the first demon I ever talked to for longer than a few minutes. How am I supposed to know the extent of your magic?"

Lorenzo nodded thoughtfully. "There's a lot humans don't know about demons and vice versa. For your information, teleportation has absolutely nothing to do with changing temperatures. Mikka is a half ice demon."

"She can freeze Tia into an ice sculpture?" I jumped up from my chair, knocking it back in the process.

Lorenzo rolled his eyes. "First, Mikka likes Tia.

Second, do you really think I would employ a demon who hurts humans?"

I put my chair upright and slowly sat back down. Shame burned my nape. "No. I overreacted." I pressed my hands together. "I know this isn't a justification, but, once again, it's just that I haven't truly interacted with any demons besides you. It's hard not to be afraid of someone so powerful, someone who might operate by other rules."

Lorenzo's gaze bore into mine. "I know what you mean. It's also really hard to trust someone who is concealing crucial information from you." He continued staring straight into my eyes, and that's when I remembered that I had plans to see Acacia this evening. To guarantee that no one saw the golden circles in my eyes, I needed to visit her every three days. Today was the fourth day. In the morning time, the gold in my eyes had been just specks. But now...

"Do you mind if I help myself to a drink?"

Lorenzo motioned to the cabinet where he kept glasses, water, and liquor. I opened it and pulled out a golden-brown, roundish decanter. "What is this?"

"One of the best brandies you'll ever taste."

"Can I get you one as well?" He nodded. I poured two fingers each into the beautiful crystalline tumblers, trying not to wonder how many months I'd have to work at the post office to be able to afford such an elegant set. I put the brandy back on the silver tray, catching my reflection and confirming there were golden rings around my irises just as I had suspected.

Carefully, I put the drinks down on Lorenzo's desk and took a sip of mine. It was strong but smooth and had notes of dried figs and plums.

Finally, I glanced up at Lorenzo and opened my

mouth, but he shook his head slowly. "You don't have to tell me. It's your secret. All I need to know is that I can trust you."

"You can. But I want to tell you. I'm terrified, but I know my secrets will be safe with you. You've revealed so much about your life. You told me what kind of demon you are, you showed me what you can do, and you told me about Mikka. You allowed Tia and me to stay at your home and work for you. It's only fair I explain my visits to Acacia, especially since there isn't much to tell."

The space between his silver brows pinched together.

I pointed at my eyes. "I don't know what they make me. When I was seven, older girls in the orphanage began making fun of me because of the golden rings in my eyes. Tia found me crying in an alley and reminded me that a woman had stopped by at Christmas, telling me to call on her when I needed her. I remembered that her name was Mrs. Woods. Thinking of her made her appear, which makes her a..."

"A godmother."

"There's another one besides the one who helped Queen Ella before she married our king?"

"Yes, there is more than one fairy godmother. However, the one that came to you might be the same one that appeared to Queen Ella."

I blinked. "But why would a godmother help me and then disappear without telling me what she was or why she was helping me? Don't they normally—?"

"Yes. My guess is that this godmother wasn't assigned and that she was helping you secretly and didn't want anyone to find out about it."

"Why would she choose to help me?"

"That, I don't know."

I sighed and continued my story. "Mrs. Wood told me that I would have to hide my true eye color unless I wanted to die. She kept changing it for me. The older I got, the shorter the intervals between her visits became. When I turned eighteen, she told me she could no longer help me and urged me to find a faerie who could hide the golden rings. She refused to tell me what they meant or why I had to hide them. Acacia doesn't know either." I paused, then added. "I don't think the rings in my eyes would kill me."

"But others, who know what those rings mean, might," Lorenzo finished.

Nobody had quite put it like that, but in my heart, I had known this to be the case for some time. Gathering all the courage I had, I asked the question that might change everything, "Do you know what the golden rings make me?"

Lorenzo's face was pain-stricken. "I'm afraid I don't. I could go to the higher demons and ask one of them, but I don't think we want them finding out about you."

"You still think that my voice is magic."

He nodded.

"Even if it is, why does it matter? It's not a very powerful ability. It's nothing compared to teleporting or freezing objects and people."

"Being able to control someone's mind can be much more powerful than any physical ability."

I took another sip of the brandy, the tension within me easing a little. "I still don't understand why that makes me a target. Aren't there plenty of fae and demons who are able to manipulate minds?"

Lorenzo rubbed his sharp chin. "There are, but they have to be full-blooded demons or fae. Even if those demons have mastered glamor, other magical creatures would be able to smell the magic they wield on them. As for fae, they can't hide what they are. Their sharp ears give them away."

And their ethereal beauty. "Are you saying that someone might be interested in me because I could spring my powers on an unsuspecting target?" Lorenzo nodded. Something dawned on me then. Lorenzo had been suspicious long before he had found out what I had done at the market to free the boy or before he had seen the golden rings in my eyes. "How did you know that I was different?"

He licked his lips. "When I handed you the microphone on the first night you played here, we touched, and I sensed the magic within you."

I, too, had sensed magic. Pushing the thought away, I sat up straight. I needed to focus. "So demons and fae can tell I have magic if they touch me?"

Lorenzo focused on his glass of brandy. "Perhaps, perhaps not, better not to test it until you have full control of your abilities."

"Control? I'm not going to train how to manipulate others."

"Do you want to hide forever? Never daring to find out what you are?"

"No, but—"

"Then, you need to train."

"How?"

"I'll teach you."

In a whisper, I asked, "What if I can't learn? What if my powers aren't strong enough, and I'll have to hide forever?"

A muscle ticked in Lorenzo's jaw. He leaned forward. "I won't let that happen."

The corners of my lips curled upward. "Thank you." I

didn't know how he did it, but I appreciated him always believing in me and having my back.

Lorenzo emptied his glass. "Let's go to Acacia's."

I bit my lip. "Actually, there's something else we need to do first before it gets dark."

He tilted his head in question, but I just stood up and motioned for him to follow me. In the corridor, I grabbed the bicycle Mrs. Flanagan had given me. "I need to learn how to ride this." At his incredulous look, I clarified. "For my job at the post office. Otherwise, I'll never manage to deliver all the mail in time."

He opened his mouth, and for a second, I thought he'd say I didn't need the job or that learning how to ride was too much of an effort, or that he didn't have the time to teach me.

But Lorenzo wasn't like my ex, Victor. Lorenzo believed in me, he lifted me up, so all he said was, "And you really think a demon is the best teacher for this?"

A laugh bubbled out of me, washing away my tension. "You teleport. It's similar to riding a bike, right?"

Lorenzo chortled as I pushed the bike out onto the street.

# 24TH JULY

The soles of my feet were on fire as I pushed the empty trolley back to the post office. I had managed to deliver all the letters before noon. To be precise, five minutes to noon, but I still thought it was impressive how much I had improved in one day and that I had been able to stay on my feet for so long despite the physical exertion Lorenzo had put me through the day before.

My fear that riding a bike would break my neck or at least end up in a serious injury hadn't come true. However, I had fallen several times, leaving both my left and right sides covered in bruises. Thankfully, I hadn't torn any skin, but I was certain that would come once I dared to ride the bike over the cobblestone streets or other uneven terrain or went a bit faster.

I sighed. As much as I wasn't looking forward to it, I would have to swing my behind back into the saddle after my shift was over. But first, I'd grab an hour-long nap on my back, trying not to roll over onto either of my aching sides. Just thinking of the bike sent a stab of pain through my lower back and into my thighs. The seat was not only uncomfortable but also crazily small. I pressed my lips together. I was making excuses, and I didn't have the luxury to do so. I had to learn how to ride. My job depended on it. On the bike, I would be twice as fast, even with all the stops to get on and off the bike.

"I'm back, Mrs. Flanagan." I waved as I stepped into the post office.

Mrs. Flanagan glanced at the clock. "Not too bad. Looks like tomorrow, you'll be ready to take the second load as well."

I forced a smile. "Of course." If I could take a draught right now that increased my stamina overnight, I would.

"How's the bike riding coming along?"

"I practiced yesterday, and I'll do some more today."

She nodded in approval. "You should ride the bike tomorrow, even if you're scared. The longer you wait, the bigger your fear will get."

I nodded while imagining how cumbersome it would be to push the bike through the city if I was too chicken to ride it. I had to find a way to learn it before tomorrow. How I was supposed to balance not just myself but also the several pounds of post remained a mystery to me.

Knowing that worrying would get me nowhere, I waved goodbye to Mrs. Flanagan. "I'll see you tomorrow."

"Keep on practicing," she called back.

I stepped outside and halted in surprise. Lorenzo was leaning against the post office, the shiny, red bike standing next to him.

I cringed. "Can't I take a nap first?"

Lorenzo shook his head. "Sorry. This is the only time I can do this."

Resigned, I grabbed the handles of the bike and took a deep breath, then pushed myself up on the bike, trying to remember what I had learned yesterday. Engage my core, trust my feet, and don't swerve the handlebars too much.

I started off well enough, pushing the right pedal hard, then the left one, keeping my upper body steady. All was going well until I realized we were heading straight for the market. "I can't ride in between all those people. I'm going to injure someone," I yelled, not daring to glance over my shoulder to see where Lorenzo was.

He appeared next to me, his teleportation coming in handy for teaching me how to ride a bike, yet also annoyingly highlighting how much control he had over his body and how little I had over mine.

"So make a turn," he suggested.

Carefully, I turned the handlebar to the left, managing to stay on top of the bike. I smiled until the wheels began to bob up and down. Cobblestone. I had gotten myself onto a cobblestone street. "I can't do this."

"You'll be fine," Lorenzo said in a maddeningly calm voice.

I slammed on the brakes and jumped down to the ground, my heart hammering.

Lorenzo gave me a few moments to compose myself. "Half of Arcadia is paved with cobblestone. I'm afraid you'll have to master this."

"But if I fall..." It would hurt a lot, way more than falling on an even street.

"If you fall, you'll get back up, and I'll be here to help

you."

Not wanting to appear like a baby, I inhaled deeply and pushed myself back into the saddle. The first few feet were so bumpy, I was certain I would fall off, yet I managed to stay on, probably due to every muscle in my body working to the maximum. Then something tiny darted in front of me.

A mouse. Harmless, especially since she got out of my way quickly, but enough for me to get distracted and lose my balance. I fell sideways. My hip groaned in protest as it hit the ground hard.

I gritted my teeth together, holding in the cry that worked its way up my throat.

Lorenzo removed the bike from me and held out his hand.

"Are you able to move everything? Are you bleeding?" he asked once I was up on my feet.

My muscles felt sore, but otherwise, I was fine. My pants and top were still in one piece, and there was no blood to be seen. "No, I've only added to my collection of bruises."

He chuckled. "At least, your sense of humor is back." He pointed at the end of the alley. "I want you to turn left and then make another left."

I propelled myself back onto the bike and executed two nice turns, ignoring trash that was blown into my path. It was only after my second turn that I faltered, realizing the next street was going downhill.

Lorenzo appeared next to me. "You can do this. You'll be fine. Remember to break gently but consistently."

With clammy palms and a tight stomach, I allowed the bike to descend. I could do this. I had to.

"Nice and steady," I whispered underneath my breath as the bike gained speed going down the hill. I pumped the brakes, taking care not to push too hard or abruptly. I was doing it. I was almost at the bottom of the hill. Tension seeped out of my body. That wasn't too hard.

Then, out of nowhere, a tabby cat jumped into my path. Instead of scurrying out of my way, it plopped down, stretching out and covering the whole road. There was no way around it unless I drove into the wall. I needed to brake, but I was going too fast to do it smoothly.

*"Go away, kitty! This is not a good place to stay,"* I sang while pumping my brakes hard.

The cat blinked at me and jumped out of my path, just as I came to an abrupt halt. The back wheel lifted, I slid forward and squeezed my eyes shut, preparing to tumble forward. Strong hands gripped the bike and pushed it back down. Then Lorenzo lifted me out of the seat and carried the trembling mess I'd become to the side of the road.

Gently, he put me down on the ground and knelt in front of me. "You're fine. The cat is fine too."

"I almost ran over it."

"But you didn't. You handled the situation really well." He pushed a strand of hair that had come loose from my ponytail behind my ear. "And you remembered to use your voice."

"Are you sure I didn't simply spook it?"

He chuckled. "I've seen plenty of people yell at cats without the cat doing anything. You didn't terrify the tabby into submission. Your singing compelled her."

I nodded. Acacia had magicked away the golden rings in my eyes yesterday, but my voice was still here, and while its abilities terrified me, I wouldn't want it to be taken away. It belonged to me. It was a part of me.

I would learn how to harness its gifts, no matter how hard it would be.

"A penny for your thoughts."

I looked up. The wind blew back Lorenzo's silver hair, revealing the strong features of his face. His nose and chin, particularly, looked as if they were hewn from marble, and yet despite the strong lines, there was no harshness.

"I would like you to be my manager if the offer is still on the table."

A gorgeous smile spread across his lips. "It is."

"And I would like to use my voice to find our missing Queen Ella by entering the national singing competition."

Lorenzo studied me. "Are you sure?"

I nodded. "It's the only chance I have to get close to the king and his court to find out what has happened to Queen Ella." The national singing competition was held by our kingdom every year. Anyone could register to participate. The winner was determined over several rounds and got to perform for the king and his court. The winner also received a private audience with the king. With Lorenzo's help, I was confident I would ask the right questions to help us discover what had happened to our queen.

Lorenzo helped me to my feet, my legs still unsteady. "We'll have to hurry to register then. The deadline is today."

I felt my forehead wrinkle. "How do you know?"

A wry grin spread across his face. "Because I hoped you would want to use your voice to help your kingdom. I didn't want to push you into the national competition, but I hoped you would suggest it on your own and would allow me to accompany you."

He pointed toward the top of the hill we had just come down. “Ready to work those legs?”

“Yes.” If I could go downhill, I certainly could make it uphill.

Going uphill felt like I was dragging a baby elephant behind me, but at least, the exertion stopped me from worrying that I would fall. After what felt like forever, we finally reached the top, and the few streets I cycled down until we reached Daydream were child’s play.

“Well done. You’ll be a pro in no time.” Lorenzo placed his hand between my shoulder blades, and warmth trickled through me. My lips tingled, and my body ached to lean into his touch. I pushed away the sensations. It didn’t matter how attractive I found Lorenzo. I could never go down this path. He was my manager. He was my landlord. He was my partner in the mission to find the missing queen. I couldn’t jeopardize all that by entering a romantic relationship with him.

Putting a lid on my feelings, I walked into Daydream to find Tia and Mikka laughing behind the bar. Mikka put a piece of celery into a tall, scarlet drink. “And this is how you make a Bloody Mary,” she said proudly.

Tia clapped, then waved as she noticed me.

I rushed up to my friend and hugged her tightly. “You gave me such a fright. I had no idea where you were.”

Tia wore a sheepish look on her face. “Sorry about that.”

“Did you go two whole nights without sleeping?”

She returned to behind the bar to clean the cutting board and throw away the leafy pieces of the celery stalk. “I stayed over in Mikka’s room. It’s next door to ours.” She didn’t look up as she spoke.

Well, I guess that solved the mystery of who was

staying in the third room. But why was Tia looking so guilty?

"I'll draft a quick contract," Lorenzo said, heading into the direction of his office. "We need to have something in place before you sign up for the competition."

"Please do." If someone found out about the special properties of my voice, I would be much safer if Lorenzo could accompany me everywhere as my manager.

Tia's forehead furrowed. "What competition?"

"The national one."

She whistled. "Wow, you've gone from not wanting to perform in public to wanting to perform in front of the king in one week?"

I twisted the end of my ponytail. "I guess so."

She shook her head. "I didn't mean it in a negative way. I'm proud of you. You're making so much progress."

"Thanks."

Mikka pushed her elbows down on the counter. "What will your shtick be?"

"What do you mean?"

"Haven't you watched any of the previous competitions? To impress the judges, it's not enough to have a good voice. Your performance needs to be full-on, and you should have an easily recognizable public persona."

"I see." Now that I thought about it, I did remember that last year a girl had been rumored to always perform with animals. Living in the orphanage, I hadn't had the opportunity to see any of her performances, but I've heard that she even had a lion in one of them. Another candidate was a sprite who always brought plants to her performances and made them bloom and grow vines around her as she sang.

I was about to say that I didn't have anything like

that when an idea came to me. I smiled at Mikka. "Perhaps you could help me?"

Mikka pointed at herself. "Me?"

"You're an ice demon."

She nodded, and Tia shifted from foot to foot, as if the conversation was making her uncomfortable.

"Would you be willing to incorporate some ice into my performance?"

Mikka's white hair fluttered like it was being moved by an invisible wind, and her black eyes sparkled like obsidians. "I would have to train and know your cues, but yes. If you're allowed to get help from someone else."

Lorenzo returned just then, holding a sheet of paper. We filled him in on our plan. "I like it," he said, then handed me the paper. "This is very rudimentary. We can draw up a more detailed contract later. Read over it and make sure you're fine with everything."

Tia took my arm. "Can I speak to you for a moment?"

"Sure." I followed her across the room.

"I think it's great how you're taking the initiative, but what's the rush? Why are you suddenly all in?" Her eyes were filled with concern.

I bit my lip. Should I tell Tia of my suspicions? Yes, she was my friend, she deserved to know. "Do you see the sculpture over there of Queen Ella?"

She followed my pointed hand. "What about it?"

"Doesn't she look familiar?"

"Of course. We've seen paintings of our queen in magazines, newspapers, and on our money."

"No, I mean, don't you know someone who looks really similar to the queen?"

She just stared at me, wide-eyed.

"Doris, the woman from the kitchen."

Tia put a strand of her blue hair into her mouth and

chewed on it, thoughtful for a moment. “Now that you mention it, there are similarities. But how does a maid from the boarding house have anything to do with the queen?”

“I’m not sure, but before the queen met our king, she was a maid too, working for her horrible stepmother and stepsisters.”

Deep creases formed on Tia’s forehead. “What are you saying?”

I sighed. “I don’t think it’s a coincidence that Doris showed up around the same time our queen went missing. I think Doris knows something. Unfortunately, she’s refusing to talk to me.”

“She’s a mute.”

“No, she isn’t. I tricked her into humming a song.”

Tia stared at me blankly. “How did you do that?”

I hated keeping secrets from my friend, but I also wasn’t quite ready to discuss my voice. So all I said was, “Apparently, the golden rings around my eyes aren’t the only weird thing about me.”

Tia opened her mouth, but I shook my head. “Not now.”

She nodded. “I’ll be here when you’re ready.”

“Thank you.” I glanced down at the contract Lorenzo gave me. “The deadline to sign up is tonight. I need to hurry.”

Tia nodded. “As long as you’re sure you want to do this, I’m fully behind you.”

I smiled at my friend. “I’m done hiding and letting people like Madam run Arcadia. Our kingdom is crumbling from within. It needs us, and I want to be a positive force within it.”

~

"Have you taken the gondola before?" Lorenzo asked once we left Daydream.

"No." I never had a reason to. As beautiful as it seemed to travel the city by the water, it seemed a wasteful pastime, inappropriate for someone of my station.

"Well, today is the day. I hope you like it."

I raised an eyebrow at him.

"Every singer needs to sign up at the Royal Opera House. It's located across the river, and the quickest way to get there is by gondola."

The gondolas were located at a pier next to the lover's bridge. A bridge I had once met Victor on. I shoved his face out of my memory. I didn't want to think of my ex, didn't want to imagine his sneer or disapproving glare at me trying out.

Lorenzo handed a coin to one of the boatmen who wore a striped shirt and tapered trousers. "Please take us to the Opera House. "

Lorenzo jumped into the boat and held his hand out for me. Carefully, I stepped onto the trembling, wooden floor of the boat. Only two days ago, I had walked everywhere. Now, I was cycling and going by boat.

The gondolier didn't sit down but remained standing at the end of the boat and paddled with a long stick. We passed Arcadia's multicolored houses, and I was surprised by how beautiful our city was from the water. I had always considered it was a privilege to live in Arcadia, but being in the gondola made me appreciate my hometown even more—the elegant church spires, the adorable, matching shutters and doors, the carefully crafted metal signs hanging above businesses, and the blooming flowers decorating the balconies.

We arrived at the dock way too soon. Lorenzo helped me out of the boat, and then I saw it. I had never been to the opera before, yet there was no doubt in my mind that the imposing building was it. Three tall columns with golden tops stood in front of the castle-like building that featured a massive balcony and was bigger than the cathedral in the market quarter.

"Not sure they will let me in," I whispered, wishing I had changed out of my simple trousers and shirt into my finest clothes.

Lorenzo glanced at me. "Nonsense. They won't deny you entry. Everyone can sign up."

Perhaps, but I had the bad feeling that given my outfit, my chances of progressing had fallen to zero. Now that I thought about the last years' competitions, I realized they had been mostly won by magic wielders that seemed to come from rich families or youngsters from well-established theater families.

Lorenzo continued toward the building, but I stopped in my tracks. Once he noticed I wasn't following, he turned around, a question on his face.

"Tell me the truth. Do you think I even have a chance of winning?"

"You do. But if you don't believe me, know this: if you don't walk inside, you have already lost."

He was right. Despite feeling small and unworthy, I stepped past the first and second rows of columns. Lorenzo pushed open the wide, wooden-and-glass doors that had the king's insignia, the crown, and the glass slipper, carved into them. The inside was even more majestic. The hall was endless. Marble and gold were everywhere. The theater staff wore red velvet hats and matching red jackets with black and golden accents.

Lorenzo led the way to the ticket booth. "We're here to sign up for the national competition."

The woman behind the glass window nodded and

pushed through a form. “Fill this out.”

The form asked for my basic information, such as my name, address, and what kind of experience I had.

It was a relief to put down that I had performed twice at Daydream. My experience might be meager in comparison to other participants, but at least I had some. After I filled out the form, I returned it to the receptionist, who looked over it and stamped it. “Take this to the competition host, Mr. Goodwin. He will give you a recording slot.”

Seeing my confused expression, she explained, “You'll record one of your songs later this week. It will be sent to the jury. The best fifty recordings will make it into the first round of the competition.”

“How many applicants are there in total?” I pressed my palms together hard.

The receptionist clicked her tongue and looked over some papers. “About 500. Probably 100 more with everyone who signed up today.”

600. The chance to get into the first round was less than 10 percent.

Lorenzo took my hand, and some of my dread eased. “Let's meet the competition host.”

Together, we walked down the marble hallway, past a wide staircase that I guessed led to the expensive balcony seats. Everywhere I looked, the white walls and ceiling were decorated with golden leaves. Massive, gilded-and-crystalline chandeliers illuminated the space. We stepped through grand double doors into the auditorium, which was a mixture of red velvet seats and gold accents. As we walked past the countless rows, my gaze went upward to the four stories of balconies. That's where the king and his court would sit if I made it to the final performance. Right now, however, the seats were all empty save for the front row. One middle-aged man was flanked by a young woman to his right and a young man to his left. The trio was whispering, their gazes fixed on the two girls on the stage. No, not girls, but women. And not just any women, but the sisters from the boarding house, Georgette and Bernadette, Madam Fontaine's daughters. What were they doing here?

"How much can we change the stage?" Georgette asked. She was the taller one, and her leading the conversation made me believe she was also the older one.

Not waiting for Mr. Goodwin's, the competition host's reply, Bernadette chimed in, "How many dress changes are we allowed to do for the recording?"

Then they both asked in unison, "How much recording time do we get?"

The older man in the middle sighed. "You get half an hour. You may change the stage as much as you want as long as you don't damage it and are able to clean it up in your thirty-minute slot. The dress changes also must happen within that time slot."

"That's not nearly enough time!" Georgette's face turned into an overripe tomato.

"Henry, can you please deal with that," the competition host gritted out, and his slender assistant jumped up and hurried up onto the stage.

"I'm sure you'll find a way," Henry said and gently pushed the sisters, who appeared to weigh four times as much as he did, off the stage.

"We'll write to you with any requests we have until our audition dates," Georgette said.

The assistant wrinkled his forehead. "But the letter won't arrive in time."

Bernadette pouted. "Fine. We'll send a messenger if

we have additional requests before our recording."

"I'm afraid we won't be able to accommodate any request," Henry said patiently. "We'll be having recordings daily, and our schedule is very tight."

"How much?" Bernadette produced a coin bag.

Henry shook his head. "We can't accept any bribes."

The competition host tapped his hand impatiently against his knee and glanced around the theater, his gaze landing on Lorenzo and me.

"Henry, please escort the Fontaine sisters off the stage. Our next singers are here," Mr. Goodwin said with relief.

The sisters shot daggers at me, but I didn't shrink back, only stood taller. I was no longer working for their mother. It was no longer my job to make them happy. I could handle their disapproval.

Unfortunately, they couldn't walk past me without making a jab.

"Aren't you the maid who worked for our mother?" Georgette turned her nose up as high as she could while still being able to glare down at me.

"She was doing room service, and then mother demoted her to the kitchens." Bernadette pointed at me like she was a three-year-old who hadn't yet learned manners.

"Good luck failing." Georgette stalked past me.

"Yes, good luck failing," her younger and plumper sister added and pushed past me, nearly knocking me to the ground.

Lorenzo's fists had gone white-knuckled.

"Leave it. They're not worth it," I whispered.

"What's your name?" the director asked.

I put on my most confident smile. "Halia. And this is my manager, Lorenzo."

# 25TH JULY

As much as I was worried about my upcoming recording, I had no time that morning to fret over what song to choose, how to make myself stand out, or what the Fontaine sisters would do. If I wanted to show up for my recording that was a few days away in one piece, I needed to focus on my balance and staying on the bike.

While the two practice sessions with Lorenzo had certainly helped me become more confident and at ease on the bicycle, riding on my own without his pointers and the knowledge that he would be there to help me if I fell, was terrifying. The several pounds of mail attached to my bike's back basket didn't help either.

The temptation to push the bike was high, but I

knew I'd only feel worse if I didn't at least try. Thus, I found myself swinging into the saddle and whispering to myself, "You'll be fine, just take it easy."

The weight at the back added an extra balance challenge and meant I had to pedal harder. Even before reaching my first destination, I was already grateful for the plastic bag Lorenzo had handed me last night. He had said I would need the trail mix, which consisted of nuts and dried fruits. I had refused the expensive food at first but had finally accepted it, something I was now very grateful for, certain the snack would be gone an hour into my shift. Keeping my gaze on the road, I watched out for uneven pavement and others. Throughout the morning, I avoided a child who seemed determined to run into my bike, a stray dog, and a coachman who acted like the road belonged to him alone.

One by one, I delivered the letters from my basket, enjoying how my load was growing lighter by the minute. There were a few times when I almost lost my balance, and twice, I had to get off the bike and take a few deep breaths when I had taken a turn too quickly. But overall, I began to feel confident about my cycling skills and even had some fun doing it.

The best part, however, was that I managed to deliver all the letters and return to the post office for the second load by eleven.

"Bravo!" Mrs. Flanagan clapped upon seeing me. "Excellent." She gave me the second load of mail, which to my surprise and disappointment, was almost as big as the first one.

Even though my thighs burned, my back ached, and I had to roll my wrists every time I got off the bike to deliver the post, I felt good. I had wanted this job, and I was grateful for Mrs. Flanagan taking a chance on me. As physically demanding as this was, it allowed me to work without being interrupted by angry customers or Madam.

With the midday sun beating down on me, I stopped off at the market and drank deeply from the water fountain, then rested for a bit on the sidewalk. Noticing a stand that sold straw hats, I wheeled my bike over there, deciding I could afford a hat since it was an investment I would wear daily.

"You look beautiful, senorita!" The young merchant grinned from cheek to cheek. "Which hat would you like to buy?"

"I'm not sure."

He began showing me different options. "Try it on!" he kept saying, pushing a mirror toward me.

I put on several styles, pausing at a wide, sandy hat. I wasn't sure I should get something quite as big, but I did like how it covered my shoulders and chest, preventing those areas from getting sunburnt. "How much?"

"For you, five marks."

I snorted. Did he think I was a silly girl who didn't know the market rates? "I saw you sell these hats for two marks yesterday, and we both know they're worth, at maximum, one mark."

Color seeped into his face. "Two marks, darling."

"I'll give you one fifty." I produced the coins.

With a sigh, he took them and handed me the wide-brimmed hat. "You drive a hard bargain."

I beamed. "Have a good day!" I swung onto my bike and pushed the pedals, a floating feeling overcoming me. I had bargained and won. No more backing down or worrying about others' disapproval. From now on, I would stand my ground. Well, at least, in daily interactions. I doubted my need for approval and being liked would ever go away completely. Plus, when it came to my singing, I needed others on my side. As much as I had signed up for the competition to help Queen Ella, I was also entering it because I wanted to know that I could make it as a singer.

I sighed. If only I had a plan on how to stand out to the judges during the recording. I didn't have the money or resources to create an impressive background. Even though Mikka had seemed excited to help me by creating some ice for my performances, the sign-up sheet had clearly stated that no element or weather manipulation was permitted in the opera house during the recording.

I chewed on my bottom lip. How could I come up with a breathtaking performance in three days□ time? What would be considered unique? I didn□t want to inadvertently choose a cliché the judges were sick of seeing. How would I know what was overdone? The best thing, I decided, was to go after my shift to the opera house and watch the recordings of my competition. Just as anyone could sign up, anyone could attend somebody else□s recordings.

Unlike the actual shows, I didn't anticipate the theater being full. I doubted Arcadia's citizens were interested in hearing everyone who had signed up for the national competition. They only wanted the top fifty.

I delivered my last letter and was about to turn to cycle back to the post office when sobs reached me. I got off the bike and pushed it toward the muffled noise.

At the end of a cul-de-sac, a woman sat on the ground. Her knees were drawn up to her chest. Her face was buried in her palms.

I stepped closer. "Are you all right?"

The woman glanced up, her blue eyes meaning mine, and I gulped. The crying woman was Doris. And she was looking much worse than she had the last time I had seen her. A blue bruise bloomed around her left eye, purple bruises covered her neck, and green bruises bloomed on her arms.

"Doris! What happened?"

She sobbed only harder in response. Setting the bike against a wall, I pulled her into a hug.

I let Doris cry for a few minutes before asking, "Who did this to you?"

She just shook her head and cried harder.

"If somebody is hurting you at the boarding house, I can help you leave."

She brushed away the tears running down her cheeks and shook her head once more, a look of resolution on her face.

I sighed. "I really want to help you, Doris, but I can't do it if you don't work with me."

She didn't reply, simply stared into empty space.

"Please let me take you to Daydream. You can stay there tonight."

She backed away from me as if I had suggested she come with me to a prison.

"How about if you come by just for a drink or a meal?"

She rose to her feet.

"Please, let me help you."

Her only response was a tight smile, which I knew was a no, even before she scurried away from me.

It was clear that going after her would accomplish nothing. As much as I wanted to trail her and see what she would do next, it wasn't feasible. Arcadia didn't have many bike riders. I would stand out like a sore thumb.

Anyway, I had to return the bike to the post office before Mrs. Flanagan wondered what had happened to me. After stopping by at the post office and debriefing with Miss Flanagan, I headed straight for Madam's Boarding House.

I walked past the main entrance toward the back of the house where the staff entered. Praying I wouldn't run into anyone, I made my way down to the kitchen. Doris wasn't there, but a young guy was scrubbing away at some pots and pans.

He glanced up. "Can I help you?"

"Ahem, I'm looking for Doris. She normally works here in the kitchen."

He shook his head. "I don't know anyone by that name."

I hit my palm against my forehead. How stupid of me. "Well, she doesn't speak, and Doris is the name I came up with for her."

"Oh, you mean Cinder."

Cinder? "Is that the name she gave you?"

The young man chuckled. "Of course not. She's a mute. But that's what Madam Fontaine told me to call her."

"I see. Do you know where Cinder is?"

He shook his head. "No idea, but I'm sure she'll be back soon for her evening shift."

"Thank you," I said, not daring to ask him about the bruises on Doris..., no, Cinder. I turned toward the door but then decided to try something risky. Turning around and tilting my head in a non-threatening manner, I said, "Have you met Madam's daughters?"

His face contorted. "Lady Bernadette and Georgette."

Conspiratorially, I whispered, "Apparently, they're entering this year's royal singing competition."

He put the clean pan away and began working on a deep pot, not the least bit impressed by my information. "They won't get far if they use their natural voices. They sound worse than a cat when you step on its tail. Of course, there are other ways to advance in the competition."

I took a few steps toward him. "What do you mean?"

He shrugged. "Madam Fontaine makes good money with the boarding house. I bet she has enough to pay a fae."

"To do what?"

He rolled his eyes as if it were obvious. "To change the sisters' singing voices."

I swallowed hard. "Is that possible?"

He looked at me as if I was born yesterday. "Why shouldn't it be? Demons and fae can do all kinds of things."

I nodded. "I suppose." Not wanting to rouse his suspicion with too many questions, I looked at the mountain of dirty dishes waiting for him and said, "I'll leave you to it."

I was by the door when he called. "Hey, what's your name?"

I debated giving him a false one, but even though I wasn't too keen on people knowing that I was here, I decided there was nothing wrong with me visiting a friend. "Halia. Please tell D—, Cinder that the offer still stands."

"What offer?"

I smiled. "She'll know."

I closed the door to the kitchen, more certain than ever that something ominous was going on at the boarding house. It couldn't be a coincidence that around the time our queen went missing, a terrified Doris, no,

Cinder appeared, and the sisters moved in with Madam. All of this was very fishy. And why were the sisters so suddenly interested in winning the competition? If they had money, there were other ways to gain fame and prestige. I had the feeling that entering the competition wasn't about them becoming famous singers or even becoming part of the court. They wanted to get close to the king.

A conversation I had overheard between the sisters almost a week ago when I was still living at the boarding house came back to me.

"There's no room for fun or balls," Georgette said. "This time, everything will be different. Being an airhead won't get you anywhere. That was cute eighteen years ago when the prince was searching for a bride, but there's no prince anymore. To live at the palace, we won't need to look pretty, fake niceties, or force our feet into a stupid glass shoe. It's all about power now. Survival of the fittest."

Bernadette had perked up. "Yes, we'll be powerful. Mother will see to it."

Madam Fontaine and her daughters were power-hungry. The question was, how far would they go? Did they want to ascend the throne? If the queen was officially declared dead, the king would feel pressure to remarry since the royal couple never had children, and he needed an heir to the throne. The king's situation didn't just make him vulnerable to pressure to take a new bride but also made him appear weak. If anyone had ever hoped to overthrow him, now would be a great time. What if that's what Madam Fontaine and her daughters planned to do?

I was getting way ahead of myself. Yes, Georgette and Bernadette were obsessed with power. Yes, their entering the competition and being desperate to win seemed suspicious. Yes, their showing up at the same time as Cinder did and the queen disappeared was odd. Yet, none of this was enough to prove that they were planning to overthrow the king. I needed more facts before I could decide what to do.

As if by a stroke of luck, just then, Bernadette's nasal voice carried from around the corner. "This better not hurt. If I turn green or walk out with horns, I'm going to sue her."

"Shush, you stupid cow," Georgette hissed. "Do you want to announce to all of Arcadia what we're about to do?"

The kitchen help's suspicions were spot on. The sisters were about to see a magic wielder. And I would find out whom they were seeing. I scurried out through the back entrance and waited in the shadowed alcove until the sisters exited the boarding house through the front.

With the sisters completely absorbed in their conversation, I had no difficulty trailing them. They didn't even as much as glance twice over their shoulders on their walk. However, the further we walked away from the boarding house, the less I liked where we were going. This was the path I had taken twice a week to Acacia. Certainly, she couldn't be the magic wielder helping them!

But it was exactly in front of her pink house that the sisters stopped. They knocked three times at the front door, and I pressed myself against the house across from Acacia's as she said in a cool voice, "Come in."

I slipped down the wall until I was sitting on the ground. No, anyone but Acacia. I had known that some of her business was in the gray zone. She collected and sold emotions, which didn't seem right, especially when somebody purchased a vial, not for themself, but to slip it to somebody else. However, as shady as some of her business was, I had never thought she would help the sisters cheat their way into winning a royal competition.

Maybe she wasn't. Maybe she would send them away.

I waited and waited. With each passing minute, it became clearer that the sisters and Acacia had reached an agreement. What were they exchanging for her making their voices sound nice? I doubted Acacia would want any of their emotions. She had often complained to me that it was hard for her to siphon off emotions of those that had a muddled head or body. She insisted I didn't drink the night before visiting her and fasted in the morning so that the emotions she took from me as payment for her changing my eye color were pure. I doubted the sisters had the willpower or interest to stick to her protocol. They didn't seem like the type to accept any inconveniences.

Finally, the door creaked open.

"That wasn't too bad," Bernadette said.

"No, the real question is if it will hold up," Georgette said sharply. "It better work during our recording session on Tuesday."

I swallowed hard. Not only had the sisters illegally enhanced their voices, their recording was also on the same day as mine. I waited until Georgette and Bernadette turned onto another street before knocking thrice against Acacia's door.

She opened the door, the slight widening of her arctic eyes the only sign that she was surprised to see me.

"How can I help you, Halia? It's been less than a day since you were here last time."

"This is not about my eyes. May I come in?"

Acacia moved aside gracefully, even though I had a feeling she would rather not talk to me. I followed her through the narrow corridor decorated with multi-colored glass paintings and into her study, which looked like a pharmacy. Cabinets lined the walls, and several tables were placed in a reversed, angular U-shape throughout the room. On top of them were countless bottles and tinctures of all sizes and shapes. A beautiful painting hung on the wall depicting a dozen fairies flying high into a starry sky. Unlike Acacia, they were tiny and had wings. Fittingly, the painting was called *The Moon Faeries' Night Sky*. Did this magic place exist somewhere, or was it only in the painter's imagination? The painting transformed as the light in the room changed from a lilac to a mint green, going through all the pastel colors. The scents in the room kept changing as well as if different perfumes were being sprayed in one-minute intervals. The citrusy scent changed into a flowery bouquet. The heavy lily note morphed into a ripe plum, which in turn transformed into a spicy scent, then back to the refreshing, lemon scent. For the first time, the ambiance didn't seem inviting or relaxing, but rather canny and manipulative. The changing scents and lights appeared to be a tool Acacia used to prevent her clients from over-thinking the transactions they were entering.

I turned to the fae, studying her. "Did you enhance the Fontaine sisters' voices?"

Acacia's face was blank, not betraying the tiniest bit of emotion.

"I saw them leave your place," I added.

"I keep my clients' business private. Discretion is important in my line of work."

"Are you aware of what they're doing? They entered the royal competition. They'll try to cheat their way into winning."

Acacia's face remained blank, and I had the sudden urge to shake her. The violent impulse passed in the next beat to be replaced by sadness. "Don't you care? I think they want to get close to the king and his court. They're thirsting for power; maybe they even wish to get onto the throne."

"And you're concerned about this because?"

My anger returned in full force. "Because I'm a citizen of Arcadia. As are you. The sisters and their mother are greedy, horrible bullies who exploit others. Do you really want them to rule Arcadia?"

Acacia examined her immaculate, silver nails. "I don't concern myself with politics."

"Maybe you should. Unless you want Arcadia to go to hell."

Acacia tilted her head, a thoughtful look on her face. "Sometimes, I forget how short human lives are. You are so young. When you've been alive for several centuries, you know that change is inevitable. In fact, change is the only constant. Nothing can stay good forever. Good and evil are always battling it out. The ups and downs are natural. A word of advice—learn to accept the hills and the valleys."

I shook my head. "Perhaps when you're an immortal, you have time to wait for fifty years for the regime to change. But I don't have that time. Most citizens of Arcadia don't have that time. Even if the Fontaines' reign lasted for only a few months, it would be too long. I'm done standing by and enduring what life throws at me. I want to help shape the world. I will be part of the change."

"That is your right. But it is also my right not to get involved."

I pressed my hands onto the glass table, welcoming the cooling sensation. How could she not see? How did she not care? "But you are participating. By helping the sisters win the contest."

"I'm running a business here."

I shook my head. "You would barely lose any of your earnings if you didn't help them. Why risk it?"

Acacia lifted her chin. "If I allowed human morals to rule my decisions, I would soon be out of business. You might be good in here,"—She pointed at her heart—"but most people aren't."

"You enable them to go from bad to worse. Don't you understand how much power you hold by being fae?"

"If I didn't help them, they would find some other fae or magic-wielder to do it."

"Is money all you care about?"

Acacia flashed her sharp teeth. "Careful, girl. I have shown you nothing but kindness, but you will find a very different side of me if you push me."

I backed away, realizing the extent of her threat. Acacia didn't even have to lift a finger to hurt me or use any of her magic. Besides Tia, Lorenzo, and Mrs. Woods, she was the only one who knew about the golden rings around my eyes.

With horror, I realized that if somebody came to her, asking if she had seen a girl with golden rings in her eyes, Acacia would betray me gladly for the right price.

I continued to back away until I reached the door. "Thank you for your time. I apologize for disturbing you."

Acacia's starred at me coolly. We both knew I wouldn't be back.

"I never hid what I was," she said in parting as I reached for the door handle.

She was right. I had forgotten that fae had different morals and rules. They could be cruel, their long lifespan making it hard for them to care about an individual or even a country. If I couldn't trust Acacia, I couldn't trust other fae either. In the future, I had to find a different way to conceal my eye color.

# 26TH JULY

With Sunday being my day off at the post office, I finally had the time to practice my singing. Truthfully, I felt awful about how little energy I had dedicated to my singing this week, but between moving, starting a new job, and learning how to ride a bike, there wasn't much of me left by the end of the day. Most nights, I collapsed into my bed and slept for a solid ten hours until my alarm went off.

Once again, Tia was missing from our room, giving me free rein to experiment and play around with different options of singing my song without having to worry about what my audience thought. Even though I was grateful for the privacy, there was also a pang in my chest. Was Tia's and my friendship crumbling?

Was she moving on with Mikka? Did the last eighteen years of living together and eleven years of being friends mean nothing to her? I bit my lip. I'd have to talk to her, ask her what was going on. But first, I finally had to practice. My recording was only two days away, and if I wanted to stand a chance at making it past the first round, my performance needed to be topnotch.

I started with a quick warm-up, then went through all the songs I had composed recently. I sang them in the order I had performed them as the opening act for the Dark Quartet as if the correct order were my talisman. Thinking about talismans, I opened my bedside table drawer and examined the palm-sized amethyst quartz Acacia had given me. I had been so grateful for her gift, but after yesterday, I wasn't sure I wanted it any longer. Then again, if it did protect me from energy stealers as Acacia had claimed, I'd rather hold on to it.

Since procrastination wouldn't get me anywhere, I repeated my repertoire: "Chains," "Through the Darkness," "Torn," "My Path," "Hope," and "Teach Me the Way." My chest felt much lighter after the second round. I wished Lorenzo was here to accompany me on his guitar but knew I couldn't use him as a crutch since the recording was acapella. The performance that followed if I made it past the first round would use bands approved by the judges.

Deciding that none of the six songs I had practiced was right for my audition, I moved on to the song I had composed right before opening night for the Dark Quartet, "Queen of Song."

*Once upon a time, there was a girl who liked to sing. She didn't have a home; she didn't have kin, but she had a voice. Her blessing terrified her for it gave her hopes and dreams she was told were impossible.*

*Years passed, and the girl only shared her voice with her closest friends, only shared her voice when it was lost in a choir. Then you came along, and you challenged the girl, you told her it wasn't right not to share her blessing, you gave her strength, you gave her confidence. You allowed her to lean on you, and she became the queen of song, she became the queen of song.*

I sang "Queen of Song" two more times, each time becoming more certain that this was the song I wanted to perform at the audition. Since it was a ballad, it allowed me to get away without having a dramatic show. However, simply standing on stage wouldn't be enough. The song had a beautiful fluidity to it that I wished I could mimic with my show. But how? An idea popped into my mind. It didn't entail the use of any elements or anything else created by a demon. Thus, it wouldn't be violating the rules outlined in the competition contract. It also should be easy enough to put up and take down without doing any damage to the theater if arranged properly. But where would I get what I needed?

Lorenzo had already done so much for me, and yet, I didn't know who else to turn to. Thus, I found myself knocking on his door.

"Come in," he called in his baritone voice that was as smooth as honey and as rich as caramel.

I entered and proceeded to gawk at his room. I knew it was rude, but I simply couldn't help myself. The floor was a light-colored oak as were half of the walls, and the bottom half was constructed from exposed, brown brick. A fireplace was built within one of them. The bed's frame was also carved from the light-colored oak, and above it was a slanted skylight. Lorenzo was lying on top of his terracotta duvet, his arms crossed behind his head, a book next to him.

"Do you like it?" An amused smile played on his lips.

"Yes, it's very rustic." And inviting. His bedroom was a surprise just as his bar had been. Both times, I had expected something modern, minimal, and traditionally masculine. Instead, Lorenzo had incorporated nature into his home and business. His bedroom made me feel as if I was in a cottage in the middle of the woods, while the bar with its different hues of blue light and ice sculptures made me feel as if I were in the middle of a lake.

"You really like the outdoors, don't you?" I asked.

Lorenzo nodded. "For the first one hundred years, I lived in a forest. Those were some of the happiest decades of my life."

A reminder that even though he looked only a few years older than I, he wasn't. "How old are you?"

"Two hundred and seventy-two."

I gulped. "Is that a lot for a demon?"

"We don't age unless we're cursed or have been severely injured with magic. Two hundred and seventy two means that I have control over all my powers. They can develop with practice, but everything has already formed. It's not considered old. I suppose it's like mid-twenties for you humans."

Trying to process this, I asked, "Why did you leave the forest?"

Lorenzo's violet-green eyes darkened. "An enemy demon clan slaughtered my family. I was the only one who survived. I had to leave."

I couldn't stop the gasp coming from my mouth. "I'm so sorry." I stepped closer to the bed and sat down on it tentatively. "I wouldn't have asked had I known."

"It's all right." Lorenzo massaged the space between his brows. "I beat myself up over it for the next hundred years, but after I entered my third century, I realized my guilt wasn't doing anyone any good. I had to let go of the past. There wasn't anything I could have done all those decades ago."

"You were only a demon child back then."

He nodded. "Yes. It depends on the type of demon how quickly we mature, but we are all born as babies and go through childhood like humans, just much slower."

"I reached adolescence around the age of 120. I wasn't an adult until I was at least 160 or 180 years old."

"How old is Mikka?" I wanted to distract him from his painful memories, but I was also curious how old the half-ice demon was who had taken my place in Tia's life.

Lorenzo chuckled. "She's a spring chicken. She's only in her fifties."

"But she doesn't look like a child."

He shrugged. "It's because she's only half-demon. Half-demons are mortal. They age, but much slower than humans."

"I see." There was so much out there I didn't know. My gaze fell on the book next to him, and I picked it up to discover it was a travel guide titled *My Journey Around the World.*

"You read human travel guides?"

Lorenzo smiled. "My teleportation allows me to go anywhere, but I like to prepare myself before I go. Human accounts prepare me for what to expect, and it's amusing to hear a different point of view."

I crossed my arms and pretended to be mad. "Do we poor, little humans entertain you?"

He didn't reply, just looked at me, and I realized he

didn't consider me human. I swallowed. Would I one day agree with him?

"There's a kingdom called Draconis," he said slowly. "It's filled with mountains, volcanoes, and dragons."

"Sounds dangerous," I replied.

"Yes, you would think the humans would stay away from the dragons, but it is rumored that some of its citizens are able to communicate with the dragons."

What an amazing skill to have.

"Then there's Atlantice," he continued, "where dolphins do your current job, delivering the mail to the merfolk."

A whole world under the sea? What I wouldn't give to see it. "Are you able to teleport underwater?"

"I am, but I can't stay long. I don't have the ability to breathe underwater. I doubt I'll be visiting Atlantice anytime soon."

"But, you hope to go to Draconis?"

He nodded. "Yes, or perhaps go see Elder, which is rumored to be filled with werewolves."

The little hairs on my arms rose. "Are there any kingdoms that have no predatory creatures?"

He took the book from me, and his fingers brushed against mine, eliciting a thrill in me that I had come to anticipate when we touched. Too soon, the contact was gone, and he opened the book onto a new page. "I think you would like this." The page showed beautiful homes built in the mountains and people sitting atop huge birds. "In Arboria, the citizens live in houses built into the mountains. They travel from place to place on birds."

"That sounds amazing." To be able to fly, what a dream.

Lorenzo closed the book, his gaze drilling into me.

"You didn't come here to talk about travel. Did you want to discuss the performance?"

I nodded. "I'm going to sing "Queen of Song." I don't think it needs a huge stage show, but I was hoping you could help me with something I have in mind." I told him about my plan and held my breath.

Lorenzo's face lit up, making it impossible to believe that this was a man who had been alive for almost 300 years and had seen horrors I couldn't even begin to imagine. "That's a great idea. I'll arrange for it."

"Thank you." I touched his arm. "But please, let me pay for the cost."

He shook his head. "Nonsense. I'm your manager. This is my job."

"You've already done so much for me."

He paused. "I'll tell you what. You can pay me back from the prize money you make when you win the competition."

"What if I don't win?"

He squeezed my hand. "You will." His fingers stayed on top of mine, and I glanced at our hands, then back up at him. Neither of us pulled back. Instead, he leaned forward and brushed back a strand of my auburn hair. "You're Halia. You can do anything."

Goosebumps exploded on my skin, and my stomach tingled with longing. His lips hovered above mine, and for a second, I was certain he would kiss me. For a second, there was nothing else I wanted but him.

A knock at the door shattered the moment. "Lorenzo, you don't need Tia or me before five, do you?"

At Mikka's voice, I pulled back and got off the bed, busying myself with studying the fireplace as my mind shrieked, *What are you doing?*

"No," Lorenzo called back. What were Mikka and Tia

up to today? It hurt that my friend didn't even consider inviting me to come along. Was I not good enough anymore? How could everything have changed so much in just one week? I really needed to talk to Tia.

Lorenzo cleared his throat, drawing my attention back to him and making my cheeks heat at what we had almost done. I had the urge to dart out of the room under his intense stare, but there was one more thing I needed to address before I could run away from my attraction to him. "I had a disagreement with Acacia yesterday. She's selling voice enhancers to Madam Fontaine's daughters. I need to find another fae to help conceal my eye color."

After I finished telling Lorenzo about my fight with Acacia, he shook his head. "That's it. No more dealings with faes."

"But I need them to hide the gold in my eyes, especially since neither of us knows what it means and what others will do once they realize I have the ability to use my voice to...to compel others." The words still tasted foreign on my tongue, and a part of me still fought this concept, even though another, wiser part of me knew it was true, and I needed to accept it. Maybe I could see it as something good. After all, my voice had allowed me to confirm that D..., Cinder, wasn't a mute and allowed me to let the young boy escape before Victor could throw him into prison over a stolen loaf of bread. What else could I do with my voice? Could I pose a singing question and get an answer from Cinder? Could I win the competition by subconsciously compelling the judges? I shuddered. If I did that, I wasn't any better than Acacia, who helped the sisters acquire better voices.

"Is that why you think I'll win? Because my voice is

compelling?" I studied Lorenzo, my shoulders tensing. "I don't want to compel the judges to give me the highest score. I don't want to win that way."

Lorenzo chuckled. "Don't worry, that's not how your gift works."

"How can you be so sure?"

He stepped toward me, making my stomach tingle with butterflies. "Because your magic is part of you, Halia. You are good. You are a light magic wielder."

"But you said others could use me to do..." I trailed off at the ticking muscle in his jaw.

"Dark magic wielders can always find a way to use light magic wielders for their nefarious purposes."

"What type is your magic?" Please don't say dark.

"Demon magic is neutral as is fae magic, allowing us to choose how we use it."

"So who is either a light or dark magic wielder?"

"Witches, healers, and poisoners."

I exhaled. "So, I'm still mostly human."

Lorenzo tilted his head, amusement dancing in his eyes. "What is it with your obsession to be human?" At my raised eyebrows, he added. "You're at least half-human. Otherwise, you wouldn't look human."

Yet the golden rings in my eyes made me "other," something that Lorenzo hadn't encountered in his two hundred and seventy-two years of living. I sighed. "I wish I knew what I am. The not-knowing is hard."

He nodded. "Ambiguity can be the worst." He took my hands in his, and calm spread through me. "Trust me, we'll find out what you are. I promise you before the end of August, we'll know."

August was only a few days away. Could Lorenzo really discover what I was in less than forty days? I hoped so. Until then, I needed to take precautions. "Do you know of any other fae nearby besides Acacia?"

He shook his head. "I'm not letting you go to another fae. If Acacia can be bought, so can others. The more people know your secret, the more exposed you are."

I had thought about this as well, but what was I supposed to do? "I can't just walk around Arcadia with golden circles in my eyes."

"You won't." Lorenzo squeezed my hand. "I'll get you colored contacts."

I blinked in confusion. "What?"

He let go of my hand. "They are tiny lenses that you put in your eyes to change your eye color. They don't hurt but take some getting used to."

I massaged my temples. "There's so much technology out there I don't know about."

He smiled. "We demons like to keep our abilities well concealed." Then his expression sobered. "I know someone who can create colored contacts for you in a day. Once I have them, I'll get what you need for your recording." He must have noticed the panic growing on my face, because he said, "I'll be back long before recording. I promise."

"It's at four on Tuesday. Please don't be late." Unable to stay away from him, I stepped closer until our noses were almost touching. "I don't want to do this without you. I need you by my side."

His breath was hot against my lips as he replied, "I will be. I promise."

I closed my eyes, ready for the kiss, but instead of feeling his soft lips against mine, there was just air. I opened my eyes to find Lorenzo had taken several steps back. Earth, please swallow me whole. Unable to take the rejection, I headed for the door. "I better get going. Lots to do."

"Me too," Lorenzo said behind me as I let the wooden door slam shut.

~

After making a fool out of myself in front of Lorenzo, I needed something to cheer me up and distract me from the critical voice in my head telling me I was ridiculous for thinking a gorgeous demon would want to kiss me. Thus, I handed the gondolier a coin and got onto the long, wooden gondola, which would take me across the river to the Royal Opera House. The sun was slowly setting and bathed Arcadia in an orange glow. Once again, it struck me how beautiful my hometown was. My mood lifted slightly. I began to hum, and before I knew it, words tumbled from my lips.

*You are my home, my beautiful home. I want to travel the world, but when I'm done, I'll always return to you, Arcadia.*

*Arcadia, you are joy, happiness, and love.*

*Arcadia, your market makes anyone feel welcome, overflowing with the most exotic spices and sweetest treats.*

*Arcadia, your street dancers and acrobats can bring a smile to anyone's face.*

*Arcadia, you always shine bright. No matter if it's day or night, summer or winter.*

I really liked the melody that came to me and wondered if I could make a full song out of it. Perhaps. A song to honor my hometown could be something for me to work on while I waited for the results of the first round of the contest to come in. But first, I had to size up my competition.

I entered the imposing theater with its tall columns,

still feeling out of place, even though today I had dressed up in a knee-length, white dress that I had purchased recently from a secondhand store and that looked almost new.

Nobody stopped me as I headed past the gilded walls and marble staircase into the auditorium. The auditorium wasn't as empty as I had expected it to be. Clearly, many of the other candidates had decided to watch the other recordings as well. I estimated that about 200 people had shown up.

I chose a seat next to a girl who appeared to be a few years older than me, who wore her hair in a braid. She didn't even glance at me as I sat down, so I didn't say anything to her either, afraid talking would get me kicked out of the recording sessions. As the competition host had promised, each candidate had exactly half an hour to set up, get the recording right, and clean up.

The recording team had several devices that stood on two skinny legs, were nearly as tall as them, and had boxes attached at the top. The whole concept of recording us on video was foreign to me. Recordings were common for the royal competitions; however, they weren't used for anything else. The technology wasn't something humans had created but rather something that was possible due to demon magic. What relationship did our king have with the magic bearers living in his kingdom?

Arcadia's policy on magical creatures wasn't very well defined. Anyone could come and live in our kingdom. Demons and faes were safe to be around in public. Yet, it was frowned upon if humans hung out on an individual basis with magical creatures. It seemed that demons were good enough when we needed something from them, like their technology, or when they could contribute to Arcadia's economy like Lorenzo did. However, the rest of the time, they were seen as second-class citizens. Second-class citizens that held a lot of power, and thus, inspired fear and even hate in some humans.

I decided then and there that if I got to talk to the king, I would ask him to create a reform that would bridge the gap between demons, fae, and humans. Right now, we all shared the city but lived in segregation. If we got to truly know each other, a lot of the tensions could be resolved.

Heat crept into my nape as I remembered how I had asked Lorenzo repeatedly if he was influencing my mind and had nearly accused him of being an incubus due to the attraction I felt. Only a week earlier, I, too, had been ignorant, and it had almost cost me the opportunity of a lifetime. If not for Lorenzo, I wouldn't be here today, preparing for the competition. If not for Lorenzo, I would still be slaving away under Madam Fontaine's violent outbursts. If not for Lorenzo, I would still be with Victor, who would subtly, and not so subtly, put me down. Thinking of Victor made sadness well inside of me. He had preyed on my naivety and loneliness. Yet, he had also been the only one to show me any interest. Lorenzo not kissing me today…I swallowed hard. It hurt. It hurt a lot. It made me feel like I was back in the orphanage. A seven-year-old girl with strange eyes and no friends.

Fireworks erupted on the stage, drawing my attention back to the performances. Even though our contracts had explicitly stated that the stage couldn't be altered in any way or be exposed to any dangerous materials, several contestants had decided to brazenly push the envelope. Besides the mini fireworks, people schlepped water fountains onto the stage, trees that almost reached the ceiling, and heavy furniture that I was certain left a mark on the floor. There was a lot of sighing and headshaking from Mr. Goodwin and his crew. However, none of the contestants were disqualified, which almost made me wonder if I should've asked Mikka to create some ice theme for my recording tomorrow. But no, just because others were breaking the rules didn't make it all right.

It was hard not to second-guess my choice to go minimal as I watched the recordings, one more impressive than the last. It wasn't just the props but also the performances that left me breathless.

A tiny girl contorted her body into strange positions and walked on her hands while singing. A man in his forties breathed fire in between the lines of his chorus. Several performers played an instrument. There were harps, drums, and cellos. Playing an instrument was not a requirement since the competition was for singing only, but I couldn't help feeling that I was at a disadvantage. Since the orphanage didn't have any instruments, I had never taught myself how to play one, but now, I wished I had gone out and searched for a second-hand guitar.

As expected, some performances were weak, but not nearly enough for me to dare to hope that I would make it into the top ten percent and progress to the next round.

It was midnight by the time the last performance finished, and everyone dispersed. With so many of us leaving at the same time, there were no gondolas left to take me across the river. Feeling restless and impatient after seeing how impressive my competition was, I didn't want to wait for a gondola and decided to walk instead. A decision I came to regret dearly.

# 27TH JULY

It should have taken me about half an hour to get home. Arcadia wasn't a dangerous city, and I wasn't worried about walking by myself at night. My biggest concern was finding my way back to the market quarter since I hadn't ever walked the route from the opera house to Daydream.

Fortunately, from time to time, flames would light up the sky, letting me know where the fire breathers and, thus, the night market were. The bursts of fire kept getting bigger and bigger the further I walked. A pleasant breeze ruffled my hair. I welcomed it. With it being the middle of the summer, many days felt sticky and hot. As I had hoped, my anxiety about my recording diminished with each step I took.

So what if a lot of the contestants had a professional

background? Putting on a show wasn't the only thing that mattered. Yes, a lot of the viewers and the court favored dramatics, but every year, there were several good voices that got really far. And that's exactly what I would focus on—my strengths, not my weaknesses.

Plus certainly, the heavens must be on my side, watching out for me in this competition. Why else give me a magical voice? The more I thought about it, the more certain I became that Lorenzo had come into my life now because the queen had gone missing, and it was up to me to bring her back. However, first, I needed to find out what the king knew. The only way I would get to talk to him was by winning the contest.

Would he know who Cinder was? Perhaps the queen had a twin or sibling she had been separated from at birth. Cinder could even be a cousin.

Another burst of fire flashed in the sky, much bigger than the last one. I wasn't far from the night market now. Confidently, I continued down the dark alley, knowing this unlit part of the path was short. It was no big deal. Rowdy partygoers wouldn't be here.

My steps were steady and confident until somebody bumped into my shoulder, nearly knocking me on my behind. A shriek burst from my throat. I quickly suppressed it and said, "I'm sorry. I didn't mean to run into you." Ugh, why was I apologizing when the man had run into me? Old habits die hard.

"Halia?"

I froze at the familiar voice. "Victor?"

"What are you doing here?" The moon pushed through the clouds and illuminated his bloodshot eyes. His usually carefully trimmed hair was a mess, and his breath reeked of cheap beer.

"I'm not doing anything." I tried to push past him.

There was no point in having a conversation with him, especially when he was in such a state.

"Hey, wait." He grabbed my arm and turned me around roughly. "You owe me an apology."

"For what?"

He let out a gurgling sound that I supposed was meant to be a laugh. "Really? You're going to pretend you're all innocent? You let that boy get away! I could've lost my job."

"You would have ruined his life if you had put him into prison over a loaf of bread."

He snorted. "Clearly, you care more about a stranger to you than me."

"I want everyone to be happy and safe."

"Is that so?" His eyes narrowed, and suddenly, he didn't seem so drunk anymore. "Your little stunt cost me. I was severely reprimanded, and now, Thomas will get the promotion I deserve."

"Is that why you've been drinking?" I asked, regretting the words as soon as they were out of my mouth.

Victor snarled. "You think you're so much better than everyone, don't you?" His fingers dug hard into my skin, bruising it.

"No, I just—"

"You just what? You think you know everything because you're a demon whore now?"

"Lorenzo and I aren't—"

"Don't deny it!" Victor shoved down the straps of my dress, ripping one of them in the process.

"What are you doing?" I tried to push him away, but he wouldn't budge. "Stop it right now!"

"I offered you my protection. I wanted to honor you, but you chose to go off with a demon. If you debased yourself by sleeping with him, I might as well enjoy you as well!"

"Let go of me, Victor!" I shoved him as hard as I could, but somehow, I was the one that ended up falling to the ground. And then, Victor was on top of me. "What are you doing?" My voice was hysterical now, and my whole body was trembling. "This is against the law!"

"I am the law."

"You can't do this!"

"I can't? I can do anything I please! Watch me."

I threw my knee upward as hard as I could, repeatedly going for his groin, yet failing to reach it. I tried to scratch him with my fingernails, but his face was too far away, making it impossible to hurt his eyes or any other vital part. And when his forearms began to bleed from my nails, he barely even glanced at them.

Pinning my arms down with one hand, he began to unzip his pants with his other hand. I bucked and thrashed underneath him to no avail. How could this be happening to me? Why wasn't anything I was doing working? I needed a weapon.

Desperately, I glanced around but couldn't find anything on the ground, not even a stone. Victor also didn't have a weapon on him as far as I could see, and anyhow, my arms were still pinned down. Breathing hard, he leaned forward, his body crushing mine, and I knew I had only seconds before he plunged himself into me. I had to think and act quickly.

What could I do? His body was immobilizing me. I had no weapons.

*Use your gift,* my inner voice whispered.

I opened my lips, but his hand came down and clamped down on my mouth. Clearly, he was afraid I would scream. While his hand prevented me from screaming, I could still sing.

*"Let go of me now, let go of me now,"* I sang.

Victor's hand came off, and he chuckled. "Really, you think your singing will help you?" He positioned himself above me, pushing my legs apart.

*"Leave me alone, leave me alone,"* I sang, willing every ounce of power I had into my voice.

He paused, hesitation written on his face.

*"I am no longer yours. I am no longer yours.*

*You must let me go, step away from me."*

Victor's face contorted as if he was in pain. "What is this witchery?"

*"You must leave, you must leave. Let me go right now,"* I belted out as much as my shallow breathing and galloping heart allowed.

A vein bulged in his neck, and his hands trembled. Slowly, his weight shifted off me. I was tempted to defend myself physically again, but my gut told me to focus on the singing.

*"You must leave now, you must leave and never come into my life again and never come into my life again."*

Victor's hands flexed and closed rapidly by his sides. His nostrils flared. And yet he took another step back.

*"Go away from me, go away and leave me alone. Forget me. Forget me completely."*

He turned around and began walking away.

Tears ran down my face, but I continued singing, sensing I wasn't safe yet.

*"Go away, go away, and leave me forever. Forget me. Forget me completely."*

It was only when I could no longer see Victor that I stopped singing and rose to my unsteady feet.

If I hadn't had my voice, if I hadn't found the courage to sing, Victor would have hurt me very badly. With my back sore from where he had pushed me onto the ground and my dress torn, I headed toward the market, singing underneath my breath, willing my voice and words to calm me and stop the trembling in my body.

*"Evil, stay away from me. Let me pass peacefully, let me pass peacefully."*

I repeated the three phrases like a mantra, like a song stuck on replay. The panic abated, but what Victor had shattered within me didn't meld.

Arcadia was my home. Arcadia was supposed to be safe, welcoming, and loving. After today, it didn't feel like that anymore. After today, it had become tarnished. No one had been around to help me when a patrolman who was supposed to protect the city's citizens had attacked me. Not just any patrolman, but one who had claimed he loved me only a week ago.

My belief in the goodness of others was splintering. First, Acacia. Now, Victor.

I knew I should count myself lucky since I had gotten away. However, as grateful as I was for my inner strength, I was devastated that Arcadia was turning into a city where only the strong survived, where money and weapons ruled.

I only stopped singing when I reached Daydream. With most patrons preparing to go back to work on Monday, the bar was open only until midnight on Sundays, which explained why there were no customers when I entered. Tia was sitting cross-legged on the bar, laughing at something Mikka had said.

I attempted to walk past them, wanting nothing more than to wash off the dirt from my skin. But Tia noticed me. From my peripheral vision, I knew she was running toward me.

"What happened to you?" She scanned my disheveled appearance and waited for me to meet her eyes.

"Victor," I rasped.

Immediately, the terror in her eyes turned into a sharp blade. "I'm going to kill him for this."

"He'll never come near me again."

There was a question on her face, but before she could pose it, Mikka joined us, asking, "Are you all right?"

"She will be once you freeze off Victor's balls," Tia said, and I managed a half-smile before my legs gave out. Luckily, Mikka and Tia grabbed an arm each and sat me down into a booth.

Tia gently pushed the hair out of my face. "Tell me."

I took a deep breath and recounted everything.

When I was done talking, Tia jumped up. "I'm going to kill him!"

I shook my head. "He won't hurt me again. I compelled him to stay away from me."

"You don't really think that your voice...he was probably just shocked."

I grabbed Tia's hand and pulled her back into the booth. "My voice has magic in it. Lorenzo confirmed it."

Tia gave me an uncertain look, then glanced to Mikka for help, who was sitting across from us in the booth.

"She's right," the half-ice demon said. "Victor won't hurt her again. In the future, he'll stay away from her."

Tia nodded slowly. Her face contorted in a grimace. "I'm sorry I wasn't there when you found out that you had magic in your voice. I should've been there for you."

I swallowed hard at the opening Tia had given me. The night had been trying enough, but I couldn't continue to push off the talk I needed to have with Tia. "We both had a lot on our minds," I began. I forced a smile. "I'm happy you found a new friend, but I have to admit that I'm a bit hurt. A lot, actually. You completely disappeared." I met Mikka's black eyes that flashed with something. "I'm not jealous of you. I just wish I would have been included in some of the things you guys did."

Mikka and Tia exchanged a meaningful glance, which only made me feel more excluded.

"The thing is," Tia began, and I braced myself, expecting to hear that it was my fault, that I had changed too much, and that now that we didn't work together, Tia simply was closer to Mikka because she saw her all the time.

"The thing is," Tia repeated, "Mikka and I are more than friends."

I choked out a laugh. "Yes, I get it. You're best friends now. I've been replaced." I hugged myself. Why did she have to rub it in, especially tonight after what had happened with Victor? "You don't have to be so cruel about it. Don't you care at all about all the years of friendship we had?"

"Of course, I do!" Tia hugged me. "You misunderstood me. You'll always be my best friend. What I meant was that Mikka and I are more than friends because we are in love."

I blinked; then my gaze zigzagged between Mikka and Tia. "But you've always dated men," I finally blurted out.

Tia shrugged. "And it never worked out. But that's not the point. I don't care whether Mikka is female or male. I'm in love with her because of who she is, not what gender she is."

Wow, that had happened fast. They had only known each other a week, but then again, that's what Tia was like—fiery and intense.

"Say something," Tia said, her voice quiet for once.

I glanced at Mikka. "Are you in love with Tia as well?"

The ice demon wrapped her long, white hair around her tiny wrist. "I'm not really good talking about all that stuff, but yes, I care a lot for Tia."

I smiled. "Then I'm happy for both of you." But not everyone would be. "It won't be easy, will it?"

Mikka tugged on her lacy top. "Demons don't care about same-sex relationships, but humans seem to. Then, there's also me being a half-demon. Neither party will appreciate that."

"Most people don't know that you're a half-demon," I pointed out, unsure whether that was helpful or not.

"They will after I help you put on your show."

I bit my lip. I needed all the help I could get to win the royal competition, but I didn't want to force Mikka to reveal herself to Arcadia if she wasn't ready. "I can't use your ice. It's against the rules and I don't want to push you into—"

"No," she cut me off. "I appreciate it, but I've been hiding for a long time. It's time to embrace what I am."

I wished I could say the same. How I wished I could stop hiding the golden rings in my eyes. Soon. Once I knew what they meant. A yawn escaped me.

"I think it's time for us all to go to sleep." Tia stood and took my hands to help me up from the booth.

"I don't want to be alone tonight," I said.

Tia glanced at Mikka, who nodded. "You won't be. I'll be right next to you."

"Are you sure?" I needed my friend, but I didn't want to annoy Mikka.

Tia grinned. "Yes. It will be just like old times."

Mikka gave Tia a quick peck on the lips, and I glanced downward, feeling like I was intruding on something private.

"Are you okay with this, Mikka?" I asked when they

pulled away.

Mikka flashed me a smile, her teeth sharp, reminding me that even though she looked like a tiny girl, she was a force to be reckoned with. "I never wanted to take your friend." She gave Tia a gentle shove, and Tia and I walked upstairs.

"I'm really sorry I disappeared," Tia said, once we were in our room and I had washed the dirt off my skin. I then turned to her so that she could examine my back, which felt like it was on fire. "It's just that meeting Mikka was like an earthquake."

An earthquake. I had never experienced one in Arcadia, but I'd heard that other kingdoms had this type of natural catastrophe. It was an odd comparison, but I knew what Tia was trying to say. Her attraction to Mikka had been sudden, unexpected, and intense. Was that what I had with Lorenzo? I wasn't sure. It did sometimes feel inevitable. At least, for me. I wasn't so sure he felt the same after he had refused to kiss me before he left on his trip.

Tia dabbed an ointment on my back, and I hissed as the tincture seemed to burn through my muscles. "How bad is it?" I gritted out through my teeth.

"A few lacerations. Not too deep." Tia inhaled sharply. "Are you sure you don't want me to go over to Victor's and hit him over the head a couple of times with a cocktail mixer?"

A weak laugh escaped me. "Thanks, but no. Please leave him alone."

She sighed. "How can you be so forgiving?"

"There's no point in hanging on to anger. It won't help me."

She shrugged. "I suppose, but I would still be angry."

"Him trying to rape me is unforgivable, but I know

he must be really messed up on the inside to act that way. He has so much rage inside of him. I would never want to live like that."

"I don't care if he's miserable. He has no right to hurt others!"

I turned off the lights, plunging the room into a comforting darkness, illuminated by Arcadia's night-lights streaming through the window. "No, he doesn't, but I don't want to focus on Victor or other people who have done horrible things and hurt me. I want to focus on the good. I want to pay attention to the light and grow it, not feed the darkness."

"Victor and Madam are sickos." Tia was lying on her side, her arm propping up her head.

"Yes, they are, and we're lucky that we got away from them. I wish we could stop them from inflicting pain on anyone else."

Tia pursed her lips. "Somebody needs to put them into their place."

I yawned. "We're not the police or vigilantes. I'll talk to Thomas."

"You think he'll believe you?"

I nodded. Yes, I thought Victor's partner would. Thomas had always been kind to me.

"Fine. But Victor better not hurt anyone else," Tia huffed. "He should keep the peace, not create fear, especially now that fights are breaking out daily. Guys are constantly punching each other. Girls are pushing each other. Men are grabbing girls' butts." She shook her head. "It's disgusting."

"At Daydream?"

"Yes. Lorenzo is pretty good at breaking it up, but it keeps happening. It's like the whole city is on edge. It's contagious. I feel on edge too."

That explained why she was so fixated on punishing Victor.

"It's been getting worse for a few months now," I agreed. "Especially in the last few weeks since Queen Ella went missing. We need to find her. Perhaps her godmother can set the situation right."

A look of uncertainty crossed Tia's face. I knew that look. Something was on her mind, and she wasn't sure if she should tell me about it. "What is it?"

She sighed. "It's probably nothing."

"Tell me." When she didn't, I added. "I'm trying to win the competition to talk to the king and figure out what happened to his wife. I need to know as much as possible to have a shot at helping Arcadia. I want our city and kingdom restored back to its goodness. Whatever is happening here right now isn't normal. And if we don't stop it—" I shook my head. "We can't let any more of our citizens get hurt." Last week, a couple disappeared from the boarding house, and a middle-aged woman had been drained of her energy and aged overnight. Now, the whole city was on edge.

Tia nodded. "Fine, but promise not to freak out." She inhaled. "You know how you said Cinder might be Queen Ella's long-lost twin or sister? Well, while it's possible, I think it's even more likely that she's the queen herself."

I jerked upright, coming into a sitting position on my bed. "What? Why would the queen be working for Madam Fontaine, scrubbing away in the kitchen?"

Tia chewed on a fingernail painted green. "I don't know."

"And why would she not be talking?"

"Maybe something traumatic happened to her. Maybe she's scared." Tia shifted onto her back and stared up at the ceiling. "Maybe I'm wrong. It was just an idea."

"Thank you for sharing. I'm going to ask Cinder about it."

She stared at me, her eyes wide. "You're going to ask her if she's the queen?"

I smiled. "If she's the queen, I'll trick her into admitting it tomorrow." I glanced at the clock that read 3 a.m. in the morning. "Or, I guess today." I had a long day ahead of me that included my shift at the post office, preparing for my recording, and confronting Cinder.

Or so I thought, because by the time I started delivering the post, Madam Fontaine's boarding house was fenced off, patrolmen swarming around it. They stayed long past sunset. With Victor being one of them, I didn't dare to get closer and decided to wait until the next day.

# 28TH JULY

The next day when I started my shift at the post office, the police carriages were still camped outside the boarding house, yet there weren't quite as many patrolmen around, giving me hope that I could sneak in, talk to Cinder, and find out what was going on. It also helped that I had several pieces of mail for the boarding house. Since I planned to spend some time inside and didn't want to draw attention by having my bike stand nearby or risk someone stealing it, I forced myself to remain patient and deliver all the other pieces of mail first. Once I was done, I dropped off the bike at the post office, then returned to the boarding house. My stack of mail contained letters addressed to Madam and her daughters, as well as a few for her tenants.

Like I had done last time, I entered through the back and headed for the kitchen. Taking a calming breath, I pushed open the wooden door, its hinges squeaking. I half-expected to find the boy from last time inside, but luck was on my side—Cinder was all alone in the kitchen. She didn't bother looking up from the dishes she was scrubbing, even though the old hinges made it impossible to ignore my entrance. I knew I had one shot to get this right.

"Ella?" I asked.

Her head shot up, her eyes wide with fear.

I brought a palm over my mouth. Tia was right. "Ella. Queen Ella?" I stepped closer. "What are you doing here?"

The dish Ella had been holding slipped from her grip and plopped into the soapy water, splashing us both with bubbles. Not bothering to wipe her hands, she grabbed a piece of paper and wrote on it hastily.

"I don't know what you're talking about."

A sad smile curled my lips. "Yes, you do. This is the first time you ever bothered to reply. You're trying to uphold a lie. The question is why."

She shook her head vehemently.

I took the piece of paper from her. "A lot of kitchen helpers don't know how to write, but even if they knew how, I doubt they would have such beautiful handwriting." The curlicues were perfect. "This is written by someone with a lot of writing experience, someone who had private tutors that rewarded easy to read and pretty handwriting."

Queen Ella's chest began to rise and fall rapidly.

"It's all right," I said. "Tell me what's going on, and I will help you."

She shook her head again, then took the piece of

paper from me and wrote on the backside.

"Don't tell anyone."

I tried to take the piece of paper from her, but she was faster. She threw it into the oven, and the flames consumed it.

Just like that, she had destroyed the only piece of evidence proving she was the queen.

Clearly, the surprise factor had worn off, but I still had one weapon left. I felt rotten using my voice to force her to reveal her secrets, but then I thought about all the unrest Arcadia was experiencing. Our kingdom needed its queen back. And certainly, Queen Ella couldn't be happy scrubbing dishes for Madam Fontaine. Whatever our queen was running away from, it was time to face it. Picking a sweet melody, I sang, "Why are you working for Madam Fontaine? Why do you allow her to call you Cinder?"

Ella didn't reply, only pressed her lips together harder. But even without her saying anything, the wheels were spinning in my mind. Madam Fontaine was in her fifties and old enough to be Cinder's mother. As for her awful daughters, they seemed to be as corrupt as the stepsisters Queen Ella had grown up with.

Everyone in Arcadia knew the story of our queen. Before she met the prince, she had been a personal maid to her stepmother and stepsisters after her father's death. Her new family had abused her and would have continued to do so if Ella hadn't found the courage to go to the ball with the help of her fairy godmother.

"Madam Fontaine is your stepmother," I said slowly, the puzzle pieces falling into place.

Queen Ella was shaking uncontrollably now.

"Georgette and Bernadette are you stepsisters."

Queen Ella leaned against the sink, her face going

ghostly white.

"But you escaped them. You married the king. Why did you leave him?"

Ella dashed past me and through the door. I wanted to go after her, but I knew I couldn't risk drawing any attention to myself or her.

I needed to return with backup. Hopefully, Lorenzo had returned from his travels. He would know what to do. What I didn't understand was that if the stepmother and stepsisters were here, shouldn't Queen Ella's fairy godmother be nearby as well? If Madam Fontaine and her daughters had something on Queen Ella, certainly, her fairy godmother could help.

About to leave, I turned around only to find a patrolman in the door.

"What are you doing here, Halia?" Thomas's mouth was set into a grim line, yet all I felt was relief that it was he and not his partner. I had told Victor to stay away, and I thought he would, but that didn't mean that if we ran into each other, his hate for me wouldn't return. Plus, seeing me might make him remember what I had done with my voice. He would be furious if he realized I could compel him. My best chance of him leaving me alone was hoping he had been too drunk last time to remember things properly or make sense of them.

Thomas raised an eyebrow, and I realized I hadn't answered his question.

"I came here to see a friend," I said.

"This is a crime scene. Didn't you notice the red rope outside the boarding house?"

If Thomas decided to lock me up for trespassing or interfering with an investigation, I would lose my recording spot and fail to tell Lorenzo about Queen Ella. I had to proceed carefully. "I also came to drop this off."

I held out the letters, putting the sweetest smile on my face. "I work at the post office now."

He sighed and extended his hand. "I'll deliver them to the front desk. In the future, don't step into a crime scene."

I nodded, but instead of leaving, I pressed. *"What happened? Did someone die?"* My questions had a melody to them and sounded almost like a song.

Thomas nodded, but then shook his head. "I can't tell you."

*"I need to know. I need to know. Tell me what happened,"* I sang, aware I was walking a fine line. Lorenzo had said my power was white magic and could only be used for good. I intended to use Thomas' information for good, but what if my magic decided that pushing him was wrong? Worse, what if my voice only worked on those that were already riled up? Every time I had used it before, the person in question was emotional, Thomas, however, was calm and collected.

Now his eyelids twitched, and he slowly said, "The guest in room two. His heart gave out. The maid found him. Madam Fontaine seemed very angry with her. Very suspicious. Worse, this wasn't the first time a tenant..." A pause. "Two guests disappeared this week without a trace. Madam Fontaine says they checked out, but their suitcases were found in the trash a few blocks away from here. It doesn't add up."

*"Was it a couple?"*

He shook his head. "Two middle-aged women."

I swallowed hard. So he didn't even know about the couple that "checked out" abruptly last week, also not bothering to take their luggage. Five guests had run into trouble after staying at the boarding house.

*"Who do you think is responsible?"* I sang.

Thomas clenched his jaw. "I don't know. Something is fishy for sure."

He blinked several times, his eyes clearing. I was losing my hold over him, best to wrap this up.

"Thank you. Now that I've given you the letters I came to deliver, I must go."

He nodded. "You have a beautiful voice."

I didn't comment but slipped past him and out of the boarding house, ready to share what I had discovered with Lorenzo.

Lorenzo wasn't at Daydream. He was neither in the bar, nor in his office, nor in his room. It was one. Only three hours remained until my recording slot. Where was he? How long could I wait for him here? It would take me a good half an hour to get to the opera house, and I didn't want to arrive last minute. I wanted to hear a few performances before mine and warm up my vocal cords.

Even though I didn't want to leave without Lorenzo, I knew I had to get ready. Tears welled in my eyes. Why did everything always have to go wrong? Why wasn't I able to do anything by myself? Why did I have to rely on others? Why was my chest constricting?

"Ready to rock?" Tia said as she entered our bedroom. I didn't glance up at her, simply continued staring at my bed and my clothes I had strewn over it.

"I don't have anything to wear," I said, too overwhelmed to focus on anything else. I had originally planned to wear the silky dress Tia had given me for my birthday, but now, I wasn't so sure.

"You can try on some of Mikka's clothes."

I let out a chuckle. "I doubt anything will fit me. She's tiny."

Ignoring my protest, Tia pulled me toward Mikka's

room. "She's only a few inches smaller than you."

Mikka was lounging on her bed, and when Tia asked if I could borrow something from her wardrobe for the recording, Mikka jumped up, her black eyes sparkling like onyx. "I thought you'd never ask. I have just the perfect dress."

She pulled out a pale coral creation that was strapless and almost reached the ground but not quite. The light chiffon number was a stunner.

"I couldn't," I said, but Tia was already unzipping it.

"It was a present, and I never liked it, but I couldn't bring myself to throw it away," Mikka said casually as I twirled and admired how the dress clung to and flared around my petite body at all the right places.

Since my hands were too unsteady and my thoughts were a mess, I let Tia apply my makeup while Mikka did my hair.

"All done!" Tia said a while later and handed me a mirror.

My hair was in a half-up, half-down style that framed my heart-shaped face. My makeup was light, shimmering eye shadow and glossy lips that reminded me of dew on rose petals in the morning.

"Thank you," I said, tears of gratefulness entering my eyes. This whole week I had been afraid I had lost my best friend, but it seemed that, instead, I had gained a new friend in Mikka.

"You're welcome." Tia beamed. "Now, let's get you to the opera house. We don't want you to be late."

"You guys are coming with me?"

Tia led the way. "Of course. Did you really think we would let you go alone?"

The three of us took the gondola, Tia and Mikka holding hands while I stared out, focusing on the rocking of our boat as it made its way across the river, which was choppier than usual. In less than an hour, I would have my recording, and Lorenzo still wasn't here.

I was grateful for Tia and Mikka's help, but I seriously doubted that my voice plus hair and make-up would be enough to get me into the next round when the competition was going all out.

Inside the theater, the stage assistant asked for my name and checked me off the list. "And who is this?" He indicated his head toward Mikka and Tia.

"My friends."

"I'm sorry. Only managers are allowed backstage. Your friends will have to wait in the auditorium."

Tia was about to open her mouth, but I didn't want to appear difficult, so I quickly said, "I'll be fine."

She enveloped me into a hug. "You'll be amazing."

"Break a leg," Mikka said. Then I was shepherded into the vast backstage room, which was filled with a long row of tables with mirrors, all seats occupied as singers put on the final touches of their hair and make-up. The rest of the room was crowded too, performers everywhere, warming up their vocal cords and stretching.

I slipped past them and into the wings to watch the current performance from behind the curtains. As I did so, a girl brushed past me, heading the other way. "Who do you think you are?" she hissed, even though it had been she that had run into me.

I stepped aside, not saying anything, deciding it wasn't worth it. Putting the rude girl out of my mind, I focused on the performance on stage. A curvy girl in a red dress was belting out a classical aria.

"Does she really think the king wants to hear something from the last century?" A guy joined me in the wings.

"She has a pretty voice," I tried.

He glared at me. "Yes, for the last century. She'll never make it to the next round." He stalked away. Before I could process why he was so aggressive, the girl walked off stage.

"Awful, simply awful," she muttered underneath her breath. "Why do I have to be such a stupid, fat cow? Mother was right all along."

I smiled at her. "Don't beat yourself up. I think your performance was great."

She put her fists onto her hips. "Who sent you to butter me up? What do you want?"

I took a step back. "No one and nothing, I was just trying to h—"

"Save it," she cut me off and stomped past me.

Annoyance bubbled up inside of me at being treated so unfairly by not one, not two, but three people. Then it hit me. This couldn't be a coincidence. I inhaled deeply, breathing out my annoyance and trying to stay rational. Then I stepped into the backstage room and observed the singers. The ones that were focused on themselves were pushing their bodies, contorting them unnaturally, and cursing quietly. The ones that came in contact with others were rolling their eyes, snarling, and some were even shoving each other.

This wasn't natural. Tia was right. Our city was boiling with unrest. And it was getting worse.

The stage assistant flew into the room, clapping his hands. "Chop, chop! Where is Eric Wells?"

The boy who had criticized the opera singer came forward.

The stage assistant grabbed his elbow. "You're up next. Don't keep us waiting. We're already behind."

The boy rushed onto the stage while the stage assistant barked, "Keep your eyes on the list." He pointed at a paper hanging on the wall. "Know when it's your turn. After Eric Wells, we have Georgette and Bernadette Fontaine, followed by Halia..."He paused. "Halia Bright."

I cringed. The signup sheet had insisted that I fill out every field, including my last name. Since I had been dropped off anonymously at the orphanage when I had been no older than a month, I didn't have a last name. The sisters at the orphanage decided to give me the last name Bright, saying that I was always a ray of sunshine. However, as sweet as the gesture was, I never used my last name. It was a constant reminder of how my parents hadn't wanted me.

If I passed this round, the reporters would know me as Halia Bright. They would look up my last name and spin my story around me being an orphan. I didn't want that. Being in an orphanage was something I had experienced and lived through, but it didn't define me.

On stage, Eric began to sing an upbeat tune. I glanced at the clock. Lorenzo didn't have long. It was likely he wouldn't make it. I would have to do this by myself. Finding a quiet corner, I closed my eyes and imagined having the best performance ever without any props and without Lorenzo. At least Tia and Mikka were here to watch me.

Much too soon, the stage assistant was back. "Georgette, Bernadette Fontaine."

The sisters pranced toward the stage in their matching, baby-blue ball gowns. What a strange outfit choice.

I glanced at the clock. Lorenzo had half an hour.

Unable to sit still any longer and needing to know

what Acacia had done to the sisters' voices, I returned to the wings.

Apparently, the sisters had decided they didn't need more than one try to get their courting right because the next fifteen minutes were spent on setting up the stage, putting down a rug that looked like a parquet floor and rolling in mirrors. They were transforming the stage into the royal ballroom. I knew that's what it was supposed to be since I had seen photos in newspapers. The sister's team even recreated the royal gardens visible from the ballroom, putting several rose bushes upstage. It was only when they began to sing that I understood their strategy:

*"Your hand on my waist. Your whisper in my ear. I'm falling. I'm falling hard for you.*

*Through a touch of faith, we ran into each other. Meeting you transformed me.*

*Your love, our love, it's unbreakable, unbreakable."*

Their perfectly harmonized voices were flawless, and yet bile rose in my throat. Not only were the sisters using voices that didn't belong to them, they were also recreating the king's meeting with the missing queen. It was as if they were taunting him. Or perhaps they hoped that by striking an emotional chord, they could get close to him and become front-runners if he decided to remarry. Either way, it was disgusting. I needed to talk to the king. I needed to tell him that the sisters and their mother had forced Queen Ella back into the kitchen.

Somebody sidled up to me, and goosebumps exploded on my back. I turned my head to find Madam Fontaine's beady eyes boring into me. "Halia, wasn't embarrassing yourself at that bar enough for you?" She tsked. "I guess you have the need to make a national spectacle out of yourself."

I stood tall, refusing to allow her words to affect me.

A cruel smile curled her mouth as she glanced toward the stage. "I would say it's a pity that you have to perform after my talented daughters, except it isn't. The sooner you are disqualified from the competition, the less you will embarrass yourself and the orphanage."

Blood rushed through my ears, and it was hard to remind myself that it wasn't like me to lash out, that I, like the rest of Arcadia, was affected by dark magic.

Knowing I needed all my energy for my performance, I pivoted and walked away from Madam Fontaine only to crash into someone.

"Don't," I said. I couldn't take another fight. However, the person didn't curse me or shove me. Instead, strong arms enveloped me, and a fresh scent of grass and lemon wrapped around me.

"Halia."

"Lorenzo," I choked out. "You made it."

His fingers moved in soothing circles over my shoulders. "Of course, I did. I'm sorry it took me so long." He took my hand and tugged me toward the backstage area, his violent-green gaze never leaving mine. I licked my lips. I hadn't forgotten that he had rejected me earlier, and yet, the desire for him was still there.

"Your eyes," Lorenzo said, mercifully interrupting my confusing thoughts. "We need to put in the contacts."

He took me into a washing room and handed me a small, plastic container that was split into two compartments, a see-through lens in each.

"It will feel strange at first, but you'll get used to it."

I glanced into the bathroom mirror to find the golden circles in my eyes were back. Who had seen them? Had

Thomas noticed? Had Ella? Knowing I couldn't afford to worry about that right now, I held open my upper and lower lid with my thumb and middle finger as Lorenzo instructed and put in the contact lens with my index finger. I repeated the action on the other eye and blinked rapidly. It stung and was strange to have something in my eyes, but I could handle it.

"Halia, Halia Bright, please get into your position," the stage assistant called.

"I'm not ready," I whispered.

"Yes, you are." Lorenzo picked up something heavy, making me realize he had procured the giant swing I had asked him for.

"How are you going to attach it?" I asked.

He shot me a lopsided smile. "Let me worry about that."

Lorenzo was true to his word. He teleported to the wooden beam above the stage and deftly secured the ropes of the swing. Then he teleported back down and pulled out a tiny container from his pocket. "This will be gone before the next performance starts," he said to the competition host, then took out a pinch of glittering dust and threw it onto the stage, transforming it into a luscious forest with tall trees. Sunlight streamed through their branches, and on the ground, wildflowers in deep blue, purple, and white grew.

He winked at me. "I hope it's all right that I took some creative liberty."

Before I knew what I was doing, I pressed my mouth to his in a quick peck. "It's perfect," I said. My words broke the spell, and my brain caught up to what my lips were doing. Quickly stepping aside, I said, "I'm ready to start the recording."

The embarrassment of the kiss was my salvation,

distracting me from imagining everything that might go wrong during my performance as the technical team went behind their devices and made a few adjustments, then waved their hands for me to begin.

I sat down on the swing. Lorenzo pushed it hard, and it rose into the sky. Clearly, it, too, was enchanted. There was no time left to wonder whom the magic for the swing and forest had come from, so I launched into, "Queen of Song:"

*Once upon a time, there was a girl who liked to sing. She didn't have a home, she didn't have kin, but she had a voice. Her blessing terrified her for it gave her hopes and dreams she was told were impossible.*

*Years passed, and the girl only shared her voice with her closest friends, only shared her voice when it was lost in a choir. Then you came along, and you challenged the girl, you told her it wasn't right not to share her blessing, you gave her strength, you gave her confidence. You allowed her to lean on you, and she became the queen of song, she became the queen of song."*

The swinging made butterflies erupt in my stomach, or perhaps it was the aftereffect of my lips brushing against Lorenzo's. Either way, singing on a swing was challenging, but also invigorating. I belted out the melody, dangling my feet as my hair bounced against my back. A few minutes of freedom, of weightlessness, of pure bliss. Too soon, the song was finished. Lorenzo helped me off the swing, then took it down. The forest disappeared just as he had promised.

"Thank you, Halia!" The assistant manager scribbled down notes, making it impossible to read his face. Confident I had given it my best, I walked off the stage and through the auditorium with Lorenzo by my side. I tried to spot Tia and Mikka in the rows but couldn't find them in the sea of barely illuminated faces.

Once Lorenzo and I were outside the auditorium in the marble hallway, I turned to him, a jolt of electricity darting through me just by looking at him. "There's something I need to tell you."

Lorenzo glanced around, then leaned his ear toward me. "Yes?"

My lips hovered above his earlobe, making it impossible not to think about the earlier kiss. Not ready to deal with it, I told him about the boarding house and Queen Ella.

"We need to get her out of there," Lorenzo said once I was finished.

Why hadn't I considered this earlier? People were disappearing without a trace from the boarding house. Nothing was stopping Madam Fontaine from making Ella disappear as well. "We have to hurry."

Lorenzo shook his head. "It's not safe for you. I'll go alone."

Before I could protest, the door of the auditorium swung open, and Mikka and Tia stepped out.

Their wide smiles vanished as they took in Lorenzo's and my solemn expressions.

"Wait for me at Daydream," he said to Mikka. Then he was gone, vanishing into nothingness.

Tia put her arm around my shoulder. "What's going on?"

"Lorenzo will retrieve Queen Ella," I said even as my gut told me it was too late.

THRONE OF SYMPHONY

# 29TH JULY

Lorenzo stood behind me as I knocked on the old door, it's peeling green paint revealing a white layer underneath. After a few seconds, footsteps thudded toward us, followed by the door creaking open.

"How can I help you?" the elderly man asked, his gaze scanning over me and the demon behind me, who looked like a human save for his violet-green eyes and silver hair.

"Have you seen this woman?" I handed the man a sketch of our missing queen. It didn't depict Queen Ella in all her queenly glory, but rather showed what she had looked like when she had worked as a kitchen maid at Madam's Boarding House.

The man shook his head. "No, I'm sorry." He coughed. "But there's a lot of strange stuff happening. A lot of people are disappearing or getting sick." He glanced upward. "Whatever luck the gods have once bestowed on us, it is no longer with us."

I agreed with him, partially. Whatever had kept Arcadia safe was broken, but I doubted it had anything to do with the gods. Everything had gone belly up when Queen Ella had disappeared. "Thank you," I said as the man closed the door.

I turned to Lorenzo. "We're too slow. We need to split up. Otherwise, we'll never cover the city in time. Why don't you use your teleportation to—"

"And leave you here by yourself? No." Lorenzo's gaze drilled into me. "If whoever kidnapped the queen realizes that you know Cinder is the queen, they'll come after you as well. I need to stay with you so that we can teleport away in case someone comes after us."

I sighed. He was right, but I hated how slow we were going. The longer we failed to find Queen Ella, the higher the chances that something bad had happened to her. Even if she hadn't been kidnapped, but disappeared of her own accord, it wasn't good. With her gone, Arcadia was falling more and more into chaos with each passing day, and our king wasn't doing anything.

I had entered the royal singing competition for a chance to speak with him. However, today while I had been delivering mail in the morning, I had heard several rumors that the king was considering canceling the competition this year even after all the participants had gone in for their initial recordings.

I didn't care about winning, even though it would've been nice to make a name for myself as a singer. What truly troubled me was that if the king canceled the competition, my chance of talking to him would vanish. As a former maid and now employee of the post office, there was no chance I would get to talk to him unless I got to the finals. Earlier today, Lorenzo had gone to the castle, trying to use his demon and business owner status to get an audience, but the guards had turned him away, stating the king was too busy to see a commoner.

This didn't sound like the king I knew, who always had an open ear for his subjects. He, like the rest of Arcadia, had been impacted by the disappearance of our queen and fallen into a deep pit of grief or indifference. His passivity, coupled with the unrest that seemed to have invaded every citizen in Arcadia, spelled trouble.

"I wish we knew how Tia and Mikka are getting on," I said. My best friend Tia had recently started dating Mikka, a half-ice demon after the two had met working behind Lorenzo's bar, Daydream.

"That I can do," Lorenzo said with his usual easy confidence.

How did one learn to become so comfortable in one's skin? "You know where they are?"

"Demons can sense each other in close distance, and I know that they're in the old town district. Once we teleport into the area, I'll know exactly where they are."

Lorenzo opened his arms, and for a moment, I froze, replaying the peck I had given him on the lips last night before my recording.

"Are you ready?" His violet-green eyes twinkled with mischief, and only then, did I realize that he had hadn't said he would teleport, but we would teleport.

"I can't teleport."

A boyish grin spread across his features, making it nearly impossible to remember that he was a two hundred and seventy-two-year-old demon, powerful enough to have mastered a glamor that concealed his demonic features. “You won’t have to do anything,” he reassured me.

I stepped closer, my body wanting to be pressed against his as my mind played horror scenarios. “What if I can’t? What if my heart gives out or something like that?”

He chuckled. “It’s safe to teleport. I promise.” His eyes softened. “I would never put you in danger.”

“I know.” Soon, we would have to talk about the kiss and the one before that that he had rejected. I needed to know where Lorenzo stood and whether he felt the same way I did. I would figure it out. Soon. After we spoke to Tia and Mikka.

Lorenzo’s arms closed around me, his scent of grass and lemon enveloped me. I wanted to press myself into him like a stray kitten. I wanted him to kiss me. I wanted him to tell me that what I was feeling for him wasn’t one-sided, that he too was interested in me.

But before I could find the courage to open my mouth, the ground underneath my feet vanished. My stomach dropped, and the air was knocked out of my lungs, the feeling similar to being on a really tall swing. I squeezed my eyes shut, petrified, expecting pain. It didn’t come. The rising and dropping sensation remained for a few more seconds, and then it too was gone, and I was standing on solid ground.

I opened my eyes to find Tia staring at me in wonder, Mikka next to her, smirking.

“First time?” the white-haired, black-eyed, half ice demon asked nonchalantly.

I nodded and stepped away from Lorenzo. I didn’t need Tia and Mikka asking me about my relationship with him when I hadn’t figured it out myself yet.

“Did you find anything?” Lorenzo asked.

Tia and Mikka shook their heads.

“There’s no trace of the queen.” Mikka pointed north. “We do still have a few streets left.”

I doubted the queen was hiding in the old town district. It was pure elegance filled with imposing buildings, the most impressive being the gilded Royal Opera House, which featured tall columns on the outside and plenty of marble and red velvet inside. The richest district was right next to the castle, making it likely that someone might recognize Queen Ella. The only reason I could think for her to return here was due to feelings of nostalgia. If she had them. I sighed. If only I knew why she had left the king and worked in the boarding house kitchen of Madam Fontaine, her evil stepmother, it would be much easier to find Ella.

Mikka’s clipped voice interrupted my thoughts. “We need to head back to Daydream after dark. It won’t run itself.”

“You do that,” Lorenzo said. “We’ll look in the other quarter.”

I turned to him. “What quarter?”

Lorenzo’s face was sober, and I knew I wouldn’t like whatever he said next.

“If the queen is still in the city but not in the market or the old town quarter, she’ll be in the Faustus quarter.”

Goosebumps exploded on my skin. After living in the Faustus quarter for eighteen years, I had vowed to never return there. It was on the southern edge of the city. In addition to being home to the orphanage, it housed other institutions filled with Arcadia’s unwanted citizens. There was the mental institution, screams echoing from its tall walls, a place for the elderly that smelled of piss, and a rundown, gray woman’s house that saw random male visitors after dark.

I hadn't been in Faustus for months, and I had never planned to return, but if there was a chance that the queen might be there, I had to go.

"Are you all right?" Lorenzo's gentle voice pulled me back to the present. "You don't have to—"

"I'm coming with you." I was done standing by, letting others do the hard things. I was done thinking of myself as weak or incapable. Yes, going into Faustus made my stomach cramp, my head spin, and my lungs constrict, but I could do it. I was stronger than my fear.

I waved goodbye to Tia and Mikka. Lorenzo's arms wrapped around me once more, and the ground disappeared as we teleported.

This time, the sensation in my stomach was much stronger. It no longer resembled swinging, but was more like tumbling down from the cathedral's bell tower. I didn't think that it was due to Lorenzo's teleporting technique, but rather, was due to my nervousness about returning to Faustus.

My feet slammed against the ground, the impact reverberating through my spine. My new surroundings came into focus. Gone were the tall buildings, white columns, and beautiful spires, replaced by houses with peeling paint, rusty door handles, and smudgy, broken windows.

I wrapped my arms around me, feeling cold despite the warm, summer night.

"Are you all right?" Lorenzo asked.

"I will be. It's just not easy to return here."

He nodded. "I wouldn't have brought you here unless I thought there was a high chance of the queen being here."

"I know. Do you think the stepmother and stepsisters

put her in the asylum?" I glanced at the tallest building two streets away from us. The mental institution was a dark column of four stories, the central point of the quarter.

"Only one way to find out." Lorenzo strode toward the asylum, and I followed him, each step heavy, my legs leaden.

"What was it like growing up in the orphanage?"

Lorenzo's question took me off guard. Nobody had ever asked me. Tia knew what it was like since she had grown up there as well. My ex, Victor, hadn't cared about my experiences, his mind made up that orphanages were the best place for orphans or children of disgraced or poor mothers who couldn't afford them. Besides him, I hadn't told anyone that I had spent my childhood at the orphanage, uninterested in their pity or disgust.

"It's probably what you would expect it to be," I said. "No luxuries, strict rules, best to keep your head down."

"That's the way you chose to survive." Lorenzo scrutinized me. "That's why it was so hard for you to stand up to Madam Fontaine."

I'd never thought about it like that, but I supposed it made sense. The orphanage had been my last resort. I had nowhere else to go unless I wanted to be on the streets. I kept the same mentality when I started working for Madam Fontaine. I had escaped the orphanage only to get myself under a new tyrant's thumb.

"You are very strong," Lorenzo continued. "I hope you know that."

I snorted. "Why, because I kept my head down and stayed out of fights? Tia was the strong one. It was because of her that the other girls didn't dare to mess with me."

“She kept the bullies away, but you protected her in your own way.”

I supposed he had a point. “Tia’s fiery temper got her into trouble. I made sure she cooled off before she said something she would regret and get us kicked out or fired. Because if Tia had to leave, I was going too. My life wasn’t always easy, but it doesn’t even come close to what you went through. I might’ve never known my parents or any other extended family, but at least I didn’t have to watch them get killed.”

Lorenzo’s shoulders stiffened, and I immediately regretted my words. What was wrong with me? Why had I brought up his past? Instead of becoming defensive like my ex would’ve, Lorenzo said quietly but with steel in his voice, “It was very hard to rebuild myself after the massacre. It makes it hard to let anyone in when I know that they, too, could be taken from me at any time.”

That was my opening. I turned around, cutting off his path. The moon illuminated his angular face that, despite its masculinity, had nothing harsh about it. “Is that why you didn’t kiss me before you left for your trip? Or is it because you have no interest in me?”

Lorenzo didn’t reply for a long moment. Then, he finally said, “I don’t think it’s wise to get all tangled up before we know what you are and what it means.”

Tears stung my eyes. “Does it really matter whether I’m a witch, a human, or something completely new? Do you really care more about what I am than who I am? I thought you were different. I thought you cared about me, and what’s in here”—“ I pumped my chest—“and here”—” I touched my temple. “But you don’t. You’re just like Victor.”

Lorenzo’s features hardened into stone. “Don’t. You.

Ever. Compare. Me. To. That. Monster. Especially, after what he almost did to you."

The memory of Victor on top of me, his pants unzipped, his leg spreading mine open flashed through me. If I hadn't used my voice, he would've raped me and taken my virginity, and he would've justified it by wrongly assuming that I had slept with Lorenzo and deciding I was a demon whore.

"I'm sorry. I was out of line," I whispered. "Who told you?"

"Mikka."

My neck tensed. Who gave Mikka permission to talk about my business? "She had no right."

"Would you have told me if she hadn't?" Fury sparked in Lorenzo's eyes.

"Just because you're my manager, doesn't mean I have to tell you everything that is going on in my private life."

A chuckle tinged with bitterness fell from Lorenzo's lips. "And that's exactly why I didn't kiss you, Halia. I don't care what you are, but I'm not willing to put myself out there when you haven't decided yet how you feel about me. You might be attracted to me, but you aren't willing to open up to me. There's no point in trying to have a relationship when you don't have trust."

"I trust you! I told you about the golden rings in my eyes. I told you that I don't know what I am. I told you about my voice and my dream to sing."

"I had to weasel all of that out of you, and even then, you stuck to fact. Just now, I asked you about the orphanage, and you answered in one sentence. Clearly, you don't trust me. If you don't trust me, I'm not interested in having a relationship with you."

I raised my chin. I had worked so hard on myself. I

had grown so much and overcome many fears, and yet I wasn't good enough. Well, he wasn't perfect, either. "What about you? Do you trust me fully? Do you really want me to believe that you came to Arcadia to open a bar because your gut told you to do so? Why don't you tell me where you got my colored contacts and the fairy dust from? What happened to hold you up on your trip that you almost missed my recording session?"

Lorenzo brought a finger to his lips, shushing me.

"Don't tell me to shut up," I hissed as he yanked me against a wall.

"We're not alone," he whispered in my ear.

As he said that, I turned my head to find a group of four women heading toward us, their features concealed by cloaks.

"I don't have a good feeling about this," one of them said. "I don't think we should be doing this."

"Be quiet, Abigail," another replied, the voice undeniably familiar. It was Acacia, the fae who knew about the strange golden rings in my eyes and who had helped the wicked stepsisters gain fake singing abilities. "We'll vote on it on Saturday. You can voice your concerns then."

"That's what the council meetings are for," a third fae said.

Abigail sighed, looking uneasy. "We're playing with fire."

Before I could hear her reply, Lorenzo's arms wrapped around me, and we vanished. I extricated myself from him as soon as we finished teleporting, a glance telling me we were almost at the mental institution. "Why did you do that? They were about to reveal the details of their secret meeting."

"We'll get the details some other way. If I hadn't

teleported, they would've sensed my demonic presence. They were getting too close to our hiding space."

"You can sense not only demons but also fae and vice versa?"

"It's not the same. With a demon or half-demon like Mikka, I can track them and know exactly where they are. I can't find fae at will. But if I'm within close range, like in a room, I'll sense it if a faerie is there. The same applies to open space like a street if the faerie is close enough. And yes, unfortunately, it works the other way around as well. I waited until the last second to teleport. If I had hesitated, Acacia and her friends would've known that I was there."

"You should've left me behind to overhear the rest of their conversation."

Lorenzo raised an eyebrow. "Are you saying you would've been able to maintain your cover if I disappeared suddenly, without any warning?"

I scowled. "I would've managed." Or freaked out.

"Well, even if you would've adjusted in time, I was afraid you would confront them directly."

I had no retort to that since I had confronted Acacia just days earlier about helping the stepsisters change their ugly voices into something beautiful. The decision had seemed right at the time, but now I wondered if it had been wise to reveal my cards. If I had gone to Lorenzo with my knowledge first, we could have watched Acacia without revealing our hand. Oh well, what was done was done. No point in beating myself up over it. At least confronting her had given me the confirmation that she was indeed helping the sisters and shown that she was willing to help whomever to do whatever for the right price.

I flipped from my conversation with Acacia to the

exchange I had just witnessed. "Do you think the fae have anything to do with Queen Ella's disappearance?"

Lorenzo considered this. "Perhaps indirectly."

A shudder seized me. If someone came to Acacia or her colleagues and asked them for an insecurity or low self-esteem potion, they could easily sell it. Acacia had siphoned negative emotions from me on countless occasions. Perhaps Ella's stepmother, Madam Fontaine, had bought a potion and slipped it to the queen, leading to her abandoning the king. "Could Madam control Queen Ella's emotions and behavior through potions? That would certainly explain why she was terrified all the time and chose to trade in the throne for the kitchen."

Lorenzo's forehead wrinkled. "A potion changes someone's emotions and behaviors only temporarily. Even with a very strong potion, Fontaine would have to administer it every day or so, and eventually, the queen would've developed a resistance. Fontaine might've gotten Queen Ella initially out of the castle by slipping her a draft, but the way the queen has been acting, refusing to even talk, tells me Fontaine must have something very serious on Queen Ella to literally silence her and make her go into hiding."

I shook my hand. "What could Madam have on Ella? She's the queen. She has countless guards, a loving husband, and a fairy godmother."

Lorenzo sighed. "Yes, in terms of brute-force and numbers, the queen is safe, but someone might still sneak into the castle and, for example, poison the king."

Madam must've threatened Queen Ella with something that was so horrendous that Ella saw no other choice but to abandon her husband and slave away once again under Madam's brutal hand. With Ella missing, the only one who could give us answers was the king. Too bad, he didn't want to see either Lorenzo or me. Something occurred to me then. "If you're able to teleport, can't you teleport into the castle?"

There was a hesitation on Lorenzo's face, which gave me all the answer I needed. "Then why didn't you do it after the guards turned you away?"

Anger flashed in Lorenzo's eyes. "Just because I'm a demon, doesn't mean I don't have morals."

"I'm not suggesting you teleport into the castle to steal gold. I'm asking you to teleport into the castle to tell the king that we know where his beloved wife is or at least used to be and have an idea of who is responsible for her disappearance."

"It's not that easy."

I crossed my arms.

Lorenzo sighed. "If I teleport into the castle, I'm broadcasting my abilities. Besides you and Tia, nobody outside the demon community knows what type of demon I am. If I do as you suggest, I risk all demons, or at least my kind, being banished from the kingdom due to safety concerns."

"But, you would be using your teleportation to help the king."

Lorenzo's face softened. "You and I know that, but all the king and his guards would see is an unknown demon invading the castle. It would be viewed as an act of aggression, and they would attack first, ask questions never."

The truthfulness of his words weighed heavily on me, exhausting me. "So, we do nothing?"

A ghost of a smile appeared on his lips, and he nodded toward the mental institution. "I'm sure we're going to find some juicy information in there."

“What about the fae?”

“We’ll deal with them later.”

Not I, but we. I smiled.

I turned toward the mental institution to see that the two guards at the gates were being replaced by a new set of guards. How many more were on the inside? “Where exactly are we going to teleport to?”

Lorenzo wrapped his arms around me in response. “Don’t worry. I have a plan.”

My surroundings vanished into a blur of colors only to rearrange themselves into a new view. The decrepit houses around me had been replaced by tiles, sinks, and mirrors. Lorenzo had teleported us into the females’ bathroom, which mercifully was empty of anyone who could scream bloody murder at the sight of us.

Gingerly, Lorenzo pushed open the door. When it became clear the corridor, too, was empty, we took a right and walked until we reached a door that read “Director’s Office.” We listened for noises coming from inside. There were none, so Lorenzo took my hand, and we teleported inside. The office was nothing impressive. A sad-looking desk and chair stood on one side of the room, a metal bookcase opposite it. Not a touch of warmth or personality. I swallowed, trying not to think about what type of person ran the facility and how he treated its patients when a cave was more inviting than his office.

Lorenzo searched the desk drawers. I went over the contents of the bookshelves, which were filled with biology and medicine titles, all the while listening for any sounds coming from the outside. Straining my ears hard for footsteps and voices, I imagined them several times only to realize there weren’t any.

After ten minutes, Lorenzo closed the drawers.

"Nothing."

"Are you sure?" I hadn't expected to find anything on the bookshelf, but I had hoped he would be more successful.

"There are only patient files, and none of them talk about the unrest or emotion and energy siphoning that is going on around Arcadia. There are a few letters, but none discuss the queen or recent events."

"Are you sure you checked everything?"

He nodded, "I speed read. The absence of any suspicious correspondence doesn't necessarily mean nothing fishy is going on."

"What are we going to do now?"

Lorenzo teleported us outside into a different part of the corridor where the lights were dimmer and the walls uneven. "Interview the inmates."

"You think they'll talk to us?"

He nodded. "Unlike the nurses and other staff members, most patients won't be here of free will. I bet they'd love the opportunity to spill the beans." We headed further down the corridor, past rooms that had small windows on the doors, allowing us to look inside. The first few patients we saw appeared to be sleeping.

Finally, we reached a door from which hushed whispers emanated.

"We should leave today," one of the inmates said. Her hair was cut unevenly, and her arms were muscular.

"No, we'll wait until tomorrow. They'll be busy with their meeting, and we can sneak out between five and six." The second girl sat on one of the cots cross-legged.

The third girl bit her lip. "Are you sure this is a good idea? Where are we going to go?" She was painfully thin, and when she moved, her long-sleeved shirt exposed red, angry scars on her wrists and arms.

The first one put her fists on her hips. "Anywhere. The streets might be dangerous, but they're better than staying here and dying. You do want to live, don't you?"

The skinny girl glanced away. The second girl wrapped her in a hug. "We'll be fine."

"We should talk to them," I said.

Lorenzo pulled me away from the room. "Not today. We'll only scare them. Tomorrow."

"What if they fail to escape, and we'll lose our chance?"

"They won't." He glanced back at the girls. "I'll send Mikka to ensure they'll get out."

My heart warmed. Even when thinking about the greater good—Arcadia's future, Lorenzo never forgot about the little people.

"Time to return to Daydream." Lorenzo's strong arms wrapped gently around me, and in that moment, I knew that to be with him, I would learn how to trust and show him all of me. For him, I would overcome my insecurities and become the best version of myself.

# 30TH JULY

My shift at the post office flew by. Only a week ago, receiving a stack of letters that needed to be delivered sent me into a tailspin. Now, I was confidently going from house to house, having developed a good route. I biked from house to house, no longer afraid that cycling would lead to a head injury. It wasn't just the path and the biking that my brain and body had memorized. I also knew what houses had a mailbox and which required me to throw the mail onto the doorstep to avoid vicious guard dogs.

Last week had been one steep learning curve. After quitting work at Madam's boarding house, I needed a job to keep me afloat while I worked on my singing career. Just like my previous job as a maid, working for the post office was physically exhausting, but in a better way. I didn't have to bend over all the time or scrub floors. Instead, I got to bike through Arcadia with its lively market smelling of spices and apples, past houses with fragrant rose gardens, and toward cottages that smelled of homemade broth and baked pastries. It was also nice not to have a boss who could appear at any moment and yell at me to release her frustration or admonish me for a perceived wrongdoing.

Mrs. Flannigan was so much nicer than Madam Fontaine. She was strict but fair. The only downside to no longer working at the boarding house was that unless I had letters to deliver, it was hard to know what was going on over there.

I had used the maids' entrance to sneak in several times to check up on Queen Ella, who went by Cinder. Unfortunately, the last time I went uninvited into the boarding house, I had been discovered by Thomas, a patrolman and the partner of my ex, Victor. Thomas had caught me trespassing when the property had been corded off after a suspicious death and told me to stay away. Since then, I hadn't dared to return, afraid that if Madam or her daughters saw me, they would call the police, and this time, Thomas wouldn't show me mercy. Thus, I couldn't snoop safely and see whether the Fontaines were involved in any illegal activity other than buying fake voices for the national singing competition.

As for Queen Ella, Lorenzo had reassured me that after teleporting into the kitchen at the boarding house and discovering she was gone, he had left a demonic device behind that would notify him if she returned. So far, she hadn't. But maybe today was the day.

I climbed up from the first level of Daydream where the bar and Lorenzo's office were to the second floor.

Upstairs, there were three bedrooms—Lorenzo's, Mikka's, and Tia's and mine.

"Come in," Lorenzo called after I knocked.

I entered his room, mesmerized by the rustic décor□wooden and brick walls and a slanted ceiling window. □Any news about the queen?□

He shook his head. "No, but I think it's for the best. It will allow us to fully focus on the mental institution."

"What do you think the patients know?"

"If they've been locked up for a while, they'll be able to inform us of any recent changes, rules, and staff turnover. Perhaps any new experiments going on or drugs administered."

"At least one of them seemed to think they'd die if they stayed. I wondered if their fears are connected to the women's house. A resident visited Acacia, reporting that she aged overnight."

Lorenzo nodded. "Life energy siphoning. It's a possibility, but if that's what the doctors are doing, they need help from magic wielders."

"Acacia siphons emotions. You think she's behind this as well?" She had acted surprised and innocent, but I no longer trusted anything she said or did. Not after I had caught her selling fake voices to the Fontaine sisters, uncaring that she was giving them an unfair advantage at the royal competition.

"Maybe Acacia is involved, maybe she isn't. It's too early to tell," Lorenzo said, and we both fell silent.

I wondered how many innocent citizens would have to suffer before we could uncover the head of the hydra and cut it off. After my conversation with Acacia and overhearing her discussion with the other fae, I was certain they were involved.

"We need to figure out when and where the fae are

meeting," I said. "I could go back to Acacia's."

"And do what, confront her?"

I clenched my hands. "I did that once."

"Which was one time too many." Lorenzo tilted his head, and his voice softened. "I'm not trying to be hard on you. But because of your confrontation, Acacia knows you're on to her."

"What if I pretend that I'm there to hide the golden rings in my eyes and sniff around while she works?"

Lorenzo shook his head. "I never liked the idea of her siphoning off your emotions. The further away from her we stay, the better."

He had a point. "But how else will we find out when the meeting is happening?"

A wicked smile curled Lorenzo's perfect lips. "Fae aren't only sellers of magic. They're also buyers. I anticipated that we might need to convince them to cooperate, so I brought something back from my journey."

"Was that the reason behind your delay in getting back?"

He nodded. "I'm sorry I cut it that close to your recording."

"Thank you." I smiled. "You showed up. That's what matters."

Lorenzo hesitated. "Now that we've cleared that up, we need to talk about the other question you asked yesterday."

I shook my head. "I was upset. I was wrong to question why you had come to Arcadia."

"No, you weren't. I didn't just come here to open a bar or because my gut told me to." He hesitated. "A demon with the ability to see the future told me I needed to go to Arcadia. That I was meant to help someone come into their own." He rubbed his chin. "At first, I thought it was Mikka. It's hard to be a half-demon, not completely human, but also not fully demon. It's even harder to be an ice demon when no one from your caste is there to teach you about your abilities." He sighed. "But now, I think I was meant to meet you. Our paths were meant to intersect."

I had to remember to breathe. What he had said was too much to take in. I needed time to process this. "What did you bring to negotiate with the fae?" I asked weakly.

Lorenzo nodded as if understanding that I needed a moment to get my bearings about his revelations. He pulled a small set of scales from his drawer that fit into the palm of my hand.

"I don't understand." The miniature thing was neither practical nor pretty enough to be considered art.

"You're holding balanced scales. They are infused with a demonic power that allows you to shift a decision or outcome in your favor. It can be used only once."

I wrinkled my forehead. "So if a faerie brought that into the meeting, she could manipulate the vote outcome?"

Lorenzo nodded. "I'll bet that Abigail, the faerie who was shut down by Acacia yesterday, would love to get her hands on these balanced scales. Obtaining them in exchange for telling me where and when the meeting will be held would be a bargain for her."

"What if she betrays you and tells the others about her deal with you?"

"She wouldn't expose herself like that. If she told on me, she'd have to admit that she accepted the balanced scales."

"What if she says you attacked her?"

Lorenzo chuckled. "She wouldn't. She wouldn't want the other fae to think that she was helpless and weak. She's not stupid enough to make herself prey. She'll accept the scales and keep quiet. The temptation will be too much for her to reject my offer."

"All right. That leaves the question of what we'll do with the information if you don't want me to go to the fae alone and you can't go with me because they will be able to sense your presence in a room."

Lorenzo's eyes flashed. "Teleportation isn't the only skill I have."

"What do you mean?"

"I can listen in on conversations without being present."

I felt my forehead furrow. "Come again?"

"Astral projection. My body can be in one place, while my mind is in another place. I can also project the image of my body into the second location if I choose to, making others think I'm there when I'm not. In this case, I won't project my image. I'll be there with my mind only, making it impossible for the fae to know I'm listening in on their conversation."

I blinked rapidly, trying to wrap my head around this information. "If you can do that, why didn't you use this skill to spy on the king?"

"Because everything has a price. I can't do astral projection for long periods of time. It's a time-bending, gravity-defying power. The universe can only tolerate it for so long. To stop demons like myself from misusing it, we're punished by a visit into hell if we astral project for too long."

I didn't like the sound of this. I couldn't lose Lorenzo. "We should look into another way."

“Why?” Lorenzo’s face sobered. “Do you not trust me?”

Trust. It all boiled down to trust. What had happened in the past to lead to this obsession? “I think you’re very capable, but I don’t want anything to happen to you.”

His Adam’s apple bobbed up and down at my admission, and the need to collapse into his arms overwhelmed me. To avoid making an idiot out of myself, I stood up and headed to the opposite side of the room, grabbed the windowsill, and stared out on the streets of Arcadia.

I didn’t hear him get up or walk over to me, but I knew he did because his fresh cut grass and lemon scent wrapped around me, and his hot breath caressed my nape. “You care about me.”

I inhaled deeply, gathering my courage. “I do. And it terrifies me.”

“Why?”

Such a simple question that didn’t have a simple answer. I turned around slowly.

“Is it because I’m a demon?” Lorenzo studied me intently as if waiting for my face to betray my next words.

I shook my head. I had gotten over him being an “other” a long time ago. I guess it had happened somewhere in between learning how much magic surrounded me and having to admit that I had magic too and that it was a gift I had to use to help Arcadia and it’s citizens.

“Caring about you terrifies me,”—I wrung my hands— “because it means I would be devastated if something happened to you, or if we were separated.” *Or if you got bored with me,* I added silently, my courage not extending far enough to express this particular concern.

Lorenzo reached out and brushed away a loose strand of my hair. "As agitating as fear is, we should be grateful for it. It tells us that we care. It makes us feel alive. It makes us fight for what we want."

I pushed away the emotions stirring within me and asked in a whisper, "What about you? Aren't you afraid that it won't work out? Are you that confident and carefree?"

He chuckled. "I don't think about what can go wrong. Not because I'm conceited or overly optimistic. I don't think about it not going wrong because this"—he gestured between us—"is already more than I ever hoped for."

"How so?"

He chuckled again, and annoyance swelled up within me. Was everything I did and said amusing to him?

"Sometimes I forget how different human culture is from ours," Lorenzo began. "In the human world, only marriages of nobility are arranged. Even in those arranged marriages, the parties often seek out someone they fancy for pleasurable pastimes."

Heat warmed my cheeks at what he was implying. "It's not the same for demons?"

He shook his head. "Many of my kind create alliances. Not because it is forced upon us, but because it's the best thing to do if we want to survive. We're always worried about power and strength. And for those of us who can procreate, we're always worried about creating the most powerful offspring." He paused, then added, "So you see, it's not just marriage but even bodily pleasures that have a purpose. And those that can't procreate stick to one-time affairs, afraid to be stabbed in the back if they let anyone too close."

That sounded dreadful. What a cruel world! "But you don't want an alliance?"

Ruefulness entered Lorenzo's face. "I lost my whole family. And while I would do anything to bring them back, there's a freedom that comes with them being gone. I'm not bound by my customs. I don't have to worry about family honor or protecting them. In a sad way, their deaths freed me to live the life I desire."

What a horrible, bittersweet, silver lining. And yet, I understood. Because I too felt that way. Sure, Madam and Victor had tried to make me self-conscious and stop me from singing, but the pressure I experienced from them wasn't comparable to being born into a family that expected me to marry well and stay under the radar like a good girl. As orphans, Lorenzo and I were free to pursue our passions without our heart's desires clashing with the respect and love we held for our families.

I had always thought that if I had the choice to give up the gift of my voice in exchange for a family, I would, but now, I wasn't so sure. My conscience told me that I was an awful person for thinking that my art and freedom was worth more than a family, but an older and wiser part within me told me that I didn't need to beat myself up. I was exactly where I was meant to be. I didn't need to censor my thoughts or feelings.

For whatever reason, only known to the universe, I was meant to go through this life as an orphan with the ability to influence others with my voice, and the desire to be a performer.

Self-flagellation wouldn't do anyone good. Self-flagellation would only distract me from what I had to do, namely, find Queen Ella and save Arcadia.

Outside, the bells on the market square rang, their

crescendo tearing me from my thoughts. I jerked into action and darted toward the door, Lorenzo on my heels. Neither of us spoke as we rushed down the staircase and then out toward the square where a crowd was already gathering.

Out of breath, I reached the king's courier, praying he hadn't come with dire news.

"I have an announcement to make regarding the royal singing competition."

I exhaled with relief. This wasn't about Arcadia or the royal family, just the competition.

"As you might remember, in previous years, fifty competitors were selected from the initial auditions. This year, however, in light of recent events, only twenty-five will be selected."

Gasps erupted around me, and my heart plummeted. It would have been hard enough to get into the top fifty, but getting into the top twenty-five? I'd never get the chance to talk to the king and tell him about Queen Ella posing as a maid and working for Madam Fontaine.

"The twenty-five selected competitors will be interviewed publicly to determine who can best represent Arcadia. The top twelve will then progress into the next round of singing."

My head spun. Even if I somehow was in the top twenty-five, I would never win a popularity contest.

"The twenty-five candidates announced today must report here tomorrow at noon and be prepared to answer a few questions regarding why they entered the competition and should represent Arcadia. The twelve winners of that round will performy a short song chosen by the king's advisors. Dates and details are to come."

I wanted to throw up and hide in my bed. Lorenzo stepped in front of me. "You'll be fine." He squeezed my hand.

"We don't even know if I made it into the top twenty-five."

"You did," he said in his annoyingly confident manner.

"These are the twenty-five finalists," the courier said, and every muscle in my body stiffened. He rattled off one name after another, most of which I wasn't familiar with. However, there were two names, two spots that I knew had been taken up illicitly. Bernadette and Georgette Fontaine, Madam's daughters. If they made it to the next round and I didn't, I would never forgive Acacia for aiding them in their deceit.

"And the final spot goes to—" The announcer paused dramatically, and my chest constricted. I needed this. I needed this so badly. This was my only chance to talk to the king.

"Halia Bright."

My knees buckled as I heard my name, and Lorenzo pulled me into a hug.

"I knew you'd make it."

I laughed, but my joy wavered as a gaze drilled into me from across the square. Victor was staring me down, his face marred with pure disgust. He walked toward us, and at first, I was afraid he would make a scene, but then he stopped in front of Georgette and Bernadette, who were there with their mother. He rearranged his face into a smile, congratulating them.

It felt as if he had slapped me across the face. I knew he hated me, but to go out of his way to congratulate the woman who had made my life hell when I had worked for her was despicable. Victor nodded at the sisters, clearly believing the credo, "my enemy's enemies are my friends." Would he still think so if he knew the sisters had bought their voices with fae magic?

Victor hated everything that wasn't human or what he deemed natural, but he also hated me and clearly wanted to spite me. Even if I submitted an anonymous tip, revealing what the sisters had done, he might choose to put a blind eye to it since he knew I didn't get on with the Fontaine's. However, there was another way to expose the sisters without getting Victor involved. Thomas, Victor's partner, was even-tempered and reasonable. He might not take my word for it that the Fontane sisters were using illegal means to win the competition, but I was certain he would thoroughly investigate my claim. Even if he didn't find anything immediately, he would be suspicious of them and ready to catch them red-handed when they pulled another trick.

I stepped away from Lorenzo. "I need to go and talk to someone."

He raised an eyebrow in question.

"I won't let the sisters cheat their way into victory like they tried to cheat their way into the king's arms eighteen years ago."

Before Lorenzo could hold me back, I pushed through the crowd toward Thomas, needing to catch him before he left or Victor joined him. If I had told Lorenzo about my plan, he would've probably tried to talk me out of it, saying it was a waste of time. I disagreed. Yes, Thomas was a human patrolman and didn't have the power or insight magic wielders possess, but he made up for his lack of magical abilities with dedication and work ethic. If any of the patrolmen of Arcadia could help me, it was him.

I was a few feet away from Thomas when he noticed me. His eyebrows drew together, telling me he wasn't too happy to see me.

"You're not planning to pull another stunt, are you?" he said in greeting.

I pressed my lips together. I wanted to scream that if not for me, he and Victor would have condemned a young boy to prison time for stealing food to support him and his mother but held my tongue, knowing better than to voice my opinion.

"What is it, Halia?" Thomas asked a note of impatience in his voice.

How I wished I had more time to get him into a better mood. However, since Victor would eventually run out of things to say to the Fontaine's, I had only minutes to make my claim. So I launched directly into the meat of the story.

"You need to keep a close eye on the Fontaine sisters."

Thomas crossed his arms. "Why is that?"

"Because they can't sing. They're using fae magic to cheat their way through the contest."

"And you know this how?"

Darn it. I hadn't expected him to ask that.

If I told him I had seen them coming from Acacia's, his next question would be why I had been hanging around Acacia's house. I could claim it was a coincidence, but it wouldn't be hard for him to prove otherwise and discover that I had visited the fae regularly. Even if she didn't betray my secret, he would know that I was hiding something.

Thus, all I said was, "It's something I heard at the market. Someone said the sisters went to a faerie in Arcadia to enhance their voices."

"So it's a rumor then, nothing more."

I groaned inwardly. If I told him more, I would look

suspicious, but if I didn't add anything to my statement, I would come across as unreliable. There was a third course of action. I glanced past Thomas to find Victor striding toward us. If I was going to do this, I had to be quick.

I opened my mouth and hit a G note. *"Please trust me on this. The sisters are hiding something. Find out their plans. Keep our kingdom safe."*

At first, Thomas had looked like he was about to protest, but as I continued with my singing, his face softened, and by the end, he nodded.

"What's going on? Is she bothering you?" Victor interrupted, and I was glad that the crowd has prevented him from hearing me sing.

"Just saying hello to an old friend," I said, then slipped away before Victor could accuse me of anything else. However, his parting words dripping with hate still reached me.

"I'm on to you, Halia. You'll pay dearly for your crimes. That I promise you."

A shiver ran through me, chilling me to the bone. Because when Victor set his sights on something, he succeeded.

# 31ST JULY

I woke up to Lorenzo shaking me gently. "Mikka's back. She brought the girls."

I opened my heavy lids, trying to make sense of what he said. The girls, right, he must be referring to the mental institution patients who had planned their escape. "I'll be down in a moment," I said, noticing that Lorenzo's silver hair was unkempt for once. Tenderness swelled in my chest, and I imagined how silky his hair would feel if I ran my hands through it. But there was no time for flirtation. We had to interview the mental institution patients.

Lorenzo closed the door gently behind him, and I jumped out of bed and threw on my clothes. It was still dark outside, and I had two hours before I had to report for my shift at the post office.

As I walked down the stairs toward the bar, three unhappy voices reached me.

"You can't hold us here against our will!" one said.

"What are you playing at? Pretending to help us only to capture us again."

"We're not planning to hold you here," came Mikka's response. "We simply have a few questions to ask you. Don't you think you owe us a bit of gratitude after we rescued you?"

"We would have been fine without you!" The brunette crossed her muscular arms, and I recognized her as the ringleader. She was the one behind the escape plan.

"Hello, girls," Lorenzo greeted them with a smile.

The smallest girl, who had angry cuts running up her arms took a step back while the other two girls scowled.

"Are you behind this?" the ringleader asked.

"If you're asking if I sent my friend to help you escape the mental institution, then, yes, I did," he replied coolly.

"And we appreciated that very much." The smallest girl bit her lip. "But we really must be on our way. We can't risk the guards catching up with us."

Lorenzo nodded. "You shall be on your way soon. We just have a few questions about the mental institution."

The three girls exchanged uneasy glances.

"You see," I began, "a lot of strange things have been happening in Arcadia lately, and we believe that the mental institution is involved." When that didn't produce a reply, I continued, "People have been getting sick, aging overnight, disappearing even. A plague has befallen our city. We're trying to figure out where it's coming from so that we can help our kingdom."

The ringleader snorted. "Isn't that the king's

responsibility?"

"I believe it is every citizen's responsibility to take care of their kingdom," I replied with steel in my voice.

The ringleader shifted from foot to foot, showing the first signs of her bravado failing. "Fine, shoot. What do you want to know?" She plopped down onto a bar chair.

"Have you noticed any changes at the mental institution in the last few months? Any increases, new things going on in the last few weeks?"

"Obviously, that's why we left," the middle girl said, pacing the room. "We were afraid that we were on the chopping block."

The ringleader threw her a glare, and she stopped talking.

"Please," I said, "We're not interested in why you left, and we're not judging you for why you were there in the first place. We just want to understand what is going on in Arcadia."

The ringleader pursed her lips. "We weren't put there because something is wrong with us, but because our parents couldn't handle us. The whole system is messed up, not us."

The middle girl slipped behind the bar. "I'll need to have a drink to get through this conversation."

"I don't think you're of age," Mikka said, but the middle girl ignored her, knowing this was not the battle we would pick, and poured herself a beer.

"We were locked up because our parents are crazy, not us," she said. Despite her harsh words, her hand trembled, betraying her feelings.

I bit my lip. I had always wanted to have a family. The few children who got to leave the orphanage to join a family had been considered the lucky ones, but now I wondered if there were families out there that were worse than the orphanage. True, the orphanage had employed extreme discipline, and there wasn't much affection or understanding, but none of us were singled out and shown an unusual amount of cruelty. We were all treated equally badly. However, if one grew up in a troubled family, I could easily imagine that the parents would take out their frustration on the one or two children underneath their rooftop.

I glanced at Tia, whose face was contorted. We were lucky to have had each other. She had stood up to the bullies and made sure with her brash behavior that they left us alone, while I, the obedient and respectful one, got us on the good side of the sisters running the orphanage.

"It started a few weeks ago," the middle girl said, tearing me out of my thoughts. She pushed a full beer toward the ringleader and took a large gulp of her own beer before inclining her head toward the shy girl, who shook her head no in response to the unspoken question..

"Inmates started disappearing without reappearing." The middle girl took another gulp as if the beer was water, and I itched to find some food for them but knew it was best to keep her talking and feed her later. "At first, we thought it was a punishment, something to scare them and to scare us. Isolate them and make us think that if we misbehave, we could be taken too."

"They never returned," the ringleader said. "We never saw them again, and when we asked what happened, we were told they were taken to a different facility. The staff wouldn't answer any other questions."

"More disappeared, almost on a daily basis," the shy girl added, staring at her fingers as if they held all the answers. "And none ever returned to the facility. There were also no new inmates."

How very careless and obvious. Wasn't the head of the facility worried that the king's patrolmen would ask questions? I made a mental note to tip off Thomas about these happenings.

"Did you see where they were taken?" Lorenzo asked. "What kind of carriage they were transported in?"

The girls shook their heads in unison.

"Our window didn't look out onto the street." The shy girl rubbed the angry red marks running up her arms.

"All we saw from our prison cell was the backyard," the ringleader said. "They locked us up inside our rooms. We were allowed to roam the halls only at certain times. Even then, we were monitored."

The middle girl jumped in. "If we asked too many questions, we were sent back to our rooms. And if we talked too long to somebody, the nurses crept toward us. They didn't want us to have any interaction with other inmates."

"They were hiding something." I bit my lip. If only we knew what.

The middle girl wiped the beer foam from her mouth with the back of her hand. "Definitely."

"We told you all we know. Can we go now?" The ringleader got up from her bar stool.

Lorenzo stepped toward her, and she balled her fists, ready to lash out.

"Please," he said, "if you can think of anything else, it would be really helpful. We're trying to help Arcadia, trying to help others in a similar position to yours."

I stepped closer, as well. "People are disappearing around the city. Widows are aging overnight by twenty years. Something very fishy is going on."

The ringleader lifted her chin defiantly. "This all sounds like a demon operation to me. How do we know that you're not in on the scheme?"

The shy girl gasped and tried to cover the sound with her hand, but the ringleader just rolled her eyes. "No need to pretend that we don't know they are demons. At least those two." She glanced between Lorenzo and Mikka. "I don't quite understand how you two fit in." She stared Tia and me down.

"That's none of your business," Tia said, but I held up my hand. Getting hotheaded wouldn't get us anywhere.

"I agree with you that magic wielders are behind this," I said. Hoping Lorenzo wouldn't mind that I revealed so much, I added. "Fae can siphon emotions. It's a big business for them. They siphon off emotions, bottle them up, and sell them. It's an ability similar to siphoning off life energy, which makes us guess they're somehow involved. However, before we confront them, we need to know more."

"Why do you care so much?"

I smiled at the ringleader. "Because Arcadia is my home and my family. I grew up in an orphanage. The city is all I have. I want to see it prosper. I can't let it wither away."

The shy girl touched the ring leader's arm, and the middle girl joined her two friends. An unspoken communication ensued between the three of them, and then the ringleader nodded. "There's one thing we know that might help you."

The room fell so silent once could've heard the splash of a water droplet.

The ringleader hesitated, and I was afraid she was playing games with us, but then she said, "The head of the mental institution said to a doctor that everything needs to be ready by the second week of August for "him." He didn't give a name, but it was clear that the leader is male."

I mulled this over. We had a timeline. Less than two weeks and the head of the chaos that was unfolding of Arcadia was male.

"Did the doctors say anything to suggest whether their client or boss was a human or immortal?" Lorenzo asked the question that was on my mind.

The ringleader shook her head, then glanced between her two friends.

The shy girl pulled on her sleeve. "I'm sorry, but that's all we overheard before a nurse escorted us back to our room."

The middle girl nodded and poured herself another beer, ignoring Mikka's and Tia's scowls.

"Thank you," Lorenzo said. "I'll get you a carriage."

The ringleader's forehead furrowed. "Where to?"

"Saxen. You should be safe there. I doubt anyone there will recognize you."

I squeezed his hand, grateful for his kindness to help the girls get away. I doubted the mental institution staff would search Arcadia for a few inmates, but one could never be too careful. With Saxen only a few hours away, the girls could return when Arcadia quieted down.

We said our goodbyes, and I watched as the carriage pulled away. When it was out of sight, I turned to Lorenzo, "What now?"

"I'll talk to the fae, Abigail. Convince her to tell me the place and time of their council meeting in exchange for the balanced scales."

Even though I believed Abigail would betray her kind to get the balanced scales so that she could influence the outcome of the meeting in her favor, I didn't think

Lorenzo should be the one to meet with her.

"She might betray us later. She might let it slip that a demon approached her, asking about the meeting. I don't think that's wise. Let me go."

He shook his head. "You can't. We can't let them know that you are on to them."

"You're both right," Tia said before I could protest. "I'll go."

"No!" I shook my head, but she just smiled.

"I'm the only human. If I wear a hat, I'll conceal my most memorable feature, and the fae won't have any idea who sent me." She pulled her blue hair out of her face.

"She's right," Mikka said. "But she'll need backup in case things go wrong."

Lorenzo nodded. "We'll go, you stay at the bar. You've already created a diversion at the mental institution."

Mikka gave a wicked smile. "Those morons had no idea what hit them when my icicles took them out. And by the time they awoke, the weapon had melted."

A cold seized me at her calculated words. The barely five-foot demon, a predator through and through.

A half an hour later, Tia strolled ten feet ahead of Lorenzo and me toward the market. The sun was just rising on the horizon, bathing Arcadia in a gentle light.

"Thank you for letting me come along," I said.

Lorenzo tilted his head. "Why wouldn't I?"

I shrugged. "I thought you'd see me as a liability. I'm glad you treat me as an equal even if I don't have your abilities."

Lorenzo gave me a long look. "We complement each other." His attention wandered straight ahead toward the market that Tia had almost reached. "She's here."

Even though the slender woman's features were

hidden by a cloak, there was no doubt she was a faerie given the ethereal grace she moved with.

As Lorenzo and I inched toward an alcove, I prayed Tia's exchange would run smoothly.

The faerie didn't even turn around as Tia called her. Thus, my friend touched the faerie's shoulder to get her attention. I groaned, knowing from experience that fae didn't like to be touched, especially by humans.

As I had expected, Abigail wasn't too happy. She whipped around, her beautiful face marred by annoyance.

Thankfully, Tia didn't show her feisty side. Her lips moved slowly, and she tilted her head slightly, making her look more agreeable.

After what I presumed was Tia explaining why she was here, Abigail glanced both ways, probably to check that nobody was watching them.

With bated breath, I stood ramrod straight, praying the faerie wouldn't spot us in the alcove and resisting the urge to make any sudden movements that would alert her fae senses. Next to me, Lorenzo stood just as still.

Finally, Abigail turned back to Tia and asked something. The two exchanged a few words, and then, Tia pulled out the velvet box that held the balanced scales.

Longing shone on Abigail's face, and she reached out a hand, but then snatched it back as if she had been burned. Her lips moved rapidly before she left.

I wanted to scream, run over to her, but I couldn't. Tia went after Abigail, but I knew she would fail to convince the fae on her own. My friend needed help. I opened my mouth.

*"Accept the balanced scales. You know you want*

*them. Accept the balanced scales. You know you want them."* I sang loud enough for Abigail to hear me, yet quiet enough so that the notes were in the background, influencing her, but not drawing her attention to our hiding spot.

*"Accept the scales. You need them. Accept the scales. They are the solution."*

Lorenzo smiled encouragingly, clearly approving of my strategy.

Tia's hand hovered over Abigail's back when the fae pivoted around. Tia dropped her hand to her side, her eyes wide at the sudden change in the faerie's demeanor. Abigail said a few things, and Tia nodded rapidly. Then she held out the velvet box once again. Abigail practically snatched it, opened it, and gazed inside.

Satisfied that Tia wasn't cheating her, Abigail said a few things to my friend before disappearing into the crowd.

As agreed earlier, Tia made her way back to the bar. Lorenzo and I watched her leave and monitored the market to ensure no one followed her. When it became clear that her exchange with Abigail hadn't attracted anyone's curious eyes, we, too, returned to the bar.

I had to force myself not to run but walk normally, my heart pounding with excitement.

Not a second after the heavy front door of Daydream fell shut behind us, I hurried to Tia. "What did she tell you?"

Tia grinned like a cat. "Nice job with the singing."

That brought me to a stop. "If you heard it, does it mean Abigail was aware of it as well?"

"No," Lorenzo said. "The individuals you focus your gift on don't know that you're influencing them. Tia was only able to discern your involvement because she's aware of your gift and knew you were nearby."

My shoulders sagged with relief. Tia said, "According to Abigail, the meeting is tomorrow at six in the evening. As for the location..." Tia hesitated, and my heart sunk in anticipation that Abigail hadn't given a concrete destination. Tia glanced at Lorenzo. "It's in the forest. At the second tallest oak, there's a cave. Abigail said that there are no directions, and whoever I was getting the information for should be able to find it."

Lorenzo's face was set with determination. "I know where it is."

Given the lack of relief in his voice, I asked, "But?"

"But, it's a magical place, where time flows differently, meaning my astral projection time will be halved."

I swallowed hard. "So we'll need to be very precise with when we do it to ensure we hear the most important part of the conversation."

Mikka stopped drying the glasses behind the bar and joined us. "That's almost impossible and relies too much on luck. Once Lorenzo astral projects, you'll have to use your voice to influence the direction of their conversation."

I blinked. "How? Won't they notice my presence?"

She shook her head. "It will be like you did at the market. You'll have to be far enough away to not hear them speak, yet close enough that your singing reaches them on a subconscious level."

Lorenzo shook his head. "It's different from the market situation. Halia has never attempted to manipulate a group of fae. If her gift isn't strong enough, our cover will be blown."

"But if she doesn't try," Mikka persisted, "the chances of you getting the information are five to ten percent, maximum."

As scared as I was to fail, I had to agree with her on that. "Please," I said, "let me try."

Lorenzo's face didn't budge, so I interlaced my fingers with his, not caring about displaying this much affection in front of Mikka and Tia, even though I hadn't had the chance to confess my feelings for Lorenzo to my friend yet.

"You can trust me," I said. "Please, let me try this. I want to."

"It's not just that your powers might not be developed enough for that." Lorenzo sighed. "There's another problem." He stared above my head, refusing to meet my gaze, so I glanced toward Mikka, searching her face for an answer.

"Astral projection is dangerous." She tugged on her white hair, a nervous gesture I wasn't used to from her. "Anyone can assist with it, but it's much more likely that the demon will return into his body unharmed if he's tethered to this world properly. You would be a much better tether than I."

My stomach cramped. Lorenzo's mind could be harmed if I failed to guide it back into his body successfully after the astral projection.

"Then I'll stay with you," I said. "I take back what I suggested before."

Lorenzo shook his head. "No, you and Mikka are right. We need you to use your voice magic. Without it, we won't get the information we need."

"I'm not leaving you alone!"

Lorenzo's violet-green eyes burned into me. "You won't. You'll do both. It's tricky but possible."

# 1ST AUGUST

I yawned as I pushed the last letter into the mailbox. After working for six hours and barely getting any sleep last night, I was ready for my post office shift to be over.

After deciding that I would use my voice to hurry along the fae meeting today to make Lorenzo's astral projection a success, I had practiced my influence singing on Mikka and Lorenzo all of last evening. Exhausted, I had tumbled into bed after midnight, but my wired mind kept me up, twisting and turning throughout the night.

My tiredness evaporated as I dropped off the bike at the post office and realized I had less than an hour until my royal singing competition interview. I'd been given only one shift because of the interview which helped me greatly

I hurried home, grateful that I could relax while Mikka and Tia worked on my hair and makeup and decided what I should wear. As much as I loved to perform in front of a crowd and write songs, I hated figuring out how to make myself presentable.

If it was up to me, I would've left my hair unbound or put it in a simple braid. Not big on makeup, I only bothered with it when I went out in the evening. As for my clothes, I liked them lightweight and non-restrictive, especially in the summer.

Thankfully, the girls took my preferences into account. As Tia and Mikka worked on my hair and face, I closed my eyes trusting their judgment completely after they had done such a great job last time.

I must've dozed off because Tia shook me gently back into awareness. "All done, sleepyhead. Now you just need to put this on." She handed me a white dress embellished with gold thread. It was tight at the top and flared out from its high waist. I put it on, liking how the weightless fabric flowed around my body, but unsure about the message my outfit sent. "It kind of looks bridal," I said. "Very innocent. I don't want the judges to think that I'm an easy target and attack me with questions."

Tia shook her head. "Nonsense. If it impacts their questions at all, I'm sure they'll give you easier ones."

There was a knock at the door, and Mikka called, "Come in."

Lorenzo's face brightened as he took me in, and I knew that Tia and Mikka had worked their magic.

"Great choice," he said, his gaze caressing my curves.

I wanted nothing more than to press my lips against

his, but couldn't after what had happened last time, and also because Tia and Mikka were still in the room. Instead, I distracted myself by throwing a quick glance in the mirror.

The makeup was light, mostly consisting of a bronzer that gave my skin a healthy sun-kissed appearance. My hair was braided sideways, a few loose strands pulled out. It all came together, and the dress no longer made me feel like I was a bride.

"Ready?" Lorenzo held out his elbow, and I slipped my arm around his.

As we headed down the stairs, my nerves kicked in.

"What if I don't have an answer to the questions of the judges?"

Lorenzo gave me a reassuring smile. "You'll be fine. You're good at thinking on your feet. Plus, I don't think they'll ask you any difficult questions. They probably just want to get to know the candidates and give the audience a feel for the different personas."

I bit my lip. Would they attach the poor orphan girl persona to me? Not wanting to think about that possibility, I asked, "What if I just blank?"

Lorenzo brushed his fingers against my shoulder. "You'll be fine. If you blank, make a joke, say you weren't prepared for the question, and then talk about your music. When in doubt, bring the attention back to your music. Maybe even start singing."

I pulled on the strap of my dress. "I don't want to do anything that would influence my odds of winning unfairly."

"You won't," Lorenzo replied softly, his lips inches from my ear. "But it's all right to set your intention on progressing further. Not only have you got the talent, but we need you to get far enough in the competition to talk to the king. With his and our knowledge combined, we can piece together what happened to Queen Ella and bring her back."

I sighed. There were so many ifs, so much that could go wrong. Even if I got to talk to the king, there was no guarantee he would believe me or know something helpful.

"If you feel guilty, remember that your competitors are using illegal magic for selfish reasons," Lorenzo added.

"But I don't want to become like the Fontaine sisters. I don't want my power to corrupt me."

"It won't," Lorenzo said. "Like I told you before, you have light magic, which makes it impossible for you to use your magic for ill purposes."

"Completely impossible?"

He hesitated. "If light magic wielders want to go dark, they can by performing a blood sacrifice. Then they can use their magic for nefarious purposes."

I shuddered. The world was filled with wonders and horrors.

We reached the market square much too soon. In its center, a stage had been erected, and around it, half of Arcadia stood expectantly, ready to judge us, the twenty-five contestants. Only weeks earlier, I would've found it unfathomable to perform in front of such a big audience, whereas now, the idea gave me a pleasant adrenaline kick. However, the speaking part worried me. What if I stuttered? What if they didn't like me?

Lorenzo brushed his shoulder against mine. "You'll be fine."

I nodded weakly and studied the performers, waiting next to the stage. Some of them had gone all out for hair and makeup, while others had chosen a more understated look.

"Wish me luck," I mumbled, not looking at Lorenzo. If I did, it would make it only harder to walk off on my own. But Lorenzo didn't let me go. He caught my hand, twirled me, and pressed a peck against my lips. "You'll be fine," he repeated. "You are Halia Bright."

I didn't say anything, too breathless. As I headed toward the other contestants, I wondered what the kiss meant. Was Lorenzo simply trying to distract me from my nerves? If so, it had certainly worked, but I hoped it was more than that. I hoped Lorenzo felt the same way about me, that he too had trouble resisting me. It was something to ponder another time.

Having learned my lesson from last time, I didn't try to strike up any conversations with the other competitors but stood quietly until the last few performers trickled in and the king's announcer, the competition host, Mr. Goodwin, and his assistant, Henry, ascended the staircase up onto the stage. The judges, three middle-aged men, whom I assumed to be part of the king's court, were already seated in wide chairs in front of the stage, their scoring cards laid out in front of them.

"Citizens of Arcadia," the king's announcer began and launched into a speech of how important the annual royal singing competition was, how anyone could win and that he wished all the participants best luck.

At least that was the gist of it. I could barely focus as I went over potential questions that I might be asked and tried to come up with the best answers.

I had expected to receive a number, but instead, our names were pulled randomly from a hat by Mr. Goodwin. His skinny assistant, Henry, held the hat and practically bounced around with excitement, while the competition host wore a more somber expression.

The king's announcer took a step back, and Mr. Goodwin pulled out the first name. "Jake Terr," he called, and I exhaled with relief, preferring to hear a few sample answers before it was my turn.

A man in his late twenties, wearing leather from head to toe, swaggered onto the stage. The crowd erupted into whispers, a reminder that our answers wouldn't be just evaluated by the king's representatives and the competition host, but also by Arcadia. Without the popularity vote, it would be hard to proceed to the end since the national competition was largely put on for the citizens of Arcadia, giving them a sense that anyone could become a celebrity and live the high life if only one worked hard enough and had talent.

"Jake Terr, is a twenty-eight-year-old builder, who has been calling Arcadia home for the last twenty years," Henry said joyfully.

"Jake, what prompted you to sign up for the royal singing competition?" Mr. Goodwin asked in a friendly voice.

"I thought it would be a fun thing to do, and the prize money sounded really good."

Jake's response drew boos from the crowd, who appeared unimpressed by his monetary motivations.

The competition host scrunched up his nose as if he smelled something bad. "Can you give us a taste of your talent?"

"Sure." Jake launched into a rock song, which garnered some applause but didn't manage to turn around the crowd completely.

Next up, was an opera singer I remembered from last time. The competition host seemed fonder of her and invited her to sing. Her aria was beautiful and showed off her vocal range, but the public seemed unengaged, many falling into side conversations or wearing a vacant expression on their faces.

Sensing the crowd's mood, Mr. Goodwin asked, "How do you plan to modernize your repertoire and approach a song that is less classical?"

The opera singer opened and closed her mouth several times, clearly not expecting that question. Finally, she replied, "If I can sing opera, I can sing anything contemporary. It's not really art. Any child can mimic modern songs."

It was the wrong answer, earning her head shakes and eye rolls.

As I watched the other contestants get up on the stage one by one, it became clear that the ones who did well with the crowd were cookie-cutter performers. They looked impeccable, answered diplomatically, adding a dash of humor or personality to stand out. Most of them were well-experienced performers and came from artistic families, adding to my insecurity.

Another thing that stood out was that they were all humans. While there had been demons and fae at the recording session, none had made it into the top twenty-five. Whether they had been lacking in talent or had been carefully weeded out, I wasn't sure, but I wouldn't have been too surprised if the judges had deliberately not let them progress to avoid the wrath of Arcadia's citizens.

My nerves kicked back in as the performers around me dwindled. We were down to eight, and the Fontaine sisters, who had been standing far away from me at the beginning, inched toward me until they were next to me. I wanted to switch positions but knew that would only draw negative attention to me. The last thing I needed was for a newspaper to paint me as a diva.

"What are you going to say if they ask you about your previous job?" Bernadette taunted.

"I'm sure Arcadia will vote for a maid—not." Georgette smiled viciously.

I inhaled deeply and stared ahead, pretending I hadn't heard them.

"Halia Bright," Mr. Goodwin announced, and I kept my back straight as I put one foot in front of the other, careful not to trip over my floor-length dress.

"Halia Bright, you're a relative newcomer. What can you tell us about yourself?" Mr. Goodwin stared at me, expectantly.

I paused, having anticipated a more concrete question. What could I tell him? I could hardly mention that I was planning to spy on a fae council meeting later tonight or that I thought my previous employer had been involved in Queen Ella's disappearance. I doubted I could mention that I was interested in a demon or that my best friend was in a same-sex relationship with a half-demon.

"Isn't there anything you want to tell us about yourself?" Mr. Goodwin prompted, his expression strained.

I glanced toward where I knew Lorenzo was standing, seeking him out for support. He nodded encouragingly, and I remembered what he had said earlier. When in doubt, always get back to the singing.

"I like to sing. I've always loved to sing. Recently, my best friend encouraged me to step it up and do it professionally. Because of her, I was able to open for the Dark Quartet at Daydream."

The crowd applauded, and my shoulders dropped half an inch.

"I also love Arcadia. Arcadia is my home, and it

would be an honor to represent our kingdom for a year and perform in front of our king. I think we have the best ruler anyone could ask for, and I hope that his wife, Queen Ella, will be found soon."

Mr. Goodwin tensed at my answer. Henry's chin nearly hit the ground, and the king's announcer looked like he wanted to gag me, but the crowd went wild, several people screaming, "Bring Queen Ella back."

Before Mr. Goodwin could redirect the attention toward my personal life, I said, "I would like to sing a sample from a song I have written for Arcadia."

The crowd cheered harder, and I launched into the song:

*Arcadia, you are joy, happiness, and love.*

*Arcadia, your market makes anyone feel welcome, overflowing with the most exotic spices and sweetest treats.*

*Arcadia, your street dancers and acrobats can bring a smile to anyone's face.*

*Arcadia, you always shine bright. No matter if it's day or night, summer or winter.*

Thundering applause followed my singing, and both Mr. Goodwin's and the king's announcer's expressions relaxed. I wondered if they didn't want me to mention the missing queen because they didn't want to draw attention to the topic until it had been resolved. If so, it was a stupid strategy. There might be people in the crowd like me who knew something about the queen. If we worked together and put our pieces of information together, we would have an easier and quicker time finding the queen.

"Thank you. Halia Bright, everyone." Mr. Goodwin guided me toward the steps, clearly not wanting another surprise. I was happy to oblige and get off the stage.

As soon as I walked into the audience, Tia fell around my neck.

"Well done! You ruled, girl!"

Mikka nodded approvingly behind her.

Lorenzo winked at me. "See, that wasn't too bad."

"No," I said and followed my three friends away from the market square.

As curious as I was to hear the other contestants' questions and answers, I didn't have the luxury. My day was far from over, and I needed all the time I could get to prepare to infiltrate tonight's fae council meeting.

Before we made our way to the forest. Lorenzo teleported inside the patrolmen's station and dropped off an anonymous tip at Thomas's desk, telling him to look into Faustus's mental institution and stating that patients had been disappearing without a trace for weeks.

Lorenzo assured me that no one had seen him, and I hoped that Thomas would take the warning seriously and not have someone like Victor talk him out of it or do a superficial investigation like they did at Madam's Boarding House after several of her guests vanished, and one died suddenly.

"If everything went well, then why do you look so conflicted?" I asked.

"Because there was a magical object in Thomas's office?"

"Why?" Thomas was human and didn't have any connections to magic wielders as far as I knew.

Lorenzo shrugged. "There could be a number of reasons. He might not even know it is there."

"What is it?"

"I don't know." Lorenzo pinched the space between his brows. "I could sense it but couldn't get close enough to see it or figure out what it was. It's a fae object, bespelled against demons."

"Interesting."

"We don't need to worry about it for now." Lorenzo wrapped his arms around me. I nodded, letting him know I was ready. The world spun as we teleported. The roiling sensation in my stomach quieted once there was hard earth underneath my feet again. I examined my surroundings. We were in the middle of the forest, but there were no tall oaks or a cave.

"We're five minutes away from it," Lorenzo explained. "I didn't want to teleport too closely, in case any fae were posted outside the cave."

I nodded. "How much time will we have once the astral projection is underway?"

"You'll see the crows, the messengers of hell. I'll see them too in my astral projection state. One crow is a warning that we only have a few minutes left. Two crows mean we only have a minute left. When the final crow shows up, you need to get the obsidian off me immediately."

"And if I'm not fast enough, you'll be sent to hell."

He nodded in confirmation, and I knew I would never be able to hold out until the third crow arrived. No matter how far the fae conversation progressed, I would remove the obsidian from Lorenzo after the first bird showed up.

"If you have any problems getting off the obsidian, just pull harder."

My gut contracted. "Do you expect there to be a problem?"

"You'll be fine." Lorenzo forced a smile, but I didn't buy it, certain he was downplaying how delicate astral projection was. This, in turn, only made my resolution stronger to get him out of there when the first crow appeared, preferably even before that.

"Let's go over the details. We won't be able to talk once we get closer to the cave."

I nodded. We had agreed that we would set up as close to the cave as possible but without the fae spotting us, so that I had a high chance to influence their conversation and force them to reveal their hand.

Lorenzo held out a satchel that contained six candles, a box that held red dust, and a hexagon-shaped obsidian. "You'll place the six candles at an even distance around me. Strew the red dust counterclockwise. It's important that the red dust connects the candles fully. If there's even a tiny gap, the projection won't work. I'll go into a deep trance as you start the circle, preparing for the astral projection. Once you have cast the hexagon, you'll light the candles, step in between two of them without extinguishing any, and place the obsidian right above my heart."

"How will I know when the astral projection starts?"

He glanced away. "You'll be able to tell. I'll no longer appear to be sleeping."

I clenched my fists, sensing that doing the astral projection would put him in a lot of pain. "Maybe we don't need to do this. I could try getting close enough to the cave to overhear their conversation."

He shook his head. "Absolutely not. If you or I can hear what the fae are talking about, it means we're close enough for them to sense our presence."

"But, we overheard their conversation in the Faustus quarter."

He shook his head. "That was different. There were others nearby, making it harder for them to spot our presence. The forest is deserted."

I sighed, hating all those magic rules.

"I'll be fine. We can do this. Do you have any questions?"

"No." But I wished he didn't have to do this and that I could help more.

His brows drew together in concentration as he studied the sun in the sky. "We need to move now. They'll be here soon." We started southwards. As promised, we didn't have to walk long until a tall oak came into view. A second, slightly smaller oak could be seen not far from it. The stone cave was right behind it.

We used a thick tree trunk as our hiding spot and waited. For what felt like a long time, nothing happened, and yet, Lorenzo shook his head every time I opened my mouth to speak. Trusting his demon senses, I remained quiet, even though thousands of questions darted through my mind, and I wished we could've gone over the astral projection a few more times.

Finally, the fae trickled in. All eight females wore dusty blue cloaks that concealed most of their features, and yet their tall bodies, ethereal grace, and the power radiating from them made it clear that they were fae. The latter wasn't something I used to notice, and I wondered if my increased awareness was because I was becoming more aware of the magic world or because my powers were developing.

After the fae disappeared into the cave's opening, we waited for a few minutes to make sure that no one else arrived.

The astral projection had to be timed carefully. We couldn't waste precious minutes on opening words, but we also didn't want to be too late and miss something important.

Lorenzo gave me a nod, and I followed him to an

area of tall, thick bushes that would cover us both from prying eyes.

In the center of the bushes was a flat area. Lorenzo lay down on the ground, his gaze focused on me.

"Ready," I mouthed, even though my hands trembled so badly, I was afraid the candles would slip from my grasp.

Lorenzo created an X shape with his body. I placed a candle above each of his palms, beneath each foot, one candle above his head, and the final one at foot-level in line with his navel.

Lorenzo nodded approval for me to proceed. He closed his eyes, and I was on my own. I took a steadying breath and opened the box of deep red dust, trying not to think whose blood had been dried as I walked counterclockwise and strew the dust around Lorenzo, starting at the central bottom part and working my way to his right foot, right palm, to the candle above his head, then left arm, left foot, and finally, back to the central candle. When the hexagon was cast, I checked to ensure the candles were totally connected by the blood-red line. Satisfied with my handiwork, I lit the candles, once again starting at the central bottom one and working my way counterclockwise.

The air shifted, growing heavier and pressing down on me as I pulled out the smooth obsidian the size of my palm.

I felt the force of the circle pushing against me as I stepped into it to place the obsidian on Lorenzo's chest, giving me a taste of what it would be like to remove the stone from Lorenzo's chest.

Trying not to panic, I placed the gleaming gem on Lorenzo's chest. A wind whipped against me, throwing me out of the hexagon. Landing on my butt wasn't so much painful as it was shocking. I even glanced around to ensure it wasn't a fae working against me, but there was no one. The circle had pushed me out.

Not having any time to waste, I closed my eyes and hit a low D, praying my efforts would pay off.

*"Tell me why you are here. What is going on in Arcadia? Where is Queen Ella?"*

I concentrated hard until a pounding started in my head. I let up a bit, reminding myself to breathe while channeling my thoughts. A groaning and rustling made me open my eyes only to realize that the noise had come from Lorenzo, who was twisting and turning on the ground as if he were having a nightmare.

*"Tell us all you know,"* I sang louder. *"Tell us about the queen and what is happening in Arcadia."* I thought I heard a noise coming from the cave and dropped my voice. I needed to be loud enough, but not loud enough for them to realize that I was out here.

Lorenzo's whole upper body lifted and crashed back down, his back and head smashing against the hard ground. Watching him being tortured and not being able to help him made me shake with rage and filled my eyes with tears. I tried to remind myself that a demon's body was much sturdier than a human's. Still, I found it nearly impossible not to tear him out of the projection as blood trickled from his nose, his eyelids twitched like crazy, and his jaw ground so hard I was certain he was about to break a molar.

To distract myself, and because it was the only thing I could do, I continued singing, *"Where is Queen Ella? Why are people disappearing from Arcadia? What is being done to them? Why is there so much tension in the city?"*

Lorenzo's body stilled, and I exhaled, naively believing

that the hard part was over. Not a minute later, the first crow appeared on his chest to the left of the obsidian.

I swallowed hard. This was too early. The meeting had just begun, and it was very unlikely that Lorenzo had gleaned any information. Still, I couldn't put him in danger.

I continued singing and stepped into the circle. As soon as my foot went over the red-brown dust barrier, a violent shaking seized me, and my muscles went weak. I dropped to Lorenzo's side, reassuring myself that I could do this. I had made it into the circle, and that's what mattered.

Just as I reached for the obsidian, a second crow appeared to the right of his chest.

"No," I breathed.

I grabbed the obsidian only to pull back immediately with a hiss from the sharp pain in my palm. There was a red mark on my palm. The obsidian had burned me. I pulled my shirt over my head and wrapped the fabric around my hands, then grabbed the obsidian again. The burning sensation was still painful but bearable.

I gritted my teeth as I pulled with all my strength while tears of pain from the burn ran down my face. Lorenzo jerked, his heartbeat visible through his chest, and his ribcage rose and fell rapidly. He was distressed. I had to hurry, yet no matter how hard I pulled, I couldn't get the stone off him.

The third crowd appeared right above his chest.

"No, please don't," I sobbed. It was clear that I couldn't overpower the stone with my physical capabilities, so I turned to the only magic I had. *"Release him, release him. Stop the astral projection and bring Lorenzo back to me."*

At first, I had no idea if it was working, but then the

stone throbbed angrily in my palms as if yelling back an angry reply.

I put every ounce of determination I had into my voice. *"I command you, release Lorenzo immediately."*

There was a pop and a crunching as I was thrown out of the hexagon, clutching the obsidian in my hand. My spine slammed against the ground hard, and stars exploded in front of my vision as my head bounced against the hard earth.

I thought I heard voices, I thought I heard footsteps, but I wasn't sure because darkness was already claiming me. I didn't mind. I had done my part. I had gotten the obsidian off Lorenzo, and he was safe.

## 2ND AUGUST

I woke up with a pounding headache, my neck and shoulders sore, and my mouth parched dry. Turning from my back onto my side was excruciating, but all the pain was forgotten when I came face-to-face with Lorenzo.

His eyes were closed, and for a moment, I worried that something was wrong with him, but then I noticed his calm breathing. He was just sleeping, recovering from yesterday. And somehow, I had ended up in his bed.

Needing a glass of water, I pushed upright and tried to suppress the resulting groan of pain as my shoulder protested the pressure on it.

"You're up," Lorenzo mumbled, his eyelids fluttering open.

"How are you feeling?"

"Shitty, as to be expected." He examined me. "I wouldn't have done it had I known the consequences for you. I've only ever done astral projection with a demon, who claimed it was nothing." He shook his head. "I should've known better. I should've asked Mikka or someone else—"

"Stop. I wanted to do it. I'm fine. I even still have all of my body parts."

He chuckled. "And your sense of humor." His face turned somber, and he held up his hand. "How many fingers do you see?"

I rolled my eyes, but replied, "Three."

"What's your best friend's name?"

"Tia, and we're at Daydream, the bar you own. I'm fine." I suppressed a cringe as I remembered the fall, the pain running down my spine, and then everything turning dark. "Getting thrown out of the circle was nothing compared to what you've been through."

"It wasn't too bad." He glanced away as he spoke, betraying his words.

"What is it like when you astral project?" When he hesitated, I pressed. "I want the truth. No more secrets, Lorenzo. You want me to be open with you. Well, I expect the same in return."

He smoothed out the bedsheets. "It feels like your body is being turned inside out. When your soul leaves, everything tenses, wanting to bring it back. Adrenaline is pumping through you, and your organs are working overtime." He must've noticed the horrified expression on my face, because he added, "It was worth it. There was no other way to find out what the fae were up to."

I sat upright. "You overheard what they're planning?"

He brushed a hand through his long, silver hair. "I

was able to overhear parts of their debate. They are connected to the human disappearances, but not involved yet."

I leaned forward. "What does that mean?"

He sighed. "The fae aren't behind the abductions. There is someone they call The Leader. Apparently, he approached them, and he wants their help."

"Why? He doesn't seem to have problems abducting people on his own." At least not when it came to the less fortunate souls of Arcadia who wouldn't be missed. The poor widows at the women's houses, the neglected and vilified patients at the mental institutions, the single travelers staying at Madam's Boarding House. If I hadn't left the orphanage a few months earlier, I could've become one of the disappearing people. I jumped up from the bed, barely feeling the stab of pain in my shoulder. "The orphanage. We need to protect the kids in there."

Lorenzo nodded. "I'll find someone who will keep an eye on them. We're needed here." He cleared his throat and poured us each a glass of water from a large jug standing on his bedside table. I accepted the glass and emptied it in a few gulps.

"Back to the fae involvement," Lorenzo said. "They're not meant to abduct any more people. They're supposed to extract something from humans. You were right; the extraction of emotions is similar to what they're supposed to do."

I put the glass down and bit my lip. "They're going to steal life-energy from the humans?"

"No, it appears that the leader knows how to do that himself."

I swallowed hard, more certain than ever that this leader was a powerful magic wielder. "Then what is the faeries' part?"

"Every human has a tiny drop of magic in them. Some have more, some have less, but everybody holds a bit of magic."

Acacia had said the same thing to me a while ago, stating that I had more magic than any of her other clients. "So are the fae supposed to target people like me who have some magic abilities but aren't demon or fae descendants and also not witches?"

A soft smile played on Lorenzo's face. "You have no idea how rare you are, do you, Halia? In my two hundred and seventy-two years, I've never met anyone like you."

"Then who will they target?"

Lorenzo's throat bobbed up and down. "The amount of magic in a person's blood changes, depending on how they lead their lives. It's complicated. There are no fast rules, but generally, those who pursue their passions, such as artists, have more magic in their blood as do people who are in love or pure of heart."

I pondered this for a moment. Those people wouldn't be as easy to get to as the unfortunate souls confined in mental institutions and widow houses. How was the leader planning to collect them? And then it dawned on me. "The competition," I breathed. "The leader will go for the singers."

Lorenzen nodded. "With so much talent in one space, it's the ideal hunting ground."

"You think he'll succeed? What about the king's patrolmen?"

"They're there to stop any unrest and protect the judges as well as the advancing candidates. Those who fail to progress into the next round make for easy pickings."

I began to pace. It was one thing to find a way to protect a place like an orphanage, but the singers wouldn't be stationary, and they would refuse to stay in a group for safety. No, we had to approach the issue in a different way. "How did the fae vote?"

"Five voted for, two against it."

"Meaning?"

Lorenzo rubbed his jaw. "Acacia was in charge of the meeting. She declared that whoever didn't want to participate didn't have to join, but that they had to swear not to interfere."

"Did she vote for it?" Even though I suspected she did, I wanted to be wrong. It was illegal for Acacia to sell the sisters' fake voices, but at least, she wasn't forcing or exploiting someone the way she would be if she agreed to extract magic from unsuspecting or unwilling humans.

"She did. Abigail and a fae named Asther voted against it."

Everything inside me tensed. I was disappointed and felt betrayed, but it was more than that. I had seen Acacia in action. I knew what she was capable of. She wasn't somebody you wanted for an enemy. "We need to change Acacia's mind. Perhaps if the king offered her a position—"

Lorenzo cut me off. "Do you really want somebody like her working for the king?"

"No, but if she allies herself with this leader, they'll succeed."

Lorenzo gave me a lopsided smile. "I like it that you aren't cocky, but a bit of confidence from time to time wouldn't hurt."

I plopped down onto the bed. "Maybe we can stop them if we prepare properly. What else did you find out?"

"Nothing, I'm afraid. After Acacia said that not everyone had to participate, I was kicked out of the astral projection. But Abigail heard the whole conversation. Now that she's accepted the balance scales, she'll be greedy for more magic. We can probably get her to tell us the rest of what was discussed"

"Why didn't she use them in the meeting?"

He shrugged. "She probably didn't care enough about the outcome and wanted to keep them for another time."

"All right. But even if she wants more magic, isn't it interference if she tells us what was discussed in the meeting?"

A cheeky grin stretched across Lorenzo's lips. "No, not according to fae law."

I smiled. For once, the bendable rules of the fae race would serve us.

Now there were only two more things to consider. "Where are we going to find Abigail, and what will we use to bargain with her?"

As Lorenzo explained his plan, my smile vanished, and worry consumed me. "No way," I said after hearing his proposal. "You will not owe Abigail an astral projection as a favor. I can't let you do it after knowing how it affects you."

"It's the only way," Lorenzo replied calmly. "I don't have anything else with which to bargain with her, and no time to find a magical item."

He was right, but there had to be another way. I didn't trust Abigail not to misuse her power and send Lorenzo into hell by not pulling him out quickly enough from the astral projection. "We can offer her my skills."

Lorenzo shook his head. "Your magic can only be

used for light. We don't know what Abigail might ask you to do, and it's best if she doesn't know about your powers. I don't think she'll betray us since she's in too deep, but we need to be careful and ensure that your singing power remains a surprise. The fae cannot know about it."

I snarled, knowing he was right and feeling helpless for it.

"I'll be fine," Lorenzo reassured me.

"Fine, we'll go with your plan, but on one condition."

"What?"

"I get to be the one assisting you with the astral projection."

"Absolutely not. I'm trying to keep you out of this. You were unconscious after yesterday. If I hadn't teleported us away, we could've both been discovered."

I shrugged. "You either let me assist you, or the deal is off. I won't let you place the safety of your soul into Abigail's greedy paws."

Lorenzo must've seen the determination on my face because he nodded. I stood tall, satisfied that he was being reasonable even as I wondered whether making a bargain with Abigail would one day come back to bite us in the behind.

Since going to Abigail's house was too risky for either of us and we didn't have the time to wait for a run-in with her, we asked Tia.

"Thanks," I said to my friend as she donned her big hat that covered her blue hair. "I really appreciate everything you're doing for us."

She waved my statement away and pulled on an oversized shirt over her cropped top. "Hey, Arcadia is my home too, and I want it to go back to normal."

I chewed on my lip. "So there's still a lot of bar fights

going on?"

"Yes, Arcadians are either extremely aggressive or nervous, almost paranoid. I spotted several people peeking from behind their curtains, monitoring the street outside their homes, and continually glancing around when out and about."

"I wonder if they're just reacting to whatever is going on, or if the fae or the leader are doing something to them."

Tia wolfed down a cucumber-and-cream cheese sandwich Mikka had prepared for her. "Either way, we need to break up their group and put an end to their plans."

I nodded, trying to figure out why the leader was interested in extracting magic. If he wanted power, even if he wanted to overthrow the king, wouldn't it be more effective and quicker to buy the loyalty of a few powerful magic wielders? But then the power wouldn't truly be his. I supposed that explained his complicated strategy. But what was the fae' motivation to collaborate with him? What were they gaining from it? They already had plenty of magic.

I turned to Lorenzo. "Could the fae use life energy for anything? They age slowly and remain young-looking even in old age, don't they?"

Lorenzo's green-violet eyes narrowed. "Life energy can be used for dark magic. It can be sold by itself or mixed in with emotion potions. It could also be used to perform draining magic rituals without having to recover in between."

Disgust rose in me. For a little bit of convenience, the fae were willing to take the most precious gift from humans. Humans who already lived only a tenth of a fae's lifespan. It wasn't fair. It wasn't right. I wouldn't let the fae get away with it.

"I'm ready." Tia brushed breadcrumbs from her lips and washed down her sandwich with a glass of water.

"You got the address? You remember what to say?"

"Yes. Tell her we have something better than balanced scales in exchange for information. If somebody else greets me at Abigail's house and asks me why I'm there, I'll say I want to buy a mood-boosting potion."

"What if whoever opens the door tries to send you away?"

"I'll claim a friend recommended Abigail, and that I don't trust anyone else."

I nodded and hugged my friend. "Good luck."

"Don't sweat it. It's nothing compared to what you've done. I'll be back before you know it."

True to her word, she strolled through the door, not an hour later. I jumped off my barstool. "And?"

"Abigail took the bait. She'll come over to discuss your proposal after nightfall."

I cursed underneath my breath. We needed to talk to Abigail before that. The announcement of the twelve candidates that would progress into the next round was today, leaving thirteen candidates undefended against the fae and the leader.

"I tried everything to convince her to come now, but she said she couldn't, and that it would be safer after night fell."

"Thank you, Tia," Lorenzo said with infuriating calm.

I whirled on him. "We need to do something! We can't just let the fae take away the losing contestants like a bag of trash!"

"I doubt the fae will move today, but even if they do, we'll get the performers back." Despite his voice being reassuring, I found it hard to believe him. I trusted him, but there were so many things that could go wrong.

However, I doubted that Abigail would appreciate it if I sent Tia back to negotiate the timing of our meeting. We couldn't afford to push Abigail too hard. She had something we needed, so she was setting the terms. Which meant I had to find another way to distract the fae from the singers that lost today. Luckily, I had a plan.

"What are you scheming now?" Lorenzo asked.

I relaxed my face. "Nothing," I lied, feeling only the tiniest bit of guilt. After all, Lorenzo had agreed with me that the police needed to be notified about the goings-on in the mental institution. Acacia was involved in Arcadia's unrest. It was time that one of the patrolmen paid a visit to her.

"I'll go for a quick walk to clear my head before the competition announcement." Lorenzo didn't look convinced, and I rolled my eyes. "I won't do anything. I just need to work off some of my nervous energy. You don't want me to be a wreck on stage while half of Arcadia scrutinizes me, do you?" He scowled, and I grabbed Tia's hand. "Here, I'll even take Tia with me."

"All right." Lorenzo agreed begrudgingly.

As soon as we were outside Daydream, my friend grinned. "So, what did you have in mind?"

"Nothing much. I just want the dirty fae to pay. Acacia hurt my Arcadia, so I'm going to strike her where it hurts the most—her business."

Tia's face lit up with excitement. "And how are you going to do that?"

"Easy. Tip off the first patrolman I see by singing in his ear that there are illegal dealings going on." And that's exactly what I did when I spotted a patrolwoman whom I remembered milling around outside Madam's

Boarding House after a guest had died from a heart attack and Madam had tried to cover up his death.

*"Interview Acacia, the fae. She's a close friend of Madam Fontaine's. She's involved in the strange death and the disappearances at the boarding house. You'll find illegal magic at Acacia's. You know that fae's always seemed suspicious."*

The patrolwoman turned around sharply and hurried to the police station, probably to get whatever papers she needed to barge into Acacia's home. I smiled with satisfaction. I would teach Acacia not to underestimate us humans.

"Very nice." Tia's smile faltered. "You're not going to get into trouble for this, are you?"

I shook my head. "It was an anonymous tip. The patrolwoman will sell this idea as her own."

The church bells rang, and Tia cursed. "Let's get you back to Daydream and into your outfit."

"What outfit?"

"The one the stage assistant dropped off while you were recovering from the astral projection."

Unlike the previous stage appearances where candidates wore all colors of the rainbow, tonight, we were all decked out in black, but that's where the similarities of our attire ended. My black dress was a flowing number, moving in the breeze. In contrast to my light chiffon, other singers wore lace, silk, even velvet, or leather. Some of us had slim silhouettes while others wore gowns. Each of our outfits represented the personas we had assumed in this competition. There was the pretty princess, the dangerous femme fatale, and the no-nonsense singer. My outfit appeared to have a touch of mystery to it, and I guessed that that's how the judges viewed me, especially after I had refused to talk about my personal life at the interview. While I thought my dress blended in nicely with the others, the same couldn't be said about what the monstrosities Georgette and Bernadette wore. Their bosoms and stomachs were squeezed into tights corsets, and their hooped skirts ensured they took up three times as much space as other contestants. Their attires were more appropriate for members of the court than performers, which I guessed they liked, given how desperate they were to leave the simple folk behind and become blue bloods.

Once everyone was assembled, Mr. Goodwin and his assistant, Henry, ascended the podium.

"Dear citizens of Arcadia," the competition host boomed. "We have come today to announce the twelve contestants moving on to the next round. Contestants, please join us."

As one, all twenty-five of us broke into motion, more akin to a funeral procession than a group of performers.

"If your name is called, please take a step forward." Mr. Goodman nodded at us encouragingly while the singers looked confused, and a few discreetly wiped their hands on their clothing, probably to get rid of sweat. I, too, was nervous. I hated unclear instructions. Were those who were called progressing or on the chopping block? I guessed Mr. Goodwin was keeping us in the dark on purpose. It made for a much better show when we looked nervous and distraught.

Even though my chances were fifty-fifty, my stomach dropped each time a name was called that wasn't mine.

I was so focused on my own name, it was impossible to remember the names of my fellow contestants even though I had promised to do just that to help me establish rapport with them later on when I warned them about the fae.

"Erik Jen, please step forward. And finally, Michele Wetherspoon," Mr. Goodwin announced with a wide smile, uncaring about our distress.

Had he called twelve or thirteen names? I couldn't remember.

"Front row, you are dismissed." There was a pregnant pause both from the contestants and the audience before Mr. Goodwin added, "Thank you for your participation, but unfortunately,, you haven't progressed to the next level."

The thirteen candidates left the stage, and roaring applause greeted us, the remaining twelve. I glanced to both sides and found, at the end of the left side, the Fontaine sisters. It wasn't fair. They should've been eliminated long ago. Instead, they were taking up a precious spot. I turned my attention back to the audience and forced a smile, which froze into place as I recognized a familiar face in the crowd. The icy blonde held my stare, and I knew this was my chance to talk some sense into her.

As soon as the competition host dismissed us, I rushed toward the lefthand stairs.

"Hey, watch where you are going! You nearly killed me," Georgette whined as my dress brushed against her wide gown.

"What's wrong with you? Why are you so aggressive?" Bernadette chimed in.

I only shook my head in response and hurried past them, refusing to add to the drama they were trying to orchestrate. My name would not be associated with theirs in Arcadia's tabloids.

Acacia moved from her spot in the crowd, not fast enough to lose me but quick enough to lure me away from the others. Clearly, she wanted to talk to me as well, which both excited and terrified me.

When I caught up to her, out of breath, she said calmly, “Halia, you’re becoming too big for your breeches, aren’t you? Just because you’re still in the royal competition doesn’t mean you run Arcadia. It would be wise of you to remember that.”

I bristled. “I’m not the one playing god.”

She clicked her tongue in disapproval. “Don’t get involved in things you don’t understand, child.”

I clenched my fists. “Why don’t you use your power for something good for once instead of filling your pockets?”

Her lips pressed into a thin, hard line. “I don’t take orders from you. I’ve warned you before, but clearly, you don’t respond to the nice way. Mark my words: You will pay for what you’ve done.”

I swallowed hard, trying to keep my face blank. She knew. Darn it, she knew that I had tipped off the patrolwoman. I had to make her doubt herself, redirect the conversation. “Why are you helping the sisters? How much did they pay you?”

She shook her head. “You’d be wise to stay out of this, or I’ll bring my wrath down on not just you, but the rest of your misfits.” Before I could reply, she disappeared inside a house.

I tried to go after her, but the door was locked. Darn fae magic.

“Halia!” I turned around to find Lorenzo had teleported in bright daylight behind me. “What were you thinking, going after Acacia?”

“What are you thinking, teleporting in front of everyone?” I hissed in response.

He grabbed my hand. “Let’s go.” Since I couldn’t open the door anyway, I followed him to Daydream where we sat in tense silence.

Hours passed, and night fell, yet there was still no sign of Abigail.

"Maybe you spooked her talking to Acacia," Lorenzo said. "Why did you have to go and tip off that patrolwoman?"

"I did what needed to be done to protect the contestants. It was an anonymous tip, and no trail leads back to me. There are tons of other reasons for why Acacia gave me a warning."

He shook his head. "I can't trust you if you're not honest. We need transparency to work together."

"Is that so? Like how you were transparent by downplaying the astral projection?"

He didn't reply, and that only fueled my anger.

"I could've lost you! Your mind could've been lost in hell! Do you have any idea what that would've done to me?"

"No," he replied quietly. "I'm sorry."

My next retort died on my lips died as the door to Daydream flung open right as the clock above the bar struck midnight.

# 3RD AUGUST

Blood rushed through my veins as Abigail stalked toward Lorenzo and me, her heels clicking angrily against the stone floor. We had closed early that day and sent Mikka and Tia upstairs. Once Abigail made sure that it was just the three of us, she threw back the cape of her dusty blue cloak. "What were you thinking, going after Acacia? Are you trying to place a target on my back?"

Lorenzo shot me an "I told you so" look, then said, "All Acacia knows is that someone tipped off the police. She has no reason to monitor the comings and goings of Daydream."

Abigail sniffed. "She suspects. All fae have well-developed intuition. For your carelessness alone, I shouldn't have come."

"And yet, you did because you know it's worth it." Lorenzo dropped his voice. "Tell us everything you know about the leader and how the fae plan to support him, and I'll personally owe you the favor of an astral projection."

Abigail's pale blue eyes lit up like that of a child who was standing in front of a mountain of presents, but she shook her head. "I have no use for that, demon." She glanced at me. "But, I'll take a favor from the mind singer."

Relief coursed through me. "Deal," I agreed.

"Halia can only use her magic for light," Lorenzo protested.

Abigail licked her lips. "Don't worry. She won't harm anyone. Let's shake on it. I want to make sure that you don't go back on your promise just because I might not have all the information you seek."

I pulled Lorenzo aside. "Please, let me do this."

He nodded slowly. "All right. But we have to be careful about how she words this." He turned to Abigail. "Swear in return to tell us everything you heard and saw at the council meeting."

Abigail motioned with a finger between Lorenzo and me. "Why do you care so much about the fae council meeting? First, you wanted to know the time and the place of it, and now, you want to know what was going on in there."

I cringed as she reminded us of our failure. If only we had gotten more information during the astral projection, we wouldn't have to strike this bargain.

Abigail tilted her head, watching us expectantly, making it clear she wanted an answer.

I glanced at Lorenzo, and he nodded, indicating that he was all right with me taking the lead on this.

"We want Arcadia to go back to normal," I said. "Awful things have been happening in the city for weeks."

"Indeed," Abigail said noncommittally, her gaze swiping across the bar.

"We won't breathe a word to anyone about who was our informant." Lorenzo stepped forward. "Let's shake on our deal."

Abigail stared at us for a long time before finally nodding and holding out her hand. "I, Abigail Asher, make this binding agreement with you, Halia Bright."

As we shook hands, electricity darted through my palm and up my arm.

"I swear to tell the whole truth about everything I know, heard, or saw at the last fae council meeting in the forest," Abigail continued. "In exchange for this, you, Halia Bright, will owe me a favor of my time and place of choosing. The favor will never expire, and you will never breathe to anyone who your informant was. You will bear the consequence of my wrath and fae magic if you or your friend betray my confidence."

"I swear," I said solemnly.

We shook hands, sparks shooting between our palms for several seconds. When the sparks died, Abigail released my hand.

I knew it probably looked weak, yet I couldn't help but grab Lorenzo's hand, needing the physical contact. He squeezed my palm, making me immediately feel better. His violet-green eyes were filled with emotion before he blinked them away and nodded at Abigail. "Tell us everything, from the beginning."

She started by explaining that the fae had been approached by the leader, a man she hadn't met. Acacia was supposed to see him after the meeting to communicate the fae's decision but hadn't revealed when and where. Abigail stated that she was free to not participate in the fae-leader deal as long as she didn't interfere. None of this was news to us, and yet I was glad that that's where she had started since it allowed us the opportunity to verify that she was telling the truth and didn't leave anything out.

Abigail's eyes slid sideways and narrowed as if she tried to remember. "Next, something strange happened. Acacia brought up the subject of the missing queen out of nowhere."

I exchanged a glance with Lorenzo's, grateful that my singing hadn't been in vain.

Abigail pursued her lips. "It's so strange that Acacia felt compelled to tell us that she didn't know where the queen was. She never admits to any weaknesses."

I chewed on my lip, wondering if Acacia had put two and two together and realized that I had been nearby and influencing her. After all, if anyone knew or guessed about my power without me telling them, it would've been Acacia, given all the time she had spent masking the golden rings in my blue eyes, which now were concealed with magic contact lenses Lorenzo had procured.

"Then she added that if anyone knows where Queen Ella is, it would be her fairy godmother. If one finds the fairy godmother, one finds Queen Ella." Abigail shook her head, looking perplexed by Acacia spitting out this information. Clearly, Abigail had no idea how valuable this knowledge was to us, and I tried my best to keep my face as neutral as possible and not to betray my excitement.

Fairy godmother. Of course. Why hadn't I thought about that earlier? The only question was, how on earth would we find her?

"Then, the conversation turned back to the leader." Abigail examined her nails. "Acacia said that to do their part efficiently, they needed to throw a party in honor of all the royal competition contestants." Abigail's gaze flew toward me, sharp as a wasp's stinger. "I suppose by now you've figured out what the fae are supposed to do for the leader."

Was this a test? Should we pretend we didn't know, or was it better to tell the truth as a sign of our trust?

Lorenzo must've decided on the latter because he said. "The fae will siphon off magic from the singers' blood. They will rob them of their talent."

Abigail nodded. "It's really not that bad. It's not going to hurt them or make them die."

"It will steal their passion, their meaning!" I couldn't hold back. How could she be so nonchalant about something as important as this?

Abigail flinched, then pressed her lips together, as if I had offended her.

"If it's not that bad, then why didn't you join them?" Lorenzo asked coolly.

Abigail smirked. "Because I don't think the leader will come through on his promise." At our raised eyebrows, she added, "I don't think he'll betray them, just that his focus will be on his own success, which will lead him to neglect his part of the deal."

"Spit it out." Lorenzo's jaw tensed.

"The leader wants to rule Arcadia."

I swallowed hard. I had suspected it for a long time, but hearing it confirmed still made me shudder.

"In return for our help, he promised to recreate our home."

I looked at Lorenzo for an explanation.

"Many of the fae who are here have been banished

from their courts, exiled for transgressions," he said.

I still didn't understand. "If this leader can recreate the faeland, he must have a lot of his own magic. Why does he need the fae?"

Lorenzo shrugged. "It seems that he doesn't know how to siphon off magic. My guess is he can weave it into something, making a vision become a reality. He's...a weaver."

I rubbed at the goosebumps on my arms as an image of a huge spider trapping insects in its web swum in front of my vision. I turned to Abigail. "Do you agree?"

She nodded. "That would be the logical conclusion, but like I said, I doubt he'll come through. I'm sure he'll make a half-hearted attempt, but he sounds like he only cares about himself. I'm not interested in bargaining with him."

Her gaze devoured Lorenzo, and I had the feeling that she was very willing to bargain and play with him. I had to fight hard not to lunge at her.

Abigail smoothed her cloak. "Either way, the fae decided that they'll ambush the contestants tonight."

And just like that, my possessiveness instantly turned into an icy panic. "Where? When?"

Abigail glanced leisurely at the clock. "I believe the party has started a while back at Dover's Tavern and will continue until two or three in the morning."

Just the mention of the run-down pub made me smell the reek of warm beer, grease, and sweat. Dover's Tavern was a seedy establishment Victor had taken me to on more than one occasion. It was the perfect place to meet for illegal activities since most patrons were wasted out of their minds and so self-focused, they wouldn't notice anything, no matter how strange it was, let alone report it to the police.

"Is there anything else you have to tell us?" I asked, eager to get to Dover's. Every second we waited allowed the fae to zoom in on their prey. My fellow competition contestants hadn't exactly shown me a warm welcome, but that didn't mean that they deserved to have their passion ripped from them.

Abigail looked me straight in the eye. "No, this is all I have to tell you."

"But?" Lorenzo crossed his arms, and I, too, felt that Abigail was holding back.

"But I think it's a trap."

I licked my lips, remembering the warning Acacia had given me earlier. "If Acacia wanted to get me out of the way, certainly she wouldn't do it in a public place." The fae didn't like to create a mess, which would be unavoidable at a bar.

Abigail clucked her tongue disapprovingly. "There are other ways to get you without killing you."

I straightened. "I'm not going to let those people down just because Acacia might retaliate."

"Very well." Abigail handed Lorenzo a piece of paper and an intricate quill that seemed to be worth a month's salary. "Write to me when you want to know the location of the godmother. I'll call on her for you in exchange for a favor."

Another favor. And somehow, I had a feeling that Abigail had cooperated with us because of it. Whatever it was that she wanted, she really needed it.

Lorenzo didn't ask any questions, simply stashed away the writing utensils in his pants pocket.

Not bothering to say goodbye, Abigail stalked out of the bar. As soon as the door fell shut behind her, I asked, "Can she really find Ella's godmother?"

Lorenzo gave a grim nod. "Yes, it's a fae ability to call

on godmothers."

And Abigail had anticipated that we would want her to. "Do you know what she'll ask for in return?"

He gave a curt shake of his head.

Something wasn't adding up. "If she wants it so badly, why not make the bargain now?"

"Because it's probably something we won't give her unless we're in a dire position, which she thinks we'll be in soon." After a pause, Lorenzo said, "Speaking of which, Abigail is right. Dover's is most likely a trap. You should remain here." He took my hand. "I'm asking you as a friend and somebody who cares a lot about you to stay back. Let me handle this by myself."

"No! You need backup."

"I'll take Mikka with me if it makes you feel better."

"I can't let you do that while I sit at home like a damsel in distress. This is my mission! I get that this is dangerous, but it's also a test I need to pass. If I don't do this now, I won't stand a chance at successfully facing whatever awaits us from the leader. Something tells me that he'll strike even if the fae fail."

Lorenzo sighed. "If I lock you up, you'll climb through the window, won't you?"

I grinned. "Yes. You better let me come with you so that you know where I am."

He stepped closer and cupped my face in his hands. "Promise me that you'll stay by my side. Promise that you'll be careful and won't do anything rash."

"I promise," I breathed, finding it hard to say anything when he was so close to me, and all I wanted to do was kiss those gorgeous lips.

When we first arrived at Dover's Tavern, I didn't see anything out of the ordinary. Beer was flowing, sloshing out of massive glasses, barmaids were pushing their breasts high up and together in hopes of higher tips, and guests were bickering with each other and lusting after the barmaids.

Then I saw the singers. They were swaying side to side, standing right below the small stage on which a middle-aged band was playing. As soon as the four men announced they were taking a break, several singers stormed the stage, fighting for the microphone.

"Hello, Arcadia!" one slurred before another grabbed the mic from him and began to sing a summer hit offkey.

The other singers watched them from below. Their glassy eyes and disbalance gave away how drunk they were. Even though they cheered and acted upbeat, it was easy to spot the downturn of their lips, the sadness in their eyes. Understandably, they were devastated that they hadn't made it into the next round of the competition.

Those who had passed weren't here, which wasn't surprising since the next round would be tomorrow, and it was preferable to show up well-rested rather than disheveled after a night of partying. Also, I didn't think that a seedy establishment like Dover's Tavern would appeal to those who still hoped to become regular court performers. For the losers, it was a different matter, however. As the saying went, beggars couldn't be choosers, and I was certain that the disqualified candidates would have accepted any invitation to distract themselves from their pain and sorrow.

While there was no sign of the fae, I was certain they lurked nearby, waiting to pounce. My guess was that they would show up when their targets were completely wasted, making them easy pickings.

To not draw any attention toward us, Lorenzo and I stayed in an unlit corner, watching as the night unfolded.

Soon, the disqualified contestants became rowdier. There was yelling and shoving from the more aggressive ones while the more sensual ones channeled their energy into provocative dancing, grinding their bodies against each other. And then, something unexpected happened. Georgette and Bernadette flounced in. They were decked out in multi-colored gowns, completely out of place in the cheap tavern.

The sisters turned up their noses and headed straight for the stage without acknowledging anyone. "Hello, Arcadia, we are Georgette and Bernadette or the Fontane sisters. We are competitors in this year's royal singing competition, and tonight we're going to rock you, Dover's Tavern!"

There were cheers from the regulars and eye rolls from the candidates that had lost. The sisters launched into a pop song, and I dug my nails into my palms, disgusted by how they flaunted their stolen voices. I wasn't the only one who resented their audacity, and soon several girls were throwing bread rolls at the sisters.

"Stop it, you losers!" Bernadette yelled into the microphone, tap dancing as she dodged the flying rolls.

The manager rang the bell. "The bar is closed for tonight." There were protests that died down as several burly males stepped forward to escort the patrons out.

Lorenzo and I slipped out first, exchanging a knowing glance. If the fae were going to strike, now was the time.

Indeed, as soon as all the singers were out of Dover's Tavern, a melodic voice sounded. "Get a free carriage ride on us."

Everything inside of me tensed as a huge, gold-adorned carriage with six horses pulled to a halt. I saw through its beauty to the ugliness underneath. The contestants were nothing but cattle that the fae wanted to drive to the slaughterhouse without blinking.

The drunken, exhausted, and devastated singers were helpless to resist the glamorous ride and walked toward it in one long procession.

"We need to do something," I said to Lorenzo.

"I'll set the horses free, but you need to stay here," he responded.

"All right." I agreed for two reasons. First, I had no idea how to disconnect the horses from the carriage, and I would probably just end up being in Lorenzo's way. Secondly, if I stayed hidden for now, I could launch a surprise attack later. In fact, I decided not to mill around but to use my voice.

But what should I sing, and whom should I influence? If Abigail was right and the fae were prepared for my interference, they would've probably safeguarded themselves against my voice, something that magic wielders could do. Thus, I decided to focus on the rejected singers, hoping I would get through their drunken state.

*"Walk home. The carriage is a trap. Don't fall for it,"* I sang as loud as I dared. But the singers showed no signs of hearing my message. One by one, they piled into the carriage, and I wondered if there had been something else in their drinks. Perhaps an emotions serum that made them more adventurous and risk-taking? Or something that made them deaf to my pleas.

Lorenzo teleported in front of the horses, taking the human coachmen by surprise and began to free the horses from the contraptions tying them to the carriage.

"What are you doing?" One of the coachmen jumped off the bench and tried to push Lorenzo away but was no match for my demon.

Then the air around the carriage glittered, and the next second, the carriage with the coachman, who had remained seated vanished, leaving Lorenzo behind with a very perplexed coachman.

I rushed toward him. "Where did they go?"

"Fae portal." Lorenzo tensed. "It has already closed. We can't follow."

"There she is!" Georgette's voice sounded from behind me. I whirled around to find her flanked by Bernadette and Victor. "She has sent this dreadful letter." Georgette pointed at me. The next minutes were a blur. Victor advanced toward me, waving a letter in my face that looked like my handwriting but hadn't been written by me.

"Halia Bright, you are under arrest for assault and stalking. This letter proves that you have threatened to harm Georgette and Bernadette Fontaine if they didn't exit the competition." As Victor cuffed my arms behind my back, a cavalry of ten guards appeared behind him. I shook my head no at Lorenzo, whose wide stance made it clear he was prepared to fight them all. While I believed that he could beat the men and free me, it wasn't worth it since it would make us public enemy number one and reveal his teleporting ability to everyone.

"I'll get you out as soon as I can," he said, his expression pained as I was dragged away.

"The letter is fabricated. The truth will come out," I hissed to my ex-boyfriend. "This will never hold up in court."

Victor smiled viciously and whispered low so that only I could hear. "It doesn't have to. All we have to do is keep you in prison today and tomorrow so that you miss the next stage of the competition."

I gritted my teeth to stop from crying out at the unfairness. There was no point in yelling at Victor. He was convinced that his actions were justified since I had injured his pride by breaking up with him and had thwarted his promotion when I had let a boy escape from his custody.

As I descended the stairs of the prison building, I prayed that Victor would throw me into my cell and leave, not stick around to continue what he had tried to do less than a fortnight ago. A shiver raked through me as I remembered his rough hands, him ignoring my pleas to stop.

Enough! I couldn't think about that. I had to be strong. I had used my voice the last time to make him back off. I could do it again if need be. At least, that's what I hoped.

# 4TH AUGUST

Footsteps pounded outside my cell, jarring me awake. I pushed off the stone floor, my neck stiff, my fingers icy, surprised that I had managed to fall asleep on the barren ground. I had stayed up the whole night, waiting for Lorenzo to come. Sometime after the sun had risen, my body must have finally given out.

I probably would have frozen to death if not for the warm light streaming through my tiny barred window. Given how bright the sun was I guessed that it must be around midday.

How could it be so late already? Where was Lorenzo? Outside my door, keys jangled, and I stood to attention. Please let it be Lorenzo. My whole body tensed in anticipation. The lock on my prison cell turned, and the heavy metal door creaked open.

I froze at the sight of Victor. He was alone. He could do anything to me without repercussions.

*"Stay away from me. Stay away from me,"* I sang, but he only smirked in response.

"Your little voice won't help you in here, songbird." He crossed his hands in front of his chest. "The prison cells are guarded against magic use."

My heart plummeted as I realized that I was helpless and that Victor knew that I had magic. When had he found out? Did he remember the night he had tried to rape me, that I had kept him off me with my singing? Whatever way he had put it together, I decided that it was in my best interest not to say anything and wait for his next move.

He took a step closer, and I fought the urge the bolt for the door or press myself into one of the corners.

"I'll make you a deal. I'll let you go and say that it was all a misunderstanding if you break up with that demon and get back together with me."

I stared at him incredulously, certain I must've misheard.

"Don't be mulish, Halia. I'm good for you. Since you've started seeing that demon, you've been ear deep in problems."

I was too shocked to respond, which he took as an invitation to continue. "I'll even let you participate in your silly competition. Your singing might actually be good for us. If you win, we can get married at court and rise up in our social standing."

I suppressed the chortle working its way up my throat. Was he for real? How could he think there was a chance of us being together after him assaulting me, locking me away, and harassing me in countless other ways?

He jerked his head at me expectantly, letting me know he would perceive it as rudeness if I remained silent.

"It's too late for us," I said softly, hating that I had to appease him when all I wanted to do was scream at him and pound him with my fists.

He shook his head. "It's never too late." He took another step toward me, and this time, I flinched backward. I expected him to lunge at me, but whether it was because he wasn't under the influence of alcohol, which had allowed him to justify his physical aggressiveness, or because he was afraid that the other guards would discover that he had roughed me up, he didn't jump me. Instead, he scowled and said tersely, "Think about my offer. I will be back in a few hours." He glanced at his watch. "It's one now. You have five hours until your little concert starts. You decide if it will be with or without you."

The door flew shut behind him, and my body broke out in a tremor. I slid to the ground, rocking back and forth and trembling for a few minutes until my heartbeat finally calmed down, and my mind cleared.

I had less than five hours to get myself out of this mess. Longingly, I glanced up to the tiny window, leading to the street above me. Even if I could reach it, which I couldn't since there was nothing I could step on, I couldn't do anything about the metal bars.

My hope that Lorenzo would come for me dwindled with each minute. If he couldn't use his magic here, he wouldn't be able to help me. If only I could get Thomas to come here and plead my case."

*"Thomas, come to me. Come to me now,"* I sang for about ten minutes without any results.

Desperate, I rattled the metal door, which predictably, didn't budge an inch. What about picking the lock? I searched myself. No hairpin or anything else I could use.

I sank to the floor and stared up at the window, begging anyone who was listening to help me. As if the gods had heard me, a while later, a letter fell through the bars, followed by a single blue hair. Tia. My dear friend had once again come through for me.

Hastily, I tore open the envelope to find two notes inside. The top one was written by an unfamiliar hand, but I recognized the handwriting on the bottom one.

I started with the first note.

*H,*

*I have kindly agreed to help you, putting good faith into you upholding your end of the bargain. As you've probably realized by now, your prison cell is guarded against magic. However, this only extends to the cells. Therefore, I suggest that you do not squander your chance when I send Thomas to you and make him take you out of your cell and into his office. You should be able to convince him of your innocence since I have vouched for you. You will also need to convince him while in his office to leave you alone for a minute. Then listen to the call of magic. It will guide you to an object that you must take from his study and bring to me. Do not disappoint me. If you succeed, I will call on the fairy godmother.*

There was no signature, but it was clear that it had been written by cunning Abigail.

The second note was also unsigned, but I recognized the handwriting as Lorenzo's. This note was much shorter than the first.

*This is our only way. I know it's not ideal, but we have to do this for her. I have no idea what it is that she wants.*

I read the two notes again before crumpling them up and hiding them in my bra. It appeared that I had no choice but to enter an agreement where I didn't know all the components. I hated how exposed and vulnerable it made me, but I needed to get out of here, and I needed Abigail's help to call on the fairy godmother. Thus, I ignored the warning bells going off in my head. Even if I didn't trust Abigail, she was my ally for now. Also, since her request involved me using my voice, I could fulfill the favor I owed her. The quicker I settled my debt, the better.

As Abigail had promised, there were footsteps a while later. The lock turned, and the door creaked open.

Thomas looked me up and down and said unceremoniously, "I'm releasing you, but first, we'll have a chat."

"Can we do it in your office, please?" I made myself tremble. Thomas must've taken pity on me because he nodded.

We didn't speak as we walked up the stone staircase I had been dragged down the night before. Thomas herded me down the corridor and into his office. He sat down in front of his desk and motioned for me to take the chair across from him.

"I know it was all a misunderstanding," he began. "But you need to be careful from now on, Halia. I can't bail you out again, and it seems that you've been getting into a lot of trouble lately."

"The sisters and Victor got me into this mess out of revenge."

Thomas interlaced his fingers. "Right now, I can't do anything about the Fontaines, but I promise I'm looking at them and their boarding house very closely. As for

Victor, I'll deal with him once I get my promotion."

A jolt of joy and excitement went through me. "You're going to be the captain? Congratulations!"

A warm smile spread across his face. "Thank you." He paused, then said, "I'm assuming the note telling me that not everything is right at the mental institution came from you." I nodded in confirmation, and his forehead furrowed. "I appreciate it. But in the future, I have to ask you to stay out of police business."

Not wanting to break a promise I would have to break later, I asked, "What happened at the facility?"

He sighed heavily. "We arrested the head doctor, and we're questioning the rest of the staff." He straightened a few papers before adding. "Patients did go missing. Apparently, they've been handed over to someone called the leader." Thomas studied me. "What can you tell me about him?"

"Not much. I've never met him. I don't know what he looks like, or what his real name is. All I know is that he's working together with the fae." I fell silent, wondering if I had said too much, but Thomas motioned for me to continue. "I believe that he's been abducting humans to extract their life energy from them. However, it seems that that wasn't enough for him, and he asked the fae to help him extract magic out of the humans."

Thomas didn't declare that such a thing was impossible. All he said was, "What for?"

"Probably to overpower the king."

Thomas inhaled deeply. "Those are very serious accusations." He thought for a minute. "I believe you, but nobody will believe it if I try to flag it. We need more proof before I can go to my superior."

I nodded.

"In the meantime, I need you to focus on your

singing and representing Arcadia. I appreciate what you've done, but please don't get involved any further."

I knew I had to tell him what he wanted to hear, even if I knew, and he probably suspected, that I wouldn't be able to keep my promise. "I'll focus on my singing." And I meant it in that moment, as I thought about the competition. I knew I had to at least make it to the next round, which would be in front of the court and thus the king, presenting me finally with the chance to talk to his majesty.

"Good luck, Halia. I hope you win." Thomas smiled, and I hated what I had to do next.

*"Thank you,"* I sang. *"Give me a few minutes by myself. Go outside, check something."*

Thomas rubbed his forehead as if he had a headache coming on.

*"You need to check on something. You'll be back in a few minutes."*

He stood, still rubbing his temples. "Before I discharge you, I need to check on something. I'll be right back."

The door fell shut behind him, and I jumped up. I didn't have to concentrate, the ancient pull of magic was strong; It pulsated; it whispered to me. It wasn't right. It didn't belong here.

I stepped to the bookcase and grabbed the book that the power was coming from only to discover that it wasn't the book but what lay behind it. The moonstone was coin-sized, easy to overlook, and not much worth to someone seeking money, but the spell in it was mighty.

I grabbed the stone, put the book back where it had been, and fell into the chair just as the door opened.

"Sorry about that." Thomas shook his head as if trying to wake up from a dream. "You're discharged now. I'll deal with Victor. See that he gets transferred somewhere else. It appears that he can't coexist with you in the same city."

I shot Thomas a grateful smile, guilt tugging at me for tricking him. "Thank you, thank you so much."

The warm sun on my face and the breeze in my hair was the sweetest sensation as I skipped down the streets toward Daydream. Lorenzo and Mikka were waiting for me inside.

"Are you all right?" Lorenzo pulled me into a hug only to release me a second later to examine me. "Has—"

"I'm fine," I reassured him.

"It's good to have you back." Mikka swung her legs, sitting on the bar. "I would've been pissed if those useless Fontaine sisters won."

A throat clearing sounded, and I turned to find Abigail in a booth behind me. She rose and strolled toward me. "I believe you have something for me," she said, not bothering with niceties.

"What does it do?"

Her lips curled back into a soft snarl. "It's none of your business."

She was right, telling me what the moonstone was hadn't been part of our bargain. I pulled it out. "You promise not to hurt Arcadia with it?"

Abigail let out a tinkling laugh, which was identical to the sound Acacia made when she laughed. The hairs on my arms stood. "Yes, I promise," the faerie drawled. "Not everybody wants your precious Arcadia. There are so many more beautiful places in the universe."

I felt the truth of her statement, and even though I didn't appreciate the derision she showed for my home, I was glad that she didn't want to dwell in my city. I handed her the stone, and a moment later, it disappeared into the inside of her cloak.

"Call on the fairy godmother," I said, afraid she'd go back on her promise now that she had what she wanted.

Abigail showed her teeth. "Very well. You better ask her everything you need to know because I won't call on her again."

My mind was a mess as I prepared to meet the godmother. Abigail closed her eyes, her lips moving silently. An invisible wind blew her blonde strands back, and her alabaster face radiated the way only a fae's skin could.

A popping sound disturbed whatever trance Abigail was in. Her eyes flew open, and next to her, appeared a hunched old lady with fine, white hair.

The old woman glanced between the four of us but focused on Abigail. "Fae child, why have you called me?"

Abigail jerked her head toward me. "This one has questions for you." With that, the fae headed toward the exit. Relief swept through me that she wouldn't be privy to this conversation. Fae were fickle and self-serving creatures. She might be working with us today, but tomorrow she might once again be on Acacia's side.

The fairy godmother turned to me. "Why have you called me, child?" Her voice was neutral, but there was a spark of recognition in her gray eyes.

"You know who I am," I breathed.

"There's a lot I know," she replied vaguely. I waited for her to elaborate, but she didn't.

Afraid that she could disappear at any moment like Mrs. Woods had, the godmother who used to conceal the golden rings in my eyes until I turned eighteen, I got to the point.

"We're searching for Queen Ella. Officially, she disappeared a few weeks ago, but I've seen her since then working in the kitchen of Madam's Boarding House. She allowed the owner, Mrs. Fontaine, to call her Cinder. Queen Ella used to be the stepdaughter of Mrs. Fontaine. I don't understand why she abandoned her husband to work as a kitchen maid. Then, a week ago, she vanished completely. No one has seen her since."

There was so much pain on the godmother's face, but she didn't reply.

"Please, we need to bring the queen back to her rightful place. Bad things have been happening in Arcadia since she abandoned the king. I'm sure her goodness can restore the peace."

"It's more complicated than that."

I stepped forward. "Just tell us where she is. We'll do the rest."

Godmother's gaze swiped from me to Lorenzo to Mikka before she shook her head. "I can't. My goddaughter doesn't want to be found."

"Why? What does Mrs. Fontaine have on her that is so bad? If her stepmother threatened her, why didn't she go to the king? Why on earth would she ever return to that monster after getting her happily ever after?"

"To protect the ones we love, we'll do anything, even if it isn't the right thing to do."

"Was she protecting the king? If Madam threatened to hurt him, certainly his guards could've prevented it."

There was a look of resignation on Godmother's face. "There has been a lot of speculation about why the queen and king never had a child. Many believed that they weren't able to have one."

Confusion spread through me at this turn in the conversation.

"The truth is that the queen and king did have a

child. It wasn't their flesh and blood but rather a newborn they took in and which they gave up when the babe was only a few months old."

I felt my forehead wrinkle. "Why?" Even if the queen had been overwhelmed with a little one, she didn't need to give it up. There were plenty of people who could help her at court. She didn't have to lift a finger if she didn't want, although I couldn't imagine Queen Ella leaving her child with nannies.

"The queen loved her child dearly and wanted to keep her, but she was afraid that if she did, the child would die. Ella's stepmother learned about the queen's daughter and promised she would kill the child."

"But weren't Madam and her daughters imprisoned at that point?"

"They were, but a few days later, someone broke them out, and rumors began to swirl that the stepmother possessed dark magic with which she could kill the child. Ella became certain that the only way she could keep her child safe was to bring it to a location where her stepmother wouldn't search."

"So they hid the child in the countryside?" There was a princess out there. An heir. "We must find her and reunite her with the king. If Queen Ella hears her child is fine, she will return."

Godmother shook her head. "The child is not at any of the lords' estates. The girl was placed into the Faustus orphanage."

My heart stopped beating. "How long ago was that?" My voice sounded weak, distant.

"A bit over eighteen years ago. The girl would be eighteen and a few months old now."

Like Tia or me. My mind broke out into a mental jog as I considered every girl that had been in the orphanage and whether any of them were of the right age. They weren't. The closest two were off by half a year each, which meant that either Tia or I was the princess.

"I turned eighteen only a few months earlier, and so did my best friend." A tremble siezed my body as I waited for the Godmother to respond, but all she did was nod. "One of us could be the princess," I added.

Still, Godmother didn't respond, and I reached for her hand. "Please, I need to know. If you can't tell me this, then at least tell me where Queen Ella is. Arcadia needs her more than ever."

Fairy Godmother shook her head sadly. "I'm afraid I can't give you the answers you seek. I swore to my goddaughter to never reveal to her child who she was. As for your second question, I wish I could help, but wherever Ella is, a spell is hiding her, making it impossible for me to know where my goddaughter is."

Lorenzo took a step forward and spoke for the first time. "What about the disruptions in Arcadia? Will they cease once Queen Ella returns to her rightful throne?"

The Godmother shook her head. "No, Queen Ella broke the last dark spell when she married the king. She was a good queen for eighteen years. Now it's the turn of the next generation to rescue our kingdom from the evil that has befallen it."

"The princess is the answer," I said quietly, a somberness descending over me.

Godmother nodded. "The princess must follow her heart and embrace her courage." The words were barely out of her mouth as the air around her shimmered, and she faded away.

I lunged for her. "Don't leave! There's still so much I need to ask you!" My pleas were in vain. She was already gone.

I grabbed a table for support as tears began to fall from my eyes.

Lorenzo embraced me and pulled me into his chest, his scent of fresh-cut grass and lemons enveloping me into a soothing cocoon.

"It's going to be all right," he repeated while I sobbed.

"All this time, Tia and I were at the orphanage, thinking we were unwanted when one of us was a beloved princess! How could this be? How could the queen have given up her daughter and not visited her once?"

"You heard the godmother. Ella was terrified of her stepmother."

"Still, I don't understand her choice." I wiped away my tears and glanced up at Lorenzo. "I think I'm the queen's daughter. Or maybe I'm just being selfish… what if we never find out whether it's Tia or me?"

"You will." Lorenzo drew soothing circles on my back.

"How? The queen gave her daughter up when she was only a few months old."

"She'll remember the color of your eyes once you remove your protective contact lenses."

I strained my mind, trying to remember if Queen Ella had seen me when the golden specks in my eyes were pronounced enough to almost create circles. Could I have worked alongside my mother without knowing it? I gazed up at Lorenzo. "You think I'm the princess?" Hope and trepidation thundered in my chest.

"It doesn't matter what I or anyone else thinks." Lorenzo's violet-green eyes softened. "You were right before. I can't keep you safe. This is your mission."

Everything clicked into place, and I knew without a doubt that I was the princess. I was the protector of Arcadia, and when all of this was over, I would find out who the queen and king had adopted me from and what my first months with them had been like. Maybe I would finally have the family I always dreamed about.

I swallowed hard. If the king and queen accepted me, my life would change completely. I wouldn't just gain a family but also a title. I would be the princess of Arcadia, which would allow me to do great things for my kingdom and its people, but also place heavy responsibility and expectation on my shoulders. I might even have to give up my singing. Could the universe really be so cruel as to give me my family and take away my most precious possession in return? If that was the price, did I even want the queen and king to acknowledge me?

"What if I'm not sure if I want to be a princess?"

"Then, we'll figure it out, as we figure out everything." Lorenzo's lips pressed against mine, and I melted against his body, molding my soft curves into his hard muscles. Time slowed, then stopped as I lost myself in the delicious sensation of his soft lips, his velvety tongue. Heat pooled in my abdomen, and I tugged on his silver hair, wanting, needing more of him. Then I remembered that Mikka had been in the bar with us and jerked backward, my breathing heavy. To my relief, Mikka was nowhere to be found. She must have crept upstairs sometime after the Fairy Godmother had vanished. After she figured out that Tia might be the princess. I needed to talk to Tia, but first, I needed to understand what had just happened between Lorenzo and me.

"Only days ago, you said you didn't want a relationship with me because I was holding back. Do you still feel that way? If you do, you need to stop kissing me, because my feelings are only growing for you, and I can't keep it casual."

Lorenzo tugged a loose hair strand behind my ear. "I was never able to stay away from you, Halia. I wanted to protect myself by waiting for you to fully commit to me." He shook his head. "But when you were seized by Victor and dragged away, I realized what nonsense I had spun in my head. The timing will never be perfect, just as relationships aren't perfect. I don't want to squander what we have or the time we have because I'm overly cautious." A smile tugged on his lips. "There's no time like now. Life is very fragile, and I want to enjoy every moment I have with you." He chuckled. "I'm done being a stupid, stubborn demon. I'm ready to jump into this with both feet."

My chest expanded, and a chuckle rippled out of my throat. "I'm ready for you to stop being a stupid, stubborn demon as well." I wrapped my hands around his neck and kissed him fiercely, not holding back any of the passion burning in my veins.

When we finally broke apart, Lorenzo pulled a box with an envelope attached to it out from behind the bar. "From the royal competition."

Since we all had been sent black clothes last time with instructions to wear them, I wasn't too surprised to receive another envelope and box. I opened the letter.

*Dear Halia Bright,*

*Please be advised that due to certain circumstances the competition has been postponed to tomorrow at ten in the morning. Please arrive promptly. Do keep your hair and makeup natural and wear the garments provided in the box.*

*With kind regards,*

*Henry, assistant to Mr. Goodwin*

I gave Lorenzo the letter to read while I ripped open

the box with a knife to find a white, long-sleeved blouse and black pants inside.

"That doesn't seem like performance attire." The clothes were more appropriate to work behind a desk at a hotel than to wear on stage. "And why did they postpone the competition?"

Lorenzo examined the contents of the box. "Postponing it for less than twenty-four hours is strange. As for the costume, maybe you'll be expected to move around a lot."

I cringed. I certainly hoped they hadn't prepared an expensive choreography for us. I was a singer, not a dancer, and I would be severely disadvantaged in learning complicated steps when I had never taken a dance lesson before.

I closed the box, wishing Tia was here to make a funny comment or cheer me up. Tia. Tia had been missing the whole time. If Mikka had gone up to her to relay what the godmother had said, the girls should've been down a long time age.

"Where is Tia?"

Lorenzo's face pinched, reflecting the worry I felt. "I was so focused on getting you back—"

"She was the one to drop off Abigail's note, right?"

Lorenzo nodded. "She was supposed to come back afterward."

I rushed upstairs and tore open the door to my bedroom. It was empty. So was Mikka's.

Lorenzo cursed behind me, and I whirled around. "What?"

"We were in the bar the whole time since Abigail left. Mikka had to deliberately take the back door to not tell us that she was leaving."

"Why didn't she tell us?" I asked as I took the stairs

two a time, darting toward the exit.

"The mating bond. When it snaps into place, it's very primal and leaves little room for reason or logic."

That stopped me in my tracks. "Mating bond?"

"When a demon finds his mate and after they consummate their relationship, an invisible connection forms between them."

"But, Tia isn't a demon."

"She can still be Mikka's mate."

I pushed away the questions this new revelation brought, and asked, "Where do we search for them?"

Just then, the door to Daydream flew open, and Mikka stormed inside. Her white hair was disheveled, her black eyes were wide, a vein in her neck pulsed violently. She was nothing like the cool and collected half-ice demon I had met. "She's gone." Her words came out as an animalistic growl. "The fae took Tia."

# GODDESS OF HARMONY

## 5TH AUGUST

As I ascended the stage with the other remaining eleven candidates, I vaguely noticed that the other performers had received much nicer clothes. Like me, their garments were black and white. However, while I had been given a simple white shirt and black slacks, other singers wore impressive floor-length gowns with complicated lace designs complemented by elegant gloves and big headpieces.

My outfit stood out in a bad way, making me the most boring contestant to look at, but I could barely summon any outrage or even annoyance at that. Who cared why I had been given such a disadvantage? I didn't care about being sabotaged or winning the competition. How could I when my best friend was gone because of me?

As I waited for the competition to begin, I went over and over what I knew about Tia's abduction, which wasn't much. Tia had delivered Abigail's letter to me in prison, then she had vanished.

My friend would never have gone away of her own free will. Someone had snatched her. But who? One of the fae after discovering that Abigail had betrayed them? The leader or Madam Fontaine, whose boarding house was getting shadier by the minute.

At first, I had been convinced that Tia had been snatched to hurt me, but since I hadn't received any demands so far, I wasn't so sure about that any longer. Either way, whether Tia had been taken to be used against me or because she had been at the wrong time at the wrong place, I needed to find her. Unfortunately, combing through Arcadia with Lorenzo and Mikka last night hadn't given us any hints to her whereabouts.

With no trace of my friend, I wished desperately that I could turn back time to when people had started disappearing in Arcadia. If I could, I would tell Tia to leave. She could've gone anywhere, found a bar job in a safe city. Or, at the very least, I would tell her to stay away from me. All of this was my fault. I should've never been so reckless and allowed her to get tangled up in the city's magical politics. What had I been thinking, asking her to deliver messages between myself and Abigail? Did I really believe that making her my envoy to the sly fae could end well?

Deep down, I had always known that there would be retribution to pay, I just never took the time to really think about the consequences, and now, it was too late.

In the best-case scenario, Tia was still alive, probably being tortured for information, or weak from the fae draining her of the tiny bit of magic she possessed as a human. I prayed she hadn't landed in the leader's hands who could suck out her life essence and make her a crone overnight.

I didn't even want to allow myself to think about the worst-case scenario. No, I refused to even consider that Tia might already be dead and that my enemies would drop off her body at the footstep of Daydream.

Disgust roiled through me, and I wanted to hit myself. If something happened to Tia, it would be nobody's fault but my own.

"Candidates, do you understand the task?" Mr. Goodwin asked in his booming bass voice, tearing me out of my self-flagellation.

I cursed underneath my breath. How could I have missed what the assignment was? I might not care about my costume disadvantage, but I still needed to win this competition or at least progress far enough to perform in front of the king and tell him that I had found Queen Ella working as a maid in Madam's kitchen before she vanished. Maybe the queen was being held where Tia was. But even if they weren't together, I needed to save the queen. All kinds of bad things had been happening in our kingdom since she had left the king, and they had only escalated when she had disappeared from Madam's Boarding House.

Thankfully, there were seven candidates in front of me, which meant I should get the hang of what we were supposed to do before it was my turn.

Thus, I didn't ask for clarification but simply smiled as I was handed a note sheet. I supposed they wanted to see if we could sing a song without any preparation, but I soon learned that it was not that simple. I hadn't been given just any song, but a rock song. I had heard it a few times, and neither the style, genre, nor vocal range fit my voice. My stomach cramped. Certainly, they didn't expect me to sing this? Unfortunately, my fears were confirmed when the first candidate stumbled forward to the microphone and began singing an extremely difficult song with an octave range that she wasn't anywhere close to being able to conquer.

The audience booed and whispered when the poor girl failed to hit the high and the low notes. Even though I wanted to look away, I forced myself to study her, noticing that her outfit wasn't much better than mine. Her simple black and white dress was unremarkable compared to the lace, silk, and fur trimmings other candidates wore.

Was our competition host, Mr. Goodwin, in charge of assigning outfits and songs? If so, someone must've paid him a hefty sum to create such an unequal competition.

I sure wanted to have a word with him after the performance and didn't feel any qualms about using my voice to compel him to tell me the truth. Not that it would do me any good. Even if I could prove that someone had paid him off, whom I strongly suspected were the Fontaine sisters, my statement wouldn't hold much weight. The audience would simply view me as a disgruntled, disqualified performer who was stirring up trouble.

The second guy did much better, which didn't surprise me since his baby blues and low-cut white shirts that exposed his muscular chest basically screamed man candy. His song "Fifth Flame" fit him vocally, and every female in the audience swooned with several yelling, "Derryl, marry me!" after he finished.

The third and fourth candidates didn't stand out in a bad or good way, and I guessed that they had flown under the Fontaine sisters' radar.

Number five had definitely been sabotaged. The guy was given an extremely girly song, and both the sleeves and pantlegs on his suit were a few inches too short, giving him an odd appearance. The sixth candidate was all right but didn't hold a candle to number seven, Hendrix Cash. In his rock 'n roll leather pants and torn shirt, Hendrix belted out a song about freedom that was exactly his style. I sighed. Seriously, not only was I given a shitty outfit and song, they also had to put me next to someone who excelled in the genre I was going to fail. As Mr. Rockstar was about to finish, I glanced at the sisters to my right side. Even though there were two people between us, I caught them whisper, "Good luck failing, loser."

I gritted my teeth at the confirmation that they were behind this. Apparently, fake voices alone weren't enough anymore for them to bolster themselves up. Now, they were taking me down underhandedly.

It was disgusting. But if they thought their little stunt would send me packing or make me quit, they had the wrong girl.

I would transform the dirty stone they had given me into a diamond. While the other seven people had performed, a strategy had formed in my mind.

As I sashayed forward, I winked at the Fontaine sisters, whose foreheads knitted at my positive mood. "Citizens of Arcadia," I began. "As you might've noticed, tonight's competition has a special flavor to it. Some of the performers have received a song that is favorable to their style and vocal range as well as amazing and beautiful outfits." I paused to let that sink in before adding, "Congratulations, Derryl and Hendrix." The females in the audience cheered. "Other singers, however, haven't been as fortunate and were given songs that didn't fit them and outfits that did nothing for them." I glanced briefly at all the candidates who had failed of no fault of their own and were now too ashamed to even meet my gaze.

I stepped to the edge of the stage and motioned at myself. "You can guess from my simple pants and shirt that I belong in the second category. I also pulled a short stick with my assigned song."

Several people in the audience shifted uncomfortably from leg to leg while others began whispering.

"But I won't let that hold me back. Tonight, I might look like a bookkeeper, but I'm going to rock your world. That is, as long as you'll let me."

Mr. Goodman advanced toward me. "What are you doing?" he hissed.

"What am I doing, Mr. Goodman?" I said loudly into the microphone, making a vein in his forehead pulse violently. "Why, Mr. Goodman, I thought it would be the right thing to do to inform the audience about what game they're witnessing."

He snatched the microphone out of my hand and said in a trembling voice, "Miss Bright, you are here to sing, not to showcase your opinions. Perhaps you got confused, but this is not one of our interviews. This round is a pure singing portion."

"Oh, I understand very well." I leaned into the microphone, fluttering my eyelashes innocently.

"So will you sing, or are you forfeiting your entry?"

"I'll perform. I like a good challenge." I grabbed the microphone from him and saluted the Fontaine sisters before turning to the audience. "Let's rock 'n roll!" I pointed at the musicians, who sat with their mouths wide open. "Hit it, boys!"

The drummer started up, followed by the bass.

*Day in, day out, it's all the same. I'm feeling dead on the inside,* I breathed in a husky voice, *but now, it's time to break out!"*I ripped off the top button of my blouse and rolled up my sleeves, which garnered me "woohoos!"

*I won't be no prisoner to the system no more, yeah, no more.*

I jumped across the stage and threw my head back and forth, and the audience went wild, joining into my shenanigans by jumping up and down, pumping their fists into the air.

*I'm breaking free from the chains you put on me. I'm getting out right now and setting sail toward a new shore.*

I strummed an imaginary guitar before motioning for the audience to sing with me. I ran up and down the stage, high fiving the people closest to me before returning to the middle of the stage and belting out the final lines.

Was my performance perfect? No.

Did I suddenly transform into a rock goddess? No.

But I was having fun, and the crowd could tell. My energy was contagious.

I might not know how to do any fancy strokes, but when thrown into the deep end, I would paddle for my life. Every. Single. Time.

The bass player hit his final note, and I bowed deeply. "Thank you for indulging me and allowing me to be your rock star tonight." My hair was wild, my shirt was torn, and for a moment, I truly felt like a rock star.

Shooting Mr. Goodwin a sweet smile, I handed the microphone back to him and wrapped his fingers around it since he looked like he was about to drop it.

My performance had left him speechless, requiring his assistant, Henry, to step in. Nervously, Henry leaned into the microphone. “Thank you, Halia Bright. Now, please welcome...”

I was riding my wave of adrenaline high for the next two performances until the stepsisters came on.

Their dresses complimented each other. One of the sisters wore a dress made of a white satin material in the front and black lace at the back, while the other one had black satin in the front and white lace in the back. The costumes were gorgeous but did nothing for their broad figures, while their heavy, smoky eye makeup only highlighted their annoyance as they took the stage for what I guessed was a duet.

However, Acacia’s magic succeeded once again as the sisters opened their mouths and sang a love song, their voices mesmerizing. The crowd swayed, pure adoration in their gazes. The citizens might’ve found me entertaining and had crushed hard on Deryll and Hendrix, but they were one hundred percent under the sisters’ spell. I wouldn’t be surprised if they believed that the sisters were the most gracious, beautiful, and talented women they had ever seen. Whatever magic Acacia had bestowed upon them, it seemed boundless. She was an ocean backing the sisters, while my efforts were a drop of water in the desert.

Exhaustion and frustration overwhelmed me, but I didn’t have the luxury to curl up into a ball or hide underneath my bed covers. I needed to be strong. Tonight, all I had to do was progress into the next round. Then, I could figure out how to break Acacia’s magic. But had my performance been good enough for me to make it into the next round? There were twelve of us. Only six would get to continue.

The crowd yelled, "Georgette and Bernadette, we love you!" while the sisters blew air kisses. The judges scribbled furiously on their scrolls, their foreheads furrowed, their lips pressed together tightly. Finally, they put down their quills. Henry collected the scorecards and delivered them to Mr. Goodwin, who hesitated before speaking into the microphone. "Thank you, everyone, for coming here today to support our competitors." His hand trembled as he glanced down on the scrolls. "I'm excited to announce the best six singers who will be progressing into the next round, which will be held at the castle, in front of our king and his court."

Whispers spread through the crowd like wildfire. Normally, the annual competition lasted much longer, providing entertainment for several months.

Mr. Goodwin must've caught onto the souring of the mood because he quickly added. "In light of everything that has happened recently, we had to cut the competition short, but our gracious king has decided to make all the concert public this year. Thus, while the next and final competition will be held at court, everyone is invited to come and watch."

A moment of shocked silence followed his declaration before the crowd broke out into thunderous applause. I, however, didn't like this development one bit. It was nice to make the competition and our ruler more accessible to everyone, most citizens had never been inside the castle's walls, but allowing so many people into the castle was asking for trouble. It would be easy for the fae and other magic wielders to slip in. If the leader was planning an attack, there would be no better time to strike the king than when he and his citizens were exposed. What was the king thinking? Or perhaps it hadn't been his idea at all. I studied Mr. Goodwin. What else had he done besides rigging the competition in the Fontaine sisters' favor? What bargain had he struck with Madam?

Mr. Goodwin patted his sweaty forehead with a handkerchief and continued. "The finale will be held in five days on the tenth of August. There will be two parts to the competition. In the first half, the top six that progress today will be whittled down to three who will compete to become Arcadia's champion."

The crowd cheered, too excited to get to witness the grand finale to worry about why the timeline had been hiked up. The only concerned face was Thomas's, and I made a mental note to ask the new head of the guards about the accelerated timeline and why today's performance had taken place this morning instead of the night before as it had been originally planned.

"With our results in, I ask you to give a big round of applause to our winners." Mr. Goodwin's thick knuckles were white as he clutched the microphone, and every cell in my body tensed.

I had to make it to the top six. Even if I didn't win this competition, I needed to get to make it to the next round. I needed to tell the king that the last time I had seen Queen Ella, she had been underneath Madam Fontaine's spell. I needed his counsel on how to find the queen, and maybe I would even find the courage to ask him if I had been the adopted child Ella had given up out of fear of her stepmother.

"Continuing this journey are: Deryll Mortimer,"—Mr. Goodwin nodded at the heartbreaker while my gut clenched—"and Hendrix Cash." Unsurprising, given that the two female favorite hotties represented the good boy and the bad boy, heartmender and heartbreaker.

"Also continuing are Georgette and Bernadette Fontaine."

As the sisters blew more air kisses, I gritted my teeth and swore I would expose them.

"As well as Lana Shay." A beauty stepped forward, and I recognized her from newspaper sketches. She had been singing for years and shouldn't be in this competition.

"And the final spot goes to..." Mr. Goodwin paused, and my legs trembled, ready to give out. "The final spot goes to Halia Bright."

Starbursts exploded in my heart. I had made it.

Before I could enjoy my win, Georgette stomped on my toe with her heel. I clamped my mouth shut. Nobody had seen her stunt, and if I screamed, I would only appear crazy.

"You squirreled your way in this time, maid. Next time, you won't be as lucky," she hissed.

Bernadette crushed my other toe. "Stop making everything harder on yourself. You think ill-chosen songs and bad outfits are all we can do? If you know what's best for you, you'll drop out of this competition."

Rage bubbled up in me, urging me to shove the sisters to the ground. But if I lost my cool, I would be arrested. Again. Thomas had dismissed the charges the sister had filed against me last time, but if I did anything publicly to them, there was no way I could escape jail. Thus, all I did was grit my teeth harder and imagine how sweet revenge would taste once I took down the sisters and their mother. They could push me down, but I wouldn't stay down.

"Do you understand?" Bernadette hissed.

"I do."

She smiled, pure satisfaction on her face, completely

unaware that she had awoken the fighter in me who would battle until her last breath. This was war, and I would win.

As soon as we were dismissed, and after the sisters walked off the stage—the last thing I needed was them pushing me down the stairs—I hurried toward Thomas.

"Thomas, may I have a word?" I asked when I caught up with him, shooting Lorenzo a look that said, "stay back." My chances of getting information out of the new head of the guards were much better alone than when accompanied by a demon.

"Halia." Thomas' surprise turned into a warm smile. "You did well up there. Even though I would lay off Mr. Goodwin."

I chuckled. "Can you blame me when he made me perform in this?"

Thomas's gaze slid down my shirt and pants, and behind him, Lorenzo's jaw tightened, and he looked ready to launch himself at Thomas. I shook my head slightly and then put my arm on Thomas' shoulder, singing above a whisper, "*Why was today's competition postponed, and why was the rest of the competition cut short?"*

Thomas blinked a few times as if trying to get dust out of his eyes. "The king," he finally said, "His Majesty needed more time before today's announcement."

*"Which one?"*

"About cutting the competition short and allowing anyone into the palace."

I went very still. *"Did someone force him?"*

Thomas nodded, then shook his head. "I think so."

*"Why? How?"*

"I don't know." He rubbed his eyes, fighting my influence, and I released him.

“Thank you,” I said brightly, knowing my smile didn’t reach my eyes. “I can use all the luck I can get to win this competition.” I waved goodbye and disappeared into the crowd. Lorenzo fell into step with me once we were out of the patrolmen’s earshot.

“Thomas is on our side,” I said as I met Lorenzo’s intense violet-green glare.

“Thomas is doing his job. He’s on the king’s side.”

I sighed. “Isn’t that the same thing?”

“You can’t trust him.” Lorenzo’s jaw was set. “He was Victor’s partner.”

“Exactly. Was, past tense. He sent Victor away once he had the authority.” Thomas couldn’t be blamed for my violent ex’s behavior. Thomas had been nothing but kind.

Lorenzo took my hand. “I know you consider Thomas a friend, but think about it, if you can manipulate him, so can others.”

I bit my lip. The truth stung. Only a while back, I had thought Mr. Goodwin to be impartial, and now, he was the Fontaine sisters’ lackey. I doubted Thomas could be bought, but he could be threatened or subjected to fae magic to change his mind.

I shivered. “I think the leader is behind the competition changes. He or one of his cronies threatened the king.”

Lorenzo stopped walking. “Do you know with what?”

I shrugged. “Maybe the queen?”

“Or maybe Tia. They could’ve lied and said that she’s the heir.”

“She might be.” I chewed on the inside of my cheek. My gut told me I was the child the monarchs had adopted, but I didn’t have anything to prove my theory, just a hunch. “Where’s Mikka?” I was certain the half-ice demon wasn’t here because she was searching for

Tia, her mate, and I needed to know if she had made any progress.

"She's supposed to meet us back at Daydream."

I quickened my step, and soon, we reached Lorenzo's bar. While it featured lots of leather and polished wood like other night establishments, what made Daydream unique were the ice sculptures that depicted different demons as well as our king and queen and were bathed in the blue lights that illuminated the bar. At first glance, everything in Daydream appeared the same, but as I crossed the floor, my feet slid on a puddle and whooshed out from under me. I landed hard on my back.

"Halia! Are you all right?" Lorenzo was immediately by my side. I rubbed my hip, staring at the ice sculptures. The sword-wielding demon's blade had been reduced to a stump, the dragon's scales were gone, and our queen's crown was dripping down her face.

"Mikka. We need to find her."

Lorenzo followed my line of sight, and his face went rigid. "If they hurt her—"

He never got to finish his sentence as a weak voice rasped, "I'm over here."

I jumped up, ignoring the dull throbbing of my backside and hurried behind the bar. Lying on her stomach, her face pressed against the tiles was Mikka. She was panting hard, and beads of sweat shone on her upper lip. "The mating bond," she rasped before her eyes rolled back, and her lids felt shut.

# 6TH AUGUST

Mikka mumbled something, tearing me out of my fitful, light doze. I pushed off the rocking chair I had fallen asleep in and kneeled by her bedside. "Mikka, are you awake?"

Her eyes fluttered open, and I grasped her hand.

She croaked, "water," and I hurried to get her a glass. I tipped it slowly against her mouth, and she swallowed. She had been unconscious most of the night. Lorenzo had told me not to assume the worst, that Mikka's weak state caused by the mating bond could mean a number of things, including Tia simply being stressed, but I found it impossible to stay positive. I couldn't help but imagine my friend being tortured by the fae. Worse, what if Madam had snatched my friend and delivered her straight to thc leader? After my altercation with the fae and my persistence in the competition, it would be easy for Madam to make the connection that I was planning something, and she certainly wasn't above torturing information out of Tia.

Mikka pushed the glass away, tearing me away from my destructive thoughts and back to the present. "I'll be fine, and so will Tia." She didn't sound the least bit convinced. Probably seeing the pain written across my face, she added, "At least, we know that she's alive. If she were dead, the mating bond would have disappeared. But I can feel her. I think she's doing better now. Maybe she's asleep."

Asleep, someplace the enemy had abducted her to. Knowing my dark thoughts wouldn't help anyone, I kept them to myself as I helped Mikka into a sitting position. Perspiration shone on her face as I placed a second pillow behind her back. "Rest and don't worry. Lorenzo and I will get Tia back."

She huffed. "I wish I could go with you, not be a useless vegetable."

I didn't know how to respond to that. Everyone hated feeling helpless, and we were beyond empty reassurances. Relief fluttered through me when the door creaked open, and Lorenzo stepped inside. The grimness on his face faded once he realized Mikka was awake.

"How are you?" He pressed the back of his hand against her forehead, eliciting a grimace from her.

"Stop it. I'm not a child."

He chuckled, his violet-green eyes twinkling. "You must be feeling much better to have your sass back."

She rolled her eyes. "I'll be much better once Tia is back."

I clasped Lorenzo's hand. "Did you find out anything?"

He hesitated, so I pressed. "Please, this is my friend. You can't protect me from this. There's a reason why I discovered that I could influence others with my voice when the queen went missing. This is my mission, and I must face the consequences of my actions."

Lorenzo didn't look happy but relented. "Our suspicions were correct. The Fontaines are working for the leader. I overheard Madam saying that old and useless people won't suffice anymore, that they need higher quality supply."

I balled my fists. "They're providing the leader with humans to siphon off their life energy and power!" I gritted my teeth. The sisters had no scruples, using illegal magic to fix their voices and buy the competition host's favor and to participate in human trafficking. "What do you think the leader promised them exactly?"

Lorenzo shrugged. "A place in the court and castle accommodations. I can't imagine he promised them real power."

I nodded. From everything I'd heard, this leader was a power-hungry man. He was already working with the fae, meaning there wasn't much of the pie left to give to the Fontaines. And since they were his lowliest supplier and had no magic of their own, they were the weak link we needed to latch onto.

We still had no idea who this leader might be, and we couldn't follow the fae since they would sense Lorenzo's presence if he was nearby. Our last attempt to eavesdrop on their meeting using Lorenzo's astral projection had disastrous results. The potent magic that had to be cast had almost torn his soul out of his body and delivered it straight to hell.

I wasn't willing to take such a risk again, and I wanted to stay far away from Acacia. Once I had considered her a friend, who hid the golden rings in my eyes with her fae magic. But now she was a foe. A foe I would bring down after I was done with the Fontaines.

With my mind made up, I rose and brought Mikka a plate with bread and a jar of honey. "Will you be all right by yourself?"

She punched me lightly on the shoulder. "Yes, but I might barf if you two continue treating me like a broken baby bird. Go and get Tia."

Lorenzo and I went to the door. "I'll put out the closed sign and add a magic barrier outside the bar," he said. "We'll be back as soon as we can."

Mikka's black eyes turned to hard obsidian stones. "Make them pay."

"We will," I promised.

Once we entered Lorenzo's room, I said, "I didn't know you could make barriers."

"I can't." Lorenzo headed toward his bed, and heat crept into my face as my stupid mind flashed to an image of us lying in his bed together, limbs tangled.

Lorenzo opened his bedside drawer and showed me a blue powder in a vial, which was similar to the red dust I had used to draw the hexagon around him when he astral projected. "I bought this while I was away. Thought it might come in handy." He ran his hand through his silver hair. "I wish I had gotten more."

"Do you still have the fairy dust?" He had used a sprinkle of it to temporarily transform the royal opera house stage into an enchanted forest.

He held out a golden box to me. "There's enough left for one more use."

I stowed the box and vial away in my crossbody purse, not arguing that he should hold on to it. For all I knew, the competition host might deny Lorenzo access into the castle for the next round, hoping to cower me into giving up without my manager.

"I'm going to get a few weapons. I don't plan to use them tonight, but it's good to be prepared." While Lorenzo rifled through his closet, I grabbed the box with the red dust from his bedside drawer. Even though our debt with Abigail had been settled after I had stolen the moonstone for her from Thomas' office, I was still worried that she might return to make another bargain with Lorenzo. There was no way I would allow him to strike a bargain in which he owed her an astral projection. I didn't trust her one bit and could easily imagine her splitting his soul from his body on purpose, and thus sending him to hell.

Lorenzo put a towel on his night table that held a plethora of knives and daggers.

I took one with a serrated edge and a ruby in its hilt, slashing through the air.

"Have you ever used a dagger?" he asked.

I shook my head, and he took my blade from me. "Your best chance of landing a blow is when you are at close range. Go for the vulnerable tissue." He pressed his finger into my neck. I knew I should've been thinking of attacking others, but instead, my thoughts went to what it would feel like if he kissed my neck.

"When do we need to leave?" I breathed.

"Nightfall. I heard the sisters say that their mother would be back at eight."

"So we have some time before that."

He nodded, his eyes growing hooded, and I pressed my mouth against his. His teeth captured my bottom lip, and I moaned. My hands ran down his powerful shoulders and back while his lips explored my neck. It definitely was a deliciously vulnerable spot. I fell down onto the bed, pulling him on top of me. Our kisses grew frantic as our hands explored each other. My finger caressed his muscular, smooth stomach while he kneaded my curves just the way I wanted him to.

We kissed until we were breathless. My heart was hammering wildly when Lorenzo pulled away. "When all of this is over, we can finally focus on us," he promised in a husky voice.

I nodded, knowing that going any further now would only make me more vulnerable to the enemy. Once the leader was defeated, and the queen was back on the throne, I would be able to do normal things with Lorenzo, not steal kisses here and there. I tried not to worry about what would happen to Arcadia if we failed or whether the king and queen would be all right with a demon dating their adopted daughter. I would cross that bridge when we got to it.

Now, it was time to pay back the sisters for everything they've done.

Lorenzo put two daggers into his boots, and four into his belt. He gave me a skinny belt that had two holsters, and I added my weapons, not ready to put blades anywhere on my body where they could injure me.

Under the cover of darkness, we strew the blue dust around Daydream's perimeter before hiding in a side street opposite from Madam's Boarding House to stake out her and her spawns.

We waited and waited, but nothing happened.

"Are you sure Madam was supposed to return here at eight?" I finally asked. "What if the sisters went to meet her somewhere else?"

Before Lorenzo could reply, one of the curtains in a window on the second floor moved, and Bernadette peeked outside, a shadow hovering behind her.

"They're still here and getting antsy," Lorenzo whispered.

I bit my lip, wondering what had postponed Madam. She wasn't the type of person who would allow anything to stand in her way.

After our brief glimpse of Bernadette, nothing happened for a long time. My legs ached from standing, so I crouched down, leaning against the wall. That was when the unmistakable click-clacking of horseshoes neared us. I chuckled inwardly. If I had known that all it would take to summon Madam was for me to get comfortable, I would've done so a long time ago.

The wooden carriage pulled close enough that I could make out the fuchsia, velvet curtains, leaving no doubt that Madam had arrived. Her lifestyle sure had improved. I didn't remember her having such an expensive and tasteless coach when I had been working for her.

I expected her to step out, but instead, the coachman nodded several times as she gave him instructions through the window. Then he rushed off into the boarding house. A few minutes later, the sisters appeared in their voluminous ball gowns.

Barely able to get into the carriage, the coachman had to almost stuff them inside. I would've laughed at the comical display if I weren't worried about how we could overhear them without them spotting us. If we stayed here, we wouldn't hear anything. But if we crept any closer, they would see us. "What do we do now?" I asked.

Lorenzo shifted. "We wait, then we'll follow the carriage." His arms tightened around me, and I mentally prepared myself for him teleporting after the carriage.

I wasn't scared of teleportation, but doing it several times in quick succession, left me dizzy and queasy. Thankfully, it had been a while since I had last eaten, making it less likely that I would spill the contents of my stomach all over Lorenzo's shoes.

Lorenzo's hands brushed my back, and I pressed my head against his chest, forgetting all thoughts of motion sickness. His strong arms felt so good wrapped around me, I never wanted him to let me go. In that moment, I realized that I was ready. There had always been a powerful attraction between Lorenzo and me, but I hadn't been completely willing to pursue it, given how my last relationship had ended. Now, however, I was ready to put myself out there, to let Lorenzo into my heart. I didn't care that he was a demon and that there was the whole immortality issue between us. I didn't care that my newfound royal family might not approve of this arrangement. I was Halia Bright, the queen of song, and I made my own decisions and dared to live fully, no matter how much it scared me.

The carriage door flung open so hard the hinge creaked. Everything inside of me tensed as Georgette stalked outside. "She doesn't understand," she hissed to Bernadette. "That stupid bitch is still in the competition. We need to get rid of her before she ruins everything. I won't have my glory taken from me a second time."

Bernadette gripped her sister's elbow. "Shut up. Mother said she'll take care of it. She'll get us more magic, and then it won't matter if the maid is still in the competition. We'll bring her to her knees just as we did with Cinder."

Georgette shoved away Bernadette's hand. "That's not good enough. Cinder got the prince in the end."

A wicked grin curled Bernadette's lips. "But she

didn't keep him. Besides, that was then. Things have changed. We have magic now. We're unstoppable. We'll make them all pay." The door into the boarding house thumped closed, underlining their statement.

I had no time to ponder my irritation or the meaning of the sisters' statement as Madam's carriage charged into motion, and Lorenzo's arms tightened around me. My surroundings disintegrated into a chaos of colors only to rearrange themselves a bit later, and I found myself two streets over following the carriage that was barreling down the streets.

My stomach roiled as my surroundings blurred again. I closed my eyes, trying to stop myself from being sick and asked, "Do you think Madam's about to meet the leader?"

"Yes," Lorenzo replied simply, sending my heart thudding with excitement and fear. Finally, we would find out who was behind Arcadia's destruction. Finally, we would find out who we were up against.

When Lorenzo's arms released me, relief swept through me, despite losing the closeness. Good thing, the teleportation had stopped now. I wasn't sure how much longer I could've gone without being violently sick.

As I gulped down the fresh air, I slowly opened my eyes to find the reason why it was a few degrees cooler here. We were at the river. Madam's coach pulled to stop at the gondolas. But instead of getting into one of the tiny boats, she went toward the nearby bridge.

Since she moved slow enough, Lorenzo and I followed her on foot, and I was grateful we were done with the teleporting. As if my thoughts had jinxed the situation, Madam disappeared. One moment she was there, the next she was gone.

“What kind of magic was that?” I asked, struggling to keep my voice quiet.

Lorenzo’s chuckle ran down my spine. “No magic. Just a door.” He stepped closer to the wall, and that’s when I saw it, an entrance made from the same stone the bridge was. No door handle, but a tiny knob that was barely visible in the darkness.

I swallowed hard as Lorenzo drew a dagger. “Are you up for this?” he asked.

I pulled out my own dagger in response. I might’ve been terrified out of my wits, but I needed to confront the monster behind the decimation of my city.

Lorenzo went first, and I didn’t mind, aware that if I got myself stabbed, it would be the end of us spying on Madam.

My lungs constricted, and my legs trembled as I stepped across the threshold and froze. Not out of fear, but out of confusion. No one was attacking us. In fact, no one was paying us any heed.

Because people, well, magic wielders to be exact, were busy shopping. Negotiations were forcefully being conducted in colorful stalls just like at the market above ground, except that this underground market served a clientele with sharp horns, spiky tails, and elongated ears. A month ago, I would’ve been terrified to be surrounded by so many magic wielders. Now, however, I was mostly curious.

A snake lurched from a basket at one of the stands, and a seller exchanged a glass jar of teeth for golden coins, confirming my suspicion that this was an illegal market.

“You’re new. Where are your access codes?” A green demon sidled up to us.

*“Relax, we’ve been here before. You know us. We’re*

*fine,"* I sang, the words coming to me effortlessly, the magic streaming through my veins as if it were the most natural thing in the world.

The green demon blinked several times, glanced between Lorenzo and me, and waved us through.

"Your powers are getting stronger. You were able to manipulate him with only a few sentences and while he was on high alert." The pride in Lorenzo's voice warmed me.

"Good, I get the feeling I'll get to use my voice a lot in the next few days." I smiled on the inside as I surveyed the market for Madam's voluptuous, tall figure.

I couldn't see her, so I made my way slowly through the rows of stalls, pretending to be interested in the dried tongues hanging by clothespins, the potions that sizzled when they bubbled out of their glasses, and the combs that had hidden blades and acted as weapons.

"Perhaps we should stock up on supplies," I whispered.

"No." Lorenzo's hard voice made me look up to find his jaw was clenched tightly. "You do not want to get involved with those who lurk around here, have them know your face, or call in any favors. They wouldn't think anything of chopping off your finger if they thought you betrayed them."

"But—"

"You being in the competition makes you a persona non grata."

I nodded, understanding sinking in. Seeing me on stage, near the king's guards, would make them believe I was a spy. Was that why Madam tended to stay on the sidelines when her daughters competed and why she hadn't brought them here? It had to be.

We reached the last stall in the final row, and panic

rattled me. We had missed her! Somehow Madam had slipped out of here. I turned to Lorenzo to voice my concerns, but he took my hand and slipped us through a set of curtains. I had believed them to be an entrance to a changing room since they were located next to a vendor who sold furs, but clearly, I had been wrong, because the curtains led into a tavern.

The room was illuminated only by half-burned candles, which worked in our favor. The stench of mold and stale beer hung heavy in the air, and the creatures around us made the hair on my nape stand up.

Thankfully, Madam's massive salmon-colored skirt peeked out from behind a wall, allowing me to spot her without circling the bar like an idiot.

"Over there," I whispered.

"Wait here. I'll get us drinks," Lorenzo replied and returned a minute later with two heavy beer mugs. We sat at the table closest to the wall behind which Madam was, and I strained my hearing.

"Haven't I done a fine job? Aren't you satisfied?" Madam asked.

"You know I am," a voice grumbled in return.

"Then give me more magic. My daughters need it."

"I'm not going to waste precious magic so that your spoiled brats can win a popularity contest!"

The air hummed with tension, and I waited for a slapping sound, but it never came. Instead, Madam Fontaine said in a menacing voice, "The girls winning the contest will give us a peaceful way into the castle. Do you really want to attack the king from outside the castle walls while he's sequestered safely with all his guards when you could slip into the castle and have a much easier time bringing him down to his knees?"

There was a long pause. Finally, the leader said, "A

valid point. Here, take this. It will ensure that no one can resist your daughters. But you better hold up your end of the bargain."

A snort. "I always do. I already have the competition host in my pocket."

"I don't care about that pompous fart. Make sure that before the eleventh, Arcadia belongs to us."

"It will. You know I've wanted this for decades, Rumpelstiltskin. I'll do anything to get onto the throne."

I exchanged a glance with Lorenzo. The name Rumpelstiltskin sounded familiar, but I couldn't recall where I had heard it.

The man, Rumpelstiltskin, laughed lowly, the nasty sound reminding me of chalk screeching across the board. "After you take down Arcadia, we'll unite with the others. We'll be unstoppable!"

Glasses clinked.

"I'll drink to that." Madam cleared her throat. "How are things going in Urbis? Is everything still on track?"

"Yes, the underground buildings with traps will be finished in no time. Everything is going the way it needs to. King Charming and Queen Ella will roll over like the pets they are, begging us to put them out of their misery." He paused, and when he spoke again, his voice was dark. "I would much rather have Arcadia ruled by you, not Acacia, but you must prove your worthiness."

My heart contracted, surprising me that I still cared. The fae had betrayed me so many times, and yet, the extent of her betrayal, the new layers I uncovered were still wounding me.

"I am worthy," Madam hissed.

"So you say, but you still haven't found the adopted princess," Rumpelstiltskin replied coolly.

"I did everything I could." Panic oozed out of Madam's

voice. "I thought for certain it was one of my maids, but neither girl had golden rings in her eyes."

So that's why she had been outside the orphanage the day we had been kicked out, offering us jobs. My fists balled, and hot anger coursed through me.

"I even snatched that stupid broad Tia, but she doesn't have more than one drop of magic in her blood."

"Then it must be the other one, the singer," Rumpelstiltskin growled, but I wasn't scared, too furious with Madam's brazen admission that she had kidnapped my friend to care. "Get her."

"It's not that easy!" Madam slammed something, probably her glass, down on the table. "She's constantly surrounded by that darn demon."

"If you can't bring her to me, then I'll ask Acacia."

"No! Don't. Arcadia is mine. I started this, and I'll finish it."

"Very well. But if this singing girl causes any problems with the takeover, Acacia becoming the ruler of Arcadia will be the least of your worries. Do you understand?"

"Yes." For the first time, I heard fear in Madam's voice.

"Good," Rumpelstiltskin replied. "A deal is a deal after all, and a promise is a promise."

Chairs scraped against the floor, and I practically dived into my mug of beer, only daring to look up when Madam and Rumpelstiltskin had passed our table. Rumpelstiltskin was a short, middle-aged, impish man. And yet, he was the one who had allowed Madam to become the villain she had always aspired to be.

# 7TH AUGUST

"Maybe you should take a break and practice your singing," Lorenzo said.

I continued my pacing. "How can I be thinking about the competition when we still don't know where Tia is or what has happened to her?"

"We know she's alive."

I threw him a withering look. Yes, Mikka was still feeling the bond, but she was also bedridden and unconscious half of the time, which made me certain that Rumpelstiltskin and his nasty fae were still milking Tia for magic, life energy, or both.

"Worrying won't bring her back." Lorenzo cupped my face, and his lips brushed against mine.

For a moment, I allowed myself to melt into the kiss and enjoy it, but then panic kicked in once again. "We need to find out where they're keeping her before they decide to kill her."

Lorenzo sighed. "I searched all of last night and asked everyone. Nobody knows."

A lightbulb went on in my head. "Madam delivers her victims to Rumpelstiltskin directly. She has no middle man."

Lorenzo nodded. "That's my guess too. I paid someone to stake out the house at dark. They'll report immediately if they see anything at all."

"But Madam would expect that and would find a way around that." I thought about all the fabrics and huge dresses she had and the trunks that were meant to transport them. "They're kidnapping their victims in broad daylight."

Lorenzo considered this for a moment. "Perhaps. Or maybe they're done with kidnapping people since they have enough magic and life force siphoned away."

I shook my head. "Madam and Rumpelstiltskin said they were almost done, but people like them are too greedy to stop at "enough." They always want more. The sisters are worried about winning the competition. They'll support their mother any way they can, becoming reckless."

"What are you saying?"

"We should follow the sisters, not their mother. We need to give them an easy target. Someone who won't fight back and won't be missed."

Lorenzo snarled. "Not Mikka. We will not exploit her current state."

"Shouldn't that be up to me?" Mikka leaned against the bar. It didn't surprise me that she had sneaked up on us, given how quietly she moved. "I want to go."

"No!" Lorenzo balled his fists.

"The sooner we get Tia back, the sooner I'll get better." Mikka's gaze softened. "Please."

I put an arm around her shoulder. "We won't let anything happen to her."

Lorenzo let out another snarl, this one softer.

"We can't let Rumpelstiltskin and Madam waltz into the palace. We need to stop them before that," I said. "I don't want to expose Mikka to danger in her current state, but what other choice do we have? If we do nothing, the situation will only get worse!"

Lorenzo must've finally seen reason because he nodded slowly.

~

I doubted that the sisters paid much attention to anyone but themselves, but on the off-chance they might recognize Mikka, I hid the half-demon's white hair in a turban. With her hair pulled back and her face pale, she looked even sicker and like an easy picking.

While Lorenzo and I waited in a side street opposite the boarding house, Mikka ambled toward the house. The plan was for her to walk up to the second floor, knock on the sister's room, and beg them for shelter. While I was certain the sisters wouldn't be able to resist the trap, I was still nervous. What if they recognized Mikka and hurt her? What if instead of ensnaring them, we were giving them our friend on a silver platter?

The seconds trickled past painfully slowly, and my urge to go inside and get Mikka out grew stronger and stronger. Lorenzo seemed to share my thoughts, practically humming with tension.

"Should we—" I began but stopped as a young boy skittered out of the house and ran, a coin bag in his hand. A messenger. Was he notifying the coachman? I received my confirmation when a bit later, an ugly fuchsia-curtained coach pulled up. The main door to the boarding house flew open, and the sisters came out, heaving a trunk between them. I was right. They did smuggle people in the middle of the day. Instead of pride, I felt angry at myself. How many people could I have saved if only I had thought of this earlier?

The sisters pulled the trunk into the carriage with the help of the coachman, and Bernadette got in while Georgette took the position of the coachman. Given the few words she exchanged with him, she probably told him to get lost since he nodded and eventually left after she gave him a few more coins.

"Bull's eye," I whispered, revenge running thick through my veins. Lorenzo's hard body wrapped around me, and this time, I didn't feel queasy as we teleported after the carriage even though we must've done it at least a dozen times. Each time Lorenzo stopped, we moved further out of the city. The shops and pubs vanished first to be replaced by cheap houses for laborers. Those, too, disappeared soon to give way to random cottages on the outskirts of the city. The huts grew sparser and sparser, and by the time Lorenzo released me, we were in a thick forest.

Unable to see the carriage or a path, I cursed. "Did we lose them?" Panic raced through me.

Lorenzo took my hand and guided me deeper into the forest. I followed him, hoping he knew where he was going. One moment, there was only wilderness, and then it appeared out of nowhere—a cottage hidden by trees. Next to it was a dirt road where the carriage was parked. I had to admit, I was impressed that Georgette had been able to get the two horses down this road without flipping the carriage. She jumped off the bench and helped her sister drag the trunk toward the house. Halfway there, Bernadette's fingers slipped, and the trunk crashed to the ground with a heavy thump. I cringed, feeling awful for putting Mikka through this and praying she didn't get a severe injury from the dumb sister's carelessness.

Once the sisters were inside, Lorenzo and I tiptoed toward the house.

"Don't look through the window," he cautioned just as I was about to peek inside. Thankfully, I ignored him because the person I saw made me grab Lorenzo's hand and pull him away a few feet.

"What?" he hissed.

"Acacia's here. You need to stay away, or she'll sense you."

Lorenzo pressed his lips together. "I won't let you go in by yourself."

"I'm not planning to. I can spy on them from the outside." When he hesitated, I added, "I'll be fine."

Finally, he nodded, I hurried back to the house, pressing my ears against the wall.

"We have another one for you," Georgette said, and there was a clicking sound, which I took to be her opening the trunk.

"Don't just stand around! Help us," Bernadette said.

I balled my fists at the thumping noise, guessing they dropped Mikka again.

"A demon?" There were surprise and a hint of caution in Acacia's voice. "You foolish girls."

"She's not a demon. She's a girl!" Bernadette protested.

"It doesn't matter what she is. She's passed out. And if you're right, that only means that she has more magic for you to siphon off, so it's a good thing," Georgette said, and I could practically see her pouting.

Acacia tsked. "You really think a demon just walked into your boarding house. Very unlikely. She works for Lorenzo."

There was a pause.

"Not anymore," Bernadette said defiantly. "Hook her up."

"It's a trap. And you went right for it, you silly girls," Acacia hissed.

"Do it! That's an order!" Georgette said.

"I don't take orders from you." Icicles dripped from Acacia's voice.

"We'll tell Mother that you refused."

"You stupid girls. Run back to the boarding house and get your Mother, now!"

"Why?"

"Because we'll be ambushed at any moment." Noises and murmurs I couldn't make out followed, and then the sisters hurried through the door and jumped into the carriage. Hidden from them, I glanced at Lorenzo, who shook his head. I agreed. We could go after the sisters later. Right now, we needed to free the prisoners and show Acacia that actions had consequences.

As soon as the carriage was out of sight, I ran to the front of the cottage. Lorenzo teleported next to me, and we threw the door open.

My breath hitched at the sight in front of us. Everywhere I looked, listless humans were lying and sitting on the floor, their limbs on top of each other. Every single person had a tube attached to their upper arm that was pulling a white, shiny substance out of them and into a see-through jar that was a quarter full.

Acacia smiled at us, her blue eyes sparkling with

pure menace. "Right on time."

Lorenzo teleported in front of her and jabbed a dagger into her stomach. A scream tore out of my throat. I knew she was the enemy. I knew she had done horrible things, but I wasn't prepared to kill her.

Blood gushed out of her stomach wound, and the thick scent of iron filled the room.

"Where are Tia and the queen?" Lorenzo growled, and I surveyed the sleeping faces all around me, belatedly realizing that neither my friend nor my adoptive mother was here.

I surged forward. "Don't kill her, or she won't be able to tell us."

"Unless a knife goes through her heart, it won't kill her," Lorenzo replied as he secured Acacia's hands behind her back. She hissed at the contact.

"If you try to pull out the knife, it's only going to hurt more," Lorenzo warned Acacia. I had no idea how one would do so with their hands bound, but I supposed if anyone could do it, it would be Acacia.

"Are you sure about this?" I whispered when Lorenzo walked over to me. "We don't want her to bleed out."

A muscle ticked in his jaw. "She won't. She's fae. Her wound is already healing. Her body will push out the dagger slowly. And then we'll have to stab her again." At my horrified face, he added. "The handcuffs are made from iron, but they alone are not enough to hold her. Let's hurry before her reinforcements arrive."

I glanced around the room at the drawn faces. None of the humans were paying any attention to us. "Can I remove the tubes?"

Lorenzo nodded. "Yes, it shouldn't hurt them."

Yet, I still cringed as I took the first person's arm and carefully eased the tube out. A few droplets of blood leaked from the wound. "I'm sorry," I said, but the middle-aged woman didn't pay any attention to me, so I moved on to the guy next to her, whom I recognized as one of the competitors from my singing contest. He also didn't react to my touch or me helping him. On and on, I went. About a dozen of the people were eliminated contestants, the others were a mix of travelers and women from shelters and children from orphanages.

A manic cackle broke my concentration on helping those poor souls, and I glanced backward to find that the dagger was no longer in Acacia's stomach, but on the floor, her wound healing just as Lorenzo had said it would. However, before she could do anything, Lorenzo grabbed the knife, poised to strike again.

"You'll never win," Acacia said, as Lorenzo brought the dagger forward.

"Is this really necessary?"

"Yes, it is." He skewered the fae deeply, and a shudder claimed me. If Acacia ever got him, she'd make him pay. No, I couldn't let myself think like that. I couldn't go there.

"Did you get everyone?" Lorenzo asked a few minutes later. I glanced around, confirming that all humans were now tube-free.

"All done. What do we do with this?" I pointed at the quarter full magic jar.

"We take it. And get the hell out of here before the others returned."

I nodded and turned to the victim closest to me. "We need to go." No response. "Wake up." I shook the young girl. "Please! We don't have time." I shook her harder, and then desperately pinched her. Still, no reaction.

"You'll never get them out of here," Acacia cackled, basically begging Lorenzo to skewer her with a second blade.

Lorenzo threw her a dark look, then turned to me. "I can't teleport them all out of here. You need to get them out while I return to Daydream with *her.*" He spit the last word at Acacia.

"What? But I can't—"

"You can, and you will. Find a way." Lorenzo jerked Acacia upright, who finally had gone pale, the sweet stench of fear emanating from her.

"Lorenzo, don't leave me here!" I screamed as his arms closed in a bruising grip around Acacia.

"It's like you said. This is your mission, so find a way." With that, Lorenzo and Acacia teleported away.

"No!" I screamed until my lungs ached, then I turned to the humans who still all looked asleep. I couldn't bring myself to stab them with the dagger Lorenzo had given me to see if they would wake up, and I couldn't drag them all outside before the sisters returned.

I rubbed my throat, trying to come up with a solution, and that's when I realized what I had to do. Of course, why hadn't I thought about it earlier?

*"Wake up, wake up. We must leave now. Awaken."*

I paused when nothing happened. Was my singing not strong enough, or had Acacia damaged the consciousness of these poor people beyond repair? I gritted my teeth. I would not allow the greedy fae and the tyrannical Fontaines to abuse Arcadia's citizens.

*"Wake up, wake up. We must leave now. Awaken. I command you: awaken."*

I put so much force into my voice that it vibrated and filled the room. When one by one, the humans' eyes fluttered open, I almost cried with relief.

Since they weren't moving, just staring dumbly at me, I continued singing, putting as much authority into my voice as possible.

*"I command you. Stand up and follow me. I will lead the way. I will be your guardian."*

I grabbed the jar of magic and headed toward the door, confident they would follow. If I acted as a leader, they would listen to me.

I was right. They were moving, well, stumbling, to be exact. At their current speed, the sisters could easily ambush us even with their silly poofy gowns and high heels.

*"Hurry up! You must hurry! Quickly now!"*

The throng picked up the tempo while I stood by the door, ushering them out one by one. When they were all outside, I let the door fall closed and took my position at the head of the line. Knowing we couldn't walk down the dirt road, I made the crowd follow me through the forest. We were far enough from the road that the sisters wouldn't spot us, yet close enough that I could see the road and know we were on the right path.

After a while, my ankles started to hurt, and so did my lower back. My vocal cords too felt tired. As much as my body wanted to rest, I knew we needed to get away from the cottage as far as possible. Ideally, we would reach Arcadia's outskirts before we rested. How much longer would that be? I guessed it took the horses about half an hour to get out here, so maybe seven miles, which at our speed translated into roughly two and a half hours.

My sluggish feet made me almost trip several times, and the words that came out of my mouth were croaky. I had to clear my throat several times.

Just as I was about to open my mouth again, trotting noises reached me. I whipped around. *"Duck!"* I sang and dropped to the ground myself. Thankfully, the fifty or so people in my group followed.

The horse hooves grew louder, and a whip rang out as it raced through the air, slashing against skin. The poor horses. And poor us if the Fontaines caught us. I tried not to think about what they would do to us. Being afraid wouldn't help us.

As soon as I was certain the carriage was far enough away from us, I continued singing. *"Walk, pick up speed, follow me, hurry!"*

The adrenaline surge at seeing the carriage wiped away my pain, and I hurried through the forest, ducking underneath branches while my boots crunched on twigs and dried grass. Abruptly, the forest thinned, and a few lonesome farmhouses came into view. Happiness welled up within my body, but I didn't allow it to take hold. Not yet. Yes, we were close, but this part of the path would also leave us the most exposed. There was nothing we could hide behind if the sisters came back now.

My leg muscles began to tremble, and faintness seized me. My body wanted rest, food, and water. But I couldn't allow it. Not now. Not when we were so close. Still, I halted for a few seconds, inhaling deeply. Nobody moved behind me, and I instinctively knew that to get this group to run, I would have to push my magic to my limits. I wiped my palms on my pants and made sure I had a tight grip on the jar of magic before I sang loudly despite the ache in my throat, *"Run, run like the wind! Run like a deer from a wolf!"*

Tears of exhaustion shot into my eyes as I sprinted. My limbs felt about as strong as pudding, and yet, I pushed them again and again with every step. I only allowed myself a glance backward to confirm the others were following. Their faces were drawn, their breathing labored. Only my magic was compelling their battered bodies and souls forward.

*"You can do this. You are strong,"* I sang, needing to hear this myself.

We passed the first farmer, and then the second, and the third. Multi-storied houses were coming into view as were proper streets. We were close, so, so close.

Hooves clacked behind me, and a loud neighing tore through the air. No, no, it couldn't be!

"Seize them!" Madam's hateful voice filled my ringing ears.

No, she couldn't get us. I wouldn't' let her. Not when we had come so far. Maybe I could compel her and her daughters. I opened my mouth and closed it again. I didn't have the energy, and switching my focus to Madam would cost too much time. I needed to act quickly. I needed to throw her off in one move that wouldn't drain me further.

I stopped and pivoted around. The crowd rushed past me, but already they were slowing, and some were tripping as the sisters were flinging stones at them out of the carriage's window.

I put the jar of magic down and pulled out the glittering powder Lorenzo had given me earlier. Mimicking what he had done for me on stage, I threw the dust into the air and whispered, "Wall of stone!" Bricks appeared, invisible hands laid row after row, blocking us from our pursuers.

Madam and her daughters gawked as the wall grew until Madam pulled the reins of the horses. "Stop, stop!" she yelled.

I smiled, even as I knew the illusion wouldn't hold long. I grabbed the jar of magic, making a split-second decision. "Serves you right that what you tried to steal will hold you back." I inhaled deeply, praying this would work.

*"Reinforce the wall, reinforce the wall, make it last long!"* I sang and threw the magic forward. It splattered alongside the wall, a drop attaching itself to each brick. Tears of relief filled my eyes. My gamble had paid off. I had compelled the magic in the jar with my voice to act on my behalf.

Even though every fiber in my body was ready to collapse, I faced my people.

*"Continue, hurry, we're almost there."*

I guided the crowd toward Arcadia's heart, toward freedom and safety.

Lorenzo joined us at the beginning of the market square. His presence helped, but I didn't dare to stop singing. To my surprise, he didn't guide the people toward Daydream, but the police station.

"It's not safe for them at the bar, and it will put a huge target on our backs," he explained.

I was too tired to argue but promised myself to give him a piece of my mind about abandoning me with all these people without even suggesting what I should do.

Thomas must've seen our strange procession because he met us outside the police station.

"Halia, what is the meaning of this?"

"Chief," I addressed him formally, and given the spark in his eyes, he wasn't yet used to his title and did appreciate me keeping it professional in public. "These people have been kidnapped. We freed them from their human traffickers." I dropped my voice. "I'll explain the rest inside." No need for anyone to overhear that life energy and magic was being drained out of people. Arcadia didn't need more gossip and for its citizens to go crazy with worry.

Thomas waved us inside. "There won't be enough room in my office for all of them," he said. "I'll have to put them into the interrogation room while we talk."

I wasn't sure that was the best idea given everything the captives had been through, but fortunately, the interrogation room was just a blank space and didn't look menacing.

As soon as Thomas closed the door behind the crowd, he crossed his arms. "Explain."

Even though I was bone tired and wanted nothing more than to collapse, I knew it was best if I took the lead on this. "Remember when you got the note about strange things happening in the asylum?"

He nodded. "It was from you. And now, you've somehow found more people that were trafficked."

I sighed. We'd have to start from the beginning. "Does the name Rumpelstiltskin mean anything to you?"

Thomas surprised me with a slow nod. "He's from the Vale. We had word that he kidnapped the young princess there a couple of months back. He shouldn't be here."

"He's milking people for their life energy, and he has employed the fae to milk them of their magic." I summarized how every person had a drop of magic and how the humans were kept in the cottage, hooked up to tubes that drained their magic.

Thomas glanced from me to Lorenzo to finally the people inside the interrogation room. Without my voice, they had gone back to their vegetative state. Some were curled up on the floor while others leaned on each other.

In a whisper, Thomas asked, "What are you, Halia?" I opened my mouth, but he must've seen the lie coming because he shook his head. "I'm not going to hold it against you. If Rumpelstiltskin and the fae are working to bring down Arcadia, we need someone with magic on our side."

I glanced at Lorenzo, who nodded. Well, if my mistrusting demon trusted Thomas, so could I.

"I don't know what I am, but my voice can make others do things. Only good things. I have white magic," I said hurriedly.

Thomas rubbed his eyes. "Good, so I wasn't going insane."

I felt my forehead wrinkle. "What do you mean?"

"Several times, after talking to you, I felt a bit funny, like I couldn't remember parts of the conversation. Things were fuzzy."

I bit my lip. "I'm sorry. I can assure you that since I discovered my ability, my intention has always been to help Arcadia and bring our queen back."

Thomas nodded. "Do you know where she is?"

Tears stung my eyes. "I thought she'd be in the cottage, but she and Tia have been taken somewhere else."

"By the fae?"

I sighed. "No, by the Fontaines. The mother and the sisters are also involved."

After I explained that the Fontaines had been delivering humans to Rumpelstiltskin and were using magic to fake their way to the top of the competition, Thomas said, "Thank you for your trust. I'll do my best. We don't have any proof about the competition bit, but I'll monitor their home."

I doubted the Fontaines would kidnap more people after today, but I kept my mouth shut. I was grateful for Thomas protecting the humans I had rescued, but I also needed him to stay busy and out of our way.

Because while having Thomas on our side was helpful, he was right, only another magic wielder could bring down the villains who had invaded our kingdom.

8TH AUGUST

I awoke to the delicious smell of roasted coffee and soft lips against my cheek. The mattress underneath me felt like a cloud, and I stretched my body before my eyes fluttered open to be met with a gentle violet-green gaze that had a hint of hunger in it.

"Good morning, beautiful," Lorenzo said, sitting on the edge of my bed, surprising me with breakfast in bed.

"Morning." I grabbed his shirt and pulled him down for a kiss.

"Did you sleep well?"

"I did." I sat up, realizing that the sun was high up in the sky. Taking in the tray on my bedside table, I went straight for the steaming coffee, not bothering to stifle my moan at its invigorating bitterness. "What time is it?"

"Noon."

"What? You let me sleep for fifteen hours?"

Lorenzo shrugged. "You were completely drained. You used up all of your magical reserves."

"I didn't realize that was possible." I sat up straighter as I remembered that it had been his fault. "You left me there. Alone." I jabbed my finger into his chest.

He sighed. "I had no other choice. I needed to ensure we got Acacia, and I trusted you'd figure it out."

I shook my head. "I did, and I don't mind learning on the go, but if I'd failed, we could've jeopardized the lives of fifty people."

Lorenzo's face turned dark. "If you fail at the palace, all of Arcadia will fall."

A shiver ran through me. "When I said this was my mission, I didn't mean that I didn't want help."

He took my hand in his and rubbed reassuring circles on it. "I'll do everything in my power, but you're the one holding the key to Arcadia's salvation."

I nodded slowly, knowing he was right. "We better plan then. I doubt the Fontaines and Rumpelstiltskin will go down easy just because we took their energy supply."

Lorenzo smiled. "That's the spirit. See, all you needed was fifteen hours of sleep."

I let out a chortle but stopped when something occurred to me. "Where is Acacia?"

Lorenzo's lips thinned into a grim line. "In my office. Bound in iron. She didn't want to talk to me. She seemed very interested in you being present."

I jumped out of bed, only a little bit embarrassed at being in my short nightgown in front of Lorenzo. "Then let's go and talk to her." The buttery smell of croissant filled my nose, but I pushed the tray away. How could I enjoy breakfast when Tia was suffering through who only knew what?

"Be careful. Her powers might be subdued by the iron, but she's still a conniving creature." Lorenzo pushed the tray toward me. "And eat up. We have a long day ahead of us, and I need you at full energy."

I couldn't really argue with that. Also, if Acacia sensed that I had come running to her, desperate for information, she would use that against me. I needed to show the fae who was in charge. Thus, I finished my cup of coffee and my croissant, applied pink color to my lips and put on a nice silk dress. Appearances meant a lot to the fae, and if me being in better shape than her would nudge her to fold her cards, I would look like a goddess.

Done with breakfast and ready to go, I descended the staircase with Lorenzo.

"If Acacia won't cooperate, we might have to rely on harsh tactics to get information out of her," he said.

I shook my head. "No, she might not be able to lie, but the fae can omit, and they can make traps."

Lorenzo stiffened. "All right. So what do you propose?"

"We wear her down."

He sighed. "That might not work."

I stared into his violet-green eyes. "It's one thing to hurt her to subdue her, but we will not torture her for information. That's not the kind of person I want to be."

He nodded. "I respect that."

We reached the door that led into his office, and I pushed it open.

Acacia was shackled to a chair. Despite the chains snaking around her arms, legs, and torso, the faerie's glare was full of defiance.

"What took you so long? Did you run into someone?" She cackled hysterically, and I wondered if not having food or water was messing with her head.

"The humans have all been freed," Lorenzo said in an arctic voice. "The Fontaines and Rumpelstiltskin will be brought down. If you cooperate now—"

"Save it!" Acacia cut him off. "You act like you're in the position to negotiate, but you're not. You want that girl back badly."

I bit my tongue hard until I tasted blood to stop myself from saying that Tia wasn't just any girl. She was my best friend. She had been kidnapped because of me, and I would do anything to get her back. Doing my best not to betray my weakness, I schooled my features into an impenetrable mask. "You're the one in chains. If you want to get out of here and not starve to death, you'll tell us what we want to know."

Acacia threw her head back and laughed, making me more certain than ever that she was losing it. "Why don't we test your theory and see if I'll die first or your human friend?"

I gritted my teeth at the threat and the truthfulness in her words. She was fae. She could endure much more than Tia. No matter how strong my friend was, she was mortal.

Sensing that continuing down this trajectory wouldn't get us anywhere, I decided to switch tactics. "Did you know that Rumpelstiltskin is searching for the golden-eyed girl?"

Acacia revealed her sharp, gleaming teeth. "Of course, princess."

My heart clenched. So I was the princess. She had confirmed it. "How long have you known?"

She shrugged. "A while. A week maybe."

"Why didn't you tell Rumpelstilksin or Madam?"

Acacia's grin turned full-on feral. "Weak hunters kill their enemy. Smart hunters convert them. You and I could do a lot of things together."

"Never!"

Acacia tsked. "Always so hasty, my child. Don't say something you might regret later."

Lorenzo stepped forward until he was only a foot away from Acacia and glared down at her. Terror shone in her eyes for a second before it disappeared.

"Are you going to stab me again?" she purred.

He gave her a feral smile. "No, I'll leave you to rot here until you tell us everything we need to know."

Acacia went pale. "Madam and Rumpelstiltskin didn't share the details of their plan, but they'll attack at the final concert."

"We already know that," I replied tersely. She shrugged as if it wasn't her problem. "Where are Tia and the queen?" She kept her lips pressed together tightly.

"The sooner you answer us, the sooner we'll let you go."

She didn't reply, even though her eyes flashed with emotion. She was considering the offer, but not with Lorenzo nearby. Because even if we freed her, he could recapture her easily. Perhaps she would be willing to negotiate with just me. While I pondered this, I asked, "Where are the other fae?"

Her eyes flashed with hatred. "The moonstone you gave Abigail allowed her to travel through the veil and into the faeland. The others chose to go with her."

I inhaled sharply. So that's what the stone I had procured for her did. "Why didn't you go with them?"

"My transgressions were more severe than theirs. There is no place for me in the homeland."

Interesting. Before I could ask another question, she added, "If you and I work together, I'll spare your parents and even allow them to pretend to continue ruling. Together, we can stop Madam and Rumpelstiltskin from taking Arcadia."

I blinked at her unexpected suggestion. Did Acacia really think that we could be allies after everything she had done? Or maybe she hoped I would accept so that she could double-cross me. She was a heartless creature, only interested in power, and most certainly, had an idea about how to screw me over.

I pointed with my head toward the door, and Lorenzo followed me outside. We stepped far away from the door so that Acacia couldn't overhear us.

"What do you think?" I asked. "Should we pretend to play along?"

Lorenzo's jaw tensed. "Absolutely not. She's protecting you from Madam and Rumpelstiltskin, which means you're valuable to her."

"Isn't that a good thing?"

I sucked in a breath, remembering all the times Acacia had siphoned off my emotions in exchange for hiding my natural eye color. "Do you think the magic in my blood, can open the veil? But how? I'm not a fae!"

His lips brushed against mine. "No matter how powerful you are, don't forget, Acacia is the queen of deceit."

I shivered. He was right, and yet Acacia's offer was too tempting to ignore. I needed to free Tia. I couldn't play cool and wait for Acacia to give us the information, but I couldn't tell Lorenzo that. So instead, I asked, "What do we do with her?"

"Nothing for now." Lorenzo's eyes flashed. "I give her a few more days in iron until she breaks. The queen and Tia mean nothing to her. Eventually, she'll tell us if only to gain your trust."

I nodded, even though there was no way I could wait for days.

"Don't worry. I'll do my best to find them before that. Do you want to come with me?"

I shook my head. "Somebody should check on Mikka."

Lorenzo kissed me again. "Yes, and you need to rest after yesterday." He paused, then said, "Don't talk to Acacia without me."

I nodded, glad that unlike the fae, I could lie.

After Lorenzo left, I did check on Mikka, who was still weak. I made her lunch and read to her. The sun disappeared behind the horizon, and Lorenzo still wasn't back. My Tia was somewhere, alone, hurt, and scared. I couldn't wait for Acacia to break. I needed to get Tia out now.

"Do you know how to pick locks?" I asked after I finished reading the newspaper.

Mikka tilted her head. "Why?"

"After I got thrown into prison last time and my magic didn't work there, I thought it'd be a nice skill to have."

Her eyes narrowed. "You're not planning to free Acacia for some crazy reason, are you?"

*"No, I'm not, just show me."*

Her face relaxed at my singing, and guilt coursed through me. I had just used my magic to compel my friend. She'd be furious once she discovered what I had done, and so would Lorenzo, but they'd understand. Eventually.

"Get me a pin," Mikka said in a relaxed voice.

Once I did, she opened her nightstand in which a

dozen locks and a pair of handcuffs were stowed away. At my raised eyebrows, she shrugged. "You never know when one might come in handy."

Two demonstrations of how to break the lock and countless fails on my part later, I finally managed to do it. I broke the lock, and then the next, and a third one.

"Thank you." I smiled at Mikka. *"It's time for you to rest now, sleep deeply."*

Her eyes fell shut, and her breathing evened out. I tugged the blanket around her.

"I'm sorry, but I had to do this."

With that, I headed down the stairs and toward Lorenzo's office. As soon as I stepped through the door, two blue headlights devoured me. "I was expecting you, Halia, dear," Acacia crooned, clearly thinking she had the upper hand here.

"You need me to take Arcadia from Madam and Rumpelstiltskin. I'm the key to your mission." Her mouth opened slightly, the only sign of her shock at my deduction skills.

I pressed on. "You'll take me to Tia now, or I'll drop you off at a forgotten place and ensure Madam finds out about your betrayal. I'll tell her not only that you knew that I was the princess, but also that you were working to take her down."

Acacia's face turned green. "How do I know you won't betray me after I give you Tia?"

I clamped down hard on the excitement that threatened to burst out of my chest. Acacia knew where Tia was. She would take me to my friend.

I lifted my head and stalked over to the fae. To squeeze all the information out of her, I needed to remain cool and collected. "Easy. After you hand over Tia, you'll tell me the general location of the queen as I undo your bindings. A piece of information for each of your chains."

She puffed her chest out. "Are you sure you don't want to get the queen first?"

"I'm the one setting the terms," I said in my coldest tone. As much as I wanted to get the queen back, I was certain that Fontaine wouldn't seriously harm her. If she had wanted to execute her, she could've done so a long time ago. Tia, however, was another matter. Madam or her daughters would kill Tia without batting an eyelash to get back at me.

"Fine. You'll need to get me off this chair."

"Tell me first where you're taking me." I made a show of taking out and re-sheathing the iron daggers I had taken from Lorenzo's room.

Acacia's throat bobbed up and down, betraying her calm face. "The opera house."

I raised an eyebrow. Was she jesting?

"It's been empty ever since the recordings for this competition. They're doing construction on the west wing."

Making the east wing the perfect hiding spot. All this time, Tia and the queen had been hidden in plain sight. I wanted to scream. I wanted to slam my fists against the wall. I wanted to shake Acacia. Instead, I walked behind her and prayed that Lorenzo would understand what I was about to do. I located the lock that bound her waist to the chair and broke it, then worked on the chains that secured her hands and legs to the chair. I left the iron shackles that bound her hands together behind her back, but had to remove the cuffs on her feet since they slowed her walk down to snail speed and we needed to hurry.

"Don't try anything." Before I turned soft, I grabbed

one of my iron daggers and embedded it deep into her shoulder, slamming it through skin and muscle. She shrieked as blood poured out of the wound.

"Why?" she whispered.

"Because I want you to understand one thing. I'm not Halia, dear or child. I am Halia Bright, the protector of Arcadia." Even as I said it, another phrase wormed its way into my mind, *Halia—goddess of harmony.* I shook my head. Where had that haughty idea come from? Yet as strange as it was, the phrase also sounded familiar, as if I had heard it somewhere before. Hot blood dribbled onto my arm, jerking me back into reality.

"Move it!" I grabbed Acacia's arm, telling myself that the better my bluff, the less I would have to hurt her to keep her in line. Fear and anticipation were powerful tools.

With Acacia walking in front of me, it was easy for me to take out the red dust and sprinkle it on the ground as we walked to the gondolas. I prayed Lorenzo would notice it when he returned. Even though I was certain I needed to do this, he was right, Arcadia was the queen of deceit, and I could use all the help I could get, once she was no longer bound in iron.

The darkness hid Acacia's shackles and the dagger protruding from her shoulder. Fortune was smiling down at me since no patrolmen came our way, and the gondolier accepted my two gold coins without asking any questions.

The ride across the river went by painfully slowly, and with each passing second, Acacia's healing body pushed the dagger more and more out of her flesh. All I could do was watch and wait for the iron to fall out. It did so just as we reached the other bank. I grabbed it, mesmerized as Acacia's wound closed in front of my eyes, and shoved her out of the boat. Then, I plunged it in again, this time, in the other shoulder.

She howled. "What is wrong with you? I'm not doing anything."

"Good. This will ensure you won't have time to scheme anything."

She threw me a death glare. I ignored it. We were past any peace offerings. Acacia would throw me to the wolves the first chance she got, and I'd be damned if I let her, leaving Tia and all of Arcadia unprotected.

Once again, I left a path of red dust from the gondola to the opera house.

Since it was long past sunset, the construction workers had finished their work for the day. No one was outside the opera house or inside its lobby.

"Where to?" I asked.

Acacia took me to a smaller staircase that led to the artists' changing room. It was empty.

"Where is Tia?" I used my anger to hide the terror clawing inside my chest, screaming that it was too late, that my friend was dead.

"Closet."

I shoved Acacia to the ground, ensuring the blade was still deeply embedded in her shoulder. Then I pulled out my other dagger and crept toward the costume closet. Keeping as much distance as possible, I threw the door open. Tia was on the ground, black mascara and eyeliner streaks running down her cheeks, a rag gagging her, her hands and feet tied with rope.

"Tia!"

At her name, her eyes flickered open. There was panic in them, but slowly happiness seeped in as she recognized me. I cut through her bindings, careful to not hurt her skin that was already chafed. Finally, I removed her gag.

She fell around my neck. “You found me!”

I hugged her back hard, needing the physical touch to process that she was alive and mostly unharmed.

“What a cute reunion.”

The hairs on my neck stood as I whipped around to find that the dagger was no longer in Acacia’s shoulder and that she somehow had managed to get out of her shackles. In her left hand, she held a black potion. Darn, where had that come from? Lorenzo had searched her. I was certain of it. That’s when I noticed the cupboard behind her. It was open and filled with potions. Her own personal supply.

“You’ll come with me, Halia, and become my voice. Together, we’ll rule Arcadia.”

“Never!”

“If you refuse, I’ll use this murder potion on you, making you kill your friend with your own hands.”

Unbridled alarm seized me, but I didn’t cower.

“Don’t!” Tia screamed, but I didn’t listen. With a leap, I tackled Acacia to the ground. My body released an oomph sound as it crashed on top of hers. She threw the potion, but I dodged it, then plunged my dagger into her stomach, much deeper than the first two times. I grabbed the iron dagger next to her and slashed deeply through her wrists. Acacia wailed. I didn’t care. I had no room for mercy for someone who had wanted me to kill my friend.

“Where is the queen? Take me to her.” I rose, and jerked Acacia upward, who froze halfway. “If you don’t behave—” I raised my blade in warning but never got to finish my statement as hands snaked around my neck and pressed down hard on my windpipe. What the... had Acacia somehow gotten reinforcements?

"Die, you stupid bitch!" Tia's hate-filled voice and the burning in my throat made hot tears shoot into my eyes.

No, I refused to die like this. Unable to hurt my friend, I didn't use the dagger but stepped on her foot hard, grinding my boot into her toes. The grip on my neck released, and I brandished my dagger while singing, *"Stop it, I'm your friend."*

Tia didn't listen. She charged, and I jumped aside a second before she would've crashed into me.

Acacia laughed. "You really think your powers are a match for mine? Foolish girl!" If she was in good spirits, she was healing fast. I didn't have the luxury to glance at her, but I could only assume she had already removed the dagger from her stomach. Thankfully, she couldn't use the iron dagger, but I was certain she would procure another potion in no time. I needed to hurry.

*"Turn around. Return into the closet."* I repeated the phrase like a mantra, putting all my conviction into my voice. To my relief, Tia took one step back and then another. When she was inside, I slammed the door shut. *"Fall asleep."* I didn't have time to check if she followed my instruction as something whizzed through the air. I dropped down to my knees just in time.

Blue liquid hit the closet door and ran down in thick rivulets. I whirled on Acacia, assessing the situation. I had one dagger and could get the other one if I made it across the room, but not before Acacia threw another potion. While I felt confident with a dagger at close range, I doubted I could throw it from here and hit her. As if reading my thoughts, Acacia purred, "Give it up! You lost, child."

She reached inside her pocket, and I raised my blade.

I was about to charge her when a figure manifested behind her. Lorenzo. He had found us. With lightning speed, he threw a chain around her throat. She cried out in pain as he wound a long iron chain around her body and slapped cuffs on her wrists.

"Lorenzo." I rushed toward him.

There was no warmth in his gaze. "You went behind my back."

"I got Tia," I said quietly.

"Where is she?"

Guilt coursed through me. "In the closet, sleeping. I made her. Acacia threw a potion at her that made her want to kill me."

Lorenzo's eyes flashed with murder. "Your behavior was reckless."

"I got Tia," I repeated again, feeling stupid.

"You almost got yourself killed."

I bit my lip, not sure how to respond since I couldn't deny it. "The queen is somewhere here as well."

Lorenzo whirled on Acacia. "Listen up, I didn't kill you before because you had information about Tia's whereabout, but now that we have her, nothing stands in my way of finishing you." As if to underscore his point, he pressed the tip of his dagger against her neck. I shuddered. If fae were able to regenerate, it probably took something like decapitation to finish them off.

"If you don't take us to the queen, I won't hesitate to end you," Lorenzo finished.

Acacia must've sensed that he wasn't playing games because she said, "I'll need a guarantee that you'll let me go and won't chase me down after I tell you where the queen is."

"Swear to never come near us again, especially Halia. Swear to leave Arcadia."

Acacia hissed. The promise would make it impossible for her to force me to become her weapon. Lorenzo pressed the blade into her skin, and a droplet of blood ran down her neck.

"Fine," she gritted out. "I, Acacia Anzu, swear to tell you where the queen was last time I saw her in exchange for you releasing me and not hunting me or sending anyone to hunt me. I swear to never come near you or Halia again."

"And also Tia and Mikka," I added.

"As well as Tia and Mikka," Acacia growled. "I shall leave Arcadia as soon as possible."

Lorenzo's blade pressed harder into her throat, and more blood spilled from the cut. "No, you'll leave immediately. No gathering supplies, no communicating with the Fontaines or Rumpelstiltskin."

"So be it."

Lorenzo grabbed Acacia's hand and squeezed it hard. Sparks shot between their palms as the agreement settled into place. Once the sparks died down, Acacia said, "The queen is in the left wing of the stage. She was locked into a clothes trunk. Now free me."

Lorenzo's hands moved quickly, only stopping when he had removed all iron chains. Acacia rushed past me. I stared after her. It was done. We had banished her, but we still had Madam and Rumpelstiltskin to contend with. And we needed to free the queen.

I glanced at the closet, not wanting to leave Tia alone for even a moment. "Can you carry her?"

Thankfully, Lorenzo didn't again berate me for my recklessness, but simply threw the closet open and heaved a sleeping Tia into his arms.

"How long will Acacia's potion last?"

"An hour, maybe. Tia will be herself in no time."

I highly doubted that after she had been captured by the enemy and endured only who knew what, but I didn't say so. One step at a time. Right now, we would free the queen.

We hurried to the stage's left wing, and I released a breath when I saw the props, one of them being a huge clothes chest. There was a lock on the chest, and I prepared to break it with the pin trick Mikka had taught me. My hands froze I realized the lock lay discarded on the ground. With trembling fingers, I opened the chest. It was empty. The queen had been moved.

# 9TH AUGUST

"Tia! You're back! You're alive!" Mikka's voice tore me out of my sleep, and I blinked, then rolled my neck, realizing, I had ended up sleeping again in a chair. Lorenzo's eyes also opened slowly, and he ran a hand through his silver strands. He was on the floor, and I felt bad about it until his glare met mine. Damn it, I guessed he was still mad about me sneaking out yesterday.

I rose and stretched my arms. Every muscle in my body ached, and my head pounded, but all I cared about was Tia.

"Are you all right?" I studied my friend, searching for any after-effects of Acacia's potion.

She brushed a blue strand behind her ear. "Yes. Are you?"

I nodded. “I wasn’t the one who was abducted.”

“No, but I almost killed you.”

“What?” Mikka nearly jumped out of bed. “How much did I miss?” She rubbed her forehead. “I was awake for most of yesterday, and then I suddenly fell asleep…” She glanced at me, then Lorenzo, who nodded.

“Halia decided to use her magic on you to go on a little trip with Acacia.”

Mikka slapped her hand against her forehead, expletives rolling from her tongue. “You made me show you how to pick a lock, and then you put me to sleep!”

“She almost got both herself and Tia killed.” Lorenzo stepped closer, towering over me.

“But she didn’t. She found me.” Tia fell around my neck. “Thank you, and I’m so sorry.”

I smiled at my friend. “It wasn’t your fault. Nobody could’ve withstood Acacia’s potion.”

Tia nodded reluctantly. Shifting on the bed, she asked, “What did I miss?”

“Ahem, quite a bit.” Mikka glanced between Lorenzo and me and then at the door.

“Right, we should give you some privacy.” I shuffled out of the room with Lorenzo. As soon as the door fell shut behind me, he dragged me into his room.

“You were reckless and impulsive. You endangered your friend and the whole mission. You could’ve died!” He held my arms in a steel grip, and I could tell it took all of his willpower not to shake me.

“I’m sorry, but I still think it was the right choice. They already moved the queen. If I hadn’t gone yesterday, they might’ve moved Tia as well. Then we would never have found her.”

Lorenzo groaned. “Yes, you took the initiative, and it worked out because I got there in time. But what if I hadn't?"

I stepped toward the window, avoiding his gaze. "I would have dealt with Acacia. I would have defeated her somehow."

His lips brushed against my nape as he whispered, "Is that what you really think?"

Slowly, I turned around, my hips flush against his. "I have to, don't I? When we get to the palace for the final competition, you won't be able to protect me every second. I have to stand on my own two feet."

His throat bobbed up and down. "The thought of losing you..." He inhaled deeply. "I don't think I could bear it."

I forced my lips into a smile. "Then let's make sure it doesn't come to that."

His lips crashed against mine, his tongue pushing my mouth open, circling my tongue. I melted into the kiss, disappointed when he pulled away much too soon. "We banished Acacia. We could leave, go somewhere else. You don't have to face Madam."

I shook my head. "Yes, I do. She has the queen. She'll use her to bring the king down to his knees. I can't leave them to their own devices. They are my family, even if I barely know them, and Arcadia is my home. I can't leave."

Lorenzo sighed. "I thought you'd say that, but can you blame me for trying? Whatever lies ahead of us won't be easy, and there's a good chance we won't survive it."

He was right. Tonight might be our last time together, and I'd be darned if I didn't make it count. My hands came around his neck, and I pulled his mouth down to mine. As I kissed him hungrily, drinking in his tongue as if were air, I wrapped my leg around his hip, pushing my body against his. Lorenzo's response was instant.

His hands explored my curves in a tantalizing motion that set every inch of my skin alight in the most pleasant of ways while desire gathered inside me. I pushed him back step by step until he sat down on his bed, and I sat astride him. Tonight was all about us. Our worries and our fears could wait. Tonight was about love.

One by one, our pieces of clothing came off. We pulled our shirts over our heads. I pressed my palms against the hard planes of his chest while he caressed my stomach. His lips trailed kisses from my collarbone to my hips.

His fingers paused at my bra straps. "Are you sure?"

"Yes, I want this."

I felt beautiful the way Lorenzo looked at me, longing and gentleness in his gaze. He lay me down on the bed, lying next to me, and continued kissing me as we explored each His touch was heaven. In his arms, I was safe.

He brought his face down to mine. "Halia."

"Mmhh."

"I'm falling in love with you."

My breath hitched, and I opened my mouth, but he continued. "We have known each other for only a short time, but I've never felt around anyone the way I do with you. You're special. You're my person."

Tears stung my eyes. Home, I had finally found my home. "And you're my person." I bit my lip. "As scary as it is, I'm falling in love with you too."

His face lit up with happiness, and I pulled him down to me, sealing our words with a kiss. At first, the kiss was sweet, but soon, it turned passionate. Everything around me exploded into a thousand beautiful stars

Twenty minutes later, I was completely spent, every muscle in my body a gooey mess.

I yawned. “We need to plan for the competition.”

“Shh. That can wait. Rest now.”

I fell into a deep, sweet sleep. At least, it was sweet for a while...

Lorenzo, Tia, and Mikka were running next to me through a field filled with thousands of different blooms and gorgeous butterflies with all kind of wing patterns. The heady scent of lilies and roses filled my nose. I made a flower crown of carnations and twirled in a circle until I dropped to the ground, the grass pricking my body.

Lorenzo threw down a blanket on the ground, and Mikka produced a delicious spread of tiny sandwiches with lobster, smoked salmon, and even caviar. Tia popped open the champagne. She poured me a crystal glass of the sparkly goodness, and I moaned as I gulped down a mouthful of the acidic bubbles. It was so good, I couldn’t stop myself from finishing the whole glass.

“That’s right, drink up,” Tia whispered in a strange voice.

I emptied the glass and put it down on the blanket only to find it was gone. I looked up. Lorenzo, Tia, and Mikka were gone too. The flowers around me were rotting away, and the butterflies were turning into nasty brown bugs and spiders. I jumped to my feet, searching for my friends. “Lorenzo, Tia, Mikka, where are you?”

There was no response. I broke into a run. The field turned into a thick forest, and wolves howled nearby. The more I sprinted, the more confused I got. Carelessly, I tripped over a root and fell forward, scuffing my elbows and knees.

“Ouch!” Tears spilled down my cheeks. “Lorenzo! Tia! Mikka! Why did you leave me?”

“They’re done with you,” a vicious voice whispered. Where had it come from? There was no one around me.

I rose to my feet, brushing off the mulch and leaves stuck to my clothes. There had to be a way out of the forest. I needed to think, focus.

"You're trapped. You'll never escape."

"Go away!" I yelled at the pesky voice and pumped my legs. No matter how fast I went, there was no end to the forest. With my chest heaving and my side stitch killing me, I sank to the ground. A spider scuttled over me, and a snake slithered by. What was this nightmare? How could everything have gone so badly all of a sudden?

I paused. A nightmare. I was trapped in a nightmare. I needed to wake up. I pinched my arm, then slapped myself across the cheek. When that didn't produce the desired effect, I rolled around the ground, hoping I would fall out of bed. Instead, all I got was mud stuck to my hair and skin.

Why wasn't I waking up?

A voice cackled. "You'll never be a match for me, child."

Acacia. But no, it couldn't be her. The magic contract was binding. She had to stay away from me. At least in the real world. But this wasn't real. This was a dream.

"Acacia, leave me alone!" No response. She had promised not to harm me, so how had she managed to trap me in this nightmare? I had heard that some people purchased sweet dreams from the faes, which meant they could create nightmares, but how did Acacia get to me? She had been forced to leave Arcadia.

I gulped hard as I remembered the storage supply in the opera house. It had magic potions. Acacia didn't take them with her. They were still there. Madam. Oh, god, no. Madam would finish what Acacia had begun. If she had somehow witnessed any of my exchange with Acacia, Madam knew that I was the queen's adopted daughter.

Something huge advanced toward me. A panther.

I tried to stay calm. "Good kitty." The beast pounced at me, and with a yelp, I darted away.

This was not real. I needed to fight this dark magic.

I opened my mouth and sang, "*Leave me alone.*" Or rather, I tried to because no sound came out. I tried again. Nothing. Where had my voice gone? The massive feline pounced again, its claws swiping for my throat. I jumped to the side. Again and again. I was getting winded while the panther seemed to enjoy itself. I couldn't keep this up. I grabbed a branch and heaved myself upward, cursing that I had never worked to strengthen my muscles. Every climb was hell, my arms protesting, my skin chafing at the rough bark. A claw swiped my leg. Pain exploded through me, and hot blood ran down my pant leg. I jerked my bleeding leg upward. The panther jumped and jumped, but I was too high.

Before I could relax, there was a caw, and a raven dived for my head. Its beak took a bite out of my scalp. Another raven ripped a strand of hair out.

"Stop it, stop it," I mouthed. More birds dived for me while the panther sat under the tree, waiting for me to fall into its jaws.

I cursed and gritted my teeth. "Stay away!" My voice was but a croak. There had to be something else I could do. The iron dagger. I reached for my weapons belt and almost cried when I found that I was wearing it, and the blade was in its sheath. I faced the next bird that dived for me and stabbed it. It burst into a thousand black particles.

"Your darn dream is finished, Acacia. It has no power over me." I leaped off the branch, angling my dagger straight for the panther's chest. I gripped the blade hard as it went through tissue, fat, and muscle. The feline mewled, and then it too exploded into a thousand black particles.

I expected the nightmare to dissolve, but instead, a crystalline laugh shook the ground, and Acacia's voice said, "Well done. I hoped you'd solve this first part, so we could really play."

"What do you mean?" There was no response. The forest dissolved and turned into a grassy field, but I felt no relief, only foreboding. Then I spotted him. Lorenzo was sitting on the blanket all by himself, staring into space. I pumped my legs, running toward him. At first, it seemed that I would never reach him, and I wondered if that was the next illusion, but then, I was next to him. He glanced at me, confusion in his gaze.

I dropped to my knees. "Lorenzo, are you all right?"

He grabbed my neck and pulled me down. "Fine, now that I have you."

"Lorenzo, you're hurting me," I breathed, trying without any success to pry his fingers off me.

"I hate you!" He threw me backward, and I landed with a hard thump on my back, pain reverberating through me, my heartbreaking.

"No! You care about me. You said you—"

"It was a lie."

Tears entered my eyes, but I swallowed them. I didn't have the luxury of breaking down. No matter how much this looked like my Lorenzo, I needed to remind myself that this wasn't him, but only a figment of my nightmare.

Lorenzo drew his dagger and advanced toward me.

"Put it down." I unsheathed my own dagger halfheartedly, knowing I could never use it against him.

"Do you know that you'll die in real life if you die in a

dream?" Acacia's voice reverberated through the empty field.

"Liar!" A shaking seized my body. "Stop it," I sang. But while I had my voice this time, it didn't stop Lorenzo brandishing the dagger at me. Dodging his swipes, I danced back until I was against a tree. The next time he lunged, the dagger got stuck in the tree. I could've struck him while he tried to pull it out, but I chose love over hate. I grabbed his shirt and pulled his face toward me. My kiss was fierce as I claimed him. His features relaxed as I broke the murderous spell that had captured him. I thought this was it, but then he dissolved right under my mouth and fingers into nothing.

"Seems like you always hurt the ones you love."

I whipped around to find Tia behind me, her arms crossed. "I hate you. I wish I'd never met you. You ruined my life."

My heart broke all over again. "I didn't mean to."

Tia ran at me and tackled me to the ground. I expected her to choke me, but instead, she pinned my hands above my head and snarled, spit flying on my cheek, "You are worthless. Nobody cares about you!"

"You don't mean that."

She let out a cruel laugh. "Both your birth and adoptive parents couldn't stand you. Both gave you up."

"It wasn't like that."

"Lorenzo was just nice to you because he wanted to get into your pants."

"He cares about me—"

"Sure, the way one cares about an object. The way Victor cared about you." Her nails dug into my wrists. "You're nothing. You're no one."

I fought her words, fought the pain they inflicted. "Shut up!" I slammed my hips upward, and her eyes widened in surprise as she fell off me. “Shut up! I don’t care about your or anyone’s opinion! I’m my own person! I know my own worth!”

My friend disappeared. Acacia slinked toward me, her silver robes brushing the ground. “Poor little Halia, scaring away all her friends and loved ones.”

I gripped her hands, the way she used to hold mine when she siphoned off emotions from me, and sing-yelled, “*Release me!*” My voice crescendoed, and my ears rang as I hit the highest note. Acacia fractured as if she were made of glass, her mouth gaping in shock.

Then there was nothing left but darkness.

“Halia, Halia, wake up!”

I opened my heavy eyelids to find Lorenzo leaning above me. Behind him stood Tia and Mikka. All three were staring at me with concern, and something cold and wet was on my forehead. I shoved off the wet rag and sat up, pulling the sheet high around my chest since I was naked.

“Are you all right?” Lorenzo took my face between his palms. “None of us could wake you up.”

I rubbed my temples. “I was trapped in a nightmare by Acacia.”

Tia grabbed my hand. “I thought you banished her.”

I nodded. “Madam or somebody else must’ve discovered the potions Acacia left behind.”

“But how did she get in here? How did she administer the potion?” Mikka asked.

Lorenzo cursed and paced up and down the room. “Somebody must’ve snuck in and given the potion to Halia when she was asleep.”

I pulled my knees up to my chest,. Somebody had slipped into the bedroom while I had been asleep, naked, and vulnerable and slipped me a draught.

"I shouldn't have left you alone." Lorenzo ran a hand through his silver hair as if he wanted to rip it out.

I shook my head. "Madam would've found another way to attack me. She must've been hiding somewhere in the opera house when we fought Acacia. She probably overheard all or, at least part, of our conversation. She knows who I am, and she's out for my blood."

"I'll go over there right now and rip off her head," Lorenzo snarled.

"No. She'll be ready for a counterattack."

Lorenzo glared. "So, what do you suggest that we do, nothing?"

I smiled. "Quite the contrary. You, Tia, and Mikka go everywhere in Arcadia, spreading the rumor that I'm not waking up, that I'm dying."

Lorenzo took my hand, his violet-green eyes serious. "I'm not leaving you alone."

"At least, let Tia and Mikka go. Then tomorrow, I'll slip into the palace with the other spectators, giving the Fontaine sisters and their mother the surprise of their lives when I suddenly show up on stage."

Lorenzo pressed his lips against my temple. "I love you." I blinked at him, and he cleared his throat, then chuckled. "I did not plan to say that. By Lucifer, you, Halia Bright, do things to me no one has ever done."

"I think we'll give you two lovebirds a moment alone." Tia pushed Mikka to the door.

"Wait!" I looked at Tia. "Can I have a word with you first?"

Tia nodded. Mikka and Lorenzo exited, understanding that I needed to have some alone time with my friend. Feeling exposed, I quickly pulled a shirt over my head, then patted the bed. Tia sank down onto it, not quite meeting my gaze.

"I'm sorry." I reached out but didn't dare to touch her hand. "If I could, I would go back in time and change everything, make sure Acacia never got her claws on you."

"I know," Tia whispered.

I was terrified to ask, but I needed to hear her answer to the questions running on repeat through my head. "What did they do to you? Tell me everything."

Tia cleared her throat, rubbing a worn-down patch on her jeans. "I was snatched immediately after I dropped off the note to you in prison. They were very quick. They grabbed me and threw me into a carriage where they pulled a sack over my head that muffled my screams and bound my hands and feet."

Those bastards. I dug my nails into my palms.

"They took me out of the city. I could tell because our surroundings grew quieter. There were so many turns, I knew it'd be difficult to find my way back after I managed to free myself."

My brave friend, never giving up.

"Finally, we arrived. I was dragged from the carriage and thrown into a room. It was a cottage." Finally, she glanced at me. "There were lots of people. Mikka said you rescued them."

I shivered, remembering the apathy, the empty faces. "They were completely out of it. I had to compel them to get them back to Arcadia."

Her hand trembled. "When they drain your magic, it does something to you."

I leaned forward, taking her cold hand in my warm one. "Did they take your magic?"

She was silent for a long moment, and I worried I was pushing her too hard. Yes, I needed to know what she had been through, but I didn't want her to relieve the trauma. "They tried. Mikka said they couldn't take all of it, that the mating bond protected me."

I let out a breath of relief. When Tia met my eyes, her gaze was stormy. "Mikka said it could take those other people decades to reclaim back a sense of hope, a joy for life. She said that at least half of them will attempt suicide."

My throat locked up. "I wish I'd found them earlier."

Tia's hand jerked involuntarily, and she put her other hand above it. "According to Mikka, I'll be fine in weeks or months."

"I'm sorry," I repeated, worthlessness and helplessness drowning me.

"I fought Acacia, so she separated me from the others and left my chains on."

In that moment, I wished Acacia hadn't been banished so that I could give her a good beating.

"She was surprised I was fighting back even after the first two days. The next day, Madam arrived by carriage, and Acacia suggested I should be moved to a more secure location. They fought. Madam didn't want me moved, but Acacia won in the end. I don't know what she said to convince Madam. They threw me back into the carriage. I could tell they were taking me somewhere into the city center due to all the city's sounds, but I had no idea it was the opera house until you and Lorenzo showed up. To think that I was only a boat ride away..." Tears were in her eyes, and she furiously wiped at them.

"It's all right. Let it out." I could at least do that for Tia, let her grieve.

She sobbed, once, twice, then pulled herself together, never one to feel comfortable with emotions. "I had no idea how long I'd be there."

Four days. I had let those bastards torture her for four days.

"Madam came a few times with Acacia. Madam watched me like a hawk while Acacia fed me and gave me some water before locking me back into the closet." Tia rubbed her wrists as if she could still feel the bindings. "I thought they kept me alive to make a deal with you, but they never talked to me about you."

I swallowed hard. So Mikka hadn't told Tia this part.

"Madam was checking on you to see whether your eyes would change and show golden circles."

At Tia's incredulous expression, I added, "Acacia never told Madam that I was the one with the golden rings. Acacia wanted me to work with her to bring down Madam so that she could rule Arcadia." I sighed. "Acacia wanted me for my magic, while Madam needed to know who the adopted daughter of the king and queen was to bring them completely to their knees."

Tia shook her head slowly, speechless.

"Eighteen years ago, the king and queen adopted a newborn but gave it away only a few months later. Queen Ella was terrified that Madam would kill the baby."

Tia stared at me, her mouth wide open. "Are you saying that you're the heir to the throne?"

I chewed on my lip. "I think so. When I worked with Ella in the kitchen, she didn't recognize me because the golden rings in my eyes were hidden." I twisted a hair strand around my finger. "I need to tell them who I am and see if they still want me."

Tia took my hand. "Of course, they do. Who could not want you to be a part of their family?"

I smiled weakly. "I don't think I'm princess material."

"No, you're not. You're much more than that. You

can be anything you want to be." Tia hugged me hard. When she finally pulled away, her expression was somber. "Do you have any clue where the queen is?"

"No, but I have the bad feeling that she'll make an appearance as Madam's hostage when she and Rumpelstiltskin strike at the contest finale."

Tia nodded. "You have to stop them."

Determination hummed through me. "I will." I had no idea how I'd accomplish that, but I knew I'd do anything to protect my kingdom and my parents. I might not really know the king and queen, but they were good people. They deserved to be happy and together. That's why the heavens had granted me the gift of my voice, to give Arcadia a fighting chance in these dark times.

"Let's get you ready. We need two outfits. Your performance outfit needs to be stunning but easily hidden underneath your regular outfit. I think I have just the right thing in mind." Mikka said as she headed for the door.

"I can't borrow any more of your clothes," I protested weakly.

She waved my objection away. "You can, and you will. You need to win, and a grand appearance is half the battle."

Didn't I know it! I hoped Madam and her daughters would drop dead when they realized that sneaking me a nightmare potion hadn't taken care of me.

While Tia and Mikka figured out my outfit, I practiced my singing. I might have magic in my blood, but I still needed to hone my instrument, especially when I had no idea what the tasks in the last two rounds of competition would be like. No one had stopped by the house with instructions, so I guessed we were free to dress however we wanted for the final event. I hoped Mr. Goodwin wouldn't try to disqualify me for appearing on the stage just as the show started. If he did, I would get the crowd riled up until he had to give in. A chuckle burst from my lips. Was I really that vain to be worried about the outcome of the competition when Arcadia's future hung in the balance? Or was this my brain's way of protecting me against everything that was about to go down? I bowed my head, closed my eyes, and brought my palms together. *Please, if anyone is listening, please let us win. We need to rescue Arcadia, the king, and the queen.* I breathed in deeply. *Please keep Lorenzo, Mikka, Tia, and I safe. I have just found my family. I'm not ready to leave this earth when I have finally found happiness.*

After a quick lunch, the time had arrived to see what Tia and Mikka had concocted for me.

"Close your eyes," Tia instructed. "Don't open them until we're done with your hair and makeup."

"All right." I trusted my friend completely and did as I was asked, even though my curiosity was eating away at me.

To my surprise, I had to step into tight pants. "Ahem. You do realize that this is the finale, right? Shouldn't I be fancy?"

The girls giggled. "Don't worry," Mikka said, and I could practically hear the eye-rolling in her voice. "You'll be very glamorous." She attached something to my shoulders that reached the ground and then moved to my upper body, carefully sliding my arms into a tight, yet light material.

Something came around my neck that felt like a long necklace. They braided my hair and pulled it up, pushing several sharp combs into it that doubled as weapons. I swallowed hard, realizing that they were making a warrior goddess out of me. My outfit would be gorgeous, but it would also be functional, allowing me to fight. Because no matter how much Lorenzo and Mikka would help me, I would have to fight against Madam and Rumpelstiltskin and whatever magic reserves they had from Acacia.

So deep was I in my thoughts that I barely noticed Mikka applying makeup until Tia said, "All done. You can open your eyes."

A gasp escaped me as I saw myself in the mirror. My body was clothed in a tight black material with a sheen to it that looked as if it had been spun by a magician. Gold thread ran down my costume in geometrical shapes that made me look like a fierce warrior queen.

My feet were in black boots, also with golden accents that ended right below my knees. My hands were covered in black gloves that didn't feel stifling despite the summer heat. The detachable cape was baby blue, its edges adorned with golden thread. It simultaneously softened the look and gave me authority and a regal air. Somehow, my friends had managed to make me look like a goddess and an heir to the throne.

"It's beautiful," I breathed. "You've outdone yourself."

The girls high-fived one another. "Do you like your hair and makeup?"

I stepped closer to the mirror and touched the diadem glowing on my head. It matched the shade of my metallic eyeshadow while my lips were painted a cruel wine red that promised pain and retribution. It was perfect. I turned and hugged the girls. "Thank you, thank you, thank you."

They smiled. "You're welcome. Now go and kick some Fontaine and Rumpelstiltskin butt."

I chewed my lip. "I'm not exactly inconspicuous in this. Do you have something to cover it up with?"

Mikka chortled. "You're already wearing it, silly." She pulled the light blue fabric around my shoulders and clasped it together in the front, making it look like a floating dress that would let me pass for a rich merchant's daughter or a lower court member.

A knock sounded from the door. "Come in," I called.

Lorenzo stepped into the room, studying me silently.

"What do you think?" I shifted from foot to foot.

"It's perfect." He brushed my lips gently.

"What's this?" I asked, noticing the gray patrolman uniform he was wearing.

"I'm your guard for the night."

"Ah, I see." It made sense I would have one if I was

pretending to pass for a lower court member. I glanced at Tia. "Are you staying here?" I wanted her to be safe, but a selfish part of me wished she could be at the palace for moral support.

She scowled. "Absolutely not."

Mikka winked. "We'll slip in with the other spectators and help if you need us."

"Please keep her safe."

My words earned me a jab straight in the ribs from Tia, but Mikka nodded in understanding and said, "Will do."

"Ready?" Lorenzo asked.

I hugged Tia and Mikka one last time, not saying goodbye because I refused to entertain the idea that this was the last time I saw them.

Lorenzo and I walked toward the river. I deliberately looked out onto the water during the gondola ride, watching the stars twinkle above in the night sky. It was around nine now. The semifinals would start at ten. The finale would happen around midnight, and the celebrations would go early into the morning. Celebrations, what wishful thinking. There was no way Madam would let Arcadia have those. Even if we defeated her, there would be losses on our side. Innocent citizens would get caught in the crossfire. Not wanting to think about what would happen to me, I focused on my surroundings, memorizing every building we passed. Lorenzo didn't push me to talk, and I was grateful for that. It was only when we got off the boat that he said, "I'm going to blend in while you make your great entrance and stay hidden so that Madam thinks you're there by yourself."

I sighed. "She'll never fall for that. Once she sees me, she'll know that you, Mikka, and Tia are there as well."

He nodded. "But she won't know where we'll attack from."

"If the situation gets out of control, I want Mikka to take Tia home."

He sighed. "You know Tia will never agree to that. And to be honest, she might be safer surrounded by people."

I nodded slowly. If I had been drugged with a nightmare potion while asleep, someone could easily snatch Tia from our home. "All right. Just please keep an eye on her."

"I will." Lorenzo smiled.

"What's so funny?"

He squeezed my hand before releasing it quickly, needing to keep up appearances. After all, a guard shouldn't get too cozy with his employer. "You. You're about to face the enemy and be in direct line of danger, and yet, all you worry about is your friend."

"And you and Mikka."

"That's not what I meant. I meant you're selfless. Another person in your position would think about themselves."

A warmth filled my heart at his words. "I don't want to die, but if I do, I'll die a happy woman. I found you. I found myself. I'll die knowing that I was loved and that I was in balance with myself."

Lorenzo's violet-green eyes glittered. "Sometimes, when you talk like this, I start to believe that you're the one who's over two hundred years old, not me."

I chuckled. "I'm an old soul."

"Indeed, you are, Halia Bright."

Goosebumps exploded over my back at the passionate way my name rolled off his tongue.

Our talk was put to an end when people pressed in

from all sides, and we were forced into a line. We were almost at the palace gates now. With so many people in front of me, I couldn't see far ahead. Thus, I stumbled along with the others, not daring to ask Lorenzo for any more advice in case a spy of Madam's overheard me. Anyhow, in the end, I would have to listen to my intuition. This wouldn't be a fair fight. Madam and Rumpelstiltskin had many more resources than we did. Anything could happen, and I was ready to deal with whatever they threw into my path to rescue the queen and the kingdom.

No one around me paid me much attention, and thankfully, the guards were more interested in checking that I didn't have any weapons on me, then my identity, which made me realize that Lorenzo hadn't brought any blades with him. How was he planning to fight Madam and Rumpelstiltskin? I was certain they would sneak in some weapons.

Once we were far away from the guards, I whispered, "Please tell me you used some magic to conceal weapons on your body."

Lorenzo smirked. "Nope. I'm trying to stay away from the fae these days."

Good call, but...

"Don't worry. I'll get some from the weapons chamber in the palace."

I swallowed hard. "Is that a really good idea?" He could teleport and all, but if he was caught, it wouldn't end well.

"I'll be careful, I promise." He glanced at my hair. "Don't forget, all of the combs are as sharp as blades."

I nodded, even as I hoped I wouldn't have to use them. I might've stabbed Acacia a few times, but that didn't mean I had grown comfortable around weapons or violence.

"I'll be back as soon as I can." With that, Lorenzo disappeared into the crowd. I knew it had to be this way, no promises, no kisses, and yet my heart ached. I really didn't want this to be our parting words. I shook my head. No negative thinking. I had no room for it. I needed to get a grip on myself.

I pushed my way toward the stage, taking in the massive courtyard. Everywhere I looked were spotless colorful buildings with gold details. In the center was the palace, its high turrets with the dark-blue roofs reaching into the sky. The palace was only minutes away from all the concert-goers, and thus, within reach of our enemies. I gritted my teeth and brought my attention to the layout of the stage and auditorium. The stage had been erected in front of one of the courtyard buildings. A bit away from it was a smaller dais with three seats for the judges, and a higher, gilded dais with two thrones for the monarchs. Additionally, there was an elevated rectangular area with fifty or so seats. It was above the standing commoners but below the two daises, making me guess that it was for the courtiers.

To get to the stage, I needed to work my way through the crowd, which had gathered in front of it. As I did so, I earned glares, which melted away as the early birds took in my getup. Thankfully, everyone seemed to see the rich court girl Mikka and Tia had made me into and didn't recognize me. When I reached the front, I waited, knowing I couldn't afford to do anything until everyone was on the stage, and Madam believed that I had been eliminated.

The minutes trickled by painfully slowly, even though I had to wait less than half an hour until the show started.

Mr. Goodwin and his assistant, Henry, came out onto the stage first and inclined their heads to the judges. They bowed deeply to the king to whom I only shot a brief glance, afraid I would miss something critical happening on stage. Then Henry made a motion with his hand, and the Fontaine sisters sauntered onto the stage. Their frothy pink gowns with white accents reminded me of a sugary strawberry cake, but the crowd applauded loudly. Next came the two male heartthrobs, Deryll Mortimer and Hendrix Cash, their scorching eyes and toned bodies sending the female attendees over the moon. Lana Shay, the female singer who looked like a model and had been securing gigs for years, also received a lot of attention. As soon as she was on the stage, I slipped toward the back of the stage, planning to make my entrance from the side wing as the other contestants had.

"This area is off-limits." A guard blocked my path.

"I'm Halia Bright. I'm the sixth contestant."

He glanced me up and down, and recognition flashed in his eyes, but he fought it. "Halia Bright won't be performing. She's indisposed."

*"Escort me to the stage,"* I sang, not wanting to have to explain over and over who I was.

He nodded slowly. "All right, but we need to hurry. You're late."

I gave him a sweet smile. "After you."

He guided me past five more sets of guards, through the changing room, and onto the steps that led to the stage.

"Thank you for welcoming our contestants," Mr. Goodwin said. "As you can see, they are only five. Miss Halia Bright had to drop out due to being unwell."

"I'm here, but thank you for your concern," I said

loudly, my voice carrying. Mr. Goodwin swayed at the sight of me as if he were about to faint. I smiled at him sweetly, then took my spot on the left side, far away from the Fontaine sisters, whom I guessed had reached the point where they wouldn't hesitate to stab me in the back in front of everyone and then claim that I had stepped into a knife.

Mr. Goodwin cleared his throat. "Halia Bright, everyone."

The crowd cheered while I allowed myself to properly take in the king for the first time. He was hunched in his throne, the seat next to him conspicuously empty. His face was drawn, heavy creases were etched into his forehead, and his eyes swam in dark circles, while his skin was a sickly gray shade. He must've been a mess since his wife had disappeared. Several guards were behind him, and more surrounded his dais, which was a safe distance away from the dais of the judges and the elevated area of the courtiers. The courtiers and judges wore stern, and in some cases, slightly bored expressions, while the commoners smiled and waved at us, excitement bubbling through them. Arcadia's people were happy, unaware that the reason why they got to be this close to the castle and their monarch was because evil forces were planning an ambush. I gritted my teeth. I had to finish Madam and Rumpelstiltskin quickly, or innocent people would get caught in the crossfire.

Taking a calming breath, I prayed Lorenzo had found weapons and shared them with Tia and Mikka. Then I prayed the four of us would be enough to rescue Arcadia.

Mr. Goodwin stepped forward. "There will be two rounds of competition today. Let's begin with the semifinals. Contestants, for this round, you are required to write an original song. You have half an hour." The curtains behind us flew open to reveal a clock the size of a massive pumpkin attached to the stage wall. "Starting now. The presentation will go from left to right."

Great, I got to go first. I caught the sisters smirking at me. They didn't seem disturbed by my sudden appearance, which I took to mean that they believed they were going to win this. They'd probably had a master songwriter compose their song and taken extra-strong potions to make themselves charming to the audience.

The ticking of the clock behind me brought me back to the task at hand. I had no time to be outraged at the unfairness of the situation. I needed to make do with what I had to ensure I progressed into the next round.

"The three finalists will get to talk to the king before the final round," Mr. Goodwin said, unknowingly providing me with the incentive I needed.

But what song should I compose? I considered writing one about Arcadia, but dismissed the idea since it was the obvious choice and probably what the Fontaines had chosen. I needed something more unique. Something that showcased what I was going through and also applied to Arcadia. Something that would let the king know who I was.

The sprout of my idea quickly grew roots and shot up, the leaves and bulbs taking shape as the words flowed onto the page, the melody playing in my head.

"Time's up!" Mr. Goodwin called, apprehension in his gaze as he glanced at me. He knew that without assigning me an unfitting song and boring clothing, my fate lay in my own hands. "Halia Bright, everyone."

I stepped toward the microphone stand and

unclasped the button of my cape, and it flew back, revealing my black-and-gold warrior queen gear. Hushed whispers went through the crowd, but their looks were full of admiration, not terror. "Arcadia, this is for you." I smiled, allowing the fierceness I felt to seep into my eyes:

*Dark times have befallen you. You're drowning in the darkness, in the evil, but you're fighting. You won't take it lying down. Don't forget, you're so much stronger than your enemies could ever be. Not giving in to evil, but choosing light is true strength.*

*I know you had to give me up. I understand. Your choice was driven by fear. I want to let you know that I forgive you.*

*The hardships I went through, the nastiness I saw, it made me a stronger, more compassionate person.*

*I'm no longer a liability. I am a warrior now. Allow me to stand by your side. Allow me to fight by your side.*

As I sang, I walked across the stage, taking in every attendee, making eye contact with everyone, memorizing every single face. For the final line, I stepped right in front of the king and held his gaze, hoping that despite the distance, he could see my eyes. The time of hiding was over. I was ready to be myself.

*Together, we'll conquer this virus together. Together, we'll eliminate all darkness with our light. Together, we'll restore love and peace.*

Deafening applause greeted me, and I bowed lowly. The king's mouth was parted, his body angled forward. Did he know who I was?

"Thank you, Halia. Arcadia, please welcome our next contestant, Lana Shay." Mr. Goodwin snatched the microphone from me and hissed low enough so that only I could hear, "If you know what's good for you,

you'll leave now, girl."

"If you knew what was good for you, you'd never have agreed to get on the Fontaines' payroll," I hissed back.

He pressed his lips together. "They'll end you."

I smiled. "I'm not afraid of them."

"You should be."

Lana Shay took the microphone, glancing between the two of us with curiosity. I gave her a tight smile and stepped back.

Lana Shay sang an upbeat pop song that sounded suspiciously like her previous songs, and I guessed that she hadn't composed it herself, but had used something that had been recently written for her but hadn't been premiered to the public yet.

Deryll's song appealed to the females and was basically a confession of how he felt lonely and was looking for his soulmate, or at least, that was what he wanted the audience to believe.

Hendrix's song was about showing the girls a good time and had a bad boy vibe to it. Neither the king nor the judges looked impressed with the two guys.

When it was Georgette's and Bernadette's turn, I tried to stay calm and breathe deeply, but that proved impossible.

*Arcadia, you shaped us into the people we are today. Arcadia, let us give back to you.*

The hypocrisy was too much to bear. I balled my fists as my magic thrashed, begging me to destroy the dark power surrounding us, throwing a curtain over Arcadia's citizens, whose eyes were glazing over. Georgette and Bernadette were using a spell. They needed to be stopped. But how?

I couldn't break their—well, to be precise, Acacia's magic. Or could I? I had done so when I had freed myself from the dream. I focused on the sister's falseness, on their words. I opened my mouth and sang quietly, *"Break the dark magic. Undo the spell. Break the dark magic. Undo the spell."*

The sisters faltered a step but then continued. What I was doing wasn't enough. I had to go all in. But if I failed, ...they would eliminate me. Worse, probably throw me into prison. And yet, I couldn't just stand by as the sisters entranced Arcadia.

I stepped right between the Fontaine sisters and risked everything. *"Let the spell be broken. Reveal the truth. Reveal your real faces. Reveal your real intent."* I hit the high G expertly, the crescendo building and building until it reached its grand finale.

There was a pop. The sisters gulped and stared at me for a second before pushing past me, clasping their microphones. But instead of the angelic voices that had come out of their mouths before, a tone-deaf, nasal mess emerged. *"We hate you all,"* they all sang. *"You will be our slaves. You will bow to us."*

The sisters exchanged horrified glances, shocked they had voiced their real intentions.

"We didn't mean it," Georgette said.

"There was a mistake," Bernadette added, but the glamour was broken. The gasping audience was inching away from the sisters. Somebody began to boo. The king said something to his guards, and they stormed the stage.

"You nasty bitch!" Georgette's hands wrapped around my neck.

I kicked her in the gut, and she released me, crying out in pain. Her sister punched me in the face, and stars exploded in my vision. But before she could get another hit in, I pivoted and put my leg out. She tripped and tried to hold on to her sister, but instead, ended up pulling her to the ground with her. The guards reached us then and grabbed the two sisters, handcuffing them.

"Release us!" Georgette screamed.

"You are under arrest for treason," one of the guards replied calmly.

"You're dead," Bernadette spat in my direction.

More guards reached the stage. Within their midst was the king, his eyes boring into mine. I held his gaze, even though I was terrified. What if he blamed me for everything? After all, all of Arcadia's problems had started when I had turned eighteen and left the orphanage. What if I was bad luck?

"Halia." The way he said my name, there was no hatred or fear; there was only hope, filled with tenderness.

I dared to step forward. Before I could reach him, the cathedral's clock hit midnight. Thunder crashed, and lightning flashed through the sky.

"Not so fast," a familiar voice came from above. Madam was levitating in the stormy sky.

# 11TH AUGUST

"If you ever want to see your wife again, you'll release my daughters immediately," Madam spat.

"You have Ella?" the king whispered next to me while I tried to figure out how Madam was flying. It must've been the magic she was siphoning off the humans with the faes' help.

And then, suddenly, she was tumbling. A hand was around her throat. Lorenzo had teleported behind her and grabbed her before gravity could pull him down, and now, they were both falling.

"No!" I rushed forward without a plan. Madam was clawing at Lorenzo. At first, I thought it was to get him off, but then I realized she was trying to maneuver them in a way that he would soften her fall. She'd crush him, and the ground would break his spine and skull if he didn't teleport in time.

I darted off the stage, down the stairs, and pumped my legs toward the center of the square the spectators were inching toward as Madam's and Lorenzo's bodies came closer to the ground.

*"Release him,"* I sang, putting all my conviction into my voice. *"Release him."*

Madam glanced at me for only a second, but that was enough for Lorenzo to shove her off him and teleport next to me.

"What were you thinking? You could've died!" I wanted to shake him, but all I did was hug him for a second.

"How dare you defy me! You shall pay! Feel my wrath!" Madam was once again levitating high in the sky, surrounded by colorful balls. No, not balls, but potions. She brought her palms down, and the potions hurtled toward us.

"Halia!" Lorenzo pivoted me, shielding me from a black potion that hit his spine. The glass exploded, and the ink ran down his back. Immediately, his face contorted in pain.

"Lorenzo!" Please don't let it be a murderous potion. I was still getting over Tia trying to kill me and me having to stop her. At least, Tia had been human. I didn't dare to think about how I could hope to even slow down a demon with teleportation skills. But Lorenzo didn't charge me or reach for his knife. Instead, he did something much worse. He collapsed to his knees.

"Lorenzo!" I took his hands. "Talk to me."

"She poisoned me," he rasped. "Get everyone inside the palace. Separate the infected ones from the others." His eyes began to close.

"Lorenzo! You can't pass out! Stay awake!" I glanced frantically around us, not willing to leave him like this, yet knowing that there was no way I could get him to safety all by myself. My gaze snagged on a familiar face. "Thomas!"

He turned in my direction, hesitating, torn between following the other guards and helping me.

*"Thomas,"* I sang. *"Come over here."*

Thankfully, my voice did the trick. I practically thrust Lorenzo at Thomas once he was next to me.

*"Take him inside the palace. To the medic."* I had no clue if a regular doctor could help Lorenzo, but I sure as hell would try everything. As much as I wanted to stay with Lorenzo, I couldn't. Once Thomas heaved him over his shoulder, I found the next closest guard to me.

*"Listen up, we need to get everyone inside the castle. The infected people, who were hit with potions, put them in the cell; the others, put them in a big room."*

I repeated my commands for what felt like a thousand times, working my way back to the stage. I kept searching the sky for Madam, but she was nowhere found. Neither was the king or the Fontaine sisters. My guess was that the daughters had been arrested as originally planned and that the king had been taken inside the castle to a safe room. I needed to talk to him at the earliest opportunity because while it appeared that Madam had retreated for now, once she realized we weren't capitulating, begging her to stop, she'd be back.

My head felt fuzzy from all the mind control I had used. When I stepped through the castle gates, I was afraid that I would have to work my way past twenty more guards, convincing them to take me to the king. But to my surprise and relief, a guard approached me.

"Halia Bright, the king wants to see you immediately."

I exhaled and followed him, hoping the king wouldn't blame me for everything that had transpired. Technically, I had set the bomb off by revealing the Fontaine sisters' real colors. Not that I had meant for Madam to attack Arcadia's citizens with potions or demand to exchange her daughters for the queen.

I was ushered through marble hallways, past elegant columns, priceless art pieces, and bronze sculptures. But I could barely take in all the splendor, my heart hammering loudly. I would finally get to speak to my father...if he chose to acknowledge me.

The guards stopped in front of a set of elegant wooden, double doors where another set of guards was waiting.

"This is Halia Bright," my escort explained.

One of the guards nodded and opened the door to announce me.

"Send her in," the king said.

I took a few steps inside and curtsied low, the door falling shut behind me. "Your Majesty."

The king motioned for me to come closer. "Do you know who you are?"

I swallowed hard and pushed the words out of my throat. "I'm your adopted daughter."

He stared at me for a long moment, and I prepared myself for him to lash out, but instead, a single tear trickled down his face. "When Ella gave you away, I thought I'd never see you again."

I rushed toward him. "We need to rescue her."

He nodded. "That woman, Madam Fontaine, she's Ella's stepmother, and her daughters are my wife's stepsisters." Pain marred his face. "I should've recognized them as soon as they entered the competition.

When Ella went missing, I should've searched for her stepmother first."

I took his hand and gave it a gentle squeeze. "Don't beat yourself up. You couldn't have known."

He shook his head. "No, I thought that they had long since disappeared. I knew they had broken out of prison, but I believed they had left Arcadia. I believed Ella was safe, that I could keep her safe."

"And you did." I swallowed hard, hoping he wouldn't hate me for what I said next. "I believe Madam Fontaine lured Ella away by telling her she found me and was going to kill me."

The king's Adam's apple bobbed up and down. "My brave wife, always willing to protect others, never thinking about herself."

As much as I wanted to hear more about the woman who had given me a home, albeit a brief one, I knew we didn't have time to go down memory lane.

"Where are the Fontaine sisters?" I asked.

"In a cell, surrounded by guards. I can summon them easily to exchange them for my wife."

I nodded. "You know that Madam won't be satisfied with that. She wants to rule the kingdom."

He rubbed his weathered forehead. "She always did."

"Your citizens are safe in the castle, but Madam will attack again. We need to be prepared."

As if my words had summoned her, there was a crash, and sharp objects rained down on me. I dove forward, using my body to shield the king. When the attack stopped, I dared to look across my shoulder to discover that the window had been shattered. A potion had made it inside, and fumes were leaking from it.

"We need to get out!" I grabbed the king's hand, coughing as the fumes filled my nose and throat and hurried to the door. It was locked. I banged against it, but no one replied from the other side. The guards must've been down.

"There's another way out."The king pulled me toward a bookshelf.

"Where does it lead?"

"Outside."

Where we would be unprotected. Where Madam wanted us. I coughed as I inhaled, and the king's eyes dropped. We had to get out. No matter how dangerous it was there. If we stayed here, we would pass out, maybe even die.

"Lead the way!"

The king jammed his body against the bookshelf, and it gave way into an underground passage wide enough for one. I shoved the secret door shut behind me and followed him. When we reached the end of the tunnel, he reached for the door, but I stopped him. "I'll go. You need to wait here."

He shook his head. "This is my kingdom. I can't hide like a coward."

"Madam is planning on you to do that."

"If I don't do what she wants me to, she'll only get madder. I can't put Ella in any more danger."

I nodded. He was right. We'd play along for now, and then I'd figure something out. I gritted my teeth. If only Lorenzo was here. He would know what to do.

Together, the king and I stepped outside.

Madam was waiting. Rumpelstiltskin was nowhere in sight, but she was surrounded by Arcadian guards, her daughters in the background.

"What is the meaning of this? Why have they been released?" the king asked one of the guards who appeared to be the most senior one given the medals adorning his jacket.

Madam laughed like a hyena, and a sick feeling twisted my stomach.

"Those guards no longer work for you, Ernst."

The king squared his shoulders. "I see. Where is my wife?"

"Cinder? Oh, you can have her back." Madam snapped her fingers, and two guards stepped forward, dragging a thin Ella between them. Her feet were shoeless, and her face was smudged with grime. I balled my fists. Madam would pay for that.

The king rushed to his wife, but a guard stopped him.

"Not so fast," Madam purred. "Hand me the crown, and then you can have your wife."

The king didn't hesitate. He took off his crown, and I wanted to scream but didn't because just then, long white hair and short blue hair flashed in my periphery. Mikka and Tia.

Madam greedily reached out for the crown only to cry out as an ice dagger slammed into her hand. "My fingers!"

Her daughters tried to run to her but couldn't, their feet rooted to the ground by ice.

*"Remember where your loyalties lie,"* I sang to the guards. *"Arrest her!"*

The guards looked from Madam to me.

"Don't listen to her!" With her uninjured hand, she pulled out a potion from her pocket and flung it at the guards. They stopped in their tracks and then turned on me. Mikka tried to get another shot at Madam but was blocked. Madam threw two more potions, knocking Tia out, while Mikka was tackled to the ground by the guards.

Madam grabbed Queen Ella. "Give me the crown! Now!"

The king extended the crown again, but before Madam could get it, I snatched it from his hand.

Madam's eyes flashed. "Halia, if you mess with me, your mother will die."

"Is that so?" I itched to use my singing on Madam, but she was prepared for that. I needed to take her off guard, and I knew just the way to do it, thanks to Mikka and Tia. "Promise me you'll let her go," I said, taking a step forward.

Madam smirked. "Why would I want to keep her? She's really not as special as you all believe her to be."

I focused my gaze on my mother and mouthed, "Duck!"

"What did you say?" Madam asked. I removed two of my hair combs and flung them at her. She managed to avoid both, and smirked, satisfied, not understanding that this was a distraction.

*"Use a sleep potion on yourself."*

Madam's features went slack as her hand moved into her pocket. "You can't do that."

*"Use a sleep potion on yourself," I repeated.*

She fished out a black potion from her pocket and began to unscrew it.

*"Use a sleep potion on yourself," I sang for the third time.*

She emptied the contents into her mouth, then yelled at the nearby guard, "Get me out of here."

It took me a moment to comprehend what was going on. I had compelled her, but she had made a move of her own. With Madam swung over his shoulder, the guard ran. I tried to go after her but was blocked by the other guards.

*"Stop it! Go to sleep! Now!"* My voice broke on the final note, knowing that it was too late. Madam and the guard were too far away. They were out of my reach. If I had Lorenzo, he could've teleported with me, but as it was, they had escaped.

"Halia! My girl!" The queen took a step toward me as guards streamed from the castle to lock up the sisters. We had lost Madam, but we had captured her daughters, and my mother was free.

~

"I'm so horribly sorry for everything I put you through," the queen said for, at least, the tenth time, still gazing at me as if I wasn't quite real.

I shook my head. "You were trying to protect me. And if you hadn't given me away, I doubt I would've been able to stand up to Madam and protect Arcadia." The queen, my mother, shuddered. I took her hand and promised, "I won't let her hurt you again."

"She won't return." Lorenzo entered the throne room and bowed lowly to the king and queen, then took a spot by my side.

"How do you know?" I asked.

He sighed. "Because she's a bully, one without magic. She can't work on her own, and she knows she's no match for you. Now that she no longer has Queen Ella, Madam really isn't holding anything over our heads."

I chewed my lip. "Yes, but I doubt she'll just lay low. I think she's going to Urbis. That's probably where Rumpelstiltskin is. Something very important is happening there. Something that stopped him from assisting Madam here today."

Lorenzo nodded. "Yes, whatever they're planning,

it's far from being over."

The queen stepped forward. "It's over for Arcadia. We are safe, and now, I finally get to make up for my mistakes." Her blue eyes filled with tears. "That is, if you'll allow me to, Halia. Please, let me be the mother I should've been all along."

I gave the queen as much of a smile as I could muster. I was grateful for her wanting me in her life, and I wanted to belong, to have parents, and be somebody's daughter, but that wouldn't change the past, it wouldn't change me growing up as an orphan. And I didn't want those things to change anyway. The trials I had been through had shaped me into who I was today. I might not know court protocol, but I knew how to stand up for myself and fight for what I loved.

"Halia, please, don't tell me it's too late," the queen whispered, making me realize I hadn't given her an answer.

"I would love to be your daughter." I smiled at the king, at my father. "It would be an honor to be a part of your family, but I can't stay here."

"Why not?" he asked.

"I need to go to Urbis. If Madam and her colluders aren't squashed, they'll eventually return to Arcadia to finish what they started."

The king shook his head. "I can send my men. You've done enough."

I put my palm over my heart. "I know in my heart that this is the right thing to do. I'm asking you not to hold me back."

There was so much sadness in the queen's face, and her throat wobbled, but she nodded. "If that's what you feel you must do, we shall not stand in your way." She tilted her head. "Before you go, will you spend some time with us?"

I gave her a genuine smile. "Of course. We still need to finish the competition." Most of Arcadia's citizens had recovered from the potions Madam had thrown at them, but they were still shocked. I wanted to reassure them that everything was fine and celebrate with them Madam's banishment.

Then, I would have to be on my way. As much as I wanted to stay with the king and queen and learn everything about them and what the first months of my life had been like, that would have to wait.

Since Mr. Goodwin had been on Madam's payroll, it was decided that his assistant, Henry, would take over the competition host responsibilities. On the one hand, it was strange to continue the competition, but on the other hand, I thought it was important to give the people of Arcadia some closure and provide them with entertainment. With the sisters locked up and officially eliminated, only Lana, Hendrix, Deryll, and I would compete in the final round. I was about to make my way to the other contestants, but the queen stopped me.

"Halia, if you don't mind, I would like you to stay with us."

"But—"

She glanced at the king, who nodded, a silent conversation passing between the two. "Now that Madam is gone and with you determined to go to Urbis, I want to do what I should've done eighteen years ago."

My breath caught. Certainly, she didn't mean...

"I want to announce you as my daughter, the princess, and heir to Arcadia."

I was too overwhelmed to respond.

"That is if you accept those titles." The queen

fumbled with a golden bracelet on her wrist. “I know we haven’t exactly done much for you.” She swallowed hard. “I truly believed that you would be safest at the orphanage. I hope you believe me when I say that I tried my best, that even though I saw no other way but to give you away, I always considered you my daughter.”

My throat laced shut with emotions, but I forced the words out. “Thank you. You don’t know how much this means to me.”

The queen’s face brightened. “We’ll send all of our best fighters with you to Urbis, and when you return, I hope you’ll accept our offer to live in the palace with your family.”

Next to me, Lorenzo, who had been silent the whole conversation, went rigid. I caught the concern in his violent-green eyes and mouthed, “I love you.” Then I took my mother’s hand. “I would love to visit often, but we can’t turn back time. I’m an adult now. I must live on my own.” I glanced at Lorenzo. “I already have a home.”

The queen’s face fell, and I hugged her tightly. “Please, don’t be upset. I’m not trying to hurt you.”

She wiped underneath her eye. “I know you’re not, and children grow up. It’s just that I never got to watch you grow up, and we had to skip to the next phase.”

My spine straightened. “Madam will pay for what she took from us, for everything she did to Arcadia.”

The king nodded. “You are our brave daughter.”

Just then, Henry approached. He bowed lowly. “Your Majesty, everyone is ready.”

The queen rested her elbow on the king’s arm, and together, they strode toward their dais.

Lorenzo gave me a peck on the cheek. “I’ll see you after the performance.”

As much as I wanted him to come up with me to the dais, I knew this was not the time to announce that the heir that had materialized out of thin air was also dating a demon. This moment was about Arcadia, not Lorenzo and me.

Thus, I followed my parents alone. With the blood rushing in my ears and my heart pounding, I barely caught what the king said about Madam and her daughters, explaining the situation to his citizens. It was only when he motioned for me to come forward that I got a grip on my nerves.

"Dear citizens of Arcadia," Mother began. "Most of you don't know this, but eighteen years ago, my husband and I adopted a baby. Due to the threat to her wellbeing, I wasn't able to raise the child, but thankfully, now that Madam is gone, I would like to introduce you all to our daughter and the heir to the throne, Halia Charming."

I stepped forward, the silence from the crowd deafening, their agape mouths making me want to shrink back. Lorenzo was the first to clap. Tia and Mikka joined in, and so did Henry and the other competition contestants, and before I knew it, everyone was clapping and cheering, "Welcome Princess Halia."

"Thank you, everyone." The crowd fell silent at my words. "I really appreciate all the support you've shown me already as a contestant of the royal competition, and I can't wait to see all the exciting things that are coming Arcadia's way." I motioned at the stage where the singers stood. "As much as I enjoyed singing, this competition is not for royalty. It's to give an opportunity to a commoner, and thus, I will have to forfeit my spot."

There were a few boos, but also a lot of applause, and the other participants looked relieved.

I nodded at Henry to start the final round and took my seat next to the queen.

"That was a very kind thing to do," she said.

“It was the right thing to do.”

The remaining three singers did an amazing job, but it was Deryll, the romantic who won. After all the carnage and the hell Madam had almost unleashed onto Arcadia, it was nice to see love win.

After Deryll accepted the golden statue, the crowd cheered for me to perform. My parents gave me an encouraging smile, and I took to the stage and sang the song I had composed earlier.

*Together, we'll conquer this virus together. Together, we'll eliminate all darkness with our light. Together, we'll restore love and peace.*

As I sang the last line, I saw them, a group of seven strangers moving toward the stage, toward me. All had golden rings in their eyes, their gaits filled with determination. I knew in my heart that they had come for me.

They each told me their stories, and as difficult as they were to believe, I knew they were telling the truth. They echoed my own, although they were all lucky enough to have grown up to the parents they had been given to. My time with my parents would come, but for now I had to go searching for my real parents.

I swallowed hard, knowing the time to leave had arrived. As hard as it would be, I would have to say goodbye to my parents, Lorenzo, Tia, and Mikka, and journey to Urbis with the seven strangers to save the world.

# IVY

## DAUGHTER OF ALICE

**GRAB THE NEXT BOXSET IN THE KINGDOM OF FAIRYTALES SERIES**

# MEET THE TEAM

The Kingdom of Fairytales Series was a team effort. Below are the people that made it possible:

EQP Management: Rhi Parkes & J.A. Armitage

Our authors: J.A. Armitage, Audrey Rich, B. Kristin McMichael, Emma Savant, Jennifer Ellision, Scarlett Kol, Rose Castro, Margo Ryerkerk, Zara Quentin, Laura Greenwood and Anne Stryker.

Our Editor
Rose Lipscomb

Our Beta Team
Nadine Peterse-Vrijhof
Diane Major
Kalli Bunch
Stephanie Woodwood

Our Proof Reader
Tina Merritt

And to all the wonderful people who loved the world we created and reviewed our stories.
Thank you

# READING ORDER

SEASON ONE
SLEEPING BEAUTY
Queen of Dragons
Heiress of Embers
Throne of Fury
Goddess of Flames

SEASON TWO
LITTLE MERMAID
Queen of Mermaids
Heiress of the Sea
Throne of Change
Goddess of Water

SEASON THREE
RED RIDING HOOD
King of Wolves
Heir of the Curse
Throne of Night
God of Shifters

SEASON FOUR
RAPUNZEL
King of Devotion
Heir of Thorns
Throne of Enchantment
God of Loyalty

SEASON FIVE
RUMPELSTILTSKIN
Queen of Unicorns
Heiress of Gold
Throne of Sacrifice
Goddess of Loss

SEASON SIX
BEAUTY AND THE BEAST
King of Beasts
Heir of Beauty
Throne of Betrayal
God of Illusion

SEASON SEVEN
ALADDIN
Queen of the Sun
Heiress of Shadows
Throne of the Phoenix
Goddess of Fire

SEASON EIGHT
CINDERELLA
Queen of Song
Heiress of Melody
Throne of Symphony
Goddess of Harmony

SEASON NINE
ALICE IN WONDERLAND
Queen of Clockwork
Heiress of Delusion
Throne of Cards
Goddess of Hearts

SEASON TEN
WIZARD OF OZ
King of Traitors
Heir of Fugitives
Throne of Emeralds
God of Storms

SEASON ELEVEN
SNOW WHITE
Queen of Reflections
Heiress of Mirrors
Throne of Wands
Goddess of Magic

SEASON TWELVE
PETER PAN
Queen of Skies
Heiress of Stars
Throne of Feathers
Goddess of Air

## SEASON THIRTEEN
## URBIS

Kingdom of Royalty
Kingdom of Power
Kingdom of Fairytales
Kingdom of Ever After

## BOXSETS

AZIA
BLAISE
CASTIEL
DEON
ELIANA
FALLON
GAIA
HALIA
IVY
JAKON
KELIS
LYRIC

www.ingramcontent.com/pod-product-compliance
Lightning Source LLC
Chambersburg PA
CBHW020451310726
48979CB00016B/2606/J
* 9 7 8 1 9 8 9 9 9 7 6 3 5 *